ADDIE

Lyn Miller

Addie ~ Lyn Miller

DEDICATION

**To God- I hope I got it down just the
way You wanted it. I am only Your pen.**

To Lela Jeannine and Susan Kay. Your strength encourages me, your
determination astounds me, your spirit humbles me. You are Addie to
me.

To all the strong women of my life, you know who you are, for I call you
friend, sister, mother, mother-in-law, grandmother.

To my beloved Jake~ you encourage me to be more than I ever thought
possible. You've handed me the world.

To the gray~ just when I think you don't fit, you pay the way for dreams
I didn't know I had. Thanks for the confidence.

As always, to God be the glory.

To Cassie, a
fellow writer -
Let your wonderful
imagination set fire to your
dreams!
God Bless you -
Lyn Miller

ACKNOWLEDGMENTS

I would like to thank my tireless editor, Arianne Hagwood. You have a way with understanding words, and encouraging me when I think I've lost the way. Your humor is priceless.

Thank you also to Sarah Damele, who rekindled a passion for art, just for my benefit. You are so very talented.

Cheryl Whiteside you help me see my writing from a different angle. Thank you for allowing me to interrupt your retirement.

Although they wished to remain nameless, I had a whole crew of technical advisors who helped me perfect all the scenes in which horses were worked with in this novel. They spent time going over historical details, and being horsemen and women themselves, painted an incredible picture in my mind. Thank you.

Cover Photo Credit Becky Lisle

Cover Design Sarah Damele

Art work within the pages of this novel Copyright Sarah Damele

Also by Lyn Miller ~

Granada

Addie ~ Lyn Miller

*A*ddie pulled her hands up into the oversized canvas coat sleeves after the hundredth time of looking up the deeply rutted road. The late October sky was a brilliant blue reflecting off the high desert peaks that were etched in a crisp brown. Nothing about the smell of the cold wind was familiar, and each inhalation was a bitter realization. No meadowlarks sang their summer songs of hope and life anew.

This was not her country.

She had never strayed like this before. The mountains above her to the north were marred with black clusters in sparse and widespread bundles that she knew must be trees. How anyone ranged to the high country to collect the necessary timber to build and burn was beyond her. She felt the desolation in the empty vastness of the sagebrush around her. She longed to see the rolling red hills of her home country.

But they were gone. Just as she was.

She had left her home in Texas willingly enough at the side of a man who had claimed her body and soul. She took to the dusty trails following the silhouettes of running horses just beyond the horizon with great anticipation and vigor. Her heart swelled with the opportunity to run with them, just as her man did. They ranged from the red clay of Texas to the stone-washed white of Santa Fe, then the deep emerald green of Colorado. Always just behind another bunch of those hard running horses.

Addie loved it. It was in her blood.

Her mama begged her not to go, that deep regret would surely follow on the heels of a mustanger, but Addie didn't care. The young rarely do. She wed Fett Loveland with nothing but a promise and hope, thinking that life was nothing but unexpected glory and hidden riches, tempered only by the radiance of love. She was addicted to a feeling of involuntary devotion to the young Fett that she couldn't tame down. His touch was like fire, and when he took her hand and led her into the future she forgot all about her mama's pleading.

Fett put Addie on the back of a bay horse and took her away from Texas and the only life she'd ever known. Needless to say, the young girl in her didn't regret the fact she might never again see her ma or papa, nor her seven brothers. Addie was a woman of adventure now, although a mere eighteen. She was going to follow her man to the ends of the earth and stand by him while he conquered it. All she needed were his blue eyes that looked at her with desire, and his promise to always be by her side.

It was enough.

It was true her life was an adventure, full of good times and rough men who cast shy glances at her over the cook fire. Men who stumbled over unfamiliar words as they grasped the importance of speaking without profanity in front of a lady. Fett knew a great many horsemen, all out combing the desert for any number of free roaming horses. They made their search and recovered as many as possible. They started the good ones under saddle, those that weren't worth turning loose to breed on the range were sold and shipped back east for meat and other uses.

It was rare Fett encountered one he couldn't tame. It took Addie's breath away to watch him, his blond hair curling out from under his hat while sweat poured down his back and chest, soaking his already dirty shirts. How she cherished washing those soiled shirts in whatever river they could find. Fett could ride like no other man she had ever even heard of, and no horse could throw him. But each horse he mounted took them farther and farther from Addie's home in Texas.

The thought of that hot summer sun burning into her skin warmed Addie's heart as she looked again up the lonely road for a team that had not yet appeared. She moved around the front of the crumbling stage stop that served the unpopulated desert country referred to as Northern

Nevada. She leaned against the bleached walls to absorb what warmth the waning late afternoon sun had to offer, her auburn hair matted from the days of dust and fatigue riding on the stage. Her usually soft and radiant face was pierced with sharp angles, and dark circles clung to the hollows below her green eyes. Again and again the returning thought filled her with dread.

What if he doesn't come?

She looked around at what was left of the day and down to the trickling creek and wondered where a woman spent the night alone. There was only a lean-to that served as shelter for the horses that lazed in the corral. They were the stage line horses who did little but wait for their turn to work. She envied them.

He said he would come, and so he would.

Addie's already gouged and bleeding heart couldn't bear the thought of lying alone to freeze to death in such a God-forsaken place, but the thought of dying cheered her some. It was not scrubbing a dirty shirt she cherished now, but the thought that the blood would someday stop pumping in her veins. Her breath would cease, and her mind would rest. It was a plague to her as it was. Even the light from the sun was weak and tired as it cast down meekly on the changing season.

The cabin she pressed her back to was little more than logs and dirt floor, the chinking having fallen way to reveal huge open slats between the logs. There was only a small potbellied stove in one corner and no food in sight. The man who tended the stage brought the food from somewhere else and made only coffee on the inadequate stove. The meal cost two bits. Addie didn't have the money to eat. Not today nor for the past two. She was wasting away.

She couldn't feel it.

She had been waiting for near three hours. Or at least as best as she could tell from the sun. Addie never rode the stage until two days ago. Now she wished she never had. She had gotten on in a small town called Otto, not much more than the shack she leaned against now. She couldn't recall much of the trip, just that it had been long and cold. Her eyes were sunken and her shoulders hunched. The stage driver continued on up the line. The man who brought the food had loaded his buckboard and gone on up the line without question. No one wanted the responsibility of a lone woman.

Not even Addie.

She slunk down the wall and settled herself against the small trunk she brought with her. It was full of all that was left of her life, right down to the petticoats she'd worn only once for her wedding and then packed away. It was light enough she could lift it and carry it herself. She hitched an arm on it and lay her head down.

Addie doubted God would make it so easy for her as to die right there a victim of the cold. No, He would make her wait the insufferable amount of time it would take for her to die an old woman. In her sleep no doubt, after a long and healthy life of misery. She really just wanted to die and show Him a thing or two.

Then she heard it. It was the slight jingle of harness, then the well-placed snort of a horse. She listened a time and heard no more. Addie lay her head down on her arm and closed her eyes. She could still see her mother, her small frame bent over the big wood table working over a batch of dough, turning it on the floured surface, pressing all her body weight down into the mass that fought back with resilience. She would hum a song to herself as she worked, sweat beading up on her forehead. Then she would look up and see Addie watching her and smile, the deeply etched lines in her face smoothing out into even planes. Addie didn't want to admit it, but she wanted her mother's comfort. Like a child lost in the darkness of the night, she longed to call out to her mother and feel her hands reach out to her and take a gentle hold of her face. Addie couldn't remember a time when her mother didn't come when she called. She wanted to feel her face pressed firmly against her mother's heart, her work roughened hands smoothing back the auburn curls from her face.

Addie wanted Texas like a dog wants water. But, Texas was far gone to the south and east.

Addie resolved not to cry on the stage, and she had succeeded a good portion of the time. But now that she was alone, looking out into an empty and lonely world she felt no need to hold up any pretenses. Twice she had been asked if she were on her way to meet her husband in this wild land, and twice she said nothing and looked out the window and away. People knew better than to ask again.

She heard the jingle of harness again, only this time louder. She raised her head in time to see a great team come into view on the rutted road that ran in front of the shack she was pressed against in an effort to warm herself. She raised up slowly as the occupants of the weathered wagon box looked at her in curiosity. Her torn and thin dark brown dress fell to the toes of her worn black lace-up boots. She reached up with a dusty hand and brushed a lock of hair away from her face.

It had been many days since she had the chance to wash or comb her hair. Truth was, she was wearing her best dress. Her only other was even less reputable than the one she wore. The team came to a halt and stood with heads low, speaking well of the journey they'd made. A man in a gray coat and stained brown hat stood from his seat at the helm, saying nothing as he looked at Addie. His dark brown hair blended perfectly with the scruff of his bushy beard where it met with his collar. His hard brown eyes glittered as he looked at what was left of her beauty. His eyes went from disbelieving to angry.

Addie took a breath and stepped away from the log shelter. "You Tom Brady?"

The man didn't reply, just set his brown bearded face into stone. He looked the beleaguered figure up and down and then shook his head. Addie didn't speak again, just looked to the two little faces that peered at her over the side of the wagon box. Another boy, the oldest by far, sat next to the man she assumed was his father up on the seat. The Tom Brady she replied to said he had four boys. This man had only three.

Addie held her hand up to her face to shield her eyes from the sun. The man just stood there looking at her, saying nothing. She didn't know if she should repeat herself or not.

"You aren't Addie Loveland." It was more of a gruff statement than a question.

Addie was dumbstruck. "Well, yeah, I am Addie."

The man shook his head violently. "No. No, the Addie Loveland I'm looking for is a widow."

Addie looked down and away as the sting of her title hit her fresh again. Tears sprang and she was sorry she hadn't cried on the stage. "I'm….. I'm Addie Loveland." It was impossible to say it.

"No." He stated firmly as he shook his head. "No. I hired an old widow woman. Who the hell are you?"

Addie wrapped her arms around her breasts. "I don't recall you ever asking my age. You sought a widowed woman, good with children. I answered you."

"No! I placed an ad looking for an older widowed woman good with children. Not a girl that was good with children!" He shouted at her.

"I really don't see what my age has to do with anything."

"Are you actually a widow? Or a woman hoping to land a man through an ad?"

Addie choked some on this. The thought of lying beside another man made her want to retch. "No, sir!"

"Well, I can't use you. We made a hell of a long trip for nothing!" He sat down and violently flipped lines, the team jerking out of their reverie and into motion.

Addie walked out next to the soggy road. "What are you talking about? I've been on the stage for two days! What do you mean you can't use me?" She shouted up at him. He drug the team to a stop and glared down at her, the deep blue of the sky making him stand out strikingly.

"What the hell are you? All of nineteen?"

Addie straightened her shoulders. "I am twenty-two. What that has to do with cookin', washin', and child tendin' I don't know!"

He leaned towards her over the side of the wagon and his brown eyes flashed fire. "I'll tell you what it has to do with cookin', washin', and child tending. I am an honorable man, not tending to take unmarried young GIRLS into my home unchaperoned. And just what kind of woman are you to willingly put yourself into a home with no other woman to watch for your well-being? It leads me to believe you are a woman of dubious repute. That's what it's got to do with it!" He started

10

the team again.

Addie flew forward and took hold of the head of the horse closest to her. He was taller than her by a ways. "I spent every last dime I had to get up here to you. You told me in a letter, a letter I still have with me, that I would have a job as your housekeeper if I were here today. You said I'd have work. You gave me your word!" She shouted at him as she was drug along with the team. Mud caked on the hem of her dress. The man Tom Brady clucked to his team. The boy beside him watched Addie with wide eyes.

"I have no money, nowhere to go!"

"That isn't my problem!" The horse she clung to turned his head to Addie almost apologetically as he pushed her aside. Her boot caught in the mud and she fell but his great strength pulled her along.

"At least give me stage fare back!" Tears of hurt, anger, and discouragement pooled in her eyes. She stared at him with all she had. "I haven't ate in two days, and I got nowhere to go. You gave me your word!"

He pulled the team to a stop again. He pointed westward. "Tuscarora is ten miles thata way. You might find something there."

"I can't walk no ten miles! This was all I have to keep me through the winter. You told me in the letter that I would have a place to live and work. You can't just leave me out here to freeze to death."

The bearded man looked down to his hands and studied the leather lines that lay draped across his palms. He looked to the boy who sat silent as stone next to him. Tom Brady sighed deeply. He raised his face to the golden light stretching out across the sky above him. The muscles in his jaw worked furiously and Addie was glad she couldn't hear the strong words that obviously coursed through his mind.

He looked down at her with dark eyes and spit off to the side. "I'll give you stage fare." He pointed at her with a straight finger. "But, and I mean but, you will remain in my home for only three weeks. Long enough to get things in order. Long enough to earn your fare back to whatever God-forsaken place you came from. In three weeks the stage will still be running to the south before winter sets in and your ass will be on it!"

Addie's hand was still wound tightly around the leather of the bridle. The great beast who resided within that leather kept his head bent to her in respectful repose while his master spoke. He neither flung Addie nor jerked from her. She could feel warmth radiating from his gentle face and her white-knuckled fingers warmed slightly. She longed to press in close to his enormous body of soft hair, to allow him to carry her to wherever he wished to go, that his back would hold her as she crept toward death in the cold.

Tom Brady's eyes bore into Addie. "If that suits, get your gear."

Afraid he was lying and would set the team to motion when she stepped away, her thin legs bounded toward the log shanty and her small trunk. It was filled with all that was left of her once great life. All the memories that would have to suffice the remainder of her life. She swooped down and heaved her trunk to her chest, awkwardly moving towards the wagon. To her surprise, Tom Brady sat waiting, but he didn't trouble himself to step down from his perch to lift her trunk into the back.

Addie fumbled with the latches to let the gate down. "Hurry up. We got seven miles to camp!"

She released the gate, and with effort raised her trunk into the bed of the wagon, then clamored in herself. She sat with her legs dangling off the back of the wagon box as it lurched forward. Tom Brady wasted no time sending the team into a brisk trot. Addie had to steady herself with one hand on the side, the other grasping tightly to her trunk. She stole a glance behind her to see two boys glowering at her from their seats below their father. As Addie turned away something caught her eye.

Under the wagon seat upon which Tom Brady sat, was a curious little bundle. It had large brown eyes and a hidden face. The child, of which gender she could not tell, peered at her from inside a swaddle of blankets. It was not a baby, but the simple set of its eyes shone with nothing akin to a child's curiosity. Addie looked at it for only a moment before turning her head to look out across the country she was leaving behind.

Every mile another mile farther from Texas.

Great sadness and isolation welled within Addie. Her icy hands clutched at her trunk, her elbows and shoulders locking with the force of it. Silent tears rolled down her face. Addie couldn't feel anymore. She lay her head down on her trunk and retreated to another place within her mind.

It was long into the dark of the night before Tom Brady halted his team. Addie was so cold she could no longer feel her legs and feet. She looked around in the dark and could make nothing out but brush. A stab of fear flashed through her.

"You boys get down out of the wagon and gather up wood." Tom Brady spoke as he lowered himself carefully in the dark and began to unhitch his team. "Luke, you get that lantern going and mind you don't break the globe."

The two boys that sat behind Addie shuffled to the back of the wagon and Addie had to jump down to make way for them. "Andrew! Be quick! Get the wood so your brother can get warm!" Tom shouted.

Addie heard a sigh in the dark. She made no move to help the boys as they climbed down from the wagon box. She was unaware of what to do with herself. She was too scared to ask Tom Brady for orders, and she was too scared to stand useless. She was also afraid to wander too far from the wagon in the dark in an unknown camp. She wrapped her arms around herself and shivered forcefully. Her mind wandered to the silent bundle beneath the wagon seat.

Was the child even alive in the bitter cold?

Addie dreaded what Tom Brady would do when he discovered his child was dead, right below his seat. Her stomach knotted in great hunger.

"Miss Loveland! If you would be so kind as to help my boys with the fire! We are all cold and long for the comfort of it."

Addie jerked and stumbled away from the wagon into the dark. Again she feared that the boys were cowering close by, and at their father's command, would return to their seats leaving her alone in the blackness to die of exposure. She fought the urge to fall to the earth and cry and plead for Fett to come to her, just as she had every minute since Pete had brought his body back to her draped across the back of his good saddle horse, Buck. She had surely fallen to her knees and screamed and pleaded then. She could not recall.

Addie pressed icy fingers to her face as she pulled what few pieces of herself she had possession of back together. She stood like that for a long time, and when she removed her hands she saw the soft glow of a lantern light reaching out to her in comfort. When she turned to look at the source, Tom Brady was holding it up high as he stared at her, his body rigid.

"Get on, Miss Loveland."

Addie just looked at him, the wagon standing resolutely behind him. She belonged to someone. Someone who had loved her deeply, passionately.

"Mrs. Loveland," she said firmly before turning and walking into the darkness and the brush, immediately stooping to grasp for any old dead kindling that might be lying about.

When she had retrieved an armload, she walked to where Tom Brady struggled to get flame to catch. His three boys stood back away from him and watched as he worked, in vain, to bring the fire to life. He stood with a curse and moved to the wagon angrily. Addie heard him rummage through a wooden box in the back.

The oldest boy stole a glance at Addie, then quickly looked away. Addie looked to the fire and pursed her lips. The boys were holding a bundle amongst them. Without a word she moved to the fire and rearranged the makings, then pulled what little dry grass she could grasp and crammed it under the stacked twigs rendered from the surrounding sagebrush. She reached into her inside pocket of Fett's coat and pulled out her flint and steel. She learned long ago never to part with it.

One strike sent the grass to smoking, then a small red ember caught as flames licked toward the twigs that looked like miniature, naked teepee poles above them. Tom Brady swore again and slammed the lid to the box down, the light of the lantern wobbling in the dark around the figures near the fire. When he returned to the fire, he stopped in his tracks and looked at it, the lantern swinging in his hand. Addie had moved away again and no one spoke as he looked at each one. He said nothing either as he handed the lantern to the second-to-oldest boy who took it reluctantly. Tom fed up the fire.

"Luke, bring 'im here and let's get the blankets off him." Luke struggled with his awkward load toward his father. Addie moved farther away, prepared for the worst.

Tom Brady unwrapped the blankets to reveal a little boy, no bigger than a sack of beans. He and Luke each took a hand and began rubbing them to warm him. The boy stood on his own and said nothing, just watched his father with flat eyes.

"Hold that blanket up behind him so the heat will catch." Tom nodded to the boy not holding the lantern. He was barely tall enough to hold up the blanket.

Addie stumbled backward even more. The sight of this lone man and the sadness he and his boys carried was far more than Addie cared to witness. She didn't want the burden of her own grief, let alone someone else's. Not to mention there was clearly something wrong with the smallest of the boys. He was off in the head, or something.

Addie no longer feared the blackness or solitude of the desert, now it seemed welcoming.

"It'll be cold supper tonight. Andrew, get the sack." Tom Brady commanded. The second-to-oldest boy handed the blanket to his father and moved off slowly to the wagon. Addie was no longer hungry, nor did she seek the warmth of the fire.

Dear God don't do this to me. Dear God don't leave me in this new version of hell. Not even for three weeks. Give me back my Fett!

Addie turned then and moved to the back of the wagon, climbing in without thought to propriety. She wrapped her arms around her trunk and shook violently.

My heart. Keep hold of my heart.

She whispered to herself as the frost began to settle on her still body. She didn't move when Tom Brady retrieved blankets from beneath the wagon seat. He didn't offer her one, nor did he offer any kind of food. She could smell coffee, but she pulled the canvas coat over her head in response, the flint and steel knocking her in the cheek bone.

Addie didn't move through that long night. She slept little, fearing Tom Brady would come and take from her all she had left in the world. Open the lid and hatefully scatter what was left of Fett across the ugly landscape that enfolded her frail body. But Tom Brady never came. He never spoke in the darkness, never reached to comfort a shattered girl.

The night was disturbed only by the low sobbing of a child.

She'd answered an ad Tom Brady placed in the Elko, Nevada newspaper. Addie was far to the south of Elko in a barren land she didn't know, staying with a homesteading family close to where she'd been when Fett died. They had kept her after the tragedy, but Addie wanted to go home. They couldn't afford to pay her for her housekeeping, not that she would have felt right about taking money after they had so graciously taken her in. She would have to earn her way back to the people she loved.

Pete Summers was Fett's riding partner for a good ten years. He stayed with Addie for nearly a week after the accident, holding her as she wept bitter tears over Fett's grave. He offered to take her on with him, but she knew he didn't want a woman along. And, he was headed deeper into the desert away from Texas. He promised to look in on her when he came back through, but, now she would be gone from that empty place when he did.

Addie was grateful Tom Brady hadn't forced her to produce his letter, or force her to read where he promised her a job. The truth was, Addie Loveland couldn't read. Never had. The rancher who had taken her in read the ad to her and replied in letter to Tom Brady's offer. Tom Brady's letter could have said anything; Addie would never know.

The pale sun hadn't yet made its daily appearance when Tom Brady kicked his boys awake from their slumber in a heap around the dead campfire. Addie had been awake for some time, having already crept off

16

into the brush to answer nature's call. She returned to her silent post next to her trunk in the wagon box and pulled her legs inside her great canvas coat and waited for the dawn.

He threw a slice of dry meat to everyone, including Addie, and hitched the team. He spoke no words unless to give orders to the boys, who in the early morning light looked even more lackluster and disparaged than they had the night before around the orange glow of the fire. They looked at Addie through sunken eyes and hollow cheeks.

No one addressed her.

The silent bundle peered endlessly from under the seat of the wagon, making no sound as they moved clumsily across great rims of lava rock and seas of sagebrush reaching to the horizon. To the west of the north-bound wagon rose a majestic range of harsh brown mountains that cragged and dipped only to round out and climb again. They were the Independence Mountains, but she had no way of knowing that. Addie felt ill looking at their altitudes, so she kept her eyes to the east and the lower hills and plateaus that ranged there.

She kept her arm draped over her trunk at all times.

When they stopped at noontime to water the team, Tom Brady made no move to light a fire nor feed any of them. Addie wasn't sure if this was her job or not, so she kept silent. They pressed on, always moving northward, stopping only when the team needed respite.

At one such stop, Tom Brady took the boy from under the seat and lay him on a blanket on the ground. He pulled the boy's trousers down to reveal a soaked cloth. He swore under his breath when he untied the knots holding the diaper on and saw what else lie in wait inside that cloth. Addie tried not to laugh when he wadded the whole cloth up and threw it as far as he could. She had offered to help and been cut short by the glare he shot her. She retreated to the back of the wagon.

The sun hovered just above the mountain peak to the west and still they traveled. The desolation of the country around her made Addie want to run screaming back the way they had come. She began to fear this man and his intent, for they passed not one cabin or ramshackle lean-to in the entirety of the day. It would be up to her to fight for herself if he

17

took it into his mind to abuse her.

She felt a fool for having trusted a stranger.

The rancher's wife, Ellie, had asked her not to do what she was doing, simply for the fact that she would be at the mercy of a man she didn't know. But, grief forces a woman's hand in ways she can't help. Addie was alone in a man's world, and she had very little skill to stay alive with. This was commonplace for those of her kind. She prayed she would not become the cast-off of that which is used by men and left to die.

The team began to lag under their burden and still they pressed on. Addie couldn't feel her bum and the boys huddled again for warmth as the sun faded away. It was pitch black and the team stumbled over rocks in the road when Addie heard the bark of a dog. It was faint, but as it grew closer, the horses moved with new vigor.

They were nearly home; to warm stalls and a feed bunk.

Addie's stomach clenched. The wagon now rolled slower as the rock gave way to mud. She craned her neck in hopes of seeing something, but she could see nothing until the outline of a building came into sight. The horses stopped of their own will and Addie assumed they were standing before the barn. She couldn't make out a cabin.

"Luke, get your brother, haul him to the house. Take the woman, too."

Addie jumped from the wagon onto sleeping feet that threatened to give way. The boys shuffled out behind her, not offering to take her the way, just assuming she would follow. Addie took hold of her trunk and stepped lightly, grasping at safe footing. The boy Luke stumbled ahead of her with his bundle, groaning at the burden. The other two boys drug along behind him.

They walked for what seemed like forever before Luke spoke. "Mind how you go. It's good and wet."

Addie sunk as he spoke and stumbled forward onto the hem of her dress and barely caught herself. The mud sucked at her boots and she could feel the seeping of water as she went.

"Step up on the bridge." Luke spoke again.

Addie did so and wobbled on the log that served as the bridge across a gently moving creek. It was then she saw the outline of another building against the starry sky. It was big, and she fell off the edge of the bridge while studying the pitch of the roof. She sunk up to her knees, but she kept hold of her trunk. She lumbered and slogged her way out of it, but she was now wet up to her underthings. She could hear Luke floundering with his burden as well.

"Get the door, Andrew!" Luke hollered.

Addie stepped up onto a porch and waited in uncertainty as the boys disappeared inside the cabin. A feeling of dread welled up in Addie. She couldn't force herself to cross the threshold. She stood in silent apprehension as colors burst in front of her eyes in the darkness while they strained to see something. Her arms threatened to drop their precious load, and her knees locked in cold, wet misery. Her heart beat faster and she felt she should do something, like she was being told to run.

Then the lantern came on. The light hurt her eyes for a moment before focusing on the source. Luke carried the lantern to the door and held it up for Addie to see by. He didn't look at her face, but he looked like he wanted to cry. Addie stiffly followed him into the house and stared.

She'd been right. She should have run.

It smelled to high heaven in that room. The mixture of burned grease and soiled diapers hit her like a punch to the face. It was a large room and the farthest reaches of the lantern revealed stacks of pots and enamel plates on the sideboard. She could see lumps of fabric that she could only assume were dirty clothes. The pine table and benches were stained black from grease spills and molded food bits lay scattered across the surface. One of the benches lay overturned on the floor and the other housed broken harnesses and sweated-through saddle blankets needing mending. Addie could also smell the dank stench of mouse urine.

Cans of liniment and pine tar sat on the pantry shelves as well as oil-soaked rags. What few jars of food rested on those shelves were pale and unappetizing. Several fox and coyote pelts were stretched on the wall

19

curing.

Addie nearly dropped her trunk.

"Best you cook somethin' before he comes up from the barn. If you don't want yelled at."

When Addie looked sharply at Luke, she saw he wasn't commanding, merely suggesting the path of least objection. His soft eyes were sad and fearful as they cautiously looked up at her, and Addie realized she wasn't much older in years or emotion than this boy was. Tears burned in her eyes. His answered in kind. His light brown hair was curly and tousled and although he was no longer a young boy, his fine features set around green eyes suggested he wasn't ready to be a man yet either.

"Well ma'am, I'll start the fire. There's fixin's in the sideboard."

Addie still clutched her small trunk to her chest, reluctant to let go of the only comfort she owned. Luke looked away from her and moved quietly to the cold cook stove. It was massive. It no doubt was an undertaking to get something so modern to this backward land.

Addie's arms began to ache. She was never one to shirk a duty. She always did as she was told, and when she became a wife, did things long before she was asked. She found she had no desire to do for another man and his children. No matter how close to Texas it got her.

Addie looked around the room through blurry eyes. The boy in the blanket that Luke had lugged to the house was now standing next to the table where Luke deposited him. He stared at Addie with an empty expression and it disturbed her to see his eyes on her. His little mouth was drawn into a flat line, blending perfectly together as if he had no mouth at all. His hair was darker, like his father's.

Addie shivered. She wanted to choke on the bitterness that rose in her chest. This was not her home. This was not her family. She wanted Fett. The very thought of him sent her mind back into his arms, and into the pain of his death. She needed to go home.

"Mama," Addie murmured. Luke turned to look at her in surprise.

Addie looked for a secluded corner to put her beloved trunk in. She decided to place it behind the door. She couldn't bring herself to take off

Fett's coat. She backed away from her trunk, looking down at it as if to make sure it didn't run away.

She kept glancing at the trunk as she moved to the sideboard and opened the cabinet. She couldn't think what to make as she stared at the ingredients she found there. What had her ma always made on short notice? Addie took out lard and baking powder in a tin can. She moved to the worktable covered in dirty dishes and pulled a handle below the table surface to find a flour bin full. She found an enamel bowl. Looking along the walls for a water barrel, she asked Luke, "Water?"

"I'll fetch it." The boy stood and left the room out into the black. It took him awhile, so Addie found the cleanest rag she could and wiped out the bowl. She glanced to her trunk. She mixed her ingredients together. The boy with the empty eyes kept watch. The other two milled about the sputtering fire. Addie needed to wash her hands.

At last Luke stumbled in out of the darkness with a heavy bucket of water. Addie went to him and took it. She caught a whiff of fresh air and realized her stomach was turning from the stench of the stale air in the cabin.

"I brought this. You might make use of it." Luke handed her something wrapped in cloth. She took it as well and moved back to the sideboard. She washed her hands as best she could before delving into the can of lard and scooping some out. The flour and lard felt smooth in her hands as she mixed and kneaded the dough. The next step in the process required that she clean off a portion of the big wood worktable along the wall. In the poor light bugs scurried as dirty dishes were moved and set somewhere else.

Disgust burned in Addie's gut. Widowed or not, Tom Brady had no sense of cleanliness.

Unwrapping her parcel from Luke, Addie found a large piece of cured beef. She set it aside. Using a wet, partially clean rag, she wiped down a spot on the worktable to roll out the dough. Addie took a handful of lard and threw it into a cast iron dutch sitting on top of the warming stove. It melted slowly, the leeching fat reaching out to the farthest edges of the dutch.

21

The boys had gathered around, trying to appear nonchalant, watching her as she prepared their meal. Addie rolled out the dough and cut it into triangles, then dropped them into the now hot grease. It took no time to get the dough to a golden brown. Knowing those growing boys had to be hungrier than herself, she handed the first to the smallest boy when it cooled slightly. The boy merely looked at her with dullness. Luke took it from her and broke off a piece and forced it into the child's mouth. After a moment he began to chew vigorously and took the bread from Luke's hand. She handed bread to each of the boys.

She grabbed another dutch oven and wiped it out. She found the bacon grease tin, and dumped several large spoonfuls of it into the warming cast iron. She sliced then diced strips of the cured beef and threw them into the bacon broth. She added flour to thicken it, then poured in cold water to finish off the gravy.

By the time her platter of bread was stacked high, Tom Brady was pushing through the door. A look of animosity glittered out of his dark eyes as he took in Addie behind the stove. The sight of her was foreign and unwelcome. The boys watched her like they would a bullfrog in a pond.

Addie quickly tried to clean out bowls on the worktable. Dried on mush made that impossible. She left them to soak overnight. Instead she washed deep-dished plates and set them amongst the tragedy atop the table. Spoons. She needed spoons.

By now, Tom Brady had righted the bench and he and the boys sat at the table impatiently waiting. Tom Brady sat at the head of the table and made no move to assist her. Addie reminded herself that if he had bothered to set the boys to washing dishes, they wouldn't be waiting for their supper.

Addie's mama had always dished up for the children, and Addie found herself at a loss to come up with her own ideas. So she kept to what she'd seen her mother do. She picked up plates and ladled hot soup into them, setting them down in front of the children. Tom Brady spooned a small amount into the mouth of the smallest. It was hot and the boy flinched. Tom Brady gave up and ladled his own.

Addie didn't bother washing her own plate, just found the least of the remaining dirty ones and turned to the table. There was no room for her. The bench opposite the boys was crowded with old leather in need of mending. They made no move to clear a place for her. She felt uncertain as to what to do. Her body was beyond exhaustion and crying out to eat something of what she'd prepared. She looked to the plate of fried bread to see it was dwindling.

No words were spoken, the only sound was the loud slurping of soup off spoons. Addie pursed her lips and turned back to the worktable as Luke grabbed two more pieces of fry bread off the platter. That finished them off. Addie quietly sorted the worst of the dishes and set them to soaking in hopes that would make the following day better.

"You boys get to bed," Tom Brady spoke low. Something in his voice set Addie's heart to racing. The fear that crept up on her in the darkness of the dimly lit cabin froze her heart. With great dread and apprehension, she searched the table top for something, anything. She found a small awl used for opening tin cans and slipped it into her apron pocket.

"Luke, take Charlie and get 'im to bed."

The boys rose simultaneously and moved without comment. All dishes were left on the table to mold and fester overnight. Tom Brady left the cabin, moving out into the darkness, closing the door behind him. When Addie turned to view the mess and destruction left behind, she hoped there would be soup left in the dutch. There was none.

Luke lingered at the table fussing over something, the smallest boy still sitting and watching Addie with stark eyes. When Luke turned and handed his plate to Addie, it was filled with soup, the last two sopapillas were clinging uncertainly to the side. She took it slowly and looked at him.

"Thank ya," she whispered softly. Luke wouldn't look at her face. As he led his brother away with a candle in hand, Addie saw how wet and soiled the boy's pants were. Her heart twisted at the thought of how badly that little bum must have been burning to have worn that all day. She remembered back to the only time she'd seen his cloth changed. That was clear back at midday.

Addie turned her attention to quickly mopping up what Luke had saved for her. It hit her belly and warmth flooded her veins. With it her attention focused on where she would be sleeping. The awl in her pocket was all she had to defend herself with. Tom Brady was a big man. Even if he hadn't been, he was still going to be stronger than she. She had Fett's pistol in her trunk, but it would be a bluff since she had no money to buy ammunition for it.

The cabin door opened and Tom Brady glared at her. "Follow me." When Addie made no move, he said, "You aren't sleeping in here."

Addie could hardly breathe as she set down the now empty plate and gathered her trunk, holding it before her as if Fett would come out and defend his love. Tom Brady didn't wait for her, just moved off the porch and waded into the black. The air was crisp and bitter against the warmth of her skin from cooking over the hot stove. There was no moon and the stars in the sky exploded in definition as they were all her eyes could see. She stumbled after the swinging lantern far ahead of her.

She slowed as she realized he could be leading her anywhere. He did not turn to see if she followed, just kept on. They crossed the creek again, this time on a bridge made of two logs, the marsh around it no less swollen and boggy.

As Addie sloshed miserably on, Tom Brady stepped up a small hill and the light of the lantern reflected off a building. It had an overhang for a porch, the old timber that held up the overhang was twisted and knotty. The roof was low and she knew it was a dugout house. The light reflected off two narrow windows, one on each side of the door.

Addie stumbled cautiously up the incline and waited on the porch. Tom Brady had gone inside, but she couldn't see him through the gingham curtains that were drawn tightly closed. She held onto her trunk with all her strength and stood just to the right of the open door.

Tom Brady stepped back out and Addie backed away. He glowered at her. "Let's get it straight. Three weeks. No more."

Addie wasn't sure what to do. Drop her trunk and go for her awl, or clutch her memories and hope for the best. It cut Addie to think of dropping all she had left of Fett. Tom Brady jerked his head towards the door. Addie refused to move.

He clenched his jaws before continuing. "You stay out here." He jammed a finger at the dugout before turning it on her. "You keep away from my boys! You don't talk to 'em, you don't look at 'em, you won't be here long enough to get to know 'em. You leave 'em be! I don't want you here and you go in time to catch the stage. You understand?" His dark brown eyes pierced Addie's soft green ones. She barely nodded before he angrily stepped off the porch and took the soft light of the lantern with him.

Addie watched the swinging light as it made its way across the bog before she turned to the open cabin door. A small orb of light was located inside on a rickety table. He'd left her a candle. A measly candle. About that time Addie figured Tom Brady wasn't a widower. Surely his wife must've ran off with the first saddle bum that came along.

Addie stepped in and looked into the darkness around her. The silence and the smell of dampness invaded her senses. It was like a tomb. She could make out a potbellied wood stove with a flat top for making coffee and such. It was cold as ice and no life radiated from it. The makeshift wood and kindling box next to it yawned deep and empty. Something scurried in the corner, making scratching noises as it went.

Addie got the feeling she wasn't going to be welcomed by the inhabitants of this home either.

Cobwebs stuck to her face and hair as she moved into the dugout. Deep misery and loneliness flooded her body as she looked at her now empty life. Racking sobs came from way down in her chest. The scurrying sounded again.

"Fett! Oh, Fett!" Her arms burned and ached from holding her trunk so long and tightly. She couldn't bear to set it down in such filth. Dust covered everything visible in the inadequate light.

"Oh, Fett!" Addie sobbed out. "Do you recall that night we stayed in the hotel in Santa Fe? You said you wanted to feel a bed under you again?" Addie let out a watery laugh. "You said we'd feel what is was like to make love like town folk on bedsprings instead of like Indians on the ground? You called quits to the whole thing at three o'clock after the mice had chewed off some of your hair? You said it weren't human to sleep on other folks' sweat stains?" Addie paused to sob out a good laugh. "Well, this is worse than that! Who's gonna kill those rats for me?"

Addie carried her burden to the table and set it down. The candlelight flickered as she did so. She was filled with fear to think it would go out and leave her alone.

"You said you'd never leave me. You said we'd always be together." She pulled the pin on the latch to the trunk and opened the lid. "Who's gonna watch out for me here? You gotta come back for me. You can't leave me here like this. I can't live without you."

Addie looked around the room. Through her tears she could make out a rope bed with a straw tick on it. It was just as dirty as the rest of the place, mouse droppings turning the white of it a dark yellow with black speckles. Next to the potbellied stove sat a curious sight. A very ornate rocking chair waited patiently under a thick layer of dust and cobwebs. Addie took hold of it and pulled it to the table beside her trunk.

Using her hands, she wiped it down as best she could. From her trunk she pulled out the one blanket she had. The quilt her mother made for her when Fett proposed. It was of many different pieces of fabric, some little

26

more than wash cloths. They were sewn together intricately with love and skill.

" I haven't spent a night without being under this. We made love for the first time under this quilt. You remember, Fett?" She sat down in the rocking chair and covered herself, careful to keep it from dragging on the floor. Addie lay the awl next to her on the table. She turned her head and lay it back towards the pale light of the candle.

A noise at the open door spooked her. She grasped her awl and looked in the dim light, squinting, to see who waited for her. She saw nothing. She clutched that awl. Then she heard a soft whine. Taking hold of the candle and lifting it up, she wondered if leaving the door open was a good idea. But, the thought of being locked away with the rats and filth was as suffocating as being buried alive in a dirt tomb.

Glittering eyes reflected the candlelight. Addie heard the whine again and remembered hearing a dog as they drew close to the house earlier. The creature dipped its head as if asking permission to enter.

"Might as well. Nothing else bothered to stay out."

The dog cautiously crept toward her, dipping her head as she came. She was a scruffy thing, the long whiskers of her muzzle covering what expression she had. The black of the dog's coat was wiry and tangled, but her dark eyes were soft and seeking. When Addie held out her hand to the dog, she sniffed it a moment before thrusting her head into Addie's palm.

It seemed to her the dog smiled as she rubbed the rough head, feeling the coarseness of her fur. She wagged a thin tail. After a long moment, Addie pulled her hand underneath the quilt and lay her exhausted head back again. The mongrel lay next to Addie as her breathing slowed and deepened, the long hours of the cold night slowly ticking away one minute at a time.

The dog lay next to Addie long after the candle burned out and darkness invaded the dugout. Every so often, she'd rise on silent feet to chase a rat away, then return to the side of the sleeping woman to keep vigil.

"You'll have a roof over your head this winter, Addie." Fett's strong voice echoed off the juniper trees that lined the wash Buck climbed out of. The air was crisp, but Addie wasn't ready to think on winter just yet.

"You said that last year. Snow and rain dripped down on our bed all through the night most nights." Addie shot him a playful glance from the back of her bay.

Fett looked back at her and his eyes were mischievous. He raised a brow as he spoke. "I think I kept you warm enough. Don't recall no complaints in the mornin's."

Addie looked away before her traitorous mouth broke into a grin. When she looked back at him her eyes were still gleaming. Fett still studied her with a brow raised, his bleached-out blond hair feathering from under a weather-beaten and stained hat. His face was covered with a scruff that was as bleached-out as his hair.

"Anyway, you'll be warm again. Even if we sleep atop the wet ground on needles and buffalo chips. Not that any reside in these parts," Fett finished as he scanned the horizon.

The pack horse in the lead stumbled and fell against Addie's bay, Paddy. "Keep yer head up, you dumb bastard," Fett chided as he struck out with his romal and whipped the pack horse with the tip.

"It's late. How far is it?" Addie asked.

"Ah, girl. You're under the stars again tonight. Last night. I swear." Fett looked at her, his eyes apologetic and pleading.

Addie looked ahead and sighed. "Well, I guess one more isn't gonna hurt."

Fett tried not to grin too widely. The effort of his attempt at seriousness made his cheek twitch. "Ah, it ain't gonna hurt none. Hell, you might decide you like it."

"Fett!" Addie chastened. Her own eyes were lit and she again turned to hide her grin.

He slowed his horse and side passed him to Addie's. "Mrs. Loveland." He moved closer and their lips nearly met.

"Mrs. Loveland." Fett's lips brushed hers.

"Mrs. Loveland." Fett spoke louder as his warmth reached out to her.

"Mrs. Loveland!"

Fett vanished as did the horse Addie sat astride. Bitter cold bit at her toes and fingers as Addie rubbed her face. Her butt was completely numb, and so was her lower right leg where it was crossed over her left at the knee. Light flooded her eyes as she tried to look around.

"I guess it's good to see you aren't froze plumb dead," the gruff voice from somewhere behind the light sounded. "Haven't you got the sense to close the door?"

He was there. Fett had been there. She'd almost felt him with her hands again. Where was he? Who was the voice yelling down at her? Addie didn't like being caught unawares. Had Fett gone to wrangle horses?

"Fett?"

"No Fett here. Get up. Milkin' time." The light faded and the sound of footsteps sounded to the end of the overhang.

Addie dry heaved. It all came back to her. *No Fett here.* The previous two days rushed back to her as did the horrific realization that she was alone. It was so real. If Tom Brady hadn't drug her back into hell, she surely would have been lying next to Fett in paradise by now.

Texas.

That was all that was left. Her mama. That's all she wanted. To go home and be with all the love that was left. Wait patiently to die. Addie was done with living.

The pain inside and out made her body old and stiff. "Mama."

Addie struggled into Fett's coat. She moved, hunched over, towards the lantern light outside the door. She didn't bother shutting it. Tom Brady glanced back at her and then stepped out from under the overhang, the darkness drawn in tight just beyond the lantern's edge.

Addie shook violently. Her breath came in short gasps and her frozen joints wouldn't bend. The wet seeped into her scuffed and worn leather shoes. The intensity of the cold in her feet made them numb to the point she stumbled.

Tom Brady kept on until he passed under the open archway of the barn door.

"Bucket's on the wall. I'll bring the cow, then wrangle the boys' horses for schoolin'." Tom Brady hung the lantern on a peg that stuck in a center pole in the barn. He left and was enveloped by the black.

It was a huge barn. Stalls lined the sides as well as two saddling stalls. It was made of great timber and the beams she could see in the faint light were massive. The team that had doggedly brought her to this place the day previous stuck their heads out of opposing stalls. It smelled of must and hay, horse sweat and urine.

As Addie stood admiring what was visible, a great thundering sounded from behind her. Addie turned in time to jump out of the path of a moving beast. The cow had a fair sized set of horns that she lowered and rooted towards Addie, releasing a loud bellow as she did. She bucked on by and into a saddling stall.

Addie stood staring. The red creature that had just nearly mucked her out surely wasn't the milk cow. She now stood motionless in the stall, staring back at Addie with a gleam in her eye. Addie slowly took the milk bucket from the peg.

She moved cautiously into the stall. The cow angrily switched a whip of a tail.

"Today, Mrs. Loveland. Them boys got schoolin' and they'll be needing a meal before they get on their way." Tom Brady hadn't entered the barn, just stood watching her outside the door. He walked on past leading a horse and was gone.

Addie stepped closer. She'd milked plenty of cows in her years, but never one that started out blowing snot and bellering low and menacing. As she approached the red horned cow braced up and put her head forward.

"Easy, easy girl. I just need to milk ya." Addie knew she wasn't convincing.

Addie's hands were so numb she had no idea how she'd get them working enough to milk. To her surprise the cow didn't move or beller anymore as she got closer. Turning her great horned head, she watched out of the corner of her eye. Addie could see no milking stool within reach, so she crouched down and very tentatively took hold of the tit on the front quarter. The red beast crouched as well, but her intentions were to jump, not squat. She blew snot and released something akin to a growl at Addie who sat motionless waiting for the cow to decide her move.

None came.

So, Addie very gently massaged the tit to convince the cow to let a little milk down. In response, the cow stamped her foot opposite Addie. Pursing her lips, Addie squeezed harder to coax a little of the life giving liquid from the cow. It took several minutes of this before a very small trickle came out. By then, Addie's legs were on fire from crouching and her back ached from being hunched. She was afraid to move and break the tenuous truce between woman and beast.

Finally, the steady *fisst fisst fisst* started to yield some tangible results. The cow began to relax and the trickle was an all-out stream. Addie was impressed. Usually the fall months saw a sharp decrease in milk as the grasses were either eaten up and gone, or dying and what was left of the nutrients were fading quickly. This old girl was going strong.

As the bucket slowly but steadily filled, Addie counted each painful second as she switched tits and reached under the cow to get each quarter emptied. She dared not move to the other side of the cow. Things seemed to be working as they were. Why mess with it.

Just as the bucket neared three quarters full, the snorting monster snapped her hind leg forward, narrowly missing the bucket in a premeditated move and swung it out in a classic cow kick maneuver. Hoof met with sternum and on its tour back to residence under the cow, it met with the bucket sending well aimed liquid to Addie's dress front and face.

Addie met with barn floor, back and shoulders first. Red Beast looked amused.

"You *bitch*!" Addie uttered in a hoarse scream-like whisper. She took a moment to feel through the wetness between her breasts. All seemed well, although there would no doubt be a bruise.

Addie stood slowly with blurry vision. Tears of anger, frustration, loss, and despair stung behind her eyelids. She gave serious consideration to having an all-out bawling fit on the floor of that bitter cold barn. It sounded very appealing.

A smug snort stopped her.

Addie angrily swiped her tears away.

Raising her face to look at the ceiling Addie ground out, "Can't You cut me a little slack?"

Face in hands, Addie gave in and cried desperately a moment as the freezing milk on her dress and coat made any kind of heat retention impossible.

"Addie, don't take no shit off a milk cow."

She'd been all of seven when her brother, Jim, said those words to her. She could see him clearly, a lock of brown hair falling across his forehead. Jim was ten and had his fair share of milk cow blues.

Addie was standing in the milking stall, crying just as she was now, milk dripping down the entire front of her pinafore. It was her first time milking alone, her father having just declared her old enough to handle it completely. That cow, however, hadn't dealt as dirty as Red Beast. Jim heard the scuffle and gave what advice he could, since Papa said Addie had to figure it out alone. Jim always helped Addie, even if he got switched for it. According to her papa, Addie's mama went too easy on her.

"Alright, Jim." Red Beast snorted triumphantly as she glared Addie down. She was well practiced in this game.

Addie left the dim stall and found a cotton rope hanging below the lantern. Tying a bowline, she carefully threw it around the cow's whipping leg. She ran the end through the loop and pulled it tight. Red Beast fought, kicking and lashing out. Addie took hold of a pitchfork and each time Red Beast blew snot and made for the door, Addie poked her with the wood end. Red Beast couldn't leave without her leg anyway. One good crack to the face had Red Beast standing quiet. Addie kept the rope tight.

She finished her milking with very little in the bucket. Red Beast had given all there was and made bad use of it. Not a quarter of the bucket was full. Red Beast thrashed and kicked at Addie as she used the pitchfork to remove the rope from the cow's leg. Red Beast swung her horns at Addie as she left the barn in the same manner as she had come in.

Dread settled in Addie's stomach as she realized she'd have to do that chore again. Most likely that evening.

Bells sounded and Addie cowered back out of the way as saddle horses flooded the barn. There were seven all told, two of which wore bells. No doubt due to the fact that they were runners. No ringing meant horses had quit the outfit.

Well versed in routine, they lined up at the bunk in the saddling stalls to eat the hay waiting there. Tom Brady rode in on the horse he had been leading earlier, no saddle, and he glowered down at Addie's bucket and dress front.

"I take it this was a first time for cow milking?" he asked flatly. "You should have told me you don't got any know how with that."

Tom Brady tied his horse and grabbed the lantern. "Guess you'll know better for next time. Don't know no better than to let the bucket get kicked," he muttered with his back turned.

Addie said nothing. She thought of how Fett would have merely laughed at her predicament with the cow. But then, Fett would never have allowed her to milk such a rip. He would have beat Red Beast with a pitchfork and turned her out onto a frozen range.

"Get breakfast on." Tom Brady lifted the lantern from the peg.

Addie stood alone in the dark after the glow of lantern light left with Tom Brady. Frost filled her nostrils with each breath and she bowed her head and listened to the sound of horses eagerly rummaging through the feed bunk for the choicest bits. The bucket hung limply in her hand, its meager contents gathering together as ice. Hooves shuffled on a packed floor.

Mrs. Loveland....

Fett looked back at her in the warm golden light of early dawn, his smile bright and full of life. Buck moved into a high lope and Fett moved with him without hesitation or awkwardness, mere extension to one body. The cold of the dark barn stung Addie's cheeks.

She moved forward through the blackness and raised her skirt to cover the ground in the general direction of the house. The mud through the creek bed was firm in the frozen hour of predawn. It didn't suck at her worn boots nor cake on her hem. There was no sloshing in her bucket any longer and she hoped the boys didn't have their hearts set on warm milk at breakfast.

It was a long walk up the gentle slope to the cabin, and each step wrenched down a deep plunge of regret and misery. Addie's body ached and creaked with each step, her knees popping and grinding as they carried her to the gloom and stench of the waiting house. What would her mama say if she saw a place like this? If she saw a man like Tom Brady?

Addie could hear plainly the click that would come from her mama's tongue readily enough; see the look of disdain on her face as she beheld what she would call a "no good". Addie's ma, Clara, called all men she found less than worthy no goods. When particularly offended at manners or actions, she'd spit in the dirt at her feet to emphasize her point.

In Texas, Clara had encountered more than a few men that caused her to spit at the mere mention of their names. She took Addie's hand and lead her away from such men at a brisk pace when she was a child. It took many years for Addie to realize what the sins of these men were. They were men who cared little for the general respect for the foundations of family life, nor did they bother with respect to the female population. These were men who moved and shifted without regard for life and its great struggles.

Addie stepped into the reek of the cabin. The stench seemed particularly debilitating after the frozen and purged air of the outdoors. The fire was young and hadn't softened the solidified greases on the dirty dishes and table top. Once it did, the smell would drive out even the mice.

Addie's empty stomach lurched.

Her body instinctively moved toward the fire and the faint heat that radiated from it. At the thought of warmth, her body began to shiver and shake violently. She set the now frozen bucket on the table and wondered what the point was. There was so little there, all it amounted to was the hassle of scrubbing out another bucket. She had plenty of those already.

"There be makin's on the sideboard there. Mind you don't waste time. The boys got to leave in time to make the bell." Tom Brady stood in the same doorway the boys had disappeared into last evening when they were sent to bed. He left the lantern on the table and moved into the darkness silently.

Addie frowned a moment before moving to the water bucket. She looked to a peg on the wall next to the stove and saw a large enamel pot for boiling water. The purpose for this water would be two-fold. It would soften the oats that made up the foundation for the mush breakfast the boys would be eating, and it would soften the crust gathered on the dishes from who-knows-when.

She hovered over the great wood stove and fussed about the placement of the enamel pot now filled with water just to buy a little time next to the heat that was generating with intention. Addie wasn't sure if she should fill the large enamel coffee pot and dig around in the cupboards for coffee makings or not. Tom Brady might have the makings, but how many creatures would reside in them?

Addie scoffed at herself. She knew of no creatures that would hide in coffee. The water began to bubble, so she crammed another quarter of a log into the fire. She went ahead and filled the coffee pot from the bucket Tom Brady set on the table sometime that morning. It took time to scrub the dishes from the previous evening's meal. She filled another pot and softened the oats. By now all water was bubbling merrily.

Scraping followed by shuffling made Addie turn her head. The boys came out one at a time and sat down at the massive wood table. They had clearly dressed in the dark for their clothes were disheveled and the second-to-youngest boy's shirt was buttoned unevenly. Addie said nothing.

At length, Tom Brady walked in holding the youngest of the children. He appeared to still be sleeping. Tom Brady carried him down a short hall off the kitchen into the dark. Upon returning, he threw a heavily soiled cloth onto the floor next to the wash basin. Within seconds a wet ring formed into the wood floor around it.

Addie stared at that cloth for a while. No wonder the place reeked of urine. It was literally imbedded in the woodwork. Surely this man and his children had sprung from the depths of some black-mudded marsh. There was no possible way a woman had been involved in the creation of this home and these imps.

Addie searched the cupboards for coffee makings. She found a tin of sugar and a small one filled with cinnamon. She couldn't remember the last time she saw cinnamon. Sometime in her girlhood. She mixed a small amount of the two and put it in the mush. Setting bowls before the hungry boys, they set to work cleaning them out.

Addie found the coffee.

"Hurry up. Horses need tended," Tom Brady ordered to the boys.

Addie wasn't sure those three boys could eat any faster or with more smacking and scraping. She filled Tom Brady's bowl and put it before him. She then returned to pull the coffee pot from the stove and add cold water to the pot to settle the grounds. She poured Tom Brady a cup and handed it to him.

The oldest boy, Luke, rose with an empty bowl and took it to the sideboard and set it down. "Thanks, ma'am. Was the best mush I ever ate."

Addie smiled a forced smile at him and nodded. Luke bowed his head and retrieved his coat from the peg next to the door, then quietly exited into the darkness. The younger two boys did the same, but left their bowls on the table, one overturned from the effort of scraping every last bit out. Addie wanted to pinch ears between her fingers.

Desperately she looked for something to send those three boys for the noon meal. She could find nothing. A few pieces of dried beef was all she came up wth. She sent that and filled a jelly jar with all the milk from the first round of battle that morning. She wrapped the jar in a dirty rag and put the meager contents in a burlap sack. Tom Brady rose from the table.

"Take that to them boys." Addie held out the sack.

Tom Brady stared at it in confusion. "What's that?"

Addie raised a brow. "Their dinner. They're boys. They need a noon meal."

"Those boys never had a noon meal. They don't need one now. They are used to eating in the mornin' and the evenin'."

Addie's mouth drew into a line. "Might be nice while I'm here to have a noon meal," she stated firmly.

The corner of Tom Brady's drawn mouth twitched beneath his dark scruffy beard and moustache. He narrowed his eyes at her and took the sack. He left without further comment. She had just enough mush left for the littlest boy, whenever he woke.

Alone in the soft light, Addie took in her surroundings again. This was the only room in the house she had yet seen. It was possible the rest looked just like this one. A strong urge to cry overtook her. This pack of wolves needed more help than one woman was capable of in three weeks.

The sorrel spun for the third time, this time his hind end raising off center line ever so slightly. His roman-nosed head tipped so his one blue eye could take in the form of the boy who sat rigidly on his back, desperately trying to suppress cold induced shivers.

"Get ahold that pig!" Luke spat as another spin put the sorrel's shoulder into Luke's soft-eyed brown. Luke could tell from Andrew's seat he was trying his best to hold on and stay warm. A bad combination.

"You ass!" The sorrel, whom Andrew had affectionately named Blue, because of his one blue eye, let out a snort.

The sun was yet to emerge, but the frozen world around the three boys was lit and the color of the world was a brown. Each time one of the boys brushed against a sagebrush it released the scent of desert that was more a part of the souls of the trio than the pine that grew high on the mountain above them. The earth was going to sleep, and in the early weeks of winter slumber it smelled of the memory of the hot months recently passed.

"Andrew, Ma didn't raise you with no potty mouth," Luke scolded.

"Ma isn't here, so's I doubt she cares," Andrew countered.

Frank, the second-to-youngest and of a wise age of six, clutched the burlap sack that held the first noon meal he'd ever enjoyed the responsibility of toting. His little mare made no fuss. She was old and on the cold mornings her joints did the talking. Mare was all they ever called her, but she'd taught all three of the boys to ride. Now she was school marm, which was alright with her, for she was glad she no longer had to contend with the studs.

Mare quit watching the trail and kept her eyes on Blue, careful to keep her cargo a safe distance. She hadn't lost a boy on the way to school yet. She had no intentions of starting with Frank. Frank cared little about himself, just that precious jelly jar filed with milk wrapped in a dirty rag at the bottom of the sack.

Luke edged in closer to Blue, hoping that would distract him from his clear intent. "Keep ahold of 'im."

Blue seemed content for a moment to walk close to Luke's brown, so the three settled into a steady pace. They were well out of sight of the house and far from the tiny one room schoolhouse where they took their lessons. Luke's stomach burned despite the sweet tasting mush that rested within it.

He wondered if all boys had to look after their brothers like he did.

"'Least she can cook," Frank said to no one in particular as his mind unpacked his meal at noon time.

Neither of his brothers replied. The truth of it was, Frank liked the way she smelled. She smelled different. He had no idea what her name was, but she smelled like nothing he could remember smelling before. Like water and......well, he didn't know what else. But he liked it.

"Don't get attached. Pa said three weeks and he meant it," Luke answered.

Andrew had relaxed some, but Blue hadn't given up on looking back at him. His head tipped constantly from one side to the next, switching eyes, and each time it was a surprise to see the boy there. The trio rode bareback, as all children did. There was very little opportunity to find small enough saddles to fit them, and they out grew them so quickly, saddles weren't something homesteading families could afford for the younger children. The boys had learned to ride with nothing between them and the smooth backline of a horse.

Luke grew impatient. He wanted the ride to be over. He wanted Andrew to get a grip on Blue. Or, at least, thread his fingers through Blue's mane and get a solid hold.

Luke watched Mare wander off the trail and into the brush, but she kept watch on her companions as she walked on.

"She ain't Ma. She doesn't belong there where Ma cooked." Andrew took his father's side.

"Well just the same, Pa never made no mush I could tolerate. That mush this mornin' plumb made me happy. What I can't figure is what she did to it."

"Black magic of the woman kind," Andrew muttered. "Next thing you know she'll be makin' cookies. Meetin' us at the door with a smile. La tee da." Andrew drawled out his finish. He tried not to speak too loudly nor move quickly.

Frank's brows knit together. That didn't sound so terrible. What was Andrew's problem?

"Well, just the same, she'll be gone soon enough," Luke replied to Andrew's speculation. "You 'spose she was ever really married?" Luke wondered aloud.

"She's a home wrecker. That's what she is. Come to wreck our home with all her doin's. Like cleanin'. Who needs their house all wrecked and neat?" Andrew's voice was firm.

"You dim wit. That isn't what a home wrecker is," Luke spat.

"Well, what is it then? What do you call it when some strange woman puts your home 'to straights' by putting all your shit where you can't find it?"

"Don't say shit!" Luke scolded. He then looked down at Brown's bobbing neck and continued in a softer tone. "I guess I don't know 'xactly what a home wrecker is, but I'm guessin' Mrs. Loveland never wrecked nobody's home before."

Mare wandered farther into the brush. Her ears were focused on Blue now.

"Well, I say she's a home wrecker and…"

Blue's head disappeared somewhere below his chest and between his front legs. Suddenly Andrew could see nothing in front of him and he was plunging first into the morning air. The feeling of rising to meet the sky overcame him just before the rapid *snap* came and Andrew closed his eyes and groped desperately for mane, or any kind of hair, to hold on to.

Blue hit the ground on his fronts and waited a fraction of a second for his hindquarters to assist him in his push into the cold air once again. As he launched with all his strength, a squeal left from somewhere deep in his throat. Andrew's fingers brushed across mane before it vanished below him again.

"Get ahold of him!" Luke yelled.

Andrew somehow found Blue's neck with his eyes clenched shut and barely had time to register its location before it moved farther away from him. Andrew opened his eyes and saw nothing but sky as he fell and hit the packed earth and the air left his body. His mind felt his shoulders hit first, then his head, then his left hip with a slight twist in his spine.

He could feel the vibrations Blue's heavy body made as he bucked away from him through the brush. Andrew's eyes closed and he decided to lay there as opposed to getting up. He heard Luke's horse move rapidly away as he yelled.

"Watch it, Frank! He's comin' at ya!"

Mare's ears focused on Blue as he hurled himself towards her and she got down on aching hocks to decide which way to go. Blue seemed determined to come over top of her. Now she pinned her ears back and a flash of anger came into her eyes. As Blue came by Mare took hold of hide between her teeth and left him a little something to think about.

Blue bucked off through the brush before he came to stop, blowing and snorting, about 50 yards away.

"You dim wit! I told ya to get ahold of 'im!" Luke shouted.

Andrew opened his eyes and looked up at Luke who had come back to stand over him. Seeing the angry look in his older brother's eyes and feeling the unnaturalness of the hard ground beneath him, tears burned in his eyes.

"You better not cry!" Luke said, but already he was softening. He well understood what Andrew was feeling. The two eldest boys were allowed to pick their own horse, and Andrew was learning that just because a horse had a unique feature, such as a blue eye, didn't necessarily make him top pick of the remuda. Luke had learned that himself the hard way with a little colt that had four white stockings.

Tom Brady made it a rule. Once you picked your mount, you stuck with him, good or bad. There was no deciding it was just a little much for you. Luke well knew this was intended to encourage the boys to pick worthy horseflesh, not shiny horseflesh.

"You hurt?"

Andrew squeezed his eyes shut and rolled over and pushed himself to a sitting position. A sob caught in his throat. "Glass-eyed sum bitch," Andrew's voice broke as he cursed his ride.

He shuffled to his feet and brushed his already dirty pants off. He had hurts, but he wasn't about to lament them in front of Luke. By now Blue had returned to the circle and stood like the rest of the group, watching as Andrew choked back sobs and pretended he was dusting himself when really he was trying to stop crying. Blue watched with curiosity, as if he really didn't know what had just happened.

Luke side passed to him and took hold of a rein. "He broke one of your reins. Pa is gonna be pissed."

"Where is it?" Andrew asked.

"I dunno, but we better go. We'll look for it after school."

Andrew's heart fell. It was impossible to ride that counterfeit no-good with two reins. Luke saw his brother's shoulders slump and his mouth droop and tremble.

He took pity. "I think you best let me lead Blue. That way we don't have to look for that rein just now."

Andrew nodded as he brushed the back of his hand across his cold, red cheek. He walked up to a skittish Blue and took a handful of mane. Luke clasped the one rein Blue still had connected to his mouth tightly and Brown braced up. Andrew clawed his way up and held on tightly to Blue's mane with both hands. Luke turned back onto the trail and moved off toward the sun that was breaking over the horizon at last.

Frank smiled and patted his burlap sack, then rubbed Mare's neck with a little hand. *There's no boy who's got a horse that will defend a lunch sack like mine will.* He thought to himself. Mare turned and looked at the brown-haired boy who sat smiling proudly on her back.

Mare moved alongside Blue. He cocked an ear at her and raised his head to look at her out of a glass eye. She pinned her ears briefly before wedging him between herself and Brown.

It seemed to take the sun longer than usual to rise that day, as everyone held their breath in anticipation and anxiousness to get the day over with. For Addie, a deep fear came with the first pale rays as she dreaded what waited for her in the dark house, trapped in the recesses of neglected space and time. For Andrew, the merciless teasing from the schoolyard kids that saw him, a nine-year-old boy, being led by his older brother. For Luke, the responsibility of his younger brothers who required more than his twelve years knew how to deal with. Not to mention the difficulty of explaining to his teacher and classmates the reason for the previous two days absence.

Addie began her day by washing the dishes she set to soaking the night before. The more she washed, the longer her mental list of chores became. She wanted to start the laundry, but she had no idea where the wash basin was. Nor did she know where the lye was kept.

Tom Brady returned long enough to eat his mush and then leave out into the darkness again. He spoke nothing, but the rigidity in his body said more than his words needed to. Addie worked in the silence after he'd gone, closing her mind to anything but the task she worked on. Her insides were fuzzy, like her emotions could go either way, steady on, or render her immobile on the floor.

As the room began to light with a pale blue, Addie turned to gather the dishes from the table and was caught off guard by the youngest child who stood in his soaked night shirt with no expression on his face. His brown eyes were opaque and reflected no thought or understanding. His lips were a soft red against the paleness of his flesh, but where there should have been rounded features in his face from baby fat, there were hollow cheek bones and sunken eyes. His curly brown hair was long, a lock falling across his forehead.

Addie stood and stared at the ghost for a moment. She wondered if it were wisdom that urged him to keep silent, or a lack of wisdom that did so. Addie pursed her lips together as she realized in the long moments she studied him, the boy hadn't bothered to blink. She'd never seen a boy child act in such a way. His body contained no wiggles, no giggles, no mischief.

"Good morning," Addie whispered in the silence of the cabin walls. She found herself afraid to disturb the tomb of filth. Something about the tiny figure that watched her made her heart surge at the unfairness of it all. Life was so unfair, and damnably cruel, even to the smallest players. Tears burned hot.

She choked them back and tried to stifle some of the anger. "Are you hungry?" she whispered again.

Addie looked out the window into the world that was now being revealed in the dawn. She needed Tom Brady to come and care for his feeble son. She stepped to the window to get a better look. Her hand brushed back the saddened curtain that was heavy with grease and dust, the cobwebs breaking years old bonds between the curtain and the wall.

It was a desolate sight as the golden light reached across the sky. Beyond the porch, the hill gently sloped down to the small creek that flowed from a spring which gurgled out of rocks above and behind the house out of sight. Her eyes took in the enormity of the lava rock and log barn that stood on the other side of the creek. The creek twisted back and under a fence line out into the pasture where it provided for the thirsty stock. Beyond the barn and the corralling system adjacent to it, the sun reflected off the same brown and steep mountains that had haunted Addie on her long journey the day previous. The gold caught her by surprise and she looked at it for a long moment.

It's a new day, Addie.

Addie clenched her jaw and stepped away from the window. The temporary reprieve looking at those mountains brought was broken when she turned and saw the boy hadn't moved, nor had the mess that waited patiently to be scoured.

"What do we do now?" Addie asked the boy who made no reply.

Giving the boy a long look of regret, Addie moved to the workbench where her recently washed dishes sat drying. When Addie picked up a bowl, it was streaked with water. That brought to mind how cold it was in the room still. Addie dried the bowl with a questionable rag and filled it with the remainder of the morning's mush.

She set the bowl of warm food on the pine table before him, but he made no move to eat it. Just stood looking at her. Addie didn't know if she should touch the boy, but Tom Brady's words from the night before echoed in her mind. He wanted her to have nothing to do with the children. So, she turned and moved to the wood stove, and picking up the lid lifter, raised the lid and began to take split wood and cram it into the hole.

She glanced back at the boy who hadn't moved, his focus still on her. The heavy scrape of the door gave evidence to Tom Brady, who entered the room and looked to both occupants immediately. Addie was glad she had chosen not to touch the boy for he would have walked in just as she was lifting him onto the bench.

Tom Brady took the boy and placed him on the bench seat, then forced a spoonful of mush into the boy's mouth. Then blinking rapidly, he chewed his food. He remained that way for a time, mulling over the mush in his mouth before swallowing. Tentative fingers reached into the bowl and scooped some up. He took lavish time licking the goo off his fingers. Tom Brady stood silently looking down at the small boy for what seemed like an hour. Addie turned from the scene and kept up with loading the wood stove.

When she finished, Addie left the cabin and stepped out onto the porch to see if she could find the wash basin. It was there, hanging from the wall on a wooden peg. She knew better than to set the basin on the board floor of the porch, knowing the hot, heavy water sloshing constant would in time rot the wood. She moved to the edge of the porch and looked around the yard for a place to hang the wash. She found it, just to the right of the house, a simple four strand line strung between hand hewn logs.

At least she could now start the wash, which she figured would take most of the day. That assumption was based solely off the pile of soiled clothes in the cook room alone. She set the basin and the ringer with tub up on the flattest ground she could find next to the clothesline. While the water boiled she would spend the time sorting laundry and gathering rags. She also found a very dusty bottle of bluing liquid for what remained of the whites.

Addie took the bucket from one of the log porch pillars and headed down to the creek to fill it. She could see a rock spring box behind the house nestled safely near the source of the spring, so the household could get the clean water first. She didn't need the cleanest water for washing, just water with no mud. She stooped to fill her bucket and paused to listen to the soft chatter of the water as it filtered by. A light mist floated up from the water and Addie was surprised at how warm it was when she touched it. While she wouldn't care to strip down and lay in it, it was far warmer than the creeks and rivers she had recently encountered. What few there were, anyway.

The sun had crept higher in the morning sky, and Addie studied the surrounding landscape. The bright gold she saw earlier was now intensified, gleaming off the sharp peaks to the west. She could clearly make out the black carpet of trees that grew in patches around the chain of elevation. Addie stood and raised her bucket, looking to the tallest of the peaks to her right and wondered at the thickly wooded hillside on the south slope. For Tom Brady, wood was not as steep a climb as it was for those in Tuscarora. The rolling sage valley she stood in stretched beyond what her eyes could see over hills and buttes.

She felt the rope handle of the heavy bucket in her hand, so she turned back to the incline up to the house and started to walk. Addie poured the water from her bucket into the pot on the stove. Tom Brady stood by the table and worked at dressing his small son, who kept up with ladling mush out of his bowl with his hand. His little face turned to Addie and he continued his scooping without looking at his actions.

After his clothes had been somewhat properly placed, Tom Brady sighed impatiently as he wiped the boy's hand with a dirty rag. He carried him to the door where he stuffed the tiny body into an oversized coat. Tom Brady tied a scarf around the little brown-haired head.

"We'll be gone awhile. I'd guess we'll need an early supper." With that, Tom Brady slammed the door, the last sight of him Addie had was his scruffy brown beard and flashing dark eyes.

Addie shook her head. Was his intent to starve his children to death? Had he not heard most folks like to eat a noon meal? She stepped to the window and watched as Tom Brady crossed the log bridge and with long strides covered the remaining distance to the barn where a horse stood saddled and tied to a hitch rail. He hucked the boy up behind the saddle before he untied his get-down from the rail. Then Tom Brady was up and the horse was gone from the view of the square paned window.

The log house was stone silent except for the occasional pop of the fire in the wood stove. Now the vibrant golden light fell upon the house. It shone through the rippled glass and beamed off Addie's tired brown dress and made her eyes squint.

Addie stepped warily back out of the golden shaft.

The large enamel pot popped and snapped as the heat wove its way into the water inside it. Addie listened to the ringing in her ears.

She wasn't sure where to start first, everything demanded her attention, and she hadn't even seen the rest of the house. She boiled water for the wash tubs and cleaned the dishes at the same time. She scoured the table with boiling water in hopes of removing the odors of festering that, once there, tend to stay in wood. She took down the pelts and carried them to the barn.

Addie spent the better part of the day hunched over the wash tub in the gentle autumn sun scrubbing then wringing soiled clothes. She hung them on the line and wondered if they'd dry before the sun set. She opened the windows in the kitchen and left the door wide open to air out the stagnant room.

After noon, Addie ventured back into the house and collected the last of the wash in the pile, and with it went a large portion of the stench. She cast a glance to the door that stood ajar which led to the rooms where she knew at least the boys slept. No doubt there would be more wash in those rooms.

As Addie boiled another round of water, she decided she best get the rest of the wash together as it was getting on in the afternoon. It would soon be time to start that early supper. She quietly pushed open the door to the adjoining room and stepped in.

It was a lovely sitting room. A row of square paned glass windows looked out to the south and the peaks that rose in contrast to the blue autumn sky as well as the barn. On the east wall was a great stone fireplace made from the rock that lined the hills surrounding. Ashes filled the box and black streaks scuffed the wood floor below it. Several wood armchairs, ornately carved, sat before the fireplace at haphazard angles.

The room smelled forgotten. It was still and silent, and the air from the open windows behind Addie didn't penetrate the space. She turned to look around the room and found on the wall adjoining the kitchen hung several shelves. Knick knacks and keepsakes sat looking out at the stranger that interrupted the solitude.

Among them were carved wooden ornaments, such as a cow, a horse, and a wagon. A beautiful bone china teacup sat in its saucer next to a small teapot with delicate roses painted in pink on the side. Dried wildflowers made up a bouquet tied together with a red ribbon. A small music box stood next to the Holy Bible whose leather bound cover was cracked and old, well read and clutched in the hours of desperation.

Everything was covered in a thick dust. With one exception.

It was a small oval tintype. It shone bright and clean from the shelf on which it sat, meticulously set back in place each time it was held. The young woman who looked out from that oval had a round face that was framed by dark ringlets. The majority of her hair was pulled back into a wavy bun, and off the dark dress she wore. Addie couldn't see much of the dress. The young woman's eyes were light and sparkling from a stilled pose, giving away the excitement behind the full lips and round nose.

She couldn't have been more than eighteen, Addie guessed.

Addie felt the worst kind of intruder. It was easier all morning to pretend this home had no previous woman to tend to it. Knowing a woman had been here to bring all of it about was one thing, to clearly picture her moving about this cabin and laughing with her sons was another. But then again, the death of two people wasn't something planned. They were gone, and now Addie was moving about the cabin, but not laughing with the woman's sons.

Addie backed away from the tintype.

Turning to the opposite wall, she moved to a wood ladder that led to the loft, where, she presumed, the boys slept. The loft was framed by a double log railing. Addie climbed the ladder. The rope beds were disheveled and the blankets were thrown carelessly into a heap at the foot of the bed. The air smelled of a body odor that came from blankets where many nights had passed without washing. A solitary window between the beds looked out to the hill behind the house where it rose to meet a wisp of clouds.

There was no time left that day for scrubbing heavy blankets. It would have to bear waiting. So, she climbed up and spent time bent over arranging the blankets, pulling and straightening, tucking when necessary. The beds were big enough for two, just enough for the boys to share each other's warmth in the winter.

When she finished, Addie gathered her skirt and turned backwards to go down the ladder. The dimension of the loft had changed, just with the small amount of tidying she'd done. Not looking back to the oval tintype, Addie returned to her wash.

Andrew slid down onto shaky legs. Blue looked back at him with a raised head out of his glass eye. As Andrew's feet met with the barn floor, Blue swung his butt away from him and raised his head higher, ears pinned. His round nostril quivered and twitched as he held his air locked deep in his chest.

Andrew's shoulder ached. He had made no mention of it all day as he worked through schooling, kept a straight face at recess during a rather rough game of tag with six other boys. Now he wanted nothing more than to sit down and hold his head in his hands. He tipped his head to look above him at Blue who needed turned out.

To say nothing of the eight stalls to be mucked.

Andrew glanced to Luke who stood in the doorway of the barn gazing up at the house. Looking as well, he saw the woman there, silently pulling an off white, used to be white, shirt off the line. She folded it carefully and placed it into a large basket, then stepped to the next one in line.

Andrew caught a glimpse in his mind of his mother. She was there, her dark hair pulled back into much the same bun as Mrs. Loveland's, but his mama's was far neater. His mama's brown skirt brushed the dirt when she turned to give him a soft smile, the light in her brown eyes reaching into his young soul and pulling out the happiness that had been there, one time, long ago.

Luke said nothing as he turned away and moved to Frank's little mare who stood patiently waiting for Frank to hand her to Luke who would gently remove her bridle, then rub her neck. Frank had previously slid to the ground, still proudly clutching that burlap lunch sack in his hand, however, now it was empty. Luke took Mare to the bunk and took off her bridle. She made no motion to run away, just happily munched on hay.

"C'mon, Andrew," Luke pulled the cinch on Mare as he spoke. "At least there'll be supper at the end of chores tonight." Luke wasn't much better off without the shoulder ache.

His recommendation to Andrew was to run Blue home as hard as he'd run, just to take a little of the edge off him. It had worked, some. All until Blue looked back out of that damned glass eye and realized he was carrying Andrew. That bastard hit another gear Luke didn't know he had. Mare was cautiously loping along with Frank, and honestly, Brown just didn't have enough start to catch Blue.

With acid in his veins, Luke watched Blue fly, unable to catch up what with his little brother loping easily next to him and Mare looking at him with reprimand. So, off Andrew went, sort of in the direction of the home place.

It did no good to talk to Pa about it. Luke had, on several occasions. But, Pa always said the same thing. "Andrew's gotta learn to think. That boy don't think reason for even ten minutes a day. Let 'im work it out and maybe next time he'll choose a mount with reason."

Sure. He'd most certainly choose a mount with reason next time. If he lived long enough to out-use Blue.

Molly nudged Luke's hand as he stood looking at Mare silently. They exchanged looks before he glanced down to the scruffy dog who licked her nose and dipped her head. Her soft brown eyes gleamed brightly as she leaned against his leg. "Hello, Molly girl."

Luke took a moment to rub her behind the ears. The admiration that shone from her was evident while she comforted him in her own way. Molly could never assist Luke with his burdens, but she could comfort him as he carried his own.

Frank finally set his burlap sack aside and picked up a pitchfork. He carefully climbed the ladder to the hay loft above them, his black scuffed shoes making small tapping sounds as he went. The smell of the sweet meadow grass hay met his nose when his pitchfork plunged in and broke the seal the outer hay made. The sweet smell permeated the air around him. Frank's small shoulders moved beneath the simple suspenders sewn to the back of his pants, and buttoned to the front.

Frank was happy. Even though he had no reason to be.

Molly moved on when Luke packed Frank's bridle to the rack on the opposite stall. Now she was somewhere in the back of the barn raising a ruckus. Growling and making low barks, she dug and moved from corner to corner in the last stall on the right. The stalls were made up of poles to separate animals. Now Molly split across the expanse in pursuit of a brown object that moved with speed.

"Get 'er, Moll!" Andrew yelled. Molly dug and raked the creature out of the corner in which it hid. It made a squeaking noise before it lit in the direction of Andrew in the first stall on the left where he stood holding a manure filled pitchfork. The dog caught hold of it just before it reached Andrew and flung it out into the alley. It hit with a squeak and moved at a run again for the back of the barn.

Dust kicked up from underneath the dog's feet as she slid into a right turn and nipped the rat in the hindquarters. It let out a loud whistle and turned to fight. Crouching and breathing heavily, Molly towered above it, poised for it to move. She made no sound, just waited for it to be vulnerable. Having spent her life chasing rats, Molly was good at avoiding getting bit.

"That dog is the ratting-est bastard ever!" Andrew hollered.

"Watch your damn mouth!" Luke hollered back.

Molly made her move and took hold of the rat and flung it high in the air. Stunned, it couldn't recover and make a dash for it before Molly had ahold of it again, flinging it higher than before. She repeated this exercise several more times before taking hold of the creature that no longer held threat of biting. She trotted to Luke and lay the dead thing at his feet. She stepped back and dipped her head at him several times before standing still with her head down, her seeking eyes looking at him patiently.

"Ah, good girl, Moll." Luke reached down to rub her head and back vigorously. When he finished, Molly bounded away to sniff the barn out again.

Andrew moved to Luke, dragging his pitchfork, and looked down at the fresh kill. "Nice big rat."

"Yeah. You ain't gonna skin this one, are ya?" Luke asked cautiously.

Andrew looked down at it a moment. He contemplated, then his eyes lit. He looked up. "Nah, not this one."

By the time what Addie considered an "early supper" hour arrived, she had a stew simmering on the stove. She'd taken time to wander outside, and in doing so found the cellar. It wasn't a large one, the thickness of the rock inside the surrounding hillside made a deep cellar impossible.

It was dark and cool, and it held treasures Addie hadn't seen in years. Dried fruit, store bought canned vegetables, flour, barley for soaking, yeast cakes, dried and salted meats, sugar, and coffee to put the sugar in. She stood there awhile and took it all in. Even her ma back in Texas didn't have these things all at the same time, just lurking there in the blackness, waiting for someone to come along and find them.

Addie took only what she felt absolutely necessary, not wanting to chip too heavily into the winter's reserve. But then again, it would surely last forever with Tom Brady's penchant for skipping meals.

Addie watched the boys ride into the yard and take their horses to the barn. She couldn't help but notice the second-to-oldest boy's horse came in long before the other two did. She was taking wash down from the line when the horse crested the ridge beyond the house. It was moving fast, and Addie wondered if it was because the boy was anxious to be home, or if he had no say in the matter.

In Texas, Addie's brothers spent much of their time breaking horses. They devoted the early years of their childhood acquiring a firm seat on horses too big and too fast without the aid of a saddle. By the time her older brother, Jim, was fifteen, he was starting horses for neighboring ranches and making a fine living at it. Jim was still somewhere in Texas riding bucking horses.

Damn buckin' horses.....

To look back now, Addie's life in entirety was flanked by bucking horses. Flecking sweat, flaring nostrils, the feel of the ground as hooves again met with earth. The soft glint in a kind eye wasn't something she saw very often. She'd felt the warm sunshine on her face and the wind as it tore her hair free and wrapped strands of it around itself.

Addie wasn't afraid of a fast moving horse. Having learned to ride young, she didn't ever think to fear them. It wasn't until recently she realized just how much they could take. How little they respected life. Now, watching men ride the fast buckers, just made her heart stop. It was not her own safety that made her uneasy, but that of somebody else.

So, raised as she was, Addie couldn't imagine a young boy afraid of his horse. Or, at least, unable to stop it from making a mad dash to the barn.

The boys took time in the barn, and Addie assumed they were about their chores.

Gathering her crisp laundry, Addie returned to the house. The air was already turning chilly, so she closed it back up and swept the floor in the kitchen. It would stand scrubbing the next day. Dropping lard into a dutch again, Addie prepared her fried bread to go with the stew, her red and raw hands working the dough quickly. How many times she'd seen her mama's hands like that on wash day.

"Evenin'."

Addie was taken back by the sound of the voice in what was once a tomb void of any noise other than what her work generated. Her heart leapt as she stopped her kneading and looked sharply to the door that hung open.

Fett stood there, smiling softly at her as he slowly removed his hat. His blond hair fell only slightly from where it had been held firmly by his well-worn hat. His blue eyes looked at her anxiously as they sought a response. The red scarf around his neck was dirty and faded, and she could smell the scent it gave off. Addie straightened herself, looked at him and sucked in air.

"Evenin'," the voice came apprehensively this time.

Fett vanished and in his place stood a twelve-year-old boy with an armload of wood. Addie looked at Luke and blinked. He took note of the change in her face as her brows knit together and her eyes began to glisten.

"Evenin'." Addie spoke lowly as she turned back to her dough.

Luke carried his load to the wood bin next to the stove and dropped it. The smell coming from the kettle was enough to make his stomach wake. Supper under his pa's directives usually didn't happen until just before bed. Then, it was something he threw together without thought or pre-determination. And it certainly never smelled like what was coming out of that kettle.

Frank ambled in behind Luke and set the burlap sack on the table. The jar that had carried the precious amount of milk made a sound as it settled on the wood. It jarred Addie's memory.

"Oh, the cow!" She stopped her kneading and grabbed a fresh rag from the top of the clean workbench. It had been awhile since she had to worry about milk cow chores.

"I'll get it, ma'am," Luke replied. "She don't give much in the evenin' anyway."

"I would be glad of that," Addie said softly. "That cow didn't take well to me this mornin'."

Luke looked down at the floor and studied his scuffed boots. "Yeah, I saw your dress front."

Addie glanced down at herself and saw the edges of the stain where the coat she was wearing hadn't protected her. It was stiff and Addie hadn't thought until that moment about how it must have smelled, too.

"Well, I'll know better for tomorrow."

Luke looked up at her then. "You must be brave. My ma never would milk that cow."

Addie scrunched up her lips. She thought of Tom Brady. "Well, I'll know better for tomorrow," she stated flatly.

"Yes, ma'am."

As the first strips of dough hit the simmering fat, Addie heard the sound of a horse. She glanced up to see Tom Brady swing off his horse and reach up for the small boy who sat hunched with head bent in front of the saddle.

"Frank! Get your brother to the stove! He needs warmin'."

Frank rose from where he had taken up post on the bench at the table. He was watching Addie with great curiosity, but now he moved off to attend to his father and brother. It occurred to Addie that she never heard the smallest boy called anything. He was like a dog nobody wanted to claim.

The sound of Tom Brady entering the cabin caused Addie's back to brace, but she didn't turn to look at him. He stood silently looking around for a moment.

The table was clean. In the center of it was the doily his wife had knitted herself the winter before she died. The oil lamp that sat sparkling on it looked proud. The workbench was clear, the stove top was polished.

The giant pile of festering laundry was gone from the floor. The hearty smell of stew permeated the room, and the oil in the dutch began to simmer happily on the stove.

Tom Brady clenched his jaws together.

Frank huddled with the silent boy who watched Addie out of flat eyes. Addie tried hard not to look at them, but her eyes were drawn to them like a magnet. She forced herself to look away.

"I 'spose it's natural for a woman to clean the room she'd be in all day." With that Tom Brady left the cabin.

Addie straightened from where she was cutting dough into strips and clenched her own jaw as she glared at the spot where he had been standing. She looked to Frank who watched her with bright eyes.

He shrugged his small shoulders.

Addie forcefully dropped dough into the dutch and the hot oil.

Addie was beyond exhausted by the time she lowered her body into the rocking chair in the dugout. She had no candle to keep company by, so she fished around in the dark until she found the quilt she'd laid atop the table that morning.

That morning.

Oh, how long ago and far into the past it felt. And yet, it had been on the opposite end of the same day. Something inside her demanded that she cry. The eternity comprising the three miserable weeks she'd spend working for Tom Brady would endure like a bad case of dysentery.

Now, Addie wasn't sure what to think. If a woman were to take up an axe and end a life that causes so much grief, would anyone really notice? She'd be so far gone into that endless cascading brush long before anyone of consequence figured it out.

Had her mama ever been that angry at her pa? Addie couldn't remember. Her mama was such a good woman. She never tired or complained when the work was heavy or the return ungrateful. She just kept at it. The only way Addie ever knew her mama was tried was when she'd sing a sad Irish ballad she'd learned from her grandmother. The rest of the time she'd sing hymns of praise.

That Irish ballad meant her mama wanted to be elsewhere. Addie hummed it to herself as she rocked in the silence and the cold.

A scurrying in the corner made her draw her quilt up to her chest. Addie looked out the open door to the one star she could see in the small patch of sky between the porch and the mountain.

She was beyond scared, beyond the woes of a bitter world. Addie just wanted to close her eyes and make her way in the night to that lone star. To feel her body pass behind her and fly on the wind away from the despair and regret.

Something wet and soft caressed her hand. The weight of the dog's head as it lay in her lap brought a shudder from Addie. The dog was more than silent. The sensation brought reality back, erased the image of Addie's ma from her view, left the star to rotate unnoticed.

The warmth she felt as she ran her hand down the dog's neck made her reach with both hands to draw more of it to her. After a moment, she lay back and continued to stroke the dog with one hand, but the other she rested against her trunk she'd brought closer.

As Addie drifted into sleep, the dog lowered herself down on the feet of the woman who bore a great weight. What it was, the dog couldn't gather, for it seemed her shoulders were empty. She kept up her watch again, the only one in a silent world with the courage to face the night.

The night carried on, with the wailing of a child moving with the wind out onto a frozen desert to go unheeded by the living.

The prairie grass bowed and swayed with the wind, the tiny yellow heads of the flowers waving to a rhythm of unseen forces. The sky above stretched into oblivion without a cloud to break or mar it. The gentle rise and fall of the land rolled as far as the eye could see, the colors of the wildflowers dotting the green of the grass like the stars in the heavens.

Addie raised her hand to shield her eyes from the sun. Her skirt moved with the grass at her feet in the fervor of the breeze. She could hear them coming, feel the vibrations in the ground beneath her feet. She felt them long before she saw them, the sun glimmering and refracting off the manes on their necks where it fanned out as they ran.

They crested a hill to her right, the mass of their bodies converging. The lead stretched and reached ahead of them to pass over country that looked untouched. The softness in the eyes of the lead gray looked familiar to Addie as it climbed the easy rise at her feet. It passed on in the lead of what seemed like hundreds, and cocked an ear to Addie to acknowledge her existence. The gray thundered on, its tail streaming out, coursing in the wind.

They passed her then, nostrils large and round, yet Addie couldn't hear the heavy breathing associated with the hard work of running like that. While they thundered on, they looked at Addie, each in their own way, quietly saluting as they passed. Some arching a neck, a bay tossing a head, a sorrel puffing rapidly. Yet another blood bay calling out to her, his voice trumpeting across the vast prairie.

Addie could smell them, the sweet scent of running horses. But no sweat flecked the air around them.

Then he came. As the mesmerizing remuda followed the contour of the hill and stretched for what looked like miles, he passed. Buck tipped his head and trained an ear on her, his brown eye reflecting the kindness he had always shown Addie when he saw her. His black mane and tail gradually fell as he stopped.

He was so beautiful. Buck's hide shone in the golden sunlight, his eyes sparkling as he turned to look back at Addie. He whistled loudly to her through his rounded nostrils. He raised his head and nickered softly.

"Buck!" Addie called.

He looked at her from where he stood a good ten yards away. He dipped his head once before lowering it in friendship. He stood like that a moment and Addie wasn't sure if she could move to him or not. He looked back and pointed his ears to the herd that moved on rapidly. When he looked back at Addie he again nickered softly.

Then he moved on. He raised his head and spun on his hocks toward the fast moving cavvy that didn't stop nor look back. His body bunched and surged as he moved down the slope and away to catch up.

Addie called again. This time, Buck kept moving. As she watched them go, she saw on a far ridge the gray in the lead had stopped and stood with its ears pointed at her. Something about it made Addie want to call to it, but her voice couldn't form its name.

Just then she remembered it. She opened her mouth and raising her hands to her face to cup the sound, she yelled, *"Mrs. Loveland!"*

Addie jerked at the sound of the incorrect name as the gray's head came up higher. The warm breeze was replaced by bitter cold, the sway of the grass at her feet now the weight of the only warm thing she could feel. Her body jerked and trembled violently.

"Mrs. Loveland. Chore time!" Addie didn't answer as the sound of boots made their way off the porch.

The dog raised up and looked at Addie patiently.

Addie sat a moment in confusion. All that had been forgotten rushed back in anguish. Addie began her new day crying silently. Like an old woman, she clawed her way out of her frozen bed of wood. She groped for her trunk and found it still there, just as she had left it. She pressed her fingers to her lips, then touched the trunk with them. She shuffled off with a new burden.

She didn't know how, or why, but Buck was dead.

Addie did try to do things differently that morning. Although, in reality, she wasn't any more prepared than the morning previous. She did, however, hobble the cow as soon as she came hooking and drooling her way into the bunk. She kept a pitchfork in hand while she dealt with Red Beast.

If Addie had learned anything milking cows as a child, it was that milk cows learn slow. They were far more apt to take offense and brace up than give in. Clearly Red Beast recalled their encounter from the morning before because she got more aggressive about turning and hooking Addie with her long horn since her leg was tied and she couldn't kick.

It took a few times of sticking her in the face with the pitchfork for her to stand, angrily, and allow herself to be milked. Making it obvious that with no attempts on her life, Addie was willing to take as little of the cow's time as possible. Her fingers were numb, and the warmth the tits on that cow provided were as welcome as the comfort of a friend.

Addie spoke to Red Beast softly in hopes the cow would understand she meant no harm. That did not mean she quit watching Red Beast for hostility. Hurrying through the milking wasn't really possible, but she did what she could in the cold pre-dawn air.

Not lingering, Addie placed the milk bucket inside the feed bunk where Red Beast couldn't take out revenge on it, then stood ready with her pitchfork as she released the red savage that was supposed to be a docile farm animal. The cow swung at her and lowered her head, long and sharp horns tipped at Addie.

Addie stood her ground, heart hammering, wondering if she would actually out bluff the old bitch. The cow stood, saliva hanging from her mouth as it would a rabid dog. A low and deep bellow came from within the chest of the animal facing off with a small and starving woman.

Addie raised her pitchfork.

Red Beast blew air out her nostrils. Then, she raised her head slightly and swung away from the points of the fork and bounded into the darkness. As she went, Addie saw Tom Brady standing just beyond the lantern light watching. She took no time to look at him, just gathered her bucket and moved stiffly out into the dark. By then he'd moved on.

The biting air made her skin tingle and sting. Addie moved to the house quickly, but awkwardly. The weight of a full milk bucket made her shoulders burn. Once in the house, she was devastated to feel the chill in the room. It was warmer than the outdoors, but Tom Brady hadn't started a fire.

She set the milk bucket down on the table and it sloshed out. In her haste to be free from the men of the house she'd forgotten to load up the stove the night before. Not that it would have lasted, but some of the heat might have remained. At least a few embers to start a new fire with. The cold had Addie shaking so badly she couldn't attend her task.

Trying to gather herself enough to cry, a long thin ribbon of orange consumed the handful of shavings she'd piled beneath the kindling. The ribbon grew wider until it was as wide as a coffee mug, but even the fire seemed reluctant to take on the task of pushing back the cold. She threw another handful of shavings in and without much control over her numb hand nearly snuffed it out.

Addie opened all the vents.

Shivering and shaking, Addie watched in the low light of the sparkling lantern on the clean doily in the middle of the table. As the fire took hold and ate away at the narrow pieces of kindling, Addie put more small kindling in. It made a roaring, rushing sound that brought life to her heart.

The sound gathered and strengthened until the room was filled with it. It surely must not have been so loud, but her ears hadn't heard much sound in the days previous, so it was overwhelming. She waited to hear the *whoosh* of steam that poured from the undercarriage of the train as it neared the platform she stood on.

Addie drifted to the one and only time she'd seen a train. Her pa held her hand tightly as it came down the track at them like a black monster, frothing at the mouth and thundering a warning. She hid behind her father. As it passed they were enveloped in steam and Addie screamed. Her pa clutched her close to him and laughed.

He'd had such big hands. Calloused though they were, he turned them to gentleness when the need was great. He'd insisted Addie grow up strong, not coddled and cossetted. He taught Addie to ride astride, not sidesaddle. His sister, Addie's aunt, was thrown violently and killed from a sidesaddle. He was merely thirteen, but he decided then some feminine traditions were stupid.

Her pa, Allen, was a quiet man, a big man, and he kept his business private. His family came first in all he did, and he took pride in them. Especially his sons. He often boasted on their talents as horsemen. For Addie, he kept a quiet admiration. She was his only daughter, and he never said much about the fact. But, he would smile a tender smile when she walked out with him in the fields, or held his hand when burdens were great.

The day Fett took her away as his wife was the only time she'd seen his eyes glisten.

Allen kept silent on the matter of Fett, all through the courtin' and shy smiles. Looked the other way when Fett smiled upon his only girl. He spoke just once on his piece, a few days before the wedding. All he said was, "Ad, it'll be a hard life. You aren't used to frills, but you haven't gone hungry neither."

He knew it was pointless to argue.

The door to the sitting room scrapped softly as Luke came through it. The boy glanced at Addie, then looked away. She moved from the fire and its consolation taking the coffee pot with her. She'd brought in a bucket of water the night before to ease her burdens in the dark of the morning. She poured water from it into the coffee pot and another pot to make the morning's mush.

Addie concentrated on a noon meal for the boys. She took a quart jar and filled it with milk. It made her heart swell to remember the feel of the pitchfork in her hands as it made contact with Red Beast...

Luke moved silently through the cabin door, as he did so Addie took note of his clean clothes. He had taken time to tuck his shirt in and brush his hair back. Smiling softly to herself, she thought of what a handsome young man he was. It occurred to Addie it had been a long time since any of the boys had clean clothes to wear into view of public scrutiny.

The coffee boiled; mush formed. Addie took leftover bread from the evening's meal the night before along with boiled eggs. The boys had gathered eggs during chores and brought what few the hens were still laying as fall settled on them. Addie watched them pecking and scratching in the yard the day previous, wondering how they maintained such a large flock.

Addie filled the lunch sack and set out breakfast before Tom Brady returned to the house. Luke returned from the dark and without words retreated to rouse, yet again, his younger brothers. When they appeared, groggy and blind, Andrew had buttoned his shirt crookedly and Frank's hair stood on end on the left side of his head. Luke attempted to tame it.

Andrew made no motions to fix his shirt.

The sound of hungry boys eating played a tune to Addie's work as she checked the yeast cakes she set to soaking the night before. She placed the coffee pot and enamel cup on the table next to Tom Brady's seat. When he came in through the door engulfed in a blast of icy air, he looked from the stove, to Addie, to the boys. The silence of the breakfast table seemed to satisfy him, so he removed his hat and coat.

He sat at the head of the table, rigid in his sovereignty. His dark brown beard was bushy and speckled with water droplets, formed by his own breath in the cold. He wore clean clothes as well, his suspenders pressing tightly into the red of his button down. Tom Brady spoke nothing, merely set his sons to moving with a look. As the sun hinted its arrival, the boys each in turn rose from the table, which was now covered in dirty dishes and oatmeal. Again, only Luke bothered to pick up after himself.

Addie again noted that he wouldn't meet her eyes.

"Andrew, fix your shirt," Tom Brady commanded between sips of hot coffee. He rose from the table and after a few moments carried the youngest soiled boy into the room. He set him down next to the fire, and out of the corner of her eye Addie noted his flat eyes looking for her.

Tom Brady ground his teeth as he noticed his shirt sleeve was wet from the boy's sleeping garment. Addie turned her back to them. The elder boys quietly pulled on coats by the door. The silence was crushing. Addie wanted to run.

She carried her enamel bowl down the workbench to the flour bin and felt all eyes hit her as she bent to pull it open. Now it seemed the boys couldn't pull coats and mittens on fast enough. Luke was the first out the door after swiping the lunch sack off the table, and Andrew fled without getting his coat on. Frank couldn't get his fingers into his holey mittens. He looked at where his finger poked out a hole and then at his father. His shoulders dropped and he plunged into the pale glow of dawn.

He didn't bother to pull the door closed behind him.

Addie watched over her shoulder from above the open bin. Her brows knit together a moment. She reached into the bin and fished around, then took hold of the metal scooper. She glanced at Tom Brady who stood hunched over as he unbuttoned the silent child's sleeping shirt.

Addie drove her scoop hard into the flour, only she struck something soft that stopped her scooper. In surprise she looked down. She sucked in air and dropped the scoop. It clanged on the wooden floor as it hit, causing a look from Tom Brady. Addie stood rigid as her upper lip glistened. She stared down at the flour bin a moment before glaring at the cabin door out of the corner of her eye.

Looking back down, she took in the body that lay in the flour bin. The long tail of bone and skin, the whiskers, the blood and fluid that soaked into the white flour around it.

Addie clenched her fist.

The rat had clearly met some kind of traumatic death. Simple death by poison or circumstance would not have yielded puncture marks. Tom Brady had gone silent behind her, the sound of fabric rustling ceasing. He now, although still hunched, was turned slightly to look at her. His dark eyes emotionless as he took in her stance.

Licking her lips and pressing them together, Addie bent and retrieved the scoop from the floor to the sound of hard running horses leaving the barnyard. Very softly Addie closed the flour bin and replaced the enamel bowl on the shelf.

Alright, you want a fight, you got one!

Once dressed in clean clothes, Tom Brady placed the youngest of the devils at the table. Addie forcefully flung mush into a bowl from the pot on the back of the stove. Her jaw was clenched and her knuckles white where she gripped the wooden spoon.

Addie had brothers. Many brothers. She knew well how to play a little game of revenge.

Tom Brady left taking the youngest boy with him again. He refused dinner, although he paused a second before denying her offer. The house wasn't much quieter after they all had gone than it was when they sat at the table eating.

Back sore from efforts made the day before, Addie boiled her laundry water again. She gathered blankets from beds and hauled them down the loft ladder. She heaved them out to the laundry area and piled them next to the line.

The dog watched her out of curious eyes, dipping its head as she went on about her way. Addie stopped a moment to rub the wire haired head that stood guard over her all night. Looking down at the dog, something passed between them. Something unspoken, that clearly gave the dog a communication that went beyond the ability to speak mere words.

After she boiled water for the tubs, she scrubbed the first round in the golden light of early morning. Her hands were dry and cracked with the hot water and the frigid air, the cracks splitting farther and bleeding with each blanket. It would take all day to dry blankets in the cold air.

Returning to the house, Addie moved to the back of the kitchen and the narrow hall that led to what she assumed was Tom Brady's bedroom. She'd not trespassed there, having left his clean clothes on the table the day before. He gathered them up and put them away himself. At the end of the short hall was another door leading to the outside.

Reaching his private threshold, she pushed open the door to look inside. The white lace curtains were drawn across the windows, but light was still able to fill the room. The sun was on the east side of the house now in the early morning, but it still brightened this dark corner.

The room was sparse, but it was a lovely room. A large round, red rug covered the floor, leaving spots where the wood floor was visible around the edges of the rug. The bed was factory made, the blankets thrown back in a haphazard way that made Addie's cheeks flush. She had never seen one like this, except for one night she had spent with Fett in a hotel. This bed had clearly been used by a man and woman who loved each other.

She stared a moment. For the first time Addie almost felt sorry for Tom Brady. He obviously hadn't bought such a wonder to sleep alone in. Thinking about her own long nights filled with sorrow and loneliness, Addie realized sleeping alone in a bed bought for his wife must have been pure hell.

But then again, from what she could see, Tom Brady spent many of his nights with a bed wetter.

She moved to strip the bed of its blankets. The top was a beautifully pieced quilt of many different colors. She went about her work until movement caught her eye. She knew it was herself reflecting out of the mirror perched atop the mahogany dresser on the wall opposite the bed. She avoided looking. But, as she gathered all the blankets to the middle of the bed, curiosity got the better of her.

Addie visibly jumped when she saw herself. It wasn't that she'd never seen a mirror before, she had, many times. Her mama kept a small one to keep herself with. It was the state she was in that cut her breath. She couldn't even recognize herself.

Her face was gray, her eyes sunken in their sockets. Deep black circles formed under her lids. Her lips that normally carried a deep hue of red were now a thin pale line. The dullness in her eyes would have given the youngest boy some serious competition. The brown and rag tag dress she wore hung off her boney shoulders like she were a mere skeleton walking around. The soft, full breasts that Fett had so delighted in were gone, nothing but sharp points that barely raised her dress front.

Addie pressed her hands to her hollow cheeks and her eyes began to drip. The life had so gone from her they didn't even glisten with the moisture they let. A shaking hand touched her hair last. Her eyes widened as she realized it had been the morning she boarded the stage that she had last brushed it.

It looked it.

Wisps hung lank down her thin neck while the bun was matted and the knot looked like a rat's nest. Thin fingers touched what had once been soft and flowing, but was now coarse and dry. This person was not a human.

"Oh," Addie sobbed. "Where have I gone?"

She stared a few more moments, crying weakened tears as her body refused to move. The room was unendurable. It was full of sorrow and dread, loneliness and the stale air of dead love and dead people. Addie gathered the blankets and left.

The air outside was still crisp and the feel of it purged her lungs.

Instantly the dog was at her side and followed her to the wash tubs. Adding the blankets to the dwindling heap, Addie stood and looked down at her hands. Her dress was torn and old.

Crying, Addie looked at the dog who wagged a tail slowly, her eyes soft and understanding. "Am I dead?" Addie whispered.

The dog dipped her head and wagged again.

"Mama always said dogs see what the livin' can't. Is that why those boys don't look at me?" Addie got no answer from the dog, but she knew Molly clearly saw her.

The dog sat and raised a paw at her, pressing ears close to her head in a gesture of subordination. Addie crouched down and realizing the size of the dog as it looked into her face said, "Is this what they call Purgatory?"

The dog placed a tentative lick on her cheek.

"The life I have left is no life. I can't live without him. He took my heart and soul when he went."

The dog let out a low whine and dipped her head again. Addie cried harder.

"I don't want to live here….I don't want to live this empty life. How can I have it all, then lose it? Why would He do that?" Addie stood on shaking legs and looked through blurry eyes, her vision rippled and distorted. She tipped her head back to the sky.

"Why?" she started slowly, then repeated the word until the peak of her voice echoed off the log of the house and the barn then reverberated into the emptiness of the land surrounding her. Her voice rose with the word until the substance of it fell away and nothing was left but the scream that shot like an arrow at the sky.

The horse Tom Brady and the youngest rode together stopped his climb up the hill and turned sharply, his ears pointed back down toward the house that sat alone amidst the vast sea of sagebrush. The sorrel moved no muscle as his ears trained back down on the spot. Tom Brady looked back over his shoulder at his homestead. It was far away, but he could clearly make out the house, and the sound coming from it.

"What the hell?" he cursed softly. Reaching back into his saddlebag he fished out a monocular he used for finding free roaming livestock. He brought it to his eye, then it took a moment to focus it. The sorrel he sat upon turned to give his full attention to whatever was happening below. Tom Brady jerked on the bridle reins to get his attention, but honestly, the old boy was so intent he didn't notice.

As his monocular focused, Tom Brady said nothing, merely watched a moment. The young boy who sat in front of him in the saddle rested his head back on his father. After a sigh, Tom Brady pushed the monocular back together and reached for the buckskin pouch he kept it in. As he replaced it in his pack he said nothing, just looked down at the house.

"Go ahead. Go ahead and yell at Him. But it won't do you no good." Tom Brady shook his head, then turned his horse and crested the hill.

As the day ground on, Addie kept contemplating her reflection. She recalled the dream she'd had the night before. She cursed the open plains and the horses she could see. All the while, the dog kept watch over her. The chickens gathered closer and chose to do their picking and scratching where they could watch the strange creature who called to the sky.

Her back bent and aching, Addie washed all the blankets in the house, then turned her focus to scrubbing floors. By early afternoon, her arms were weak and she couldn't move them anymore. So, she dumped her water bucket and moved slowly back out to the line where she checked the blankets. They would be dry in time to make beds for the night.

Stopping to ladle out a dipper of water, Addie again caught her reflection. She tried not to think about it as she took her drink. She only had one other dress, and she had refused to wear it again after Fett's funeral. But it ate away at her. It continued to eat away at her as she returned to the kitchen to accomplish a few chores there.

The boys milled about in the barn doing chores as long as possible. They rode in to see the woman pulling blankets off the line, then carry them into the house. At the sight of her, Luke's face turned red. He had no part in putting the rat into the flour bin, but he hadn't stopped it either.

What made it worse was not knowing how much his father knew. No matter who put the rat in the flour bin, they'd all get the leather strap across the butt just the same. It made for a long day of schooling, wondering what would happen when they got home.

Andrew rose out of bed that morning and told Luke what he'd done the night before after his father had gone to use the outhouse. Luke was glad he didn't know the minute Andrew did it or he wouldn't have slept all night. As it was, school had been unbearable enough. Frank was quiet and contemplative, for even at his sum total of six years he'd felt the strap often enough.

Now Andrew looked stricken. He had the entire school day to sit and think about what he'd done, about the consequences of such actions, and worry about just how mad the woman would be. His father didn't like her, but being the cause of wasting an entire bin of flour would gall his father past any lines of allying with his son against a foreign woman.

Andrew glared at Molly who lay in the doorway of the barn thumping her tail on the ground at him. Moll had started the whole thing, catching that damned rat. She was the only one who wouldn't get the strap over it! The whole thing was so unfair.

Glancing to Luke who hadn't spoken to him nor looked at him since the fast ride to school that morning, Andrew felt the weight of guilt tenfold. Not only would he get the strap, but worst yet, so would his brothers who would never speak to him again on account of it.

Isolation was a heavy burden to bear.

"Boys!"

Luke and Andrew met eyes for the first time in many long hours at the sound of the woman calling from the porch. Luke looked to where she stood, hands on hips, skirt moving in unity with the breeze. Luke licked his lips. Andrew swallowed hard.

"Come on up to the house." With that she disappeared through the door.

All three boys stood rooted, the pressure of reprimand palpable between them. The corner of Andrew's mouth twitched. Would she taunt them with the strapping they had coming? Would she attempt to strap them herself? It would be possible. That damn strap hung on the wall by the door for all the world to see and fear. Andrew became indignant.

I'll be damned if some home wrecker woman is gonna strap me!

"Well, come on. You started this, you can take your licks," Luke growled at his brother.

The three boys slowly made their way to the house, shoulders slumped, heads bowed. They made quite a noise with the scuffing of reluctant feet. Mrs. Loveland reappeared to meet them on the porch.

"How was school?" she asked nicely.

Luke looked up at her out of the corner of his eye and took note that her hair was tidied. It was pulled from her face and repined.

Then it hit him. It was like a punch to the groin, a shock so deep he almost fell over backward. He wondered if Andrew felt the same way.

It was the smell of fresh baked bread, laced with that of sugary delight. His stomach flipped and started to growl, then plummeted into nausea. Elation at a long forgotten treat gave way to stricken grief.

"Sit down at the table. I figured you boys would be hungry after a long day. Was your dinner enough?" Mrs. Loveland's voice was so kind and warm. At a inconspicuous glance her eyes and face didn't reveal anything menacing.

There it was. Right there on top of the table. Just past the loaves that sat cooling on clean kitchen rags. It was a stack so large Luke hadn't seen the likes of them since his mother's time. Even then, he wasn't so sure.

Cookies. Little blonde delights with tiny brown speckles of cinnamon. He stopped in his tracks only to be hit by Andrew who couldn't take his eyes away either. Saliva involuntarily filled Luke's mouth only to evaporate and leave nothing by a dry sticky tongue in its wake. Oh, the happy delirium, and the plunging reality.

"Come. Sit." Mrs. Loveland sounded so chipper. Almost happy to see them. Could it be? Had she really not found the rat? Was her eyesight poor? Had she scooped flour without noticing it? Would they now have to endure the agony of telling her that her goods were no good? How would she take that?

The three boys sat in a line on the same bench. Mrs. Loveland sat across from them. She smiled pleasantly. "How was your day?"

Nobody answered. They shrunk down into their suspenders and looked warily at the stack of cookies.

"Oh, come now. Don't be shy. Take one. Each of you. I made them for you."

Was Luke crazy or did he catch a note of sarcasm there? He and Andrew glanced at each other out of the corner of their eyes.

"Take one. Please. You don't want to hurt my feelings, do you? I make very nice cookies." At the end of her statement she threw in a down stroke that all women use against men. That note of desperately rendered feelings that a man was now stepping carelessly on. It was working. Luke knew what was happening, for his own good mother used this tactic many times. He tried to fight it, but he couldn't. He slowly reached out to take a cookie. Mrs. Loveland's eyes twinkled.

"You both better get one." It was still there. Accusing, baring a raw nerve. She wasn't letting anyone off the hook. Not even Frank who was littler and cuter.

Luke ran an elbow into Andrew. "Take one," he whispered.

Once each boy had a cookie in hand, she smiled pleasantly again. "Go on, take a bite. I want to know if they are any good."

Andrew clapped a hand over his mouth briefly. Luke elbowed him again. She clearly had no idea about the rat. Should they roll with it? Play it out like they didn't know about it? Spare themselves the strap?

Yes. If God was going to give an out, this was what Luke had prayed for all day. If they ate the cookies, then surely that would exonerate them of guilt, right? Surely if three boys knew about a rat in the flour bin they wouldn't eat the baked goods made from that flour, would they? No, to Luke's thinking they wouldn't. Now it came down to choice. Take the strap or eat dead rat.

He chose dead rat.

With a trembling jaw, Luke opened his mouth. He elbowed Andrew harshly and hoped the idiot would take the hint. His lips closed down on the warm cookie and......it melted in such a delightful way on his tongue..... the sweetness of it nearly overpowering the image of Molly tossing a screeching rat in the air...... lurching stomach!

"I've been baking all day," came the sweet feminine voice from somewhere across the mile wide table.

Luke looked to the loaves of bread, then to his brother, Andrew, whose eyes were clenched shut as he mechanically chewed. Frank seemed to have forgotten all about the rat and reached for another....

"Eat them all. Growing boys need good feed. We have bread for dinner."

Andrew dry heaved.

With surmounting effort, Luke finished off the cookie. Frank was well into his third. Andrew looked green.

Mrs. Loveland smiled softly. "Were they alright? You boys looked like they didn't taste very good. Don't you like cookies?"

It took all of Luke's effort to reply when he realized Andrew wouldn't. "Yes, ma'am. They were good."

"Good. If you like them, I'll make more tomorrow."

"No, ma'am! Uh, what I mean is, don't trouble yourself." Andrew hurriedly replied.

"Oh, it's no trouble. I like to provide for hungry boys." A look of fondness crossed her face.

"I'm glad you like them." Mrs. Loveland put her arms before her on the table and leaned against them. "I guess now all you have left to wonder is, did I or didn't I clean out the flour bin?" With that she narrowed her eyes and left the table.

That was something none of the three boys had contemplated......

She didn't tell.

Luke sat through dinner that night in fear that she would, but she said nothing as she stood by the workbench, washing and drying dishes.

The only close call was when his pa looked up and saw the loaf of sliced bread sitting on the cutting board in the center of the table, untouched. He reached and took two slices for himself and then said, "What's a matter? Don't be wastin' food."

Each boy took a slice and ate it under his watchful glare.

Luke trudged off to bed, thankful to be away from both adults. He still wasn't speaking to Andrew who hung his head and spoke nothing either. Luke nearly felt sorry for him, but he deserved to be in complete silence.

The truth was, Luke would just as soon have his ma back. But, Luke was old enough to understand that death was a permanent thing. She wouldn't come through the door on a spring breeze, no matter how hard he prayed for her to. Andrew, Luke decided, really didn't understand that.

Luke had a hole in his life. Not that Mrs. Loveland would fill it, but, she provided a sort of buffer between him and his father. Although Luke knew his father understood death, he just wasn't so sure he had accepted it yet.

"Here now, Addie."

The golden light of evening touched everything, turning the hard work of the day into a memory. Addie's ma, Clara, reached back for her hand, the faded blue of her gingham dress warm and familiar. A small hand fished in the space between two beings. When the fingers met, her ma clasped tightly to her hand and smiled down at her.

"Sweet girl."

While still bent towards Addie, her ma shielded her eyes from the brilliance of the sun. She then looked back at Addie's small face that was framed with short auburn curls. Her tiny feet wore no shoes and the feel of the waving prairie grass was soft beneath her feet.

"Look, honey. There he comes." Clara took her hand away from her eyes to point toward the horizon. Being very small, Addie couldn't see much between herself and the ravine that separated her from the horizon her mama wanted her to see.

Addie reached out a small and wobbly hand towards a bluebonnet that struggled after the sky. It waved and bowed in the movement of air that swayed Clara's skirt. Addie couldn't feel it on the bare skin of her arms.

Clara bent low. "There, child. There he comes."

Addie looked where she pointed this time. He stood tall, his ears pointed to her as he watched her from the opposite side of the ravine, the prairie grass waving elegantly at his feet. His color was a dark gray, the points of his ears etched in black. His eyes were a gleaming brown as his nostrils flared and his great neck arched. He then lowered his head and shook his mane and advanced. He picked up a lope and started into the ravine.

Like a grown woman, little Addie shielded her eyes from the sun. His ears still trained on her, the magnificent gray moved easily across the ground and up the hill. Addie couldn't make out who the rider was, for some reason her eyes wouldn't focus on them the way they did on the gray.

Clutching her ma's skirt, Addie hid behind them, only her small head still visible. *"Come, Addie, say hello."*

The great beast stood before her now, blowing through his nostrils and shaking his head. He worked the cricket in the bit in his mouth as he collected himself. His etched ears cocked towards her and he lowered his head. The black of his mane parted halfway up his neck and fell to the opposite side. Still collected, he stepped closer to Addie.

Stepping aside, Clara took hold of Addie's small hand once again. Although sustained, she stood alone. The gray quit working the cricket and stood still, the only sound was the puffing of each exhalation from the rounded nostrils before her. The grass tickled her bare arms as she reached out her free hand to touch the velvet that extended to her. The gray's eyes turned soft as she came closer.

The sharp whine cut between girl and horse. The grown Addie that sat bound in a quilt on the hard rocker groaned slightly to feel the familiar ache and numbness of bitter cold. Her arms weren't bare, but the cold bit them as if they were. The darkness surrounding her was silent and still, the only comfort before her was the twinkling stars and the weight of a dog on her feet. Addie had no idea why the dog chose to stay with her, but she was grateful she did. The scruffy thing was all that kept her from extreme solitude.

In the distance, Addie heard the sound of the cabin door to the main house scraping. The cold and stillness refracted the sound back to her as if it were the door standing before her that was opened.

The dog stood.

What little warmth she had was gone. Standing slowly, Addie started the portion of her day where violent shivering obstructed movement and feeling. Pulling Fett's coat closer to her, she started forward in a bent position.

"Mrs. Loveland." The sharp and unwelcoming voice echoed off the cabin walls to start another desolate day.

"I'm here," came the flat reply.

"Well, let's get on with it then."

Time waits for no one, even when it appears it isn't moving. Even when it has no forward motion. Even, as it were, when it seems to have fallen off track altogether. It moves on, carrying the rest of the world straight toward the sun and relentless rises and sets, always aging the body and soul.

For Addie, this was no different. While her heart and mind stayed on Texas, her body stayed on her tasks. She moved slowly, from one room to the next, always with her tin pail of hot water and soap. Rag in one hand and weariness in the other, she scrubbed and polished Tom Brady's home. She fed his children and washed his clothes. But, never, for any reason, did she clean his room. She left his clean and folded clothes next to the closed door.

That room reminded Addie of times past.

She was numb and humbled, quiet and angry. Her body needed rest, food, and comfort. But, she refused to rest, her dreams more haunting than her wakeful memories, and out of spite she refused to eat more than a few scraps of Tom Brady's surplus. As for comfort, there was a dog.

While that left something to be desired, she was grateful for the patience the dog displayed.

As the days grew ever shorter, ever colder, and ever more bleak, time kept moving. Revolutions brought Addie right back to Red Beast and milking time, then the awkward hour of avoiding the table of men who ate supper behind her as she washed and dried the dishes.

She was grateful she only had to endure three weeks of them.

Each time she felt as though she couldn't go on, Addie thought of her ma, and just how it would feel to board that stage, knowing it would take her home. Home. Addie had no idea how easy it would be to return to Texas knowing Fett would not be there. How hard it would be to see things that she last saw as a new bride.

Well, that couldn't be more painful than living on alone. Existing in a plane of death where she wasn't really alive, nor really dead. The comfort and courage her family would offer would be enough for her to stand on. She kept on with that in her mind.

As for the men who had intruded into her life, Addie took no notice of them. It seemed as though the eldest, Luke, had been quicker to smile, ready to help, less willing to quarrel with the next to eldest, Andrew. Something about the way Luke came out to breakfast every morning dressed in clean clothes made him smile more. He seemed to be making amends for a rat in a flour bin, which Addie already knew he had nothing to do with.

Addie was a week out. Time had slowly brought her to the last of the days she would be trapped with the Bradys. The hours of the day filled with sunlight had decreased to a point where Addie spent much of her time working by lamplight. Soon the boys would no longer have school due to the weather and the impossibility of getting to school in the snow.

Addie didn't know what winter was like in that country, nor did she care to know. Something in the air led her to believe the winter was not going to be kind to an already harsh and barren land. Texas hummed in her heart like a song. Images of her home popped into her mind throughout her day and kept her moving.

Addie had seen no other human life in the time she had worked for Tom Brady except his sons, so as she dried a dutch and listened to the shuffling feet of tired boys as they moved off to sleep, she was surprised when Tom Brady spoke to her. It was said quickly, with no time for return comment.

"Tomorrow we'll be gatherin' yearlings. Boys will be home from schoolin' to help. There'll be six more men for a mid-afternoon meal." Tom Brady moved towards the door to the sitting room as he spoke. Addie paused mid-swipe to look at him in silence.

"There needs to be coffee on the branding fire, too." With that he was gone, his silhouette visible only for a moment as he followed the lamplight to the loft ladder. Addie supposed he was off to issue work orders to the boys.

Addie's heart filled with dread.

More men. As if she didn't have more than she could handle with the five she was stuck with already. She thought a moment longer and realized it wasn't as bad as having to explain herself to another woman. Her situation wasn't a common nor accepted one, and having to explain the depth of her loss was not something she could form the words for.

She'd rather be thought a loose woman than have to face telling another woman about Fett.

But on the bright side, men rarely asked. Perhaps watch her out of curiosity, but somehow, men just knew when it wasn't a good idea to pry into a woman's heart. Addie couldn't figure if it were because they were wise, or if it were because they were only wise enough to realize they weren't wise. Now a woman, that was different. They would pry and poke until Addie was broken and bleeding again.

Which brought to mind another problem. While the Brady family had steadily gotten cleaner, their clothes bright and pressed, Addie had steadily gone the opposite direction. She didn't slip into a cotton night gown at night, mostly because she didn't own one, her silky skin having been Fett's cloth of choice. And, with the fact she didn't put some other kind of sleeping clothes on, that meant she never took off her faded and worn dress.

Clara had helped her make the dress she was wearing. They carefully stitched it with loving hands a week before the wedding, admiring the tiny white flowers against the brown of the fabric. Her mother smiled through tear-filled eyes as she spoke of the days when she herself was a new bride. They'd made one other for her to start her new life with, but it lay in her trunk, untouched since the day Fett was buried.

She pursed her lips and forced herself to look to her idle hands that lay still as she stared into the dutch, remembering. This was not the time to delve into memories. Nor was it the time to remember the feel of her mother's last embrace as she prepared to ride away with Fett.

Already Addie's throat hurt. If she kept up, she'd cry all night.

She placed the dutch at the back of the wood workbench. She went to the door and soaked up as much of the last heat she'd feel until sometime the next morning as she pulled on Fett's coat. She looked down at her dress. Several weeks' worth of scrub water, not to mention the first morning's milk harvest, all resided within the woven thread of that brown dress. It occurred to Addie she must be a spectacle of the dirtiest sort. She might even stink. She had no idea.

Addie grasped her skirt in her hand and brought it closer to her eyes to examine the distressed print. Her eyes welled and she recalled her mother's smile.

"Mama," Addie whispered.

Her fingers lightly traced over the work-roughened exterior of the coat that kept Fett warm, been filled with his heat and smell. A rough exhale came from her chest. As it did so, a small movement made Addie look back towards the sitting room door.

Luke stood in his long night shirt, quietly watching her, listening to her murmurings without comment. Their eyes met and an unspoken understanding of misery met with confusion. His deep eyes reflected his bewilderment at a grown woman and the agony she only revealed when she thought no one was looking.

The moment was broken when Tom Brady stepped past Luke into the kitchen. He looked at Luke and then to what he studied so intently. With that look Addie lowered her tear-filled eyes and pulled the door open and stepped into the darkness. She'd slipped a candle into her pocket earlier that day, along with some matches.

A familiar nudge was at her right hand as she made her way in the black to her dugout. Addie reached out her fingers to feel the dog's head as she went. Her escort was always waiting to guide her through the dark.

As she felt her way along the wall of the icy home she shared with the creatures of the night, she fumbled also for her candle and matches. She struck life to the phosphorus, light blazed bright for a moment as she brought it to the candle. Dripping wax onto the dust covered table, Addie welded the candle to the wood.

She ran her hands along the top of the trunk as she gathered her courage for a moment. Then, removing the pin from the latch, Addie raised the lid. A soft and pleasant smell reached out to her and brought to life images of happiness she no longer felt. After breathing deeply for a time, Addie reached into her trunk.

The day dawned bright and clear, but the air was filled with a certain bitterness to it. Addie watched as the boys bundled into whatever they could find lurking by the cabin door. It was a rare occasion when their father allowed them to drink coffee at breakfast. It was still black outside when they shuffled out the door, spirits high with boyhood spent doing a man's work, instead of trapped in the schoolroom.

Tom Brady lingered about the kitchen as Addie picked up the breakfast dishes scattered across the table top. When he turned to her finally to say something he stopped short and his brows knit together.

It's just a dress, Addie.

The corners of her mouth twitched as she reminded herself, not for the first time that morning, that the memories weren't in the fabric, but in her mind. She'd changed into the dress that had covered her in her sorrow as they lowered Fett...

She stood straight and looked at Tom Brady, the lamplight clearly showing the dark circles under her eyes. The gray color of her dress intensified this reflection. Tom Brady looked away.

78

"Uh, I need you to watch the boy. It'd be best if he didn't have to ride the circle with me." Tom Brady put his hands on his hips and as he finished speaking looked directly at Addie with no please in his features, the brown of his beard wild and frazzled at the ends. He was a tall man, and he looked down at Addie.

Addie thought a moment, then nodded her head before returning to the morning's mess. She wondered if it would be best to handle Tom Brady the same as she did Red Beast. Perhaps not, but it would give her great satisfaction to jab him with the pitchfork.

He left after bundling himself up, and she looked at the door as he walked out. The boy was still sleeping, but she had no idea where in the house. She frowned slightly to think of spending the day under that empty stare. Well, maybe he would sleep late. He normally had to rise to accommodate Tom Brady and his death march, so it was possible. Returning to the workbench, she set to making fresh loaves of bread. By the time they had risen and been punched down, then left to set and rise again, she would hopefully have the wood stove warm enough to bake in.

Addie had never baked in an oven before. When she did for the first time a few days before, several loaves had to be thrown out due to the fact they were scorched beyond redemption. Not one to enjoy a double round of failure, she dreaded the use of the modern convenience a second time. Her ma had a great fireplace in the kitchen back in Texas, and Addie herself in her married life had never cooked on anything except an open fire. Tom Brady's kitchen only boasted the wood stove. Although, she could use the fireplace in the sitting room, for it had been lit against the cold that morning.

Having been to the storehouse and seeing the supply of potatoes and dried vegetables, she decided on stew for the mid-afternoon meal. That and a mostly-scorched slice of bread would do nicely on a man's stomach.

It took the sun a miserably long time to rise, and Addie didn't envy those three boys riding across the sage-covered ground, over rocks and badger holes in the dark. She really didn't envy the boy named Andrew who was no doubt flying across that sage-covered ground, praying he missed the badger holes. She'd watched him come and go on that tall and goofy horse of his many times only to wonder how he survived it.

When the sun's rays finally did illuminate the solitary mountain tops, Addie's dough was well into its first rise. Working alone, she longed to hear the familiar tone of her ma humming as she worked. Addie had no heart to do it for herself.

Having all but forgotten about the boy, she was surprised to turn and see him standing in the doorway leading back to his father's bedroom. He stood against the wall and peered out at her, his dark little eyes glittering as he took in her movements. With no energy to smile, she stood straight from her sweeping to look at him.

Addie considered a moment how difficult his life must be. Not one person in his life wasn't suffering. Not one person ever smiled in a way that showed him how.

"Good morning," she whispered.

Standing there watching him, she saw his little lips move, not with any sound, but almost as if he were attempting to mimic her. The movement was so vague she wasn't really sure she actually saw it. Addie knew he must be cold, for despite the warm fires in the two rooms, he'd been sleeping in the bedroom with the door closed.

"Come. Come now. Come to the fire," Addie said softly. He made no move to follow her voice, but watched her. Setting her broom aside, she took Tom Brady's chair and set it near the big wood-burning cook stove. Filling a cup with the morning's milk bounty, she placed it up high so it would warm on the stove but not scorch. When she turned she saw the boy staring at that enamel mug.

"Are you hungry?" He gave no indication he understood her, nor did he look at her.

Moving to him slowly, Addie reached out a hand for his. He wavered for several moments as he looked at it, a lock of dark brown hair falling over his eye as he did so. He looked back at the mug of milk warming above the bread box. As he reached up to take her hand, Addie realized just how cold he was, it was like holding on to a rock pulled from the river.

She led him to the chair and helped him on, the feel of his small body, cold and sharp, beneath her hands. Once settled, she handed him the mug of milk. He took it and within a few seconds had the creamy contents consumed. As soon as it hit the belly, his body came alive. Upon doing so, it began to shiver violently with the chill in his fragile bones.

"Oh, you are alive. I was beginning to wonder." Addie smiled softly at him, but his blue tinged lips didn't respond. He watched her out of dark eyes, but something in them wasn't as shocking.

Addie stepped away and into the sitting room, on past the warmth of the fire and to the ladder to the loft. She climbed with a weary body. Stripping a quilt off the closest disheveled bed, then painstakingly straightening the blankets on each sleeping place, she descended once again. The boy stood in the doorway to the kitchen watching her, still shivering. When she reached him, he stood resolutely staring at her dress. Addie bound him up in the quilt, then lifted his light frame and carried him back to his chair. He was stiff and awkward in her arms.

That was it. He was content.

Slicing into a loaf from the day previous, Addie slathered it with honey from the cupboard. The boy ate with a few fingers out the top of his quilt and watched Addie as she worked. When the bread was gone, she bundled him tight again. He made no move for a great length of time. In his shimmering eyes was a look of vague curiosity, and each time Addie looked at him and offered a weak-hearted smile, the corners of his mouth twitched.

A solitary bark from the porch brought Addie to the window about noon. The grizzled dog sat in rapt attention, her bent ears forward as she looked out past the barn, over the corrals, out into the vast space between sage and sky. Addie saw no movement on the horizon, so she went back to work for another quarter of an hour.

She'd dressed the boy and kept him occupied with bits of food, and in pursuing her own work gave him something to watch. He was a silent partner, and unlike boys she'd known, didn't involve himself in mischief

81

when things got slow.

Another bark sent Addie again to the window, and this time the dog was running across the barnyard, tail out, ears back. She was bound for somewhere. She pulled the latch on the door then stepped out as she dried her hands on a clean kitchen cloth. Addie watched the horizon. She felt them long before she saw them. The low and steady hum of vibration as it traveled along through the ground. The dog was nothing but a bounding black dot as Molly dodged and jumped the sage in her path.

They poured over the hill from every direction in every color, thundering as they went, nostrils flaring and manes flying. What Addie had assumed were cattle, indeed turned out to be horses. Near thirty of them in the single band, streaking out of the emptiness and barely contained in a specific direction at the vague urgings of the men working twice as hard to keep up. Smears of sweat drenched the flanks and necks of the beasts pressing on towards the homestead. A man in the lead over and undered his horse with the need to overtake ground on the lead horses before they saw their destination and veered away.

Addie lowered her hands.

The men and boys in the back closed in and pressed tightly, seeing that no doubters in the bunch listened to conscience and turned back. The wooden gates to a huge corral stood gaping open, and for the first time Addie took in the enormity of it. The wood posts were high, laden with heavy poles. A horse in the lead second guessed his direction, and for a moment Addie thought the herd would be lost. But, Tom Brady pushed in from the side on a sweat-soaked bay. Like a tide of water, the horses flooded through the gate, only to hit the dam of back fence and fan out to the left and right and hit another gear and rush the gate again. But, as the bunch kept coming, the colors and bodies mingled in mass confusion and all speed was stopped. They milled and spooked, snorted and raced along the confines of their enormous entrapment.

The final insult to freedom was the closing of the gates, one by Luke, the other a tall man Addie had never seen before. He patted Luke's shoulders and smiled down at him just before they turned to the waiting, sweating horses to remount. From inside the corral Tom Brady shouted something to Luke and his counterpart. They moved at a brisk trot around the fence line to a smaller, easier gate to handle horseback. The tall man made short work of it and within seconds and a few fine-tuned maneuvers had the gate opened and shut with Luke and himself inside. They rode to the center of the pen where Tom Brady sat, bullwhip in hand, looking at individual horses as they ran by in a great circle. The horses moved as one great body, young ones from the past spring whinnying frantically for their mothers lost in the fray, mares pushing and fighting to keep the mass moving.

Out of the bulk of the moving animals came a great beast, black in color with a white star beneath his long forelock. He screamed a violent threat before he charged after the group of geldings that stood quietly in the middle of a storm of chaos and panic. Without much distraction from the conversation with the man and boy, Tom Brady stepped away from them and cracked his whip. With teeth bared and ears back the stud reared and struck at the bay Tom Brady sat on. Looking irritated, he cracked his whip, but this time the tip mercilessly bit the end of the stud's tender nose. Not one to back down from the defense of his band, the black stud charged. He stopped short when the whip bit again. He spun to double barrel the nervous bay with both hindquarters, but instead squealed and ran when the whip spoke yet again.

"How'd he end up in there?" the tall man shouted to Tom.

"Ah, he's always workin' his way from the geldings and headin' back to the mares. Even when the season for workin' is done and gone," Tom replied. "I just know some wild stud is gonna kick his ass one day and break a leg on him. We'll sort him and put him back with the geldings for the winter. If he'd just stay where he belongs..." Tom didn't complete his thought.

Tom Brady wound the whip and threw it to Luke, then took his rope down from where it rested, coiled neatly and tied by a leather strap to the saddle. Tom Brady built a loop and without visible encouragement his horse started forward. His loop floated, open and direct, and settled over the neck of a sorrel mare running on the outside of the bunch. She looked poor, her hip bones protruding sharply and her ribs like that of a scrub board. She stopped and jerked violently once, but after a stout pull from the bay dropped her head and came willingly enough. Her mane and tail were full of witches knots and sticks, all dreaded together. Out of the band with her came a shaggy little foal, stunted in his mama's poor condition, as she obviously wasn't making enough milk to raise a babe.

Tom Brady led the mare to Luke and passed the rope over to him. Luke dallied and took the mare to a gate north of where they stood. The running bunch bowed out around Luke as he made his way with the mare and shaggy little foal behind her. Luke opened the gate and put her in a pen by herself with her foal, where she would wait doctoring.

Addie watched all this from her vantage point on the porch of the cabin on the rise. Seeing that band made her stomach flip and go all queasy. Where before she would have stood to take in each horse's color, conformation, and gauge temperament, she turned away and went back to her work in the cabin. A female role she'd never bothered to take before. If it had been Fett, she would have made ready the meal in time to watch the horses come in, then be sorted. She never missed a chance to watch him work. And, on many occasions, aided him in the sorting and held herd. Not this time.

Addie put more wood on the kitchen fire.

At what Addie would have considered close to mid-afternoon, she began to put things in wooden crates. Plates, spoons, enamel mugs, the coffee pot with freshly ground beans. She sliced and wrapped three loaves of bread in clean towels and put them on top of the cutlery. She took deep plates and stood them up next to the coffee pot. Then as she contemplated the first of her trips to deliver the meal, she heard heavy foot falls. Looking out the window, she saw Andrew leading one of the work horses hitched to a simple cart, not more than a large wooden box on wheels. It seemed a bit more horse than the weight of the stew called for, but Addie was sure the beast was chosen based on his ability to be gentle with the cart.

Addie loaded all her wares into the empty cart and looked it over one last time. She then smoothed her apron down, but she realized that really made no difference. All she had to do was set the coffee on the fire, leave the meal in the cart ready to dish up, and head for the house.

It was then she remembered the boy.

Returning into the house, she took him by the hand and led him out the door. He came methodically enough, and when she lifted him into the cart he huddled to one corner. That prompted her to get his wee little coat from the peg next to the door. It should have prompted her to get her own, but she gave no thought to herself until somewhere by the barn when the bitter wind bit into her flesh through her dress.

Andrew led the work horse and cart while working at not looking at Addie. Horses were still thundering around the corral, but now Addie could see that the mares and foals had been parted off from the yearlings. The stud marched back and forth along the fence in his own solitary confinement screaming at the mares in the next enclosure who took the opportunity not to listen. In frustration he bucked violently before returning to his post, head up over the fence, mane shaking and flying in his exertions.

Damn studs.

Two men worked over the fire at the south side of the pen, a strong and healthy blaze that consumed the wood above it. Tom Brady, the tall man, Luke and another sat in the center of the pen discussing particular horses, a few that were clearly older than the yearlings they ran with. Tom Brady still had his loop down, but his hand rested atop his saddle horn. The tall man pointed to an animal and nodded vigorously. Tom Brady stepped away from the rest and threw a loop. It settled easily over the head of a chestnut filly. She ran and fought wildly for a moment, but the bay Tom Brady rode kept up with her without much problem.

Frank opened a gate on the west side for his father who ran the filly into an alley. Once there, two other men ushered her into a round corral and replaced Tom Brady's rope with another. It was then the first saddling process began for the young filly.

Addie looked away. She'd seen it many times before, and she had no desire to watch men get themselves killed.

Sighing heavily, Addie took her coffee fixin's crate and slipped through the poles in the fence. She caused quite a stir with a bunch of young horses who had taken refuge in the corner close to her. They spun in a tangled mass before one caught the idea to run. Away they shot to the south corner, too afraid to pass in front of the men who surveyed the prospects. Silently, Addie passed behind the men whose horses tipped their heads to watch her pass out of the corners of their eyes. She could hear Andrew's blue-eyed goof calling from the saddling stall where he was tied.

So far, no one had noticed her. She set the filled coffee pot on the fire's edge, arranged the crate with mugs and stood to leave. The horses were moving again, fast, as the tall man this time swung his loop. Hovering at the fire, Addie waited until the tall man passed with the bunch of running horses, but he didn't. Instead, his eyes met with Addie and he let the bunch go, the black he rode collecting for the stop it made just in front of her.

The horse dropped his head as the man leaned forward and rested on his elbows against the saddle horn. He pressed a thumb to his lips as his blue eyes sparkled. His cheek twitched with the effort it took not to smile. He stared at her face a moment as Addie listened to the sounds of the filly grunting as she flung herself around the round pen in attempt to remove the saddle she now wore.

The tall man had light colored hair and a smooth face. He shook his head just before he spoke. "You must be the housekeeper."

It came out more a statement than the accusation Tom Brady made several weeks before. Addie just stared as his face broke into a grin and he laughed once. "You're not old."

Addie decided to leave as Tom Brady, Luke and the others were now watching. Even those with the rollicking filly forgot their duties and gaped. The tall man laughed again.

"I told him. I told him some soured old hide would do him no good. He needed life to brighten up those boys. Now look. Here you are," he smiled as he spoke, clearly proud he'd been right.

He stuck out his hand as his horse side passed to her. "Roy. Roy Albert, ma'am."

Addie hesitated a moment before taking his large and rough hand.

86

"Addie Loveland." The boys in the round corral were now standing at the fence, arms draped through, the filly pitching and writhing unnoticed behind them.

Roy pushed his hat back. "Tell me, Addie Loveland, where do you come from?"

Her eyes shimmered some as she replied, "Texas."

Roy's eyes and face grew serious. "Well, it's a pleasure to meet you, young lady."

Addie smiled reservedly as she stepped away from him, her head down, but she could feel all eyes on her as she made her way across that wide corral. Even the horses that had once been running frantically were now paused in their tracks not far beyond to her right watching her. The filly that pitched and writhed now completely forgotten of her burdens pricked her ears forward in silence to see Addie go.

She quickened her pace. Addie slipped as gracefully as possible through the corral fence and stepped to the lunch cart. She finished arranging lunch before asking Andrew to bring the cart to the house when the meal was over. He nodded an unhappy agreement.

Work had mostly returned to normal in the corrals behind her when Addie gathered the smallest boy in her arms and lifted him to her. He, in his customary fashion, said nothing, but moved in closer to her to secure some warmth. Addie doubted she had any.

He stood not twenty yards from her, quietly watching, quietly waiting, for her to turn and look at him. When Addie did finally turn towards the house and saw him, she stopped and felt what little strength she had go from her. The boy in her arms became an unbearable burden she could not hold up.

She recognized him instantly. He was no doubt the same, the dark etching around his ears as they stood prominently pointed in her direction. His deep brown eyes were bright in the gray light of the afternoon. His dark gray coat had not yet grown out into winter's shag. It was thick, but still short and handsome. He dipped his head at her, but his focus remained on Addie without breaking.

As she stood in stunned shock, reliving the moment her tiny hand had reached out to his velvet muzzle across the waving prairie grass and bluebonnets, the tall gray horse took a giant lunge towards her. His whole body rose and lengthened out as he moved closer. Addie backed away from his advance quickly. He again lunged at her.

"He won't hurt ya." Addie looked back to see Roy had come to the fence and side passed to it to speak encouragement to her.

At the sound of another jump Addie returned focus to the gray whose eyes were intent, yet kind. Looking down at the big feet that prepared for another lunge, Addie realized he was hobbled. The leather that tied his front legs together at the cannon bone kept him from advancing to her normally. Addie felt her mama's hand holding hers. Tears began to burn about the time the gray reached his nose out for her to come to him. She balled her hand over a wad of the boy's coat.

"He don't mean harm, ma'am."

"It's not that," Addie replied in a small voice.

Roy was silent a moment, then said, "Maybe more the fact that he thinks he knows you."

Addie answered nothing in return, just gathered her courage and left, ignoring the apparition standing before her, beckoning for her to come to him. His great neck arched as he turned to watch her leave, part of his mane falling to the other side of his neck as he did so. His nostrils flared as he took in her scent on the breeze.

Roy turned to look at Luke who rode up beside him and watched as Addie headed to the house quickly. Luke gave Roy a partial smile out of the corner of his eye.

"She goes Friday."

Roy nodded his head in a way that said it was natural for her to. After a moment he looked up at the graying sky. "The weather is changin'."

Luke looked up also. "Yeah." He paused to gather his thoughts into words. "She is real sad."

Looking down and over at Luke, Roy again nodded his head. "Sad is a part of life. But only a part."

"What's gonna happen to her?"

Roy shook his head as he again looked at the sky. "The weather is changin'."

On Thursday, it was all Addie could do to get through her day. She rose before Tom Brady came to her dugout to shout at her to rise. She ignored Red Beast's threats and snot strings, giddy with the promise this was the last time she would have to bother with her. No one spoke of regrets at Addie's departure at the breakfast table. Nobody said it, but Luke felt it.

Addie spent the morning making bread and cookies while the wind whistled out a tune as it came round the edges of the log cabin. The sunlight was dull and listless as it filtered through high, thin clouds. The air bit crisply the day before as she had labored over the wash tub and the Brady family's clothes one last time.

Addie was gonna see her mama again, and Texas moved through her like a river, sometimes gentle, sometimes rushing as her blood quickened at the thought of seeing it. It would not yet be blustery there. How long would the stage ride be? She had no idea. Days on days, she figured, but a day on the stage getting closer was far better than a day spent dreaming about it. Addie wasn't slow or sluggish, she moved through her last day with ease, almost careless, even.

A three-week eternity was now ending, and Addie couldn't have found greater relief. She looked at the faces of her family in her mind one at a time, held them in her heart with strong arms, saw her mama's face as she both cried and laughed to see her girl back again under such devastating terms. Her pa wouldn't say much, just hold her tight and try to think of a way to set things right again.

Tom Brady spent the last several days since the gathering of the yearlings putting work into the filly that had been saddled for the first time that day. He took time with her, and although he was pushing her way beyond her limit, he was making steady progress. The day passed with her under saddle, going out and carrying him while he went about his duties, doing what, Addie really didn't know.

The filly was a gentle beast who really had no desire to spend her time fighting. After the first day Tom Brady took her out into the hills to check one of his other broodmare bands, the filly learned not to waste her precious energy bucking and fighting, for in the end, Tom Brady would not be unseated, and she would still have to complete her tasks by the end of the day. No matter how tired and weak she was.

For Addie, this filly was the world. The little red mare was her ticket to Texas. It was Tom Brady's intentions to tie the bright-eyed filly to the back of the wagon and take her with them as they journeyed to Tuscarora and the stage line. Tom Brady did not have the cash to pay a housekeeper who was meant to stay the winter. After colts were sold he'd have cash, but not yet. He merely hoped she'd bring enough, fillies not being worth as much as a gelding. But, he'd had no time to gather a gelding from another far roaming band.

She would have made not only an excellent saddle horse, but a great contribution as a broodmare, too.

The wind gathered speed as Addie's last day with the Brady's passed. The sky didn't change much, but the whistling soon became a great moan. The boys returned from school with red noses and red cheeks. Addie wondered briefly if they had scarves somewhere, but dismissed it since she wouldn't be around to worry about it later.

Supper was a quiet affair, nobody speaking, which didn't matter since Addie was already hundreds of miles away. She put everything back in its place, setting out breakfast makings early as to make things quicker in the morning.

Addie closed her door that night against the cold that rushed through the dugout door like a train. Her companion stayed with her to guard her last night with vigilance, but Addie was thankful she wouldn't need her anymore. The wind would make for a terrible traveling partner, but, Addie was willing to partner up. Gathering her quilt around her, Addie listened as the scurrying turned into the running footsteps of her younger brothers as she stepped through the doorway to her dreams.

The brilliance of the dark blue sky against the setting golden sun was blinding as Addie looked out across the vast prairie. The grass blew softly in the twilight, moving out across the earth as Fett walked to her, hands in his pockets, his clean white shirt gleaming. The top two buttons were undone in his usual fashion, and his skin was clean and pure. The suspenders on his trousers melded against the muscles in his chest and shoulders.

Addie cried instantly at the sight of him.

Fett stopped and smiled softy at her, just out of reach. His sandy blond hair ruffled with the wind, the lines around his blue eyes crinkling a bit as he looked at Addie. She wasn't sure why she couldn't go to him, touch him, nor why looking at him made her miss him deeply. Surely they had ridden to this spot together?

"Listen to that wind, Addie. Listen to the wind."

The breeze she heard was soft and compliant. As she so often did when she saw Fett anymore, Addie felt confused.

"Sweet Addie, listen to that wind change your weather. Listen to your weather change."

Addie shook her head. The breeze was barely enough to tease the wisps of hair around her face. Fett's blue eyes were full of sympathy as he stood there, perfect, looking at her.

"What wind?" she asked in a panicked voice.

The roar came from somewhere out on the prairie. As it engulfed her it brought a deep blackness with it, smothering everything in its wake. Addie heard a sharp whine as the dog laid her head on Addie's lap. The extreme bitter cold that covered everything with death was unlike any cold Addie had ever encountered in her life before, and despite her coat and quilt, she felt the impossibility of rising and moving ever again. Instinct told her to make her way to the main house, but she really didn't think she could make it, even if she tried.

The dog moaned loudly now, right into Addie's face as she lay her head back against the hard rocker. It seemed an easier option to lay back and sleep in shivering fits until dawn came. But the dog howled now, nudging her and whining, trying to get her to raise her head.

"Let me go," Addie whispered.

Beyond the dog, the wind had moved from a moan as it came

around corners to a roar rivaled by that train her pa took her to see. It made no attempt to slow with the slacking of the gusts that rattled the panes in the window. Addie could hear something as it blew in underneath the door, skittering as it swirled and sought a home. Behind closed eyes, she envisioned dust collecting in the corners of her mama's well-kept house.

A huge gust blasted the door to the dugout open with an explosion of cold. Addie could feel something pelting her face, biting as it stung her bare skin. The cold ache in her neck wouldn't allow her to raise her head, nor reasonably think how to get the door shut. It was difficult to think with the barking going on in her face now.

"Get up. Get up, Mrs. Loveland."

Hands grasped at her arms through the quilt and coat and Addie couldn't understand why milking was so important. Let Red Beast waller in her own agony.

"Get up, woman. Mrs. Loveland!" The harshness of the voice caused her to groan loudly at it. The shivering had ceased, but she couldn't make herself push the source of the voice away.

She was roughly pulled to her feet, the kink in her neck screaming violently. "Come on, we gotta go. Walk with me."

Tom Brady had brought a lantern on his snowbound journey to the dugout, but the force of the wind and driving snow had snuffed out the faint life without hesitation. Now he struggled on through the driving snow and wind on instinct. The woman he drug along behind him stumbled and tripped with full desire to lay down and drift away. Angrily, he pulled her forcefully with him.

When they reached the creek, his first step broke through the newly formed ice and plunged his foot into the frigid waters. He had no hope of finding the footbridge. It did give him relief to know he was at least heading in the general direction of the main house. Tom Brady paused in his relentless march against the snow and wind to gather the failing woman into his arms, the mere bones and skin of her, and hold her against his chest as he stumbled through the ice and water, over the mounding snow, following the impatient bark of the dog who walked ahead of him a few feet. The sound seemed miles away through the wind.

There was nothing to her. Tom Brady could feel the protrusions of her sharp bones even though a bulky coat and thin quilt enshrouded her. Nothing about her struck him as delicate femininity while he hauled a mere girl towards warmth.

"I hate you," she'd said it with what must have been the last of her strength.

"I hate you, too," he replied vehemently.

"Take me to the stage."

"You're plumb froze stupid. Won't be no stage now 'til spring," he spat.

The dog barked from the porch now. His feet wet blocks of frozen water, Tom Brady stumbled up the steps nearly going down and dropping the silent woman. In his mind he wondered if she were dead, way past the point a warm fire would do her any good. The door flung open and light reached out to him, who hoped she wasn't dead, the time consuming task of notifying family really didn't appeal to him. While he would have a pang of guilt, he doubted he'd waste his time with it.

Luke watched anxiously from the doorway of the cabin.

Tom Brady set Addie down in the chair Luke drug to the fire in the sitting room. The room was light with the blaze that raged and popped, lighting the room without the aid of a lamp. Luke stood behind his father and watched through fearful eyes at the pale woman who made no sound. Her head fell back and nothing in her face moved. Tom Brady, despite jerking movements of his own, pulled the quilt free and unbuttoned her man's coat to let warmth reach her body. Something about the way she lay there struck him, for his father's hard face changed in a way Luke had never seen. Realization hit him as he looked at the frail body before him, hunched and bent, sharp and unmoving. He stopped shivering and a great sadness crossed his hard mask of a face.

Tom Brady lifted a hand to his mouth and covered it for a moment before turning his hand and rubbing his chin with a knuckle. Luke watched his father in horror, just standing there, helpless.

A great and terrible sound came from somewhere in the room, the source Luke could not identify for several seconds. After a time he wanted to clap his hands over his ears and run from the sound of suffering. He looked to his father who stood watching the woman with agony in his own face, the sadness there reflecting that of the sound she made.

Mrs. Loveland finally moved with the break in the sound and with an inhalation continued the wail that came from somewhere in her soul. She molded herself into a ball and covered her head with her arms.

Tom Brady turned to Luke. "Come, boy."

Luke was reluctant to leave, so his father took him by the shoulder and led him out. Luke turned to look at Mrs. Loveland who wept with intensity.

"Is she scared about nearly dyin'?" Luke asked after his father had shut the door and walked to the bench and sat to remove his wet boots.

Tom Brady was silent for a great length of time. "No." After a pause he continued, "No, she's grieving that she didn't."

Luke swallowed hard and looked down. "Should I do somethin'?"

"No, just let her be."

It was a great and insufferable blow. The kind that wraps the insides up into a ball then squeezes them in a fist until all life has dripped out. When Addie had wept out all her meager strength, she just sat, unmoving, crushed, and hopeless, until the fire burned low and the sound of the wind drove her to near madness. She couldn't think of one good reason to be left in this horrible home to die.

That was how she felt, and yet she had multiple opportunities to die and hadn't. That was rather disappointing to her. Addie had no way of knowing what Tom Brady would do now. The bargain had been for three weeks and money to get her down the line. It was an open fact now that they hated each other, and how he would react to that was anyone's guess.

But, although she had no idea where she would go, it would be a great relief to her to be free of the house where he lived and avoided his duties as father. Addie certainly didn't want to spend her time caring for a pack of ungrateful boys who thought up terrible ways to annoy her. She was now completely on her own. It may be she would have to make her way to Tuscarora for the winter.

The sound of the door opening and closing behind her brought dread into her soul. Tom Brady came around to poke at the fire and throw in several more logs. It would be a day for stoking fires to ward off the chill the wind drove into any cracks and holes it could find in the house.

He stood with his back to her while he used the poker to arrange the logs. After he had a good blaze going, he turned and looked down at her. "What are your plans now?"

Addie looked up at him and replied, "I guess that depends on what you say next."

He shook his head. "There must be damn near a foot of snow out there right now. No way we'll get to Tuscarora today or tomorrow. Not to mention I can't leave my stock out there after all this. Soon as possible, I gotta get out there and gather what I can."

"Then what do I do?" Addie asked.

Tom Brady again shook his head, a lock of dark brown hair falling across his forehead. The scruff of his beard made it hard to see his features very well.

"Well, I don't see how you got much choice but to set where you are. What I'm gonna pay you won't see you through to spring, let alone get you wherever it is you want to go. Unless you have a mind to earn wages some other way." Tom Brady avoided looking at Addie.

"I don't want to set up here. I don't want to set up anywhere."

"Well, tell me a better idea! You don't want to be here. I don't want you here. I think we both agree on that. But you need a place to hide out the winter, and I need somebody to look after things I can't get around to. It's a simple matter of necessity."

Addie felt the last shred of give-a-damn drain out onto the wood floor. "When will the stage lines run again in this country?"

Tom Brady rubbed his face with his hand. "End of March on a good year. April to first of May on a bad year."

Addie closed her eyes and stopped breathing.

"You got no choice, woman. Accept it for what it is. You'll be outta here come warm weather time with winter wages in your pocket."

They both fell silent, Tom Brady's mind drifting with the sound of the wind to the stock out on the range and the task of sorting off the poorer ones and driving them to his meadows where they would be fed through the winter. The rest would make out for themselves. Already he knew it would be a hard winter what with the snow piling and drifting in the middle of November.

Addie was searching for a reason to breathe again. She couldn't find one suitable enough. The thought of a long day trapped in the cabin with the Bradys was enough to choke the air out of her lungs anyway.

"Woman."

Addie looked at Tom Brady with derision.

"Eat something. Or at least leave an address where I can notify kin of your departure." With that Tom Brady stood and left the room leaving Addie to stare into the fire.

By the time the sun rose and struggled to filter through the thick layer of gray and white, it had little effect on the world around the main house. Addie had finally stood and wandered to the window to look out at the bleak world around her. It was like watching death claim everyone she loved then carry them off to a place she could not follow. A terrible feeling of dread consumed her and made a tragic form of panic rise up into her throat. She gripped the window sill to keep her sanity and reject the notion to run out into the storm in the general direction of home.

At the sound of Frank and Andrew coming down the loft ladder, Addie folded her quilt and lay it on the chair by the desk for safe keeping. The flood of memories it brought back caused her to look away. The stark reality of her situation was enough to drive Fett away.

Moving into the kitchen, Addie found Luke staring into a rare cup of coffee. He looked up at her through shining blue eyes that reflected deep uncertainty. As for Tom Brady, he made the most of his time by spreading harness out on the table and added to the grease spots on the table with his oil. Addie flashed back to the animal skins on the wall. She had thrown them into the barn. The youngest boy stood on the bench in his night shirt and watched her with wide eyes. He looked like a little scarecrow perched up there.

Watching Addie as she moved through the kitchen, he moved slightly and nearly fell off the bench. "Boy, watch yourself," Tom Brady stated in an unfriendly voice.

Stopping in front of the big cook stove, Addie balled her fists and turned slowly to Tom Brady. "Has the boy no name? I've been here for three weeks and never in that time did anybody call him anything other than boy."

Tom Brady's hands stopped, but he merely raised his eyes to her. His look held fire in it. "Charlie. His name is Charlie."

Addie sighed as she looked at the boy who stood on the bench watching her out of empty eyes. His little shoulders slumped and he looked like he carried his world between his shoulder blades.

The storm raged on as Addie begrudgingly made breakfast. Hot, angry tears threatened to spill the entire time, making it nearly impossible to carry out the process. Everything had to be done by lamplight. Many times Tom Brady rose and went to the window and looked out, sighing heavily then rubbing the back of his neck. The boys gathered at the table said nothing, just watched their father with looks that ranged between understanding and fear.

The livestock.

It was an unexpected blow with little or no time to get somewhere with adequate shelter. But, the air had been cold for several weeks, so it was not as if the animals hadn't been somewhat hardened off. But, Tom Brady feared some of his stock was still high, still foraging on what was left of last year's summer grass.

Waiting out the storm with little to no hope was a painful thing to endure.

The day wore on. Soon after breakfast, Tom Brady and Luke bundled up and made their way awkwardly to the barn for chores. Even in the daylight the blowing snow made it hard to make way. By mid-afternoon it quit snowing, but the wind kept up with its insatiable gusting. Addie would have chosen a large project to occupy her mind, but the fact was she had to split her time between the two fires in the house that had to be minded constantly to prevent the bitter cold from gaining a foothold.

After evening chores, Luke commented on the severity of it all. Tom Brady spoke to comfort himself more than anyone. "The wind is good. It blows open stretches bare so the stock can forage easily."

Luke nodded his head and reached out to the fire to warm his cold and stiff fingers. After the evening meal, Addie gathered her coat with a deep feeling of dread and shrugged slowly into it. Tom Brady was now working in a ledger at the table by lamplight, his pencil making scratching noises as it wrote in small columns.

"No way you'll make the night out there. You won't even make it to the creek." He hadn't looked up.

Addie was just about to open her mouth and let something nasty fly, but he interrupted her. "Stay in here by the fire. That's gotta be better than waiting for death."

Addie wasn't so sure. He still hadn't looked up from his ledger. In her hesitation he made up her mind for her.

"Stay by the fire. You sleep sittin' up anyway. At least there will be a fire."

It was an end to a very difficult day. She had thought that by now she would be close to Tuscarora, sleeping under the stars, dreaming of getting on that stage come morning. But, as it was, she spent her day silently crying, avoiding the Bradys in a very tight space, and feeling like what Fett hadn't taken with him was slowly dying too.

Addie felt her shoulders must look like little Charlie's. Slumped and sagging, crushed under the weight of her world. Addie turned to the sitting room and left, the weariness in her bones drawing her to the fire after she collected her quilt and moved to a chair where the heat out spoke the cold.

Tears running down her face, Addie listened to the wind that kept up with its game outside.

I'm broken. I'm broken, God. You've wanted it done and now it is. You took my light, my life, and now you've left me with this. Just whose side are you on?

Addie dreamed no dreams until just before the fire burned low and she woke to tend it. The gray stood on a hill across a ravine from her. Addie watched him from her own hill, and had it not been for the ravine it would've seemed he were merely a dozen or so yards away. But the ravine was deeply cut into the earth, its sides steep and made of slippery shale that would break away with the slightest touch.

The gray called to her, his nostrils flaring as he snorted his finish. He dipped his head to her, calling again. But Addie could neither make her way to him, nor did she want to. The gray stepped to the edge of the ravine and pawed the ground before him.

Then he was gone. And in his wake was nothing but the familiar hardness of a chair Addie slept in and the ache in her neck. The dim light of the fire hardly offered any comfort, so Addie rose and built it back up. The chill in the room was gathering strength, but she could no longer hear the force of the wind as it made its way around the corner of the house.

She wasn't going home.

Tears burned unwelcomed, and she wondered if she would ever gain control over her emotions again.

The sky was still gray, but the snow had gone, and light penetrated the clouds above easily. Addie stood on the porch a moment before stepping down into the snow to make her way behind Tom Brady to the barn for chores. A light and bitter breeze pierced her dress and prickled her legs as she avoided a tall snow drift. Her hand carrying the bucket was already numb from cold.

Red Beast was even angrier than usual, as if she too thought the number of days she would have to contend with Addie was up. As she milked and dodged feet, Addie sent out an irritated prayer that the old snot would dry up like all good cows do in the winter.

After a particularly painful hit to the knee, Addie slapped the cow's side. The strike made a loud sound that reverberated through the barn. Red Beast swung her horn at Addie who moved away. "I hate you. In fact, I think I might hate you more than I hate Tom Brady! What breed of milk cow are you anyway?"

Clara had often told her pa, Allen, it did no good to beat on a milk cow. It was like beating on the mentally slow. It did no good and you didn't come out of it a better person.

"Huh. Mama didn't know Red Beast," Addie muttered.

Addie trudged through her morning, avoiding looking out the window into the stark world that dawned. It being Sunday, the boys frolicked about in the snow and made a sled run off the drift that butted up against the barn. Being taller than Luke, it made for a good, but short, ride. After a while, they drug the toboggan off to the hill up behind the house that was still covered in snow and made quite a run off of it. Tom Brady rode out after the chores that morning to survey the damage.

Now, just past noon, Addie gathered up her bucket and broom with intentions of finding a shovel in the barn. Having been left with Charlie, she bundled him up warmly and awkwardly carried him and the cleaning gear. She made her way down across the narrow bridge and over the creek, winding her way around the tallest of the snow drifts. Depositing Charlie on the porch of the dugout, Addie made a dash for the main house and robbed kindling, wedges of split wood, and matches.

When she returned, Charlie stood right where she left him, his empty eyes looking at the corner she had disappeared around. His little hands were red and cold, as was his nose.

"You gotta keep moving if you want to keep warm out here."

Addie busted open the door and dropped the fire making goods into the wood box near the little wood stove that set like ice, lonely and lifeless in the cold dugout. Drawing back the stained and faded curtains on the two windows, light flooded the one room.

It looked even more desolate in the light than it did in the dark.

Addie had determined that if she were gonna be forced to stay the winter with the Bradys, she'd do it in her own space. Not to mention have a retreat to escape to. Her first job was to light a fire to work on the chill. It was no surprise that the remains of an old bird nest lay in pieces in the stove where it had fallen down from the top of the chimney. Once that was cleared, Addie pulled the chimney apart at the joint to clear everything else out that may have blocked it up. As she fished around with her broom handle, pieces came out, but the nest had been the worst of it.

When the pipe was back together, Addie lay her makings out and lit them in the stove. It crackled to life, and as it did so, the smell of burning dust brought life back to the room. She drug the old rocker closer and placed Charlie in it. As she looked down at him, he looked up at her with a blank stare.

"You know, mamas everywhere pray for a good boy like you. To actually see one puts to mind how disturbin' such a boy is."

The fire was gaining some ground and the hum that came from within was a great comfort in such a drab place. Addie turned and sighed at the sight of the great task before her. Something scurried across the bed. Addie shivered. How would she ever gain the courage to sleep there? Lying there, waiting for the feel of little claws.....

The loud sound of falling wood made her jump. Turning abruptly, Addie saw Luke standing above the wood box that was now half full. Behind him, the dog stood crouched, her eyes locked on something under the rope bed with the straw tick mattress.

Frank waddled in, his spindly arms full of all he could carry. He dropped it proudly in the wood box and beamed at Addie. She couldn't help but offer a smile in return.

"Well, I expect the first chore is to let Ol' Moll at those rats. We'll never get 'em all if we do it ourselves." Luke looked at Addie with seriousness.

"Yeah. Best we have shovels or somethin' to get the ones that we can."

With a grin Luke was out the door. The dog was still crouched and waiting on go, looking at Addie out of the corner of her eye.

"Alright," Addie said to the dog with apprehension. She hated rats, and this wouldn't be much fun.

Molly burst forth in a great surge of energy and somehow, with great effort, slid her entire frame under the low standing bed. The bed shook and rattled as a great squeak wailed out from under it. Charlie's eyes were wide as he watched the bed frame wiggle.

Several rats darted out, and Addie's own eyes went wide as she let out a scream. Realizing she was defenseless, she made a lunge for the broom as one made way to her. In a greatly exaggerated movement, Addie brought that broom down on top of the rat that took several stunned steps before she cracked him again. It rolled over on its back and its legs twitched. For good measure, she hit it again.

Frank hopped up on the table with a squeal. "Get it! Get it!"

Addie looked to where he pointed to see a rat, a rather large rat, climbing the shaking bed. Snarling noises mixed with squeaks came out from underneath.

"Luke! Luke!" Addie yelled. Where had the boy gone for shovels? Tuscarora?!

Crawling out from under the bed, Molly looked at Addie. "Get it!" She screamed and pointed. The dog turned to see a hissing rat mocking her from on the bed. With a jump the fight was on. Growling and pouncing, Molly nipped and flung the rat repeatedly, going for a slow and sure kill that resulted in less bites to her own tender mouth.

Having clearly stirred up the nest as several smaller rats dashed out from under the bed, Frank hollered and Addie grabbed up Charlie and moved back to the wall. One headed towards them, but out of nowhere Luke sailed in and a shovel crashed down on it. Addie dashed for the table and put Charlie on top. She grabbed up the shovel Luke handed her and went to whacking. Mice, rats, whatever Molly unearthed in the corners of that dugout. The battle raged for what seemed like hours, but in reality must have been only minutes. Wielding shovels, the fighters claimed many of the enemy, while Molly satiated a long burning desire that had ground away at her in the torturous hours of the many nights she watched over Addie. It was time to kill her taunters.

Frank cheered and laughed, jumped and shook the table. Charlie watched with the same wide-eyed expression frozen on his face. It was the longest Addie had ever seen the boy look alive. He spoke nothing.

When finally Molly wandered the room, sniffing and digging at piles of rubbish and coming up with nothing, Addie lay her shovel against the wall. "Well, I guess the next step is to take everything out. Then I can clean the floor proper."

Luke nodded and took hold of Charlie and returned him to his rocker by the fire Addie was stoking. Then he turned the table sideways and he took one end and Addie and Frank took the other, awkwardly carrying it out the door. The few other meager pieces of furniture were easy to dispose of. When it came time for the rope bed, the stained straw tick mattress was drug outside and the old straw dumped into the hen house. Addie scrubbed the tick in the spring, not having heated water for the purpose. Although the air had warmed some and the snow was turning sticky, she strung it up in the main house. Pegs lined the walls where winter laundry could be set for drying near the fire. Addie stoked the fire and gathered bread and butter for the boys to snack on. She checked Andrew who sat in an armchair in the sitting room sulking. She offered him bread, then left the house for the dugout.

They shoveled the rat and mouse nests out, throwing them into a fire Luke started outside the door. Luke smiled a satisfied smile at Addie when the floor was bare. Taking a large enamel pot off the wood stove that generated enough heat now to keep the room decent even with the door open, Addie, Luke, and Frank began scrubbing the floor made of rough cut lumber.

"Pa had to put in a board floor, on account of the rocks. He couldn't get the floor level. He just kept diggin' up more rock," Luke explained of the fancy floor.

When late afternoon came along, Luke and Frank took the now dried tick to the barn and filled it with fresh hay. Addie wiped down the front wall made of log, then the few pieces of furniture. While she made the bed with her quilt and a wool blanket Luke produced, the boys did their chores and finished filling the wood box. Addie stood back and admired the work they'd done. Looking at Charlie who had moved from the stove to the floor and sat in the ray of golden light that now filtered through the window, she felt tears burn. His little hands were held flat as he looked at dust that danced in the light. It was time to feed her crew.

"Charlie," Addie spoke low and soft. The boy didn't move or look at her. She walked to him and reached down for him. He looked at her with an expressionless face, but made no protest to be held. The boy still looked at his flat hand as she carried him to the house.

Sitting him at the table, Addie studied him several moments. He was still examining his hand that hadn't moved or changed since the dugout. He merely held it before himself and stared, almost as if his mind were gone and his body was frozen like that. Addie rubbed her face then moved to the workbench. Plucking a large wooden spoon from the tin that sat clean with utensils waiting to be put to use, she moved to the shelf near the giant stove and retrieved a match. Lifting one of the lids on the cooking surface, she lit the match and let it burn for only a moment.

Addie blew out the match, then taking the charred end drew two little eyes and a nose in the dish of the spoon. She made a large "O" for the mouth.

She placed the spoon gently in the boy's hand and stepped back to watch him. His little brows knit together briefly as he looked at the face where nothing but flat palm had been. After a moment he tilted his head to look at it from a different angle.

Addie went to making the evening meal.

When the boys came in from chores they marveled at Charlie's new friend, but none of them took it from the boy to get a closer look. When Tom Brady returned from his ride to check stock, the meal was on, and Charlie held tight to his spoon that the boys were now calling "Spoony". Addie didn't look at Tom Brady through the meal to see any looks of dismay.

Being Sunday, Addie took hold of the bathtub when she left the house that night. The boys had gone to ready for bed and she had no doubt they were exhausted. Tom Brady sat at the table working over his ledger again. He watched her take the tub out but made no comment on it. He'd seen the burn pile outside the dugout when he rode in on a tired horse.

The woman needed a bath.

"I promise you, Addie. You'll have a roof over your head this winter and a warm body beside you. I swear it this year."

Fett was turned in his saddle grinning back at her. Buck's head was tipped slightly as he, too, looked back at her. Addie felt herself roll her eyes and suppress a grin. "Uhmm hmm."

"Come on, girl. I mean it," Fett laughed. That usually meant he had something else up his sleeve. Like a wild idea to winter in Mexico. Addie laughed out loud.

Fett stopped Buck and reached out and took hold of her reins to stop her horse. His look turned serious. "I promise you, Ad. You'll have a roof over your head and a warm body to keep you this winter. I promise you that."

The dream echoed on long after sleep melted away and left her to stare into the darkness. The bed she lay on was comfortable, and the body next to her was warm, but the scent of dog laced it. As a tear traced her cheek, Addie withdrew a hand from the blanket and touched Molly's head. She let out a soft whine to let Addie know she was there. She had no idea what time of night it was, nor why she couldn't sleep. Not once had the dog left Addie's side to chase away unwelcome rodents.

Since the storm moved on leaving only blue skies and a cold wind behind it, the boys returned to school Monday morning. Tom Brady bundled the boy Charlie and took him out on a circle with him. Addie had no idea if he was finding his stock or not, nor did she ask. But that morning he said he'd be back mid-afternoon.

Charlie held tight to Spoony, who now had hair. At the breakfast table that morning, Luke quietly got up from the table and went to his coat hanging on the peg by the door. When he returned, he pried Spoony out of Charlie's hands. Addie watched out of the corner of her eye as

Luke dipped the back of the spoon into the sorghum and pasted a little square patch of hair from one of his hides now hanging in the barn to the spoon.

Had Charlie not already been speechless, he would have been speechless. Luke beamed at his brother.

So they had gone, leaving the house to silence. Addie took a scrub brush to the sitting room floor, then to the rock that made up the fireplace. The more she wanted to cry, the harder her arms worked until the burning wiped out all energy for it.

Addie did feel different on the outside. Her hair was soft and clean from her bath the night before. She'd washed her ragged old dress and was wearing something clean for once. Her neck wasn't kinked from sleeping in the chair. But her insides were the same. In fact, probably worse on account that the light at the end of the dark Brady tunnel was snuffed out. Spring was so desperately far away.

The days drug on, and by the time Wednesday fell, Addie had Molly in the house with her all day. No matter how she stoked the fires in the main house, she couldn't keep warm. The dog drove some of that away.

As Addie struggled over a batch of dough she was kneading at the table, Molly let out a friendly growl. She was careful not to let Tom Brady catch her with the dog in the house for she had no idea how he would feel about it, female sentiments be damned. Molly lowered her head and lay back down, so Addie left it at that. Perhaps the dog could sense the boys would soon be venturing home from school. She worked on.

"Hello the house!"

The sound of the unexpected voice caused Addie to jump and her stomach to burn. She looked at the dog who stood at the door wagging her tail, waiting for Addie to open it. With caution, she picked up her apron and wiped her hands on it, sending flour cascading down onto the floor.

Addie couldn't open the door wide enough to let the dog out fast enough. She touched her hair self-consciously before stepping out herself. The cold air outside made her realize how hot she'd made the house.

Roy Albert sat atop a sorrel and held on to the lead of a string of five head of horses, all standing patiently save one, the last in line who snorted and side passed as Addie came out the door. Molly happily danced around Roy's horse as he spoke to her softly.

"Mr. Albert."

At the sound of Addie's voice, he looked up and smiled, then straightened in his saddle. "Well, I wondered if you were still here."

Addie didn't trust herself to respond, so she nodded.

"That was quite a storm. You must be big medicine if the good Lord needed that kind of power to stop your leavin'." He grinned at her as he finished.

Addie couldn't remember the proprieties in these cases. Did she ask him in or was being alone with a strange man in a house impolite? She had so little practice in the art of conversation of late she felt awkward and clumsy when it came time to speak. And something in his eyes made her want to cry every time she looked at him. It wasn't that he reminded her of anyone, but rather the deep understanding that stirred her emotions. As if all she felt was just a line in a book for him to read.

"Uhm, would you like, coffee?" she stammered out without looking at him.

He studied her a moment. "I would," he replied cautiously, as if he knew that might be hard for her. Suddenly she understood what she dreaded was what he'd ask and what she'd have to tell.

"I brought back some colts I started for Tom, I'll just put them in the corral."

Addie nodded. "I'll get some coffee on."

By the time he returned to the house, Addie had the coffee on. She'd smoothed back her hair several times and berated herself for inviting him in. Truth was, she still couldn't remember if it was polite to allow him in the house or not. But, she was living as a housekeeper to a man she hated with no one to "watch out for her well-being" as Tom Brady pointed out. Might as well invite a strange man to coffee.

Addie was back to wearing her old worn-out dress, but there was nothing she could do about that. Shabby was her outlook right then anyway.

She heard him step up on the porch and thought of what a big man he was. He tapped softly on the door before opening it. Addie was busy slicing bread and gathering honey to put on it. The coffee water was hissing and sighing as it came closer to boiling.

"Please, sit," Addie told him.

He removed his hat and put it under the bench beneath him after he sat. He'd chosen the opposite end from where she was working dough. His large frame folded into the space provided and he clasped his hands together as he smiled softly at Addie. She put the bread and honey on the table before him, then moved to add the fresh ground beans to the pot.

"The place sure looks different."

Addie nodded her head in his direction, but said nothing. Roy's presence was not like Tom Brady's. He was not judging or disgusted, merely observing and comfortable. He had no investment here, no ties to keep him locked in the past.

"She'd sure be grateful to ya. All you've done here," Roy stated softly.

Addie wasn't looking at him, she was facing the stove and the coffee pot, holding the tin can with the ground coffee in it, ready to scoop some into the pot. She stopped what she was doing and looked back over her shoulder at Roy.

"I guess I don't know how grateful I'd be to the one who took my place."

"I think it's different when you go 'cause you can't be here anymore. I'm sure it makes a mama feel good to know her boys are watched over."

Addie raised her eyebrows and turned back to her task. His voice was low when he spoke again. "What about you? Don't you think it brings your man great comfort to know you are watched over?"

Addie stopped moving and her face lost all expression. Her lips quivered a moment before she replied without looking back at him, "I doubt he finds much about this circumstance comforting."

"Well, I guess the Lord knew few of us would rejoice in our circumstance. Perhaps that's why they made the word "circumstance" to begin with."

Addie chuckled to herself. "I think there's a few better words to use for it."

Roy chuckled himself. "Yes, ma'am. I would agree with you. A few times in my life there was no way I had the patience to come up with the word circumstance."

Addie brought the coffee to the table and poured him a cup. Then she returned to rolling out her bread dough and shaping it into loaves. "Where do you live from here?"

Roy took a sip of the hot coffee then set his cup down. "North and east of here. I guess it would be about seventeen or so miles. I'm the Brady's closest neighbor by far. Tom claims this piece of ground you're standing on all the way to the mountain. Takes alotta room to run horses."

"And what do you do?"

He took a longer sip of the hot coffee and helped himself to the bread and honey. "Cattle. I raise beef cattle."

Roy smiled softly as he looked down at his bread. "How long are you staying?"

She sighed before replying, "Mr. Brady assures me the stage lines stopped running out of Tuscarora with the storm. So, I guess I'm on the payroll till spring."

"Good. That'll give the gossips fodder for the winter. You can't understand the favor you've done them. All the speculatin' around the fire they'll get to do on a snowy day."

Addie was serious for a moment, then let out a small chuckle. "Well, I guess they got reason. Just judgin' by me giving a strange man coffee in another man's house."

Roy smiled. "You don't strike me as a woman who'd give reason for doubting her character."

"You must not be quick to judge then. I 'preciate that."

Roy was silent a moment as he studied her. "May I ask you a question?" He waited for her to look at him. "How old are you?"

Addie looked back to her work as she replied, "Twenty-two."

Roy whistled as he sighed. "That's awful young. Awful young to be bearing up trials like Job did in the Bible."

She knew he wasn't referring to her age in life, but rather to be carrying such burdens. She'd already enjoyed four years of a wonderful marriage, traveled the country from Texas to Mexico, then up to this God-forsaken place. She'd buried her man along with her soul, and survived the shock only to attend another man's mess. It seemed surely she was near the end of the ride. What else was there left to experience? She'd seen it all.

"Does your mama know where you are?" he asked in a quiet voice.

Addie started to shake. He was damn good at getting to his point. It took her a moment to respond with the shake of her head. Roy sat absolutely still and gave her a moment, but it did no good. This wasn't something you overcame in a few moments.

"Can you send word?"

Addie's face burned red at her shame. She knew few women, and men for that matter, could read and write, but it made her feel simple not to know these things. Her brothers could, barely, but she didn't know even that much.

"Would it help if I wrote a letter to them? Let 'em know where you are?"

Addie always sent word in the fall. Just to let them know she and Fett had survived the summer and where they anticipated spending the winter months. Fett wrote it for her, but Addie mailed it. She rarely got word back, by the time a letter came, Fett would have moved them on beyond the letter's reach.

"Don't tell 'em." Addie blurted out. "Don't tell 'em he... don't tell 'em he..... that he's..... gone." She looked down at her hands holding the dough. "I'll tell 'em when I get there. Just tell 'em I'm alright. Tell 'em I'm setting up here the winter. That's enough."

Roy nodded his head. "Now I have another question." With fear in her eyes, Addie looked at Roy. "Can I have some sugar for my coffee? Tom Brady is the only man I know who buys bulk sugar."

Through tear-filled eyes, Addie laughed.

"It's kinda my way of getting back at him for being such an asshole all the time. I steal his sugar a teaspoon at a time." Pausing there with his serious face and coffee lifted halfway to his mouth, he looked at Addie with blue eyes and soft lips. Then he broke into a grin and laughed loudly.

"I'm glad I'm not the only one who silently thinks of ways to get even," Addie replied.

"Where is he anyway?"

Addie shrugged her shoulders. "He never says where he is going. Sometimes he says when he'll be back for a meal."

"Well, I suppose, as it is a long trot back to my place, I best get after it. I thank you for the coffee. I'll be going to Charleston in a few days, I'll post your letter from there." He unfolded himself from the bench after reaching back to grab his hat from beneath where he sat.

As she watched him, something occurred to Addie.

"Would you wait? I'll get you postage."

"Oh, that's no trouble. Best you hang on to what you got, just in case ol' Brady stiffs ya on your pay come spring." He smiled as he spoke, to let her know he was kidding, but Addie took no concern from it.

"Please, wait." She hurried out into the cold air, across the yard and over the creek. When she reached the dugout, she left the door open as she flew to the table where her chest sat perched like an honored guest in an unacceptable home.

For the first time since the big storm, Addie felt a shred of hope. Although she wouldn't be able to hear back from her mama, nor would she feel her strong arms comforting her, it was enough to know that her mama would know where she was. Like her hands always finding her in the dark of the house as a child, she would know where Addie was in the big, dark world. And surely, she would pray for her. That was something that held weight with Addie, for she'd always felt that no matter what she prayed for, God listened to her mama. Even when he didn't listen to Addie.

Deep down, Addie found an envelope that had come from her pa several years before. It had a return address on it. She took the letter out of it and clutched the envelope as she found the small coin bag Fett had kept their meager fortunes in. Addie dug around and came up with the last five cents to her name. She was glad to let it go for such an important purpose.

Roy stood bridling his horse by the porch where it was tied to a heavy railing, then tightened the cinch. He glanced back at Addie over his shoulder when he heard her running back towards him. He turned to face her as she came to a stop.

"This has their address. Take this, too, to pay the postage."

Roy looked down at it, then took the envelope. He shook his head slightly. "It don't cost that much to post a letter. You keep it."

Addie shook her head and pursed her lips. "No. You take it. Whatever is left you take for writing the letter and posting it."

Roy swallowed hard before replying. "Now, I'm not doing it to make a few cents. And I'm goin' to Charleston for other reasons. I don't need paid for the trip. Keep it."

Addie thrust her hand at him again. "No. You take it. Then I know you'll do it. You don't understand what it means to me."

Roy studied her determined face a moment from beneath his brown hat. He sighed before the corner of his mouth twitched and he spoke. "Alright."

He took the last money Addie had in all the world and tucked it, and the envelope, safely inside the breast pocket of his coat. Roy looked down at Addie and their eyes held for several moments. He reached out to her, and with reluctance, she took his hand.

"I'll be back around. 'Til then, you take care of yourself, Mrs. Loveland." When he released her hand, he swung up into the saddle and was gone with a tip of his hat.

Addie watched him go, the small speck of hope he carried tucked in his pocket and mind was all she had left in her life to keep her going. It was word to her mama. Words was all she had left to tell the world she was alive, although barely. All the word left to let her mama know, they'd meet again.

As Roy topped the rise headed east from the Brady homestead, he was greeted by the thundering of hooves. A tall sorrel blazed by about ten yards to Roy's right, not bothering to break stride even after he saw the other horse and rider. The reins blew back behind him as he ran, the void on his back starkly evident against the empty land beyond.

Even at that distance Roy could see the horse had a glass eye.

He rode on, looking for the boy who was supposed to be attached to that glass-eyed bastard. After riding on a ways, he could see the boys. The wind was right to carry their raised voices off in the opposite direction of the setting sun. Roy could catch snippets of what was being said, but beyond the occasional word he had no idea what they were shouting about.

Luke pointed angrily in the same direction the horse had run off in. About that time, Mare raised her head and nickered. Frank looked up and saw Roy approaching and waved. Neither of the other two boys noticed him until he was upon them. Then, Luke looked up surprised, but the red anger in his face did not melt or soften for several moments. Andrew immediately hung his head in shame to be caught out on that desert without his horse. Roy could see that his britches were torn a bit and were scuffed with dirt. His bright eyes flashed unshed tears he was desperately trying to keep in check. The boy wasn't happy his beast got the better of him.

Roy brought his horse to a quiet stop. He looked at each face, Luke's bright with anger, and wouldn't meet Roy's eyes. Andrew who was roughly wiping something from his cheek, and Frank, who smiled with relief at seeing him. "Howdy, fellas."

Mumblings of greeting came from the bunch.

"I can't help but notice, you appear to be afoot, Andrew." Roy leaned on an elbow atop his saddle horn. He tipped his hat back.

"Yessir," Andrew replied as he rubbed his back.

113

"How'd that happen?"

Andrew scrunched his face and looked away. It was Luke's clipped voice that answered, "Andrew won't get ahold of that dip shit!"

Roy nodded without speaking for a moment. "Perhaps it not that he won't, Luke, but maybe he can't."

"I don't give a damn! He chose that turd! Now he gets to ride him!"

The deep stress of the situation rode on Luke's shoulders like a pet raven. Roy could see the shimmer of oncoming tears welling up in the boy's eyes as he spoke. It wasn't that Luke was upset Andrew couldn't ride the horse, but rather that he had to keep trying. Roy raised an eyebrow and looked to Frank.

"Frankie, why don't you let Andrew ride up behind you?" The boy nodded, but that was cut short by Luke.

"Oh no. Nope. He got himself bucked down, he can walk home!"

"That's not so! You know it! I was going along fine 'til that jackrabbit run beneath him. You know it!" Andrew shouted up at his older brother. This released the rage that simmered in Luke.

"That's a lie! A bald-faced lie! You were clutchin' on for dear life when that dip shit sailed over that brush there and you lost your grip!"

"Aw hell! Was not! Just 'cause your horse can't outrun a sack of beans in a cook pot you gotta 'cuse me of poor ridin'!"

"Andrew Brady! You fell off that horse when he jumped that brush! Don't go lyin' about it!"

"I did not....."

It was about this time in the screaming match Roy decided he'd best cut them off as Andrew had balled his hands into fists and was near to making a plunge at Luke's horse, who was clearly seeing it coming.

"Boys! *Boys!*" he shouted. Two bright red faces looked over at him. "Now, seems to me, it doesn't matter how he got there, but Andrew needs a ride home. Might I suggest a truce for the moment?"

Neither boy replied. "Luke? Sun's going down. It's an awful long walk."

Luke tipped his head away from Roy as the corner of his mouth quirked. He wasn't quite ready to forgive and forget. "Come on, Luke. I know for a fact Mrs. Loveland has fresh bread just waitin' for you boys to come eat it. And if I know your pa, he'll want chores done before any bread gets eaten."

Luke's head snapped up at this. "You saw her?"

"Yes, I did."

"What was you doin'?"

Roy tipped his head back and laughed. "Making passionate love to her."

Frank's brows knit together. He had no idea what that was nor how to go about it. Luke, however, flushed deeply, and he got a look on his face like he'd walked in and caught them.

"I didn't mean..." Luke began.

"I know what you meant." Roy's eyes danced with merriment. He sat and watched the boy's tortured expression for a moment before relieving him. "I brought back five head of geldings your pa had me start. She was gracious enough to give me a cup of coffee."

Roy turned and looked at Andrew. "There's a nice little bay in that bunch. Not real big, probably never will be. But, he's good and gentle. He's young, but he won't need bucked out every morning either."

Roy looked back at Luke who really hadn't recovered. Roy turned serious and his features meant there would be no more quarreling. "It's getting late. You boys get on home. Let Andrew up behind you and get on home."

Luke nodded his assent. Side passing his horse over to Andrew, Luke reached down for his brother. Andrew took his older brother's hand and scrambled up behind him.

"I think you boys would agree that all you got right now is each other. Don't waste your time screamin' over some damn useless horse. Get on home 'fore your pa finds that beast sailing the desert and comes lookin' for ya."

"Yessir," Luke mumbled.

Roy stood and watched them go for a long time, until they disappeared over the brow of the hill. They were three lonely figures in a world of hurt. He couldn't imagine what their life was like in that cabin full of loss and regret. He didn't blame Luke for his feelings. No twelve-year-old boy should have to feel personally responsible for his kid brothers.

Roy thought of Mrs. Loveland's desperate face.

God had strange ways of healing the broken.

Addie stood still, rug in her hands, particles of dust filtering softly through the air from the last violent shake she'd given the rug off the porch. Her lips scrunched together and her teeth ground. Molly let out a whimper.

That blued-eyed turd sailed into the barnyard like he did it every day and cut a hard left into the barn. Addie heard his feet clomping on the wooden floor of the saddling stall. She knew that his next move was to eat contentedly until the boy Andrew showed up to pull the snaffle bit and put him in the corral with his evening meal.

It was the fourth time that week he'd done it to the boy. The boys had said nothing to their father about it at meal times. Not that he would have listened.

Addie pretended to work at sweeping the porch, her breath coming in short puffs of anger, until she at last saw the figures of two horses with riders crest the hill to the east. She exhaled and lay her broom aside.

Enough was enough.

Addie made her way down to the barn with Molly at her heels, and as she stepped into the saddling stall, good ol' Blue Eye raised his head and snorted, then made a exaggerated jump to get away from her. Addie didn't stop, just pushed him into a corner, her own boots making slight tapping noises on the wood floor. She took hold of one rein and drug him from his contented eating.

The boys were just riding into the barnyard themselves when Addie brought Andrew's horse out. She was met with three sets of wide eyes and the tear-stained cheeks of the boy who belonged to the Blue Eye. With frustration evident, Addie looked right at Andrew.

"Come here."

Luke looked back over his shoulder to his brother that took an

116

agonizingly long time to slide down from the back of the horse. Andrew walked toward the woman who stood with her fists doubled over the rein she held. Blue acted like he'd never seen a person before. He snorted and jigged this way and that.

"This horse throw you?" Addie demanded.

Andrew jammed his hands down in his pockets and looked at the ground. His shoulders drooped and he made no return comment.

"Get back on 'im."

Andrew's head shot up and he looked square into the determination on the woman's face. Addie could plainly read fear in the boy. She guessed he had once been a fearless rider as most boys are, but Blue had done his best to see all his boyhood brash confidence was eliminated. Addie leaned over to better look into Andrew's face.

"You get back on him," she again stated.

Andrew shook his head. "No. No I ain't gonna."

Addie took hold of his arm in a quick move that sent Blue flying backward to the end of his rein.

"You get back on 'im, you take him by the face."

"Mrs. Loveland," Luke began.

Addie shot him a dark look. "You get back on. He's beating you 'cause he can." She tried to speak softer.

Andrew fired at her a look of burning indignation. "No! And I won't take no horse talk from a woman! A *housekeepin'* woman!"

A deep conflagration flared up inside Addie's belly and soared up her throat. She looked at the boy whose brown eyes shimmered with determination. She wanted to smack him as the vision of a rat oozing in a flour bin flashed in her mind.

"Is that so?" she ground out.

"Yeah, that's so!" Andrew spat back.

Blue was catching on. He jumped back and forth as the feel of tension zinged down the rein directly to his mouth. Addie jerked hard to bring him to a standstill. Blue stood, the whites of his eyes showing in a wide band around his shining brown eye.

"Alright. You just keep standing there and watch what this

housekeepin' woman can do better than a *rat killin'* boy like you!"
Andrew's eyes went from mad to fearful once again. He swallowed hard.

Addie didn't seem to notice or care that Blue was hopping around
and snorting as she led him into the saddling stall where several saddles
rested up on the railing. Taking hold of the first one that appeared to
have the right stirrup length in a line of three, she threw it and the blanket
beneath it up onto the dancing, blue-eyed sorrel. Throwing up the stirrup
and hooking it on the saddle horn, Addie jerked on the cinch to secure it
tight for the flight Blue was about to make. The stirrup hit his side with a
thunk when Addie dropped it. She took Blue's head away from him and
brought it back to his shoulder and held it there firmly. No matter how he
tried to blow away from Addie, he could not free himself from the bit.

Leading him back out into the sunlight of the barnyard, Addie
firmly took a hold as she slid her hand into the space between withers
and pommel. Addie hiked her skirt to reveal her worn stocking and
scuffed boots to the sound of boys gasping. She doubted any of them had
seen a woman's leg before.

"Mrs. Loveland!" came Frank's shocked exclamation. Molly barked
a short, frantic yip.

"No!" shouted Luke. Even Blue met her eye with mortification.

Addie swung into the saddle, still holding Blue's head with one
hand, her skirt clear up past her knees. She took no time in shifting it, nor
did she care about impropriety. Blue figured he'd just get a jump on the
game at hand and before she could get a foot in the off side stirrup,
started bucking in a circle. His first jumps were mere crow hops, but he
gained confidence with his momentum and arched his withers with as
much room as his head would allow.

Addie laughed.

The boys watched in awestruck horror, eyes wide and full of fear.
What would Pa say when he came home to a busted up housekeeper?
Mare raised her head to watch in anticipation. She had never spent much
time around human women.

Blue was gaining more momentum as his jumps rhythmically
sounded off the barn walls. He was now making that deep and throaty

grunt that spoke of his efforts. Addie reached back and seated herself by holding the Cheyenne roll. When she had her seat firm, she let go of the cantle binding and began to slap Blue on the rump with all the strength her thin arms could muster each time his haunches left the earth. When that wasn't enough to shake his course, she took the tail of her split rein and cracked him between the ears.

One hit was all it took. Blue stopped bucking and looked back at her with sharp surprise, his head raised high in the air. He didn't have time to contemplate her motives before she lunged forward in the saddle and over and undered him. He broke forward and shot past the onlookers who were unable to move before horse and rider were gone. Molly went with the woman at a fast pace.

"Oh, shit!" Luke shouted as he jerked his horse in the direction Addie had gone. He sprung after her leaving Andrew yelling behind him to stop, take him along too! Frank paid his brother no more mind than Luke did. The chase was on.

Addie gathered Blue in her hands and took his head away from him in squeezing motions on the reins. With her legs she pushed him with all her strength. Just as she knew he could, Blue set his head and collected his body beneath her. She sent him on as fast as he would go, urging him with the tail of that right rein. Once he was at top speed, she kept him there, racing down the road in the gathering dusk. The bright gold of the sky blinding all sight above that chain of mountains to her right.

Blue sailed on. His mane whipped out at Addie's face as his neck raised and lowered in his gathering and releasing of his body to produce the pace he maintained. He sailed on at a momentum he'd never carried anyone at before, causing tears to stream out Addie's eyes and down her cheeks to her ears. Addie could hear nothing but the roar of breath as the horse flew further down the road that she'd come in on. Blue at times left the earth to clear a snow drift, but he always lit and kept moving, too afraid to undermine the demon on his back.

As her ride intensified, Addie started to yell. It was the most enthusiastic burst of energy she had let out since Fett died. She wanted to laugh. She wanted to cry. She wanted that glass-eyed bastard to run until his heart burst and he fell, skidding and rolling her to her death. But on he pushed, pounding harder and harder into that golden light, not breaking his stride until at last he calmed, and just ran. His legs stretched and reached, breaking over quickly, bunching then reaching again.

Luke and Frank gave up the chase early on. They stopped on the highest rise they could find and just watched her go. Neither spoke, and eventually even Molly gave up and found high ground to watch from as well. The sun reached out to fill the sky with exploding light, the gold of the grassy hills reflecting it endlessly.

Addie felt consumed by that light. It froze time and engulfed her entire being. Blue could feel it too, and he ran to it like a safe haven. He no longer looked back at the woman he carried, just held up the weight of her soul. The warmth of that early winter sun warmed the bare skin of her face and melted away the stinging in her exposed legs.

"Dear God," Luke whispered as he watched Addie go, farther and farther into space and time.

Molly stood from where she watched on a knoll above the road and raised her nose to the sky. From deep within her chest, she let out a mournful howl that lasted what seemed like an eternity. When she ran out of air, she inhaled, filling her lungs to capacity, and let loose again. The sound floated after Addie, but she was going too fast to hear it.

When the last ray of sun was barely peeking over the high mountains to the west, Addie slowed Andrew's beloved Blue. The horse instantly slowed and set himself into a walk. He made no move to double back the way he came, just lowered his head and traveled. After a moment, Addie stopped him. He stood quiet as a mouse, tipping his head to look back at her out of the corner of his eye.

Addie watched the last of the day go.

Tom Brady saw the whole thing from the hill behind the house. When Blue took off at a dead run, so had Tom, clutching tightly to Charlie who said not a word from his perch in front of Tom in the saddle. He ran into the barnyard and stopped next to Andrew and lowered Charlie down.

"Watch your brother!"

Andrew said nothing in reply, but he was gone so quickly there was no time to. As his father left the barnyard at a dead run, Andrew kicked a rock so hard it hit the barn with a loud cracking noise. It was his horse, why the hell hadn't someone thought to take him along!

When Tom Brady caught up to the two boys watching on the hill, he told them to get on back and finish their chores. Luke looked at him with consternation in his eyes, but Tom Brady's answered with hardness. The boy bowed his head and moved off with his brother.

Tom Brady watched until the sun was behind the hill. Then he turned his own horse and headed home. By then, Addie was lost to the twilight.

She rode back to the Brady's homestead silent, working hard at remembering the way the horse felt as he ran, not at the way she had fallen back down in her soul when he stopped. The air was cold now, and she shivered some. In reality, she hadn't been gone long. The sun sets fast, and night in the winter claims the world easily.

She was just barely able to make out objects and what they were in the remnants of the sun's glow when she wandered into the barnyard. She caught movement out of her left eye in the doorway of the barn and she focused on it. She made out the shape of Tom Brady leaning against the doorway, his head down, his hand lightly whipping something she couldn't make out against his leg. For once, Blue let the mystery of it escape his notice. She stopped him and he hung his head. He'd covered plenty of desert since school let out.

Addie sheepishly pursed her lips and slid down. She lit on the balls of her feet and made very little sound. She silently went to pulling cinches.

"I seem to recall telling you to mind your own business." His voice was loud and accusing in the near darkness.

Addie stopped pulling her cinch and looked back at his figure.

"What the hell were you thinking?"

Addie folded the latigo back through the riggin'. She answered quietly, "I guess I was thinkin' somebody ought to help that boy. His horse has come home without him four times this week."

"Well, that's his problem, not yours."

Addie moved to the off side and hooked the cinches in the keeper. "Haven't you ever fought somethin' you can't win against? When just a little help would have won you the world?"

Tom Brady snorted in the darkness. "That boy badgered me for damn near a year for that horse. I told him. Again and again. I told him that horse was too much for a boy. Although I doubt he'll offer much trouble tomorrow."

Addie moved back to the near side and reached up to jerk the saddle off. "Leave it!"

She jerked some at the sound of his tone.

"Who taught a woman to ride like that?" his voice demanded.

Instantly Addie could hear Fett's voice as he helped her ride through one that was bad to buck. He hollered for her to tuck her chin, sit deep, then laughed joyously as she got hold of the colt's face and took it away from him. He had promoted her abilities the first time he saw she had some.

A tear rolled down her cheek as she answered Tom Brady's question. "My husband. He didn't always have help to get the green ones rode. So he had me do it."

"I'm not sure he had your best interest at heart at all times," Tom Brady said sharply.

"He knew I could handle myself." Addie jerked that saddle down anyway, then faced Tom Brady.

He stood, braced, looking at her in the dark. She could see his outline, but nothing in his features was visible. "In the future, I would appreciate it if you didn't ride all the life out of my horses. And, I would appreciate it if you didn't scare them boys half to death, either."

"Can't think what would scare 'em about what I did."

His reply was slow in coming. "Luke already watched one woman die. He don't need to see another depart. His heart ain't strong enough to live through it again."

Tom Brady stepped to her and took hold of the saddle in her arms.

"And since you'll be leaving anyway, don't make yourself a hero to those boys' thinkin', either."

When he'd taken the saddle, Addie handed him the rein she was holding. "I think you put too much store in what I do here. You forget I wouldn't be here but for that storm. And I would gladly go, if you thought of *any* way I could leave this country."

"Aside from you riding Blue hard to his death in the direction of Texas, I got nothing."

"Well, then maybe that's just what I oughta do." Addie stood tall and looked at the shape of his face in the dark. He was silent a moment.

"I believe you would. You got way more determination than sense." He paused a moment, holding that saddle, looking down at the frail woman before him, held up merely by strength of spirit. He laughed a short, humorless sound. "Just going on what I saw today, I can't even dream up what you must have been on your best day. God help the poor bastard you were married to."

Tom Brady snorted as he walked away, leaving Addie to feel the cold after the horse departed. Addie stood a moment looking up at the brilliant night sky. Right then, stealing Blue and running hard for Texas was the best idea she'd heard in a long time. In the end, Tom Brady would be so glad to see her go, she doubted he'd make much fuss over the horse.

Froze and again empty inside, Addie made her way to the main house. When she came in, the boys were gathered at the table surrounding a glow of lamplight. None of them said a word when she quietly opened the door and entered. They looked at her without raising their heads, save one, little Charlie, who looked down at Spoony with a terrible contorted look on his face.

Addie looked at them for a moment realizing they had been prepped to ignore her, which they clearly weren't able to do, completely. She understood what Tom Brady wanted. For them to not love another woman who would in the end just leave them to a dark and lonely world. She understood that. And she agreed with him. She had no heart to love these boys as a mama should. But, that wouldn't stop them from forming

123

an attachment. The winter would be long.

She looked again to little Charlie. Half the patch of hair Luke had affixed to Spoony was peeled back, and she guessed, without assistance the rest would go. She turned away. She worked at a meal she would not sit to eat.

That great herd was running again. Addie could see them in the distance as the tall grass waved in the wind. The sun was setting and released a bright glow on the earth, but Addie couldn't smell the plains of Texas like she thought she would when she inhaled deeply. Raising a hand to shield her eyes, she looked for Fett. He'd no doubt be working the herd from the back somewhere, tipping and tucking, ever so gently, as to not start a run away again. She couldn't see him, but she knew he was there by the way the leaders moved and watched behind them. She smiled when he did finally come into view. Buck worked beneath Fett like an extension of his body.

Out from the lead came a gray, and he moved away from the bunch, traveling up the hill where Addie stood watching. It was her first instinct to shout at Fett he'd lost one, but she decided against that. The sound of her voice would no doubt scatter the herd. To her surprise, none of the other horses made any judgements to follow the gray, just kept on their course, easy moving up the country.

Addie couldn't think where the trap was.

Then she looked at the gray. He was locked on to her, his black etched ears pricked forward and head up, his eyes bright as he looked at her. It was concerning, she thought. If he were the stud for that massive bunch, she was a goner. In a panic, she looked for somewhere to hide. The vast and open prairie afforded not one tree nor rock to get behind.

Looking back, the gray moved steadily towards her, head still up. *"Fett!"* she screamed.

In terror, she looked down to Fett. He wasn't moving anymore. Buck was still, standing and watching the gray move up the hill. Fett watched too, but no panic showed in his eyes and he didn't break into a fast run to her aid. The panic in Addie exploded as she turned and ran,

124

moving awkwardly across the grass-covered ground. She clutched her skirt, raising it to free the movement of her legs. She looked back. The gray was gaining in his steady gait.

"Fett!" Looking for him, Addie was shocked to see both Fett and Buck were gone, as was the great herd that snaked across the emptiness. Only the gray remained in his pursuit.

Addie stopped in stunned silence. Fett had left her. Alone. She would have to stand alone and fight a stud, with nothing but her hands and voice. Tears welled and fell. The sun fell beneath the horizon, taking with it the warmth of light. Just as it did so, the gray stopped, outlined against the brilliance of the purpling sky. His broad chest widened as he dipped his head at Addie. He raised his head again, his bright eyes never leaving her.

Addie shook with fear. When the gray took a step towards her, Addie jumped backward. At the sudden movement, the gray stopped and stood still, intently watching her, his nostrils wide as he took in a deep breath. Steadily, patiently, he tried again. Addie stumbled backward.

"No! No, stay back! Fett!"

The gray inhaled deeply again and dropped his head, this time keeping it low, ears forward. He reached out for her with only the tip of his nose.

Addie screamed and ran, the heads of the grass breaking and scattering seed as she brushed them, the sun's light waning, the way before her dark and endless. Addie stumbled but kept going.

She felt something warm and wet cross her face. Then she felt the warmth of something next to her, smelled the short burst of what could only be dog breath. Addie opened her eyes in the darkness, she couldn't see anything. But she knew Molly was there. She threaded her fingers in the fur at the back of Molly's neck.

"I was dreamin' again," Addie whispered. "I hate those dreams."

She had no time to contemplate it before Tom Brady pounded his wake up call on the dugout door.

The wind was back. The stars twinkled brightly in the black sky, but the air moved like a train, howling around every sharp corner and claiming anything it could carry away. Addie braced against it as best as she could, then headed into the night to follow Tom Brady, who hadn't bothered to wait for her. By the time she stepped into the shelter of the barn, Red Beast was snorting and hooking her way into the milking stall.

Addie procured her usual pitchfork and set to work. She dodged feet, hovering in uncertainty, moving as the occasion called for it. Red Beast just never did give up, and the cold froze Addie's hands into permanent fists. Again she uttered a silent prayer the cow would just dry up for the winter.

Addie pushed the cow out just as the boys' saddle horses were driven into the barn. With them was the little red filly Tom Brady was making. He came in right behind the bunch and started putting neck ropes on all of them, then tying them to the rail above the feed bunk. Addie watched him for a moment through exhausted eyes.

He must be as tired as she. At least he was as home as he could get.

As he tied Mare to the bunk, he glanced back over his shoulder at her. She stood with sagging shoulders in Fett's oversized coat, her eyes dull and her face drawn. When they met eyes, Addie looked away and started out of the barn. She carried her bucket in one hand, and the other she pulled into her sleeve. She walked slowly, but determinedly, the promise of the warm fire waiting on the other side of her walk. The wind pushed at her, knocking her off course as she made her way to the creek.

She had to cross the log slowly, the pressure of the wind nearly taking her legs out from under her. The log was laced with frost now too, so each step had to be very carefully placed.

Addie made the house, and stumbled through the door. The room wasn't as warm as she hoped, but it was still better than the wind. Setting the milk on the table, she moved to the lamp on her workbench and turned up the wick. Soft light encircled her. Cramming logs into the hot embers in the stove, Addie soon had fire roaring again.

As she turned back to the workbench, Addie was startled enough to gasp and jump back. At the table sat the ghostly little figure of Charlie whose white night shirt gleamed in the soft light. He was hunched forward, and Addie couldn't make out his face. How long had he been there? She was almost too afraid to move to him, afraid she would find that he *was* a ghost. That all of them were. Including herself.

Shaking some sense into her head, she cautiously stepped forward. "Charlie?"

He didn't move or acknowledge her. So, Addie advanced to him, lightly, quietly. When she stood over him, she again said, "Charlie?"

Not appearing to even be breathing, Addie crouched before his hunched figure and touched his small back. Moving closer she could make out his face, his eyes squeezed shut. On his cheek rested a single tear at the end of the trail it had traced down his cheek. Addie touched his hair. He finally looked at her, and for once, there was emotion in his little brown eyes.

"Charlie?" she asked with emotion. She thought perhaps he was sick, that his stomach was in great pain, for he remained hunched over, clutching at something in his bulky night shirt. Feeling along his arm to his stomach with care, she felt something sharp against the back of her hand.

In surprise she pulled her hand back. Then, pulling away the excess of his night shirt, Addie saw the tip of a wooden spoon. "What do you have?"

He looked at her mouth, but didn't answer. He relented it easily. When she looked at it, Addie could see that it had been Spoony. But now, only a corner of his patch of hair was affixed, and his soot drawn face was faded away. She looked to his face, and there in his eyes, was Charlie. His eyes reflected thoughts he couldn't convey. Thoughts all his own. She could only guess what they were, or how to comfort him.

Then it came to her. Standing quickly, Addie moved to the pantry shelf and pulled out the sorghum. Dipping in a spoon from the workbench, she smeared it along the back of Spoony's head and pressed his hair back into place. Then, lighting a match and letting it burn a moment, she blew it out and used the black of it to draw Spoony a new face. This time, however, he had a great big grin, teeth and all. Turning to the boy who remained hunched at the table, Addie walked to him then crouched down beside him again. She tucked the spoon back into Charlie's wee little hand and stood. She could hear Tom Brady's footsteps as he stepped up onto the porch. Addie got after the coffee.

When at last Addie finally looked back over her shoulder at Charlie, long after Tom Brady had entered the house, he sat, bright-eyed, tracing a finger lightly over Spoony's new patch of hair. The tear was long since dried, and although his face again reflected no emotion, at least it had been there once.

Breakfast was finished, the boys dressed in clean clothes and bellies full ready for school, Addie watched out in the very gray light of predawn. She smiled a crooked, lopsided smile when Blue *walked* out of the barnyard, last in the line of the three horses.

Take that Tom Brady. Wind and all.

Addie returned to her butter churning. Tom Brady, however, paced and wandered the room, looking from Charlie to the howling wind outside the window. Addie could read his every movement behind her, knowing with great satisfaction he was about to eat crow. Charlie wouldn't make the barn, let alone another circle to push horses closer to the feed ground.

Tom Brady ground his teeth and rubbed the back of his neck. Addie pretended not to notice.

"Ahhh," he growled out. "I can't take the boy with me. He's gotta stay here."

Addie stopped her churning and turned to look at him, her face set into hard lines. "I don't get paid to watch young 'uns."

Tom Brady ground his teeth.

"You want me to watch the boy, you best be ready to pay extra."

Tom Brady's arms fell at his sides. "I don't recall paying you anything yet. Seems you've been doing this for free before."

Addie's head came up. "You're right." She dropped the handle of the butter churn. "Seems to me you don't pay real regular. Perhaps I should just find things in the house I feel equal to my pay."

Tom Brady narrowed his eyes at her. "How do I know you aren't already doing that?"

Addie crossed her arms. "Guess you don't."

Another gust of wind made the logs of the house groan and pop.

They stood like that a moment, staring each other down. Addie had her arms crossed; Tom Brady had a hard set to his face. Addie didn't back down. She had this fight won before it started.

"Fine. Extra pay. Five cents a day."

Addie would have done it without being paid extra. But, Tom Brady liked to play the game a man's way. All business, no sense to the emotional side of things. Nor with any sense at all.

He pointed a finger at her. "Don't let that boy sleep. He sleeps all day and then cries all night."

Addie was shocked to hear he made noise at all. With that, Tom Brady gathered his winter gear and left the cabin, Addie chortling to herself. If she had met a more stubborn individual, she couldn't recall.

Addie turned and looked at Charlie. How on earth did he sleep all day in the saddle? How did Tom Brady hold him up without dropping him? But, Tom Brady never said he hadn't dropped him. He merely stated Charlie slept all day. The wee boy still sat, his head bent, brown hair falling down over his eyes as he traced Spoony's face. No wonder the last face didn't remain.

Mare was walking smugly along. She kept glancing back out of the corner of her eye at Blue, who trudged along with his head down. Each time she looked at him his ears would prick forward at her, then return to a comfortable position. It was the first morning in many she wasn't running that ignorant turd down. Blue always set the pace, no matter where those boys were headed. Mare watched the woman sail out across the desert on Blue and give him a strong dose of his own medicine.

The wind whipped and howled along through the sagebrush and rock around her, but Mare didn't let that bother her. She'd lived amongst the brush her whole life, and she'd seen many a storm come and go. Now that she was older and Frank's mount, she got to sleep in a nice clean stall every night. The rest of the boys' school horses stayed in the pasture along the creek, but Tom Brady insisted Mare stay in the barn.

More than a few of Mare's babies grew up to make Tom Brady a fair amount of money. Mare put as much heart into those foals as Tom Brady did. Not a one walked away without cow savvy and the build to back it up.

Unlike Blue, whose mama had bothered only to gift him with a glass eye.

Luke looked back at Andrew and smiled. Andrew smiled back, a confident smile. Luke said nothing to Andrew, for despite the truth, he knew Andrew would try to take credit for Blue's new attitude.

It was a new day, and Luke again thanked God for that ridiculously powerful storm that left Addie Loveland a prisoner in the Brady home.

Addie scrubbed away on the washboard through the morning. She made no comment to Charlie, and he none to her. Several times that morning she fetched him a cup of milk, or a heel of bread. Always he ate it with an appetite fitting a boy twice his size. It occurred to Addie his little body was craving sustenance. Tom Brady needed to pack the boy a snack, or a meal, or anything.

A thought came to Addie. But time would have to prove the theory.

After lunch, Addie took a basket of socks into the sitting room by the window where the light was good and sat. She took out a darning needle and thread from the little wicker basket that sat on the shelf above the desk. Charlie was in by the table tracing the cracks in the wood floor with his little finger. He'd been at it awhile, so Addie left him be. He seemed to like the way the floor felt on his hands.

As Addie worked, the warmth of the fire warmed her blood and made her sleepy. She worked on through closing eyes, the fact that so many socks needed attention keeping her going. At last, her hands became heavy and she rested her head on the back of the chair in the warm sunlight that filtered through the window. From her seat she had a perfect view of one of the mountain peaks to the west, and she could see much of the barnyard. The wind still whistled and fretted, but Addie was warm.

She dozed like that for a few minutes, nothing but the sound of the popping fire and the moaning of the wind to play a lullaby. Then she thought of Charlie and opened her eyes.

Addie spooked when she saw the boy standing right before her, his dark eyes watching her with no emotion. He clutched Spoony in one hand, the other resting at his side. He was so small to be so serious. A lock of brown hair fell across his forehead. Addie pursed her lips and sighed.

"I've seen the look of longing in a man's eyes before. What, pray tell, is it you be longing for?" Addie asked softly.

His thin mouth twitched as she spoke, his gaze intent on the movement her lips made. They looked at each other for a long time, then with uncertainty, Addie held out her arms to the boy. His little forehead creased in confusion as he looked at Addie's open arms. As he contemplated something, Addie thought about what the dangers were of such an offer.

Addie hadn't held another human being close to her since Fett died.

Oh sure, she'd carried Charlie around a few times, hoisted him someplace, but that wasn't the same as inviting him in to share warmth and comfort. She nearly took her arms back before Charlie took just one small, miniscule step into her embrace. With trembling lips, Addie lifted the passive boy onto her lap. He sat there rigid, unsure of what he was supposed to do. He had a knack for staring at her face without blinking and it set her soul uneasy. Addie knew he couldn't help that, but still, it was unnerving.

"What was he thinking? Leaving us here together. Might as well tell the cat to stay out of the cream," she said with low sarcasm.

As she spoke, Charlie reached up with a wrinkled brow and laid heavy fingers on her lips. When she quit speaking, Charlie looked up at Addie's eyes as if to request another sentence.

"You are a strange boy, Mr. Charlie," Addie whispered.

Charlie moved his fingers from her lips and with a stilled expression traced the contours of her face for quite some time. He felt of her hair, her nose, her eyes. He tugged at her ears and then looked down at her breasts. His brow wrinkled more.

"You don't see a whole lot of those, do you?" Addie said with a smile. "Come, I'll show you what they are best at."

With that, Addie gathered Charlie close to her, pressing his head down until his head lay in the hollow of her shoulder, his forehead resting against her neck. He sat very stiffly for what seemed like an eternity before his body slacked and melted against her. The warmth that passed between them and surrounded them was the first time in many long months Addie was warm on the inside of her soul.

Memories flooded her mind, dreams and wishes that were buried along with Fett ached and burned inside Addie as she held that boy. As was only natural, Addie began to cry. Tears rolled down her face and she wiped them away with a hand. Charlie raised his head to look at her with confusion.

Addie traced his cheek with her finger and tried to smile. Charlie reached out a finger and touched the tear that rested on her cheek. He moved his lips, but no sound came out.

"I'm sad," she stated in a whisper. "I'm alone, and I'm scared. My love is gone." With the last she cried harder.

Uncertain of how to fix the matters of mystery, Charlie lay his head back down on Addie's chest. Wrapping her arms around him tightly, she cried while the boy drifted off to sleep. When she realized he was unconscious, Addie laughed.

Tom Brady was losing battles all over the place.

Tom Brady took off his hat and rubbed his forehead with his forearm. He looked down again at the mare, then sighed. He looked up at the clear sky, wondering what the purpose of such a stout wind was. If it wasn't going to blow in a storm, then why blow at all? But he felt that way about everything. If you can't get something accomplished with your hard work, you've wasted life. Get something done.

He turned and looked at the mountain that towered behind him. He was miles from home. So many so that he stood at the base of the mountain and had to crane his neck to see the top. The trees up there had long lost leaves if they were aspen, but the pines were a dark green against the brown of the dead grass. He studied the contours of it a moment, but really he was just avoiding what came next.

Brushing off a few pieces of grass and dust from his hat with his hand, he moved toward the red filly that stood quietly watching him. It was late in the day, and if he didn't start home soon, he'd be traveling in the dark.

He'd made a wide circle and started pushing a few bands towards the meadows he opened up before he rode out that morning. It seemed obvious that December was on them, and with a few snow storms already gone by, the winter was just going to increase. School for the boys would be over as he would need them for feed crews.

Tom Brady ran a gentle hand down the red filly's neck to settle her. Moving to her side, he grasped the butt of his rifle and pulled it out of the scabbard slowly. The filly cocked her ear back, but remained still. Tom Brady took a moment to hobble her, for there was nothing but sagebrush to tie her to. Her warm and kind eyes questioned him, so he rubbed her forehead.

"Right in the middle," he said silently to himself.

He opened his gun to make sure it was loaded, then he stepped away from the filly and looked back at her. Tom Brady clenched his jaws, unable to look away from the red filly. When he did, he saw again the mare, down and struggling. She had been struggling for so long she had ruts dug out where her feet had scraped and tried to gain traction. Tom Brady wasn't sure what had happened to her, but clearly something had.

Her back end just wouldn't answer her command to rise.

Standing above its mother, all gaunt and drawn up, was a pretty little dun colored horse colt. He nuzzled her and nickered, urging his mama to rise, but she could not. Her skeleton was sharp and severe under her hide, and her eyes were dull and sunken in her head. The colt trotted around her as Tom Brady approached.

Tom Brady had seen this mare only a few weeks ago.

She wasn't a young mare, but she'd looked well at the time. Perhaps one of the studs had gotten rough with her. She could have been running down a rocky slope and fallen, hurting her pelvis so severely that she finally went down and couldn't rise. Either way, she was down, and Tom Brady knew she wouldn't rise again. She would lie out in the bitter cold, perhaps for days, until at last she would die. And, eventually, the colt would too, as he waited for her to get up.

Tom Brady approached, and the mare lay still and watched him with relief in her eyes. It always astounded him how animals knew intent. Whether it be good or bad, they can read the soul of a man just as well as God. He was here to end her misery, and she knew it. Now the trick was pulling the trigger. How devastated would the horse be if he couldn't?

It wasn't that he had no ability. He hunted often, and he put down any suffering thing, just as his pa taught him to. But the truth was, his beautiful wife picked this mare. Out of a bunch of seventy horses, she walked right in and pointed to the dun mare that lay before him now. That was a good sixteen years ago.

He could still see her smile in the sunlight as he teased her about her pick. He claimed the mare was pigeon-toed, cow-hocked, and parrot-mouthed. But, Edith just smiled and laughed at him. She'd made her pick and that was that. The little dun mare made good on her potential, and now she left behind a six or seven-month-old colt to her credit. He looked just like his mama.

Edith lived to see most of the dun's babies born, started, and sold, or kept for ranch use. One was now a brood mare out with a band somewhere. Another carried Luke to school each day. Up to the last, Edith had gotten a fair amount of enjoyment out of teasing him about her pick turning out to be so wonderful.

Tom Brady clinched his eyes shut. He didn't want to think about her. Not right now. Not on the long ride home. Not when he lay alone in the dark.

"Say goodbye to her, little man."

He spooked the colt off a ways, then stood with his gun leveled and against his shoulder. The mare waited patiently. She was in so much pain, and the only reason she would try to rise was now standing a ways off, nickering frantically. She relaxed her ears and lowered her head. She was ready to go.

Tom Brady's eyes burned as his finger rested on the trigger. His breathing was loud and rough as it rasped in and out of his chest. He clinched his eyes shut and forced them open again. Forgiveness was in the mare's eyes as she waited for the call to God's country.

Tom Brady lay his head against the gun and felt his body weaken. In his mind he saw Edith laughing. It was like saying goodbye all over again. Only this time, it was a horse that ripped him apart. He took ragged breaths as he lay his head down against the rifle, knowing the outcome was not in his favor. He'd already explored the options of using the red filly to pull her up, but he knew she would never be able to stand, let alone make the miles to the barn. Not to mention the red filly wasn't big enough to haul the mare's weight and his own. No, that would be cruel to pry her off the ground just so she could fall again. He forced his breathing to steady with deep inhales and slow exhales.

He opened his eyes.

The sharp sound cracked off the rocks and sent sage hen flying. The red filly reared high into the air, the hobbles making her unable to bolt as she would've preferred. She bounced and hopped until the sound and the ringing left her ears. Tom Brady turned and walked away from the mare with his eyes shut tight. He didn't want to think of the fine meal the coyotes would have. His breathing was worse than it had been.

The colt ran to his mother as soon as Tom Brady walked away. He nudged her and made throaty noises as he moved around her. Tom Brady rubbed the red filly's neck to settle her, then he put the rifle back into the scabbard. He took the hobbles off, then swung up into the saddle. He moved the filly out who still danced and shook all over. He took down his rope.

It was an easy catch as the rope settled on the colt's neck. He hadn't even run, he didn't want to leave his ma. It took some schooling, but after a while, the colt finally led decent, and they started out on the long trek home, the red filly pulling the colt.

The dun looked back and nickered for his mother who lay behind him, unmoving, with the wind blowing wisps of her mane. He couldn't get enough of his last sight of her. Tom Brady couldn't get away fast enough.

In the last of the light, Addie watched from the spring were she filled a bucket for the morrow's coffee. Tom Brady rode in on a tired horse pulling a very downtrodden little colt. It wandered helplessly behind Tom Brady, his little head low to the ground. Atop his horse, Tom Brady didn't look any more enthusiastic. His shoulders sagged and his head was bent forward. She watched until they disappeared into the barn, the colt balking for several seconds before his strength gave out and he lunged inside.

Addie returned to the house. When Tom Brady came in, she had his meal on the table and his boys gathered around it. He shrugged out of his winter gear and hung it on the pegs next to the door. Then he moved to the wash stand that had to be brought in from the porch due to the freezing temperatures. Tom Brady washed and dried his hands and face, and then he sat down to his meal.

He said little, answering only what questions his boys directed his way, and even then they chattered on amongst themselves. Addie stood at the workbench setting yeast cakes to soften overnight. Tom Brady watched her out of the corner of his eye in quick glances.

"Pa?" Luke's voice cut into his thoughts.

"Hmm?" Tom Brady asked without looking at his son.

"Are they all down?"

Tom Brady looked sharply at his son, the big hand that held his coffee mug falling back to the table. "What?"

"The horses. Did they all come down out of the hills?" Luke asked again.

Tom Brady's brows knit together a moment. "Oh. I didn't get too far south. But it seems so."

"Why didn't you get south?"

Tom Brady looked steadily at his eldest son, his shoulders sagging as he leaned against the back of his chair. He set his fork down. Luke watched him expectantly, his own fork hovering above his plate.

Tom Brady clenched his jaws together, then glanced away from the boy who looked just like his mother. His eyes sought Addie Loveland who stood at the workbench, still pouring water into a big enamel bowl. She'd fiddle around there awhile, waiting for the Bradys to finish their meal, leave the mess and go. Then, without words, she'd clean it up and disappear into the dark.

"Pa?" came a voice from somewhere else.

Her dress hung on her like the hide on that mare. It was faded from the sun and rubbed nearly clean through from the struggle of getting up every time she was down. Her weak legs dug and dug at the earth to gain a foothold, but she was too weak to get up and going, no matter how she tried. Sharp shoulders jutted out from the hide, just as they did from gingham. Dull and sunken eyes took in what was around her, but really what they sought was relief. The look of gratitude in the mare's eyes would be the same look in the woman's if she was staring down the barrel of relief.

"Pa."

Tom Brady dropped his fork and stood abruptly. "Mrs. Loveland."

She jumped at his voice and stopped what she was doing and looked at him suddenly. Her face didn't change, and the silence in the room was so loud it would crush the tide. Her hollow cheeks and gray skin betrayed the fire in her eyes.

Tom Brady sighed deeply and looked down at the wood table before him. "I think it best you come sit down and eat somethin'."

"I've ate already," Addie replied as she turned back to her work.

"I doubt that." Tom Brady's firm retort echoed off the cabin walls. All four boys watched between the two adults without movement.

"I've ate," she answered.

"Yeah, you look on the gain. I believe I'd feel better about it if you'd sit and eat. Won't be nothing left to take back to Texas with you come spring."

Addie stood a moment before she sighed and looked back to the enamel bowl.

"Frank, you're closest, fetch a plate off the shelf."

The boy jumped to do as he was told. All the while Tom Brady was thinking of how sharing a table wasn't exactly putting distance between her and his sons. The mare flashed in his mind again. "Mug too, boy."

When Frank returned to his place, he set the mug and plate next to himself. They all turned faces to Addie, who clearly wanted no part in meal time. "Get a fork."

Tom Brady remained standing. Addie picked up a fork and with shoulders drooping and jaw clenched, sat down next to Frankie.

"Pass her the food, boys," Tom Brady said as he sat down after Addie did.

Thanksgiving came late in the year of 1886. An early winter set itself upon the land, and there was no turning back to the few days of Indian summer that graced the land weeks before. The bitter storm that took Addie Loveland's one chance at Texas also robbed what precious little fall was left. It was now nothing but the harshness of winter.

On the Brady homestead, no thought was given to the day of gratefulness. Addie had no calendar to know what day it was anyway, and Tom Brady must've just lacked the gratitude necessary to request the special meal the day deemed. Or, perhaps it was the fact he was scrambling to get the last of his horses off the mountain and where they needed to be to pass the winter.

Those that were strong and healthy would spend the winter months on the meadows surrounding the homestead foraging for themselves. The others, the older mares and the weaker ones, would winter on the long meadow near the cabin where Brady and his boys would pitch hay to them through the winter. They would also have a full-time job breaking ice in the creeks and few ponds where the horses would water. But, the first job was to wean spring foals off their mamas. Those mares would already be preparing for foaling again in the late spring, so last year's young ones had to go. They would be in the east meadow with the two-year-olds, and the few old mares Tom Brady left with them to keep the bunch settled.

It seemed odd to Addie that the Bradys had no hired hands. She asked Luke once how many head of horses they ran, and he guessed around a hundred, give or take a few. But, she didn't know if that included previous years' crops that were waiting to be started. It would be impossible to start all those colts himself. Although curious, she never asked.

The small school over Charleston way went six days a week. While a few of the closer students could make it year round, the majority were like the Bradys and had four or so miles to ride to make it for their education. The day was long at around six hours of schooling, then traveling horseback tacked on each end. The school teacher was a young woman from Elko who came up in the fall and spring to teach the children, and when the times of year came that her students couldn't attend, she'd travel back and teach there. She stayed in a tiny room at the back of the schoolhouse. She was a strict and determined thing, and the Brady boys had crossed her more than once.

On a Wednesday, what would have been the week after Thanksgiving, Tom Brady announced at breakfast it would be the last day of school for the fall term. He would have a crew the next day, and weaning would commence. The grins on the boys were obvious, but it also meant feeding time would begin, too. Long ago Luke had graduated from driving the team to pitching the hay. So had Andrew. This year the team would be entrusted to the smallest, Frankie. He was too small to pitch hay and break ice all day.

Addie took it as her cue to provide a meal for the crew. That was easy enough. But, this time he informed her, they would need coffee at the fire, and then they'd come to the house for the mid-afternoon meal. That way, they could warm up some. She wasn't sure if that was better or not. Then she'd be trapped under the scrutiny of the men. No, she decided she'd set out the meal, then leave the room. Nobody said she had to be there to serve it.

Tom Brady looked particularly exhausted that morning, and little Charlie slept again after his breakfast. He'd disappeared, and after a short search, his father found him curled up in his bed holding tightly to Spoony. With tired eyes, he looked down at the sleeping child and sighed heavily. Charlie spent the day with Addie again when Tom Brady gave up waking the boy. Again, a theory occurred to Addie, and she figured now was as good as any to try it.

That night after she'd washed the supper dishes, she took a mug and poured the last of the day's cream into it. Then, she covered it and put it into the pie safe next to the hall to Tom Brady's bedroom. It took nerve to decide she'd tell him as he sat at the table working figures in his ledger.

Addie put on her heavy coat without his notice. She laid a hand on the latch of the door, and looked at the wood as she spoke, "There is a cup of cream in the pie safe. It oughta stay cold there. Give it to the boy when he cries. Little fella just be hungry at night. That's all."

With that she pulled the latch and was gone into the night. Tom Brady remained where he was, staring at the door with his brows furrowed. If it were that easy to solve the sleepless nights, wouldn't he have thought of that on his own? Charlie was the youngest of four, surely it would be within his realm of understanding to know the boy was hungry at night. And to be told by a woman with no children. Not likely.

But, a voice cut in, Edith had risen with the other three boys at night. He had no idea what she did to settle them.

And Charlie was particularly small for a near three-year-old.

"Bah!" he growled. Damn women always think they know best.

But, as the night wore on, little Charlie began his usual wailing ritual around two. No amount of holding or coaxing convinced him to calm himself and lay quiet. Charlie never would listen to coaxing or shushing. He always just kept on crying and sobbing. Tom Brady knew he must be keeping the whole of the house wide awake. The only thing that saved the boys in the loft was the thick timber that made up the walls of the cabin.

As he bounced and cradled the fitful child, Tom Brady lost all his patience, the tiredness seeping out of his every pore. He closed his eyes and even Charlie's wailing joined with his walking legs couldn't keep him from falling asleep. His head jerked and his arms slacked, nearly dropping the boy. He growled at the injustice of it all. He roughly bounced Charlie which only served to make him howl louder.

Again, Tom Brady thought how odd it was that a boy who never made a noise during the day could split the heavens at night with his carrying on. A man has to sleep! Sometime! Why can't God help a man out and give him rest! Why! Surely this never happens to a mama!

God, help a man out!

Near ready to throw the boy on the porch and leave him there, a picture burst into Tom Brady's mind. The pie safe.

No. No way was it that simple. No possible way.

"Ah!" he yelled as he jerked open the bedroom door. Charlie's cries filled the kitchen before he was even in it.

Turning up the lamp that sat on the table, the room brightened with a soft glow. With a clenched jaw, Tom Brady turned to the pie safe and stared at it. A man has work to do during the day. He can't be up all night adhering to the whims of a woman. He took a few angry steps with Charlie screaming directly into his ear, as if he felt he couldn't get his dull father to understand something.

Jerking the safe open, Tom Brady took hold of the cup of milk. He had to shake Charlie a bit to get him to stop screaming in his ear and open his eyes. He was shaking his head in doubt when Charlie stopped wailing and took hold of that mug like he'd been crossing a desert wasteland and that was the first water he'd seen in weeks. He spilt some down his shirt front as he slopped it to his mouth and gulped the entire contents in a mere two seconds. When he was done with the precious liquid relief, he dropped the mug on the floor and lay his head on Tom

Brady's shoulder and was instantly gone, a huge cream moustache coating his upper lip.

Tom Brady stared into the pie safe for a long time. He clenched and unclenched his jaw while he listened to Charlie's heavy breathing in his ear. The word stubborn kept rolling around in his mind. He denied it might have been directed at himself.

Yep. Now I really hate that woman.

When Addie came in the next morning, she decided a bear had broken into the pie safe. The little cupboard door had been flung open, the mug tossed carelessly to the floor, dried milk drops on her clean floor. Yep, nothing but a grizzled old bear would have done that. And, she was pretty sure she'd met that bear before.

For some reason, the humor of what that scene must have looked like made her chuckle. And, in her heart, something told her to go ahead and feel justified in an "I told you so" sort of way.

It lightened her load just a touch, and made the breakfast getting a little less unbearable. Bear. The very thought of it made her chuckle each time. In her mind she started seeing that grizzled old bear throwing open the pie safe, unable to grasp the mug with his huge paw. Then she could see him roaring in great anger at that pie safe. By the time Luke wandered in to stand by the fire, she had a grin from ear to ear and she couldn't stop herself from laughing.

"What'd I miss?" Luke asked just before his father burst through the door bringing with him a blast of cold air.

Addie just smiled quietly at Luke.

"Get your brothers up if they ain't already." Tom Brady commanded.

"Yessir." Luke moved off immediately to rouse his brothers.

The men of the house left earlier to reach the meeting grounds for all the additional help that would be there to assist with the gather. It was pitch black when they rode out of the barnyard, and Addie didn't envy those boys who sat atop fresh horses in the dark. She was glad she'd done her part to curb old Blue, who was still minding his manners. At least as far as she knew.

Charlie slept late, then tottered out rubbing his eyes. Addie, knowing the distance his little body had to go to make up for his lack of growing, immediately put him up to the breakfast table. He ate happily while she cooked and prepared the makings for the coffee fire. Charlie spent the majority of the morning eating little tidbits he could get from Addie. He would look from one hand that had his snack, to the other that held Spoony who wore a brand new face.

Addie heard and felt the herd being brought in about noon. The ground rumbled under the fast moving hooves and she could hear the nickering of the bunch as they entered the corral. Surely nothing is as devastating as realizing your freedom has been taken from you, all the while thinking you had it beat. She didn't go to the window. She didn't want to see more horses.

She did know, however, Tom Brady would want the coffee boiling on the fire, so she bundled little Charlie up, and put her own coat on. She'd have to make her way without the wagon box this time, and she had Charlie to think after. He played with Spoony next to the door, so Addie held out her hand to him. It took a second, but he came to her and gave her his hand. Addie had to pry it open a little, but then she took a fold of her skirt and put it in his little hand. She closed his hand tight over it and smiled at him. When he tried to drop it, she repeated the motion. After a few tries he seemed to understand she wanted him to hold on while she walked.

She picked up the giant chuck coffee pot by the handle, and put the small box of fixin's under her arm. She went slowly to keep Charlie coming. He was quite pleased to have something in both his hands. As they moved to the corrals, Addie could see Tom Brady had quite the crew assembled. She saw Roy Albert and he tipped his hat to her from a distance. She could see his smile as he did so. She waved in return.

Horses ran and bucked, colts squealed and bolted, looking for the mothers they wouldn't be with anymore. In the middle of it all were the men, cutting and sorting, roping and dragging. Addie found each of the boys, young Frankie sitting on the fence watching and hollering his support, Andrew standing in a hole, moving occasionally when the men pushed a colt to the alley. Luke was next to his father, listening intently as his father pointed out colts and mares, what he said Addie couldn't hear.

Gently taking Charlie's hand from her skirt, Addie placed it on the rail of the fence. She slipped through and then gathered her coffee makings. She looked down at the brown-haired boy that peered up at her.

"You stay, Charlie. I'll be back quick." Addie figured she'd better hurry before his hand got cold, resting there on the rail as it did.

Addie had brushed her hair that morning and rolled it back into a bun. She made sure to wear the cleaner of her dresses. And now she felt all eyes, human and horse alike, on her. The young man who tended the fire stood as she approached and removed his dirt stained white hat as she came to his fireside. He nodded his greeting to her. Addie didn't see much of his face, she kept her eyes down and replied with a "Mornin'."

It seemed the horses had forgotten to run about and squeal as she set the coffee on to start boiling. Awkward.

As the horses resumed their running behind her, Addie stood from where she had crouched by the fire and looked to Charlie. She could see his little hand still on the fence, his expressionless face peering at her from between the rails.

"Thank you, ma'am. That'll taste real good after a cold, fast ride."

Addie turned to the young cowboy and nodded. With hat in hand, his green eyes looked at her from beneath hat-flattened hair. His expression was still, his eyes searching. Addie had seen that look before, followed by a comment made useful as a gateway to another. She turned and walked away, not bothering about the running horses, nor the casual watching of the men around her. Addie had no intentions of comments making gateways to conversations that led to deeper things. Cowboys had their ways of doing things, and as appealing as those ways might be to a young woman, Addie couldn't survive the hurt the last gateway led to. Let alone survive the next one.

Charlie was the only cowboy who got a smile from Addie Loveland that day. The thought occurred to her, he wasn't as benign as he appeared to be either.

Without hesitation, when she stood after crawling through the fence, Charlie grabbed a handful of her skirt. Holding Spoony tightly next to his chest, Charlie squinted when he looked up at Addie. She looked down at him with deep apprehension. She had done something. Something without intention, but none the less, Charlie was different.

Winter was a lifetime to a small child.

Addie led Charlie away. She spoke nothing and he made no conversation as they went, just followed her, looking like he found an island in the middle of his ocean. Addie looked like a lone tree, bending in the wind of a violent hurricane.

Roy Albert pulled up next to Luke, who was now watching Addie go as he kept colts from balling up in a corner. The two men, one old and wise to the ways of a woman, the other still uneducated to the disasters of wearing his heart on his sleeve, made silent notations of their own.

"Sometimes I wish I could help her," Luke said, then quickly became embarrassed and looked down.

Roy sat up straight in his saddle and looked at Addie who walked slowly for the sake of the boy. He could see her hesitation each time she looked down at him. She was not going to lose her heart again.

"Luke, I'm gonna tell you a little somethin' about women most men never do figure out." He looked to Luke who watched him intently. "It doesn't matter what she says, or how she acts, the strength you *think* she's got. There comes a time, even when she says she don't need or want it, but a woman just needs to be held in the arms of a man. She needs to let a man hold her burden, even if just for a moment. Do you understand what I'm saying to you?"

Luke's brows furrowed deeply. "I...I guess so?"

"There's no, 'I guess so'. It's simple. God made a woman to comfort a man. But He made a man strong enough to share the burden of sorrow in a woman."

Luke looked back to Addie who was now stepping up onto the porch. "Yeah, I think I understand," he said a little more confidently.

"Your pa used to know this, but he just doesn't care much anymore.

So, maybe it's up to you." Roy left Luke to chew on this a bit.

When the work was done, the men made their way to the main house. They brought saddle horses with them and tied them to the hitch rail next to the porch. Luke rode his horse to the house just to be part of the men. Andrew had asked for a ride, but Luke told him to get lost. It was his own fault for leaving his horse in the barn. Frank rode up behind his pa. Only Andrew was left to foot the distance. Andrew kicked what rocks weren't frozen down.

Addie had a meal ready. She'd made a huge dutch of beans and chunked smoked bacon into it. Then she'd made a stack of biscuits to rival those mountains to the west. When the men had pushed the colts out of the pen and to the east, Addie put more water on for coffee. By the time they came to the house and loosened cinches, she was ready.

She poured fresh warm water from the stove top into the wash basin. The table was set and Charlie was already enjoying his lunch. He had helped himself to the cookies several times that morning, so he knew well what dessert would be.

Each man who entered the house removed his hat and made his greeting to Addie with a "ma'am". They hung coats on the peg near the door and washed in the basin. Then they turned eagerly to a meal prepared by the woman who stood at the workbench pouring coffee. She set a cup of steaming liquid by each plate. All except for Andrew's. He looked a little bent about this.

The men spoke all at once and some of the talk was business. Tom Brady and Roy spoke of what they figured next years' horses would bring. Several of the younger men, including the one who had greeted Addie at the fireside, took note of Andrew and Frankie's mugs of milk. Due to the distress on Andrew's face, they took to teasing him.

"Aw, you don't want coffee anyway. That just puts hair on your chest and the girls don't like that," said the man from the fire.

"Nope," replied a young man with brown hair. He wore a moustache and had mischievous eyes. "It gets in their nose," he added quieter. Both he and the man from the fire laughed wickedly. Andrew flushed. Frankie was too intent on a perfect milk moustache.

146

As Roy sat next to the brown-haired one, he slapped him in the back of the head. Roy was a big man, and when he'd sat he looked over and down at the man, who really wasn't much more than a boy. "What are you talkin' about James? You ain't got no chest hair to tickle a nose with."

James got his head up. "I do so."

Roy took a finger and gently pulled James' collar away from his neck. Arching a brow high, he said, "Hmm. I guess you got one or two sprigs."

James slapped his hand away as the rest of the table laughed. Addie placed the last cup of coffee in front of Tom Brady. He didn't say thank you, but he stopped Addie from leaving to make introductions around the table. Not for her sake, but to ease the curiosity of the men.

Addie balled her hands in her apron. As Tom Brady pointed to each man and stated his name, she knew with certainty she wouldn't remember them. There were six men at the table. The two young men who'd made Andrew uncomfortable about the coffee, Roy Albert who Addie would never forget, an older gentleman who looked as though he'd seen the west on the day it was created, and two men who looked to be about Tom Brady's age. Each was the same in the color of shirt, for in truth, brown or tan fabric was about all that was available. Each shirt was in its own state of wear, some just had deeper set stains than others. All had creases in their hair where hats sat day after day, although not preventing the crinkles around squinting eyes. Despite its life force, the sun took just as much as it gave. Life for beauty. As each man was introduced, he stood partially to tip his head at Addie.

As Tom Brady introduced a man of about his own age, he said to Addie, "You sure got the place to straights, ma'am."

"What does that mean?" Tom Brady asked. "You sayin' I don't keep house like this woman?"

The man smiled broadly and it warmed his sharp features. "I'm sayin' there's a reason the good Lord didn't make you into a woman."

Tom Brady narrowed his eyes from beneath his brows at him. "I think I did alright. The coyotes weren't trying to move in and make a den."

Snickers came from the older gentleman and Roy. Roy said, "That's only because your true diligence lay in closing the door."

An incredulous look came over Tom Brady's face as he set his coffee cup down with a thud. "I don't claim to be no butler, but I made it livable!"

It was Addie's turn to snicker softly. She kept her eyes away from him, but the sound had caught his attention. Addie set down honey for the biscuits. All grinning faces looked at her. "Hey. You stay outta this. I don't pay you to tout your opinions."

Addie looked at him on the level. "That's true. I can't imagine the difficulty of raisin' boys alone." Tom Brady nodded in smug approval of her comments and again raised his coffee to his mouth. As Addie turned away to the workbench she said, "I was just confused for a few days as to which was the barn and which was the house."

Laughter shook the room. Addie looked over her shoulder at Tom Brady whose face was pinched into a look of disapproval. She smirked impishly at him. Again he narrowed his eyes at her.

"And I don't think it's real fair to say he's diligent in closing the door, Mr. Albert. When I came in this mornin', a bear had clearly broken into the pie safe and stole a mug of cream during the night."

"Damn bear! Ah, hell!" Tom Brady roared. He slapped the table and the older gentleman next to him nearly fell off the bench with laughter.

Addie's face went serious. "I'm corrected. Perhaps it really wasn't a bear..."

Roy Albert nodded his head in approval. "Yes ma'am. I think you got this figured out."

As the meal was eaten and the sun set farther into the afternoon sky, the men stood to leave. By the time they did, Addie had all the dishes washed and dried, and sitting back on their cupboard. She listened quiet like a mouse to the conversation of the men, and it brought memories of listening to her father and brothers talk man talk. She could close her eyes and see her mama's own workbench and dishes in her hand. Addie watched as her mother smiled at a round of teasing amongst the men.

Those rough men Tom Brady brought to aid him in a job had brought a great amount of comfort with them.

When at last they stood to leave, the older gentleman, whose name was Josiah, came quietly to Addie. He fumbled with his hat in his hand as he found the words he sought. Finally he said, "Ma'am. It's been a long while since this house was warm. Been a long time since there was cause to laugh here." With that he smiled awkwardly and turned to leave.

Behind him was Roy, tall and silent, waiting his turn to speak. When he stepped forward to talk to Addie, his green eyes sparkled with life, his lips drawn into a smile. He stepped close so no one would hear what he had to say. "Addie, I sent your letter. Left with the post a few weeks ago. Can't say when they'll get it, but, it's on the way."

Instantly Addie felt her mama's hands as they reached out into the dark to gently take hold of her face. If ever she needed the comfort of her mama after a nightmare, this was it. Addie's wounded soul needed a mama's healing touch, to take hold of her and soothe the pain it found there. She closed her eyes to hold back the tears. They squeezed out the corners and melted down into the black hollows beneath her eyes. With a strong hand Roy squeezed her shoulder.

Addie so badly wanted to be held.

Just the warmth of Roy's hand was more comfort than she'd had for months. Roy said in a low voice, "You best watch out, pretty Addie. Those two young cowboys will be back. And the next time they won't be here to help Tom with the colts."

When Addie opened her eyes and looked up at Roy, his smile had turned sympathetic. He looked down at her for a moment, then he stepped away and shook Tom Brady's hand, but Brady was still watching Addie, a look of suspicion in his eyes. As Roy left, he winked at Luke.

He gleamed in the midday light like an orb. His mane flowed out behind him as his neck arched and stretched with each step. The black in his mane sparkled like diamonds, and the black etching around his ears stood out like ink on white paper. His nostrils were round and large with inhalation. His back flexed great muscle.

149

His gray hide was smooth and clean.

His tail fanned out in the wind behind him like a flag. Although he was running, he was slow, slow enough to see the definition in all his muscles. He moved on like the wind, leaving no trace of himself, just the rustle of the grass. It was the first time Addie had ever seen him in the midday light. He moved on, outlined against the blue sky, shimmering in the light.

Addie lay in the dark for a long time. She listened to the popping of the fire in the little stove. The logs on the front of the dugout cracked occasionally with the cold. She lay still, knowing the day would come. The sun would rise, and so would she.

She had no idea what time it was, nor how long it would be before she heard the door to the main house bang. Molly lay still next to her, but she doubted the dog slept. Honestly, the dog kept watch all the time, never faltering in her self-appointed duties. She kept some of the dreams at bay, but she never could keep that damn gray bastard out. He let himself in, and let himself back out again. Molly never stood to stop him from coming and going.

Addie had no idea what he wanted. She wanted him gone. She'd seen horses before, hundreds, probably thousands, but none like this one. He spoke with no voice, commanded with no actions, beckoned with no pleading. He just was.

And in all their dreamed meetings, he was just as real to Addie as the dog who kept watch over her. She had never touched him, couldn't bring herself to. And then to consider the fact that he *was* real. Somewhere out on the sage-covered desert, he combated the cold or stood in Roy Albert's barn.

With a disturbing realization, she knew just as surely as she dreamed of him, he was dreaming of her.

He had to be. He had reached and called for her the one time she'd seen him in the flesh. He knew her, demanded her, sought her out. The day she laid Fett in the ground, Addie cursed all horses, living and dead. She screamed out at the sky as she wept and wailed the death of her love over his fresh grave. She jammed her fingers into the cold earth where he lay and tried to claw her way to him in her weakened state.

She'd carried on like that for hours upon hours, until at last Pete could watch from a distance no more. He came and pulled her away from Fett for the last time. He picked her up in his arms and drug her away, his own eyes threatening to spill over. Addie could still smell his scent buried deep in his skin as she tried to get away from him and back to all she had of Fett.

She cursed the horses then, and she cursed them still. She cried out to God to wipe them from the earth like the plague they were, to bury them deep in the earth and rot their hide and flesh until nothing but worms had use for them.

Pete held on to her for days. He forced her to eat and drink. Then, when he could take no more of the sitting, he saddled her little bay and asked the woman they were staying with to dress Addie, and to pack her meager things. He was taking her on up the country with him.

Addie wouldn't go.

She stood out in the dirt and sun and looked at that little bay. She told Pete she couldn't do it. That she couldn't set another day with those damn things. Pete was so torn. He couldn't stay, but he didn't want to leave Addie. He pleaded for what seemed like hours. He coaxed and bargained. But she wouldn't go. His heart couldn't take just leaving her where she was. Finally, the man of the house came out and spoke reason to him. Said Addie was better off with them. That they'd see her home however they could.

Still Pete would not go.

It wasn't until he looked deeply into Addie's eyes that he saw she had no strength to leave. He swore he would return, that in time he would wander back through and take her to her mama in Texas. Addie couldn't wait that long. Now she knew.

She should have climbed up on her little bay and left with Pete.

Addie listened as the wind began again with its slow moan, quiet at first, but as she lay there and listened, it grew in strength. She heard the door slam up at the main house. Molly raised her head and yawned.

Addie buried her face into the bed. That wind blew away any ambition she might have had.

A welcome bonus came to Addie in the form of the cow. Red Beast's milk was finally down. But, now that little Charlie was dependent on his midnight snack, that kinked up the works some. Addie's ma would always save a biscuit or bread for the little ones who needed extra at night.

Red Beast was no less cantankerous for Addie, even after being part of her morning routine for so long. She bellowed like a mad cow and snorted at her, flinging long strings of saliva. Addie kept her pitchfork ready, and Red Beast kept it at verbal threats. Why in the world, like any good milk cow, couldn't Red Beast just bloat and be dead? All the good gentle ones died that way. Get in the garden and eat the potato vines, break into the granary and gobble up three times what a cow can handle. The good ones never lasted.

Addie knew Red Beast hadn't given up on her ideas of running her through with one of those horrid horns of hers. Addie followed the cow out of the stall and stood in the doorway of the barn looking at the black sky that was perforated with millions of stars. The wind teased at the hem of her dress. Her fingers were aching from the cold, and Addie knew the warm kitchen fire was hers to make, but she couldn't bring herself to make the trip to the house.

Behind her, Tom Brady led the work team to the stall Addie just occupied. Now instead of saddle horses waiting to take school boys to their education, the work horses ate out of the bunk as they waited to be harnessed for the hay bed.

"If you're waitin' on the wind to stop, you'll be here till June," Tom Brady muttered.

June. Oh, how long that was from now. If she thought the trek to the house was near impossible, the passage of that kind of time would never end. Addie's shoulders dropped. Tom Brady stepped out from the stall. The big horses rummaged through the feeder noisily.

"Don't tell me heavenly Texas has no wind," he said with mock surprise.

Addie turned her head to look at him out of the corner of her eye. "Do not mock the fair country that made me."

Tom Brady rolled his eyes. "You Texans are all the same. You think you are the only ones alive. That ain't no Garden of Eden you come from."

"Well, it sure is better than this rock heap you call home. The deer won't stick it out here."

Tom Brady merely shook his head at her, his dark eyes barely visible from beneath his hat and above his wiry beard. Addie frowned at him and narrowed her eyes. She wasn't going to stand there and take his insults. That fire was waiting.

Addie shot him a nasty look and stepped out into the wind that had decided to kick up pretty hard just before she took her first step. It came around the edge of the barn and met with the air being sucked forcefully through the barn and out the door that was open in the back. Before Addie could get hold of her what-nots, the wind ignorantly trapped itself beneath her skirt. Not to be trapped and held, the wind forced against the fabric and pushed with all its might to free itself. It worked. Addie's skirt rose up like a great balloon, full and taut, just before it flipped itself inside out; above Addie's head.

Tom Brady wasted no time. He watched with burning amusement and without any kind of regret or understanding, a low chuckle started deep inside him. It rose out, deep and mirthful, followed by another, louder, more profound one. The more that came, the more that followed.

Without intention, Addie squealed. With a milk bucket in one hand, she couldn't do much except pull and yank on the one side she had a free hand. The more she pulled, the more the wind caught and forced it up. The rush of that ice cold wind took away all her thought and rationality with concern to the situation. She couldn't think of anything but the dual fold sting that was hitting her about then: the cold and the deep embarrassment. By now, Tom Brady was bent over laughing so hard. The sound was so deep, it shocked Addie further to realize the old turd had a sense of humor.

Another blast sent her skirt up and over her head this time. It hung there. In aggravation, Addie dropped the milk bucket sending it sloshing and spilling. She stepped back into the barn to the sound of Tom Brady nearly suffocating, and wrenched her skirt back down into place. Her chest heaved as her heart ignited with mortification. The crimson on Addie's cheeks flushed deeper when Tom Brady couldn't get ahold of himself. On seeing her discomfiture, he tried to compose himself. He slid his hands into his pockets, and his cheeks twitched from the effort it took to hold it in.

Addie sighed deeply as she looked up at him, a look of utter defeat crossing her features. She wanted to say something ornery to him, but it wouldn't matter what she said. It would never rival seeing her with her skirt up over her head. Clara would be so ashamed, and Addie knew it was only because the fabric was so threadbare. It had no weigh to hold it down. The reality of her situation hit her fresh: her loss, the lack of comfort, and now this, Tom Brady laughing at her. If things in her life could get worse, she couldn't see how. Tears sprang into her eyes and she turned to leave. This time with a firm hold on her skirt.

Tom Brady was still sputtering, but he was trying to hold it together. Addie bent and picked up her milk bucket that was now full of blowing dirt. All her hard work in the cold was for naught.

"Mrs. Loveland," Tom Brady spoke softly. "While it ain't the first skirt I seen go over a woman's head in my presence, I think this one made me happier than all those other times combined. Leave your bucket. I'll take care of it." With that he turned from her, a half smile still playing out on his face. He walked back into the stall where the team was tied.

Addie stood there a moment, the wind coursing around her, her hair being slowly pulled from the hasty bun she'd wound a few minutes before when she heard the main house door slam. It was disturbing, the feeling she got, staring back into the barn and the soft glow of the lantern where it hung on a peg in the saddling stall. All Addie had a view of was one of the work horse's huge rear quarters and tail. It felt as though a seeping had started in her soul. A small piece of the dam she'd built had fallen away and now a tiny jet of water trickled out. If it kept up, the water would work a bigger hole and then the whole wall would crumble away.

It was raw human emotion.

The fact that an ignorant man had broken her wall was unfathomable. There she stood, completely unnerved, uncovered and unprepared to make it through her day. She'd see him at the breakfast table. Then she'd see him at the dinner table, then the supper table. Fett's smiling face flashed into her mind. That was it. She was done. The wind pushed her along in deep sobbing fits as she trudged her way across the log bridge, stepping carefully along the ice that threatened to spill her. That's all she needed, a serious butt ache to round out a perfectly miserable morning.

By the time she reached the porch, her face was soaked and frozen, her air was gone, and she couldn't feel her fingers or toes. She fumbled with the latch and grimaced with the effort it took to open the door. As she pushed it open, warmth hit her face and caressed her bare skin. The smell of coffee tickled her nose. She stepped in and shut the door, then leaned against it.

Luke rose from where he crouched loading wood into the kitchen stove and looked at Addie. In the weak light he could see clearly that she wasn't alright. His arms dropped at his side and his bright eyes shone in the light.

"What did Pa do?" he asked cautiously.

Addie just looked at him like a kid caught crying in the barn after the horse stepped on her foot. She shook her head. Then she began to wipe her face with her coat sleeve, feeling guilty to be bawling in front of this young man. The smell of the wood smoke in her nostrils a welcome friend.

As she wiped, Luke pursed his lips and looked down at the floor. His hands twitched and he looked to be arguing with himself. Addie slipped her coat off and hung it on the peg. She avoided Luke's eyes as she muttered, "I'll get breakfast on."

He barely stepped out of her way as she moved past him to fetch her skillet. It crossed Addie's mind to send him on his way, but the tears were stinging her eyes and she didn't trust her voice not to commit the ultimate betrayal and crack. Luke didn't move away from the stove, and the warmth rolled from it like a steam train lets steam. Surely his backside must be on fire by now.

Addie fetched flour off the shelf. Still he had not moved. Then, a soft clearing of the throat, followed by a small voice. "Mrs. Loveland?"

Addie looked over her shoulder at Luke and was caught by surprise. He stood there, his arms out, his face painfully uncertain. Addie's brows knit together. She shook her head in lack of understanding. As she stared at him, Luke nodded his head and stretched his arms out to her further. Addie choked back a small laugh that was overcome with a sob. She covered her mouth with her hand.

Luke had come this far, he figured he best go the rest of the way. The awkwardness of rejection would chaff at him the rest of the day. He'd seen few women cry, and most of those were shorter and younger than Mrs. Loveland, and it usually happened in the schoolyard. He certainly never offered to hold any of those females.

Stepping forward, he closed the already narrow gap between them, Addie didn't move to him, but she didn't back away either. With the uneasiness of a near grown boy, Luke folded her slowly into his arms. She was taller by a few inches, but Addie wasn't a tall woman, and Luke was big for his age. He was stiff and uncomfortable at first, Roy Albert's face in his mind the whole time. Addie covered her face and laid her head in her hands on Luke's shoulder. She let out a snort in an attempt to curb the tears.

With loose arms, Luke rubbed her back gently. He gritted his teeth some, unsure at what point Mrs. Loveland was just miraculously better. Or, would that actually happen? He had no idea what would take place.

For Addie, something happened. That tiny trickle that was jetting out the crack in her dam turned into an all-out rush of emotion. It gushed and crumbled the remainder of the wall, flooding the bottoms of her soul with uncontrollable water that filled her with rock-shattering emotion. The part of Addie that had been held and consoled by Pete was now held and consoled by Luke. As she started to cry harder, Luke tightened his hold on her. In response, Addie wrapped her arms around Luke's shoulders and buried her face between her arm and his neck. He increased the amount of his holding until he was squeezing Addie as tight as his arms could hold her.

In one swift lesson, Luke fully understood what Roy had been telling him.

Addie cried until the strength to do so was gone. Although the ache was always going to be present, the dam waters had rushed out and the pressure on the wall was gone. It would not trickle out slowly through the day, it was gone. She could build up from there. When Addie raised her head and looked into Luke's tear-filled eyes, she put her hands on both sides of his face and held him there. She smiled dimly at him, then covered her mouth. With the sound of footsteps on the porch they broke apart, each turning from the door in an attempt at nonchalance. Addie hurriedly wiped her face as the door opened, and Luke fiddled with arranging the wood box.

The wind brought with it thick gray clouds to accompany its howling. By noon, snow started to fall, hard frozen little balls that hit the windows with a vengeance. Within an hour, Addie could hardly see the barn from the kitchen windows. Everything was slowly becoming blanketed in a layer of white. It was a lonely feeling, knowing the outside world was slowly becoming unavailable.

Addie thought about the letter Roy sent to her family.

How long would it take to reach them? Would it reach them? Would she step off the stage in the spring and walk home because they had no idea she was coming? No. She shook that thought away. She'd take some of her hard-earned money and send them a telegram. Addie watched the snow come down sideways and wondered what life was like in Texas right at that moment. What was her ma doing? Each of her brothers were moving and alive, participating in a journey all their own through life. Addie had no idea what they would be doing now. Her youngest brother would be twelve. The young ones were growing up without her.

She sighed and wrapped her arms around herself. The youngest would be near Luke's age. Dear Luke. It brought her close to tears again to think of him. He was a good boy, well on his way to becoming a man. It was unfortunate for him his mother passed. Much of what a woman needs to teach a young boy would never be taught. A ma teaches him what to look for in a wife, whether it be good or bad. How a woman acts, or shouldn't.

Ah well, not really her problem. He was mostly grown anyway. It was Andrew who needed a ma most. He mostly just needed a ma who'd give him a good lesson with a wooden spoon to the backside every now and then. Frankie was such a dear sweet oblivious little creature. And Charlie, well, who could help him?

Addie turned to look at him. He was sitting on the wood floor eating a slice of bread. He was tearing little bits off and putting them in his mouth. Whatever Charlie did, it took him all day. He never asked for anything, and he never became agitated, with exception of the time Spoony's face had worn off. And even then, he brought his burdens to no one. He just wore them. Even if Tom Brady had welcomed her help, Charlie was a mystery.

The noon meal came and went. The boys and Tom Brady returned from feeding to eat and warm up, then they were gone again. Tom Brady made no reference to his fits of laughter that morning, just ate and left, never acknowledging her. Addie had forgotten one thing when she lamented sharing the table with him. He would have to actually see her to continue his laughing fit. He did not.

That was good with Addie. It had been a strange day anyway. She'd endured many strange days in the last few months, but this one was different somehow. It felt like forces were working against her. Addie longed for the comfort of her ma's table, with the laughter and poking fun at everything. Tom Brady's table was quiet and remorseful. The young boys gathered around it made a job of eating quickly and sullenly, then leaving their dishes behind for the help to gather.

Addie looked again at the snow blowing.

Tom Brady clutched his collar closer to his neck. Every so often when he raised the maul over his head, the frozen balls of snow would see an opening, shoot down his shirt and melt against his skin. His shirt was slowly getting wet, and it chilled him. They were a good three miles from the house, and Frankie was now burrowed beneath the hay that was left on the sleigh.

The team stood facing the onslaught with their heads low in the attempt to find relief. They kept their ears pinned close to their heads to keep the stinging ice from going in, but the ice was forming on the wet of their hides. The line of ice-laced horses bent against the wind and driving snow huddled in bunches down the meadow as they consumed the hay the Brady men forked off the feed sleigh.

Andrew struggled in shivering fits with a smaller axe a little further down the creek, raising it over his head into the force of air and with all his might brought it down on the ice below him. Tom Brady covered all the boys' faces to ward off the cold, but now the boy was jerking so violently he feared he'd drop the axe on himself.

The sorrel team moved impatiently in the desire to turn their backs to the wind and storm.

"Luke!" he hollered to the boy on his right up the stream a ways, diligently chipping at the water. He stopped to look at his father.

Tom Brady motioned him to come back. He then moved to Andrew and sent him to the sleigh. The boy walked carefully on frozen feet. Feeding would be ten times harder the next day; they'd have to shovel down to the water, then chip it out. Luke moved to Andrew and took his axe from him. Tom Brady braved the snow down his collar and finished breaking off chunks of ice to make a hole big enough for the horses to drink from.

As he finished, he raised his eyes to the gray of the sky, just as the clouds parted.

The gold light filtered through the blinding snow, making a shaft that cut between two peaks way up high. The sun hit the country to the west of him and moved quickly to engulf the valley the Bradys stood freezing in. The snow kept at it without reprisal, but the sun lit everything, revealing a streak of blue sky above with brilliance for a moment. It captured Tom Brady's attention as it reflected off the snow and nearly blinded him.

Then it was gone.

He turned slowly and moved to the sleigh where Luke already held the lines in his mittened hands. He had thrown hay over Andrew for the excruciatingly long ride back to the barn and the cook fire.

Nobody said it, but great relief lived in the hearts of the feed crew. For everybody already knew Addie Loveland was tending the home fire to warm the house.

The last few winters had been so very hard. The cold was bad, yes, but the greatest difficulty had been Charlie. When it was possible, Tom Brady brought him, but those days were so few, he could count them on one hand. And, it was obvious that a clear, calm sky in the morning did not reflect what would come of the afternoon. He was left with no choice but to leave Frank in charge of his baby brother through the winter previous. The winter before that, just after his wife had died, Andrew had been left to tend both Charlie and Frank.

Luke worked like a man for the first time in his life that winter.

What would have been an easy break in, turned out to be intense labor for a ten-year-old boy. Many times when it was the worst, Tom Brady would look to his son and see him crying silently, still forking hay as the team moved slowly up the meadow. Or, he would catch him hugging the shoulder of one of the great, patient work horses, his arms unable to cover the expanse of horseflesh. Tom Brady called him firmly back to his work. He had no idea what else to do.

Luke didn't cry anymore, but he wore a deep burden in his eyes.

Andrew and Frankie both proved to be miserable mothers, and the confinement of being stuck in the house with a small baby was more than any young boy should bear. The hours of worry about them stoking the fire alone took years from Tom Brady's life. So, in the end, he told them not to, that he would do it when he came in, which resulted in a freezing house.

As much as he hated to admit it, Mrs. Loveland proved to make his life immensely easier.

He set the team into a willingly brisk trot. Feeding was done, and they knew it. They turned the sleigh in a big circle, then headed home in a new set of tracks, out and away from the eating bunches. Tom Brady took time to look over the horses, but it was snowing so hard now, their backs were covered, making it impossible to see anything about their condition. The team charged forward with the wind and raised heads to cock ears back at Tom. They'd travel every bit as fast as he'd let them.

When they finally made the barn, Tom Brady sent Andrew to the house with Frankie. They stumbled and slipped their way up the frozen slope. Andrew went down when his numb foot couldn't get feeling. That was it. Frankie did the best he could to haul his bigger brother up, but the crack Andrew's knee had taken ached and throbbed like he'd hit it with an axe. He started to cry.

As they started out again, in agonizing steps, the door to the cabin flew open and Addie rushed out. She made her way down the steps and through the snow to take hold of Andrew around the shoulders. He shook and sobbed, the last of his big boy strength gone.

"Go Frankie! Get in the house!" Addie gave him a gentle nudge to get him moving faster. Frankie moved off and left Andrew to Addie.

Addie had no coat on and the bitterness of the wind and snow took her breath away. She shuffled Andrew along as fast as she could, and he was making progress as he could now see the end. The warmth of the fire no longer a distant hope. It was a promise in the flesh.

They broke through the door, closing it harshly behind them, almost as an insult to the storm. It went unheeded. Addie pulled off Andrew's green and white striped stocking cap and threw it aside. Then she began to pull off his multiple layers of mittens. Frankie stood by the fire with all his layers still on, watching silently as Andrew sobbed and Addie worked.

"It's alright. You'll be warm in a moment. Come boy, pull hard so we can get these mittens off."

Andrew was still crying hard enough to distract himself from the task at hand. Addie worked and pulled until she had most of his clothes off. Frankie and Charlie watched with silent faces as Addie stooped to take off Andrew's snow-covered boots. As she knelt the bright red ring encircling Andrew's knee stopped her. Without comment she quickly pulled off his boots.

"Frank, pull a chair to the fire for him."

The young boy did as he was asked in a hurry. Addie helped Andrew to the open and waiting comfort of the fire. She then dragged another chair over and propped his leg up on it. Andrew was trying harder to control his crying, but Addie knew he was so cold, emotion had the reins.

Working the pant leg up, Addie saw he had on several pairs of long underwear. She stood and pulled him up. "Come, we gotta get those off. We gotta get a look at your knee." With great effort, Addie pulled off Andrew's pants first, then slowly two layers of long underwear. When she was done, he stood in his white under shorts.

Setting him back in the chair, she again propped his leg. Blood ran everywhere and Addie reached for a rag to sop it up as best she could. The white gleam of bone shone through the opening where Andrew had clearly fallen on a sharp rock, or something in the cold that was willing to break through the skin in such a manner. Addie knew how to stitch things up, but, she wasn't sure how Tom Brady would like it.

Best he tend his own boy.

"Frankie, get your pa."

The wide-eyed boy left the room without comment into the fading light of day, and the enraged wind that spit snow in violent bursts. Addie rubbed Andrew's fingers and toes to bring life back into them. Then, when the sting of blood flow became enough to remind Andrew he was alive, Addie stood and poured him a cup of coffee. Andrew was still trying to keep himself together, and the hot coffee seemed to hold his attention enough to stop the little gasps of breath. Addie soaked a rag in warm water and laid it over the deep wound.

When the door opened and Tom Brady stepped through, for some reason, Addie was relieved. It might well take two to stitch that wound, one to hold, another to stitch. The sky behind both Tom Brady and Frankie was all but black, the last glow of the day fading fast above the thick clouds and swirling snow. Luke did not appear with them. Frank moved in shaking fits to the stove where Addie could see his little face was red, and white etched around the crimson of his cheeks. The boy was near frozen like Andrew.

"Frank, see to the chores with Luke." Tom Brady said as he lowered himself to look at Andrew's knee. He pulled off his gloves and set them on the table.

Without hesitation, Addie said, "I'll go." With that she quickly turned and grabbed her coat and a pair of Andrew's mittens that lay on the floor. Not bothering to look at Tom Brady, Addie yanked the door open and stepped out into the blinding snow and pulled her gear on. She could hardly make out what direction the barn was, but she could still see the faint glow of the lantern.

Addie entered the barn to shake the snow from her hair. She had nothing to cover her head, and the bitter cold had instantly frozen her ears and nose. "Luke!"

She sat a moment and listened. "Luke!"

Finally, he came in the back door carrying a pitchfork. "Where's Pa?"

"He's in the house seein' to Andrew. I'll help you finish chores. What needs done?"

The corners of Luke's mouth twitched, and the look in his eyes spoke of how being alone in the great storm had scared him. "I need to feed two pens out back. Then the stock in here needs fed. I'll push the cow in and leave her in here tonight."

"She need milked?"

"No, Pa said don't bother with it. He kinda acted like we needed to get in the house quick."

Addie nodded her agreement with that thought. "I'll climb up in the loft and start forking hay down."

Luke gave her a short and uncertain smile, then forked another huge bunch of hay and moved out into the dark and blinding snow. Addie moved to the ladder and held up her skirt as she climbed the rungs. A pitchfork waited for her at the top. She took it in her hands and started forking hay down to the floor below to be fed to the beasts in the barn. It took several minutes, and in that time, Luke did not return. When she was done, Addie climbed down the ladder and looked to the back door for him. He did not appear out of the howling.

"Luke!" she shouted. He did not reply. Addie walked to the back of the barn and called again out the door. "Luke!"

Panic seized Addie. She looked out into a dark world. She could see nothing, but the sting of needles on her face told her it was still snowing with harshness. She could make out nothing but the darkness, fear the only thing charging through it to slam into Addie forcefully.

"Luke! Where are you?!" Oh, why had she let the boy leave the barn? What had she been thinking?

He's not yet a man, Addie! Don't abuse him as such!

"Luke!" The panic rushed into her heart and tears sprang into her eyes. This was it. This was the losing point. That point where you wait to know for sure someone has died. The point where you know for sure you've lost, and hope has gone. "Luke…"

It was a small sound, but it was sharp. Addie strained hard to hear it over the incessant moaning of the wind. "Luke!" Addie again hollered into the raging storm. Again the sharp sound followed her voice.

Without thought, Addie plunged out into the storm in the direction she thought she heard the noise come from. As her ears froze, she ignored her own comfort and stumbled through the mounting snow to the rail fence. She flailed a minute as she waited to feel it beneath her hand. When at last she did find it, she moved along it as quickly as she could.

"Luke!" The sound moved out into the empty night, away from Addie as far as it could, but Addie suspected it wasn't much past her. The noise came again, only now as she moved away from the barn, Addie could tell the noise was actually constant, either brought to her by the wind, or away as the storm dictated. Addie tried to move her feet faster.

The sound. It was familiar. The steady stream of it……

Addie moved on, shouting when she could find enough air. The sound, now piercing the storm in bursts of regularity kept up as well.

When Addie finally neared it, she realized what it was.

Molly.

"Molly!" The dog's excited yipping increased. Addie came to a corner in the fence, where a gate must have been opened. Addie kept following the fence, until, at last, the yipping of the dog was directly to her left, but away from the fence. The thought came to Addie, what if the dog were merely barking at one of the stock? What if Luke were somewhere else? No, the dog was far too panic-stricken to be merely barking at one of the horses.

Stumbling away from the fence, Addie moved off to the sound of the dog. Already Addie had a hard time keeping her direction. She knew if she couldn't find the right fence, then remember which way to turn, they'd wander helplessly until the cold claimed them.

Addie was now just above the dog. "Luke!"

She stepped onto something firm. She took her foot back and knelt down. She groped around in the dark until her hands met with Luke's. "Oh, Luke!"

She bent to get closer to his head when she found it. "M..mm…my ffeet, M..Miss Addie,"

"I know… mine, too. Stand with me," Addie tried not to cry, although she wasn't sure if it was from the pain of freezing, or at the relief she found Luke, or the fear she wouldn't be able to save him. Awkwardly they stood, hunched and weak, leaning heavily on each other.

Bent and slipping, Addie set herself to thinking on what direction to move. Thinking she knew the way, the wind pushed at her from that direction. No, the wind was at her face as she traveled down the rail away from the barn. That must be the wrong direction. The wind should be at her back as she goes back to the barn. Or did the wind shift directions? She took a moment to try to remember if it had. She could remember nothing. Not even her name. She felt rather than heard something move up beside her, heavy and determined. Then Addie felt the sharpness of a horn as it pushed past her.

Red Beast. *Red Beast!*

"Hold on and walk with me!" Addie bent to shout into Luke's ear. She raised a hand and rested it on Red Beast's back, which the animal couldn't feel through the thick ice formed on her back. Addie's hand followed the contours of the cow's back as it moved by. When her hand dropped down with the tailhead, Addie latched on to a handful of tail and clamped it in her frozen hand. She prayed the cow wouldn't act in her usual manner and try to kick her, or swing and butt her with those piercing horns. Luke slipped and fumbled along beside her, and Addie couldn't feel her arm where she clutched him to her.

Red Beast moved on. Addie's instincts told her that despite the blinding dark and snow, the cow knew just where she was headed; to the barn at milking time. The cow's basic instinct was far better than her own. They trudged on for what seemed like the duration of the night, the cow moving quickly and steadily, dragging Addie who kept Luke against her, and Luke, who moved, it seemed, without his own consent.

At last, Addie nearly fell when the snow beneath her feet disappeared and the walking became instantly easier. Addie opened her eyes and could see the beacon the lantern had made of itself, and the whining of the dog who moved beside Addie and Luke, completely unnoticed in the violence of the storm. When Addie released Red Beast's tail, she lost her balance and fell to the barn floor in a heap with Luke. Red Beast looked back at them and moved on to her usual eating place.

"Luke, are you alright?" Addie asked in a stricken voice.

The boy shook and jerked violently as he tried to nod his head. Addie looked from him to the back door. The wind was blowing swirling snow in. So, Addie rose and looked to the door.

Addie was at a loss.

She looked back to Luke who lay on the barn floor still, trying to wad himself into a ball to generate a little heat. The horses who stayed in the barn watched between snatching up hay from their bunks. At the opposite end of the barn the door stood like a black hole.

She would never be able to get Luke to the house.

She had one chance to save him, and that was to get him burrowed into the hay somehow. But first, she had to stop that wind from cutting through the barn like a knife. Unless she got that air stopped, she'd never get Luke to warm, no matter what she did. Moving on a thousand needles, Addie made her way to the barn door. Her aching hands couldn't get a hold on the handle to yank it closed as the wind pushed against it. Her grip would slip and she'd stumble backwards. If she could only get it away from the barn, then she could get behind it and push it closed, plowing the drifting snow with it as she went.

Gripping as tightly as she could, Addie summoned the last of her strength to pull with all her might to get the door away from the wall the wind pressed it against. Yanking hard, Addie felt her grip slacken and the handle slip from her hands. Then she felt herself falling backward, flailing, headlong into the storm. She hit the ground with a great thud that forced all the air out of her lungs. The sharpness of the cold in her body made the fall hurt far worse than it should have.

Grasping and gasping, Addie kicked feebly in an attempt to roll herself over so she could get up. She couldn't get her body to roll. Desperation settled upon Addie's soul. This was it. If she couldn't rise in the next few moments, she'd be gone. Then what of Luke?

Strong hands clutched at Addie, grasping for her shoulders. Pulling with all the strength they possessed. They made short work of pulling Addie to her feet, then an arm with the strength of a mule clutched her close to a firm body. Carrying rather than assisting, Addie was taken back towards the barn.

Fett... he's come at last.

When they entered the barn and the soft glow of the lantern, Addie looked up with joy in her eyes to see....a grizzled beard. The smile that was forming on her lips faded as she met the dark eyes of Tom Brady.

"Stay with Luke."

Addie realized her mistake. The bitterness of the storm raging around her had taken her senses and vanquished them of reality. She forced herself not to think of it and looked down at Luke. As she did so, the wind was cut short when Tom Brady closed the barn door behind them. Molly lay atop Luke, her wiry tail thumping the floor as Addie looked at her. The old dog was doing her best to save her beloved boy.

167

Luke clutched her with all the strength he had left.

"Come, woman. We gotta get back to the house." Tom Brady took Addie by the hand after he took the lantern from the peg. He handed her the lantern and stooped to drag Luke off the floor.

"Stand, boy. We gotta get to the house." Luke stood on shaking feet looking down at the dog who kept close to him. "Hold on to me. No matter what, keep a hold on me." Tom Brady said as he moved to the main door of the barn.

Without stopping to close the door, he plunged into the black and wind that immediately claimed the life of the lantern flame. Addie prayed Tom Brady had better directional sense than she did. He clutched her hand in his left, Luke in his right, pressing forward with as much determination as the storm. Addie slipped and nearly lost the lantern, but she was able to keep it in her hand. Tom Brady's grip never wavered nor

slackened.

It was hard for her to tell when they'd crossed the creek, for it was

168

frozen over, only a small trickle of the warm water in the center still moving without solidifying. Addie had no wherewithal to know anything about their direction, or their location on the journey to the house. It was black as the center of the earth, and as she held coherency a moment, realized the wind was indeed shifting directions. With every gust.

Addie and Luke both fell when it came time to step up on the porch. With patient strength, he pulled both to their feet again and drug them to the door. For Addie, it was like arriving at Jesus' feet in heaven. She had never seen a more beautiful glow coming from a lantern, nor smelled anything as wonderful as old grease soaked into the wood of a table. Had the hides still been on the wall, Addie would have rejoiced in the gift of them. The wide eyes of Charlie lit on Addie and something flashed behind them.

Frankie slammed the door behind the trio. Molly had followed them in, and she stood back a ways looking anxiously at the boy and the woman. Tom Brady immediately took to assisting Luke out of his winter things. Addie shook her head and bent to untie Luke's boot laces. Her fingers wouldn't work. Addie lost her ability to control her body. Tom Brady released Luke and pulled Addie up.

"Stoke that fire, Frankie." At his command, even Andrew rose and hobbled to assist his younger brother. When that was done he went to Luke to unbutton his coat for him. Molly whined softly her concern.

Tom Brady said nothing as he pulled Addie's one layer of mittens off and threw them away over his shoulder. Addie met his eyes as he reached for her collar and unbuttoned the top button on her coat. His mouth and eyes were set into a firm line, symmetrical to each other in flat, unreadable emotion. He looked down at her buttons and quickly finished despite the shiver Addie saw in his arms.

He pulled her coat off and led her by the arm to a chair next to Luke's by the fire. "Rub Mrs. Loveland's hands and feet, Frankie."

The boy jumped to do his father's calling, and with small hands rubbed Addie's hands between his two own. His little palms generated a small amount of friction and heat, warming the skin first, then the bones. Tom Brady worked on Luke, who was far worse off than Addie. By the time Addie could move her fingers again, Frankie had started on her feet. When he lifted a foot, she noticed Tom Brady look down briefly and see her stocking riddled with wear holes.

The warmth trickled its way back into her body and mind. Cold pockets of blood eased into Addie's heart and brought on the shivers again, then it would pump out again, to be warmed by the friction of blood in the veins and vessels of her body. In time, no pockets of cold blood were left, and she was able to stop shivering, although clearly still chilled. Molly lay at her feet, the ice melting off her back, licking the snow that was packed in little balls between her toes.

Addie rose, while Tom Brady still worked away on Luke, who fussed quietly, his spasms controlling him. She didn't have the heart to ask if he would he suffer great damage from frostbite. She should not have let him go back out into the storm to tend those last few chores. She should have insisted he desert all of it and head to the house. But, those animals gave life and sustenance to the people they served. Without them, life wouldn't just be hard, it would be impossible. Addie knew well the care of animals came before people. For without them, there was no people without horrific toil and poverty.

Turning silently away, Addie moved to the stove and began to dish up supper for the younger children. She placed the stew on the table as well as sliced up fresh bread. She called Frankie and Charlie to the table, avoiding looking to the eldest boy. She thought of finding him in that blizzard. Her shoulders dropped and her heart ached.

Sweet Luke….

The overwhelming thought of losing him to the cold clutches of a frozen death left Addie back at Fett's grave again. It was as her mama always said, "God takes the good early. He doesn't leave them with copious amounts of time to go bad. It's the rest, those who need more time to seek His face, that remain." Addie wanted to throw up, the feel of close death touching her skin.

"Food for Luke, please." Tom Brady's low voice cut into Addie where she stood looking down at the bread. She reached for a plate and dished up both Luke and Andrew's meal. Then she dished up for Tom

Brady.

Having completely forgotten about Andrew's knee in the stone silence of the room, she was reminded of it when he stood and limped to his meal at the table. His pant leg bulged where his knee was clearly wrapped beneath it. He made no reference to it, he must have figured he got off easy. Even Charlie avoided the usual gaping, empty stare as he sat at the table. He kept his little face down as he attempted to feed himself with his spoon, the beloved Spoony next to his plate.

At last, the dishes were washed, the boys off crawling into bed under heavy blankets, Molly lying silently by the fire twitching in fits of dreams. Luke had recovered adequately, although Tom Brady was sure his right foot had some frostbite on his smallest toe. That was lucky. It could have been his whole foot. Andrew's knee was stitched as good as his rough hands could manage. Now the boys crowded together in beds to keep warm, Tom Brady assisting them in the effort to get into bed. Addie could hear their quiet voices drifting from the loft.

Addie stood at the worktable and put plates back on the shelf. She did so very quietly as not to disturb the sound of the tomb. The fires of the house were warm, but the feel of it was distant and lonely.

"Mrs. Loveland." Addie finished placing an enamel plate on the shelf before she slowly turned to look at Tom Brady. He stood in the doorway to the sitting room with his hands on his hips, his brown hair flat and tired, his bushy beard full of itself and fluffed up to show it.

"I guess I don't have to tell you there ain't no way you'll make the dugout."

Addie merely nodded her head and looked down at the floor. After a long moment passed, Addie looked up to see that Tom Brady hadn't moved. He still stood, his face very grim in the soft light. When she met his eyes, he looked away. "I have blankets if you want to make a pallet."

"No," Addie sighed out.

"Well, anyhow, there's blankets in the armchair." Tom Brady turned to walk down the short hall to his bedroom.

"Mr. Brady," Addie spoke softly. When he half turned to look at her, the dull of his eyes reflected the weak light. Addie swallowed.

"Thank you. I was certain I couldn't save him," her whisper cut short.

He said nothing for a moment, just looked back at her while she tried not to cry, her eyes glittering with the effort. He sighed before saying, "Luke assures me you're the only reason he didn't die." Then he was gone, swallowed by the dark in the hallway. Addie then heard the soft scrape of the door as it closed.

She moved to the sitting room and gathered up the blankets off the chair and thought of her quilt. It was so far away. Molly wandered in and sat down to watch the woman as she spread blankets down on the rug before the fire. When she lay down, the dog was with her, right by her side. She pressed close to Addie's back and curled her head around to drift back into her dreams. At last, Addie's heart pumped warm blood as she lay before that great fire.

Addie could see nothing on the horizon. The vast country before her was empty, the sun gleaming off the waving grass just as she had seen it a hundred times before. The clouds formed and raced across the sky, never stopping nor gathering to bring about a storm. They just drifted quickly on, leaving streaks of open sky behind them before another cloud formed and raced.

It was entrancing. The warmth of the sun on her face warmed her entire body. The passage of eternity could be spent in that very spot, watching those happy clouds form and fly. The color of this country was beyond golden. The light seemed to be brighter than the sun, but came from no sun Addie could see.

She closed her eyes and inhaled deeply the scent of the grass. The country was empty, yet Addie didn't feel desperate in being alone. She was at peace. There was no need for another to be with her.

When Addie opened her eyes, he stood there, quietly waiting. The black etching around his ears as he kept them pricked forward gave him away. His brown eyes were soft and deeply kind. He barely moved his head, as he waited patiently for his presence to register.

He was not more than twenty feet away. The wind teased at his mane and tail, but he seemed not to notice. It was in Addie to panic, but for some reason, the extremity of his attempt to be passive struck her. His nostrils expanded as he took in a deep breath, then reached his nose out to her. Addie didn't move.

When he'd stretched as far as he could, he took a tentative step. When she held her ground, he took another, all the while his nose stretched out before him.

"What do you want from me?" she spoke in a very soft voice that made the gray's head go up and ears stand at attention. "What do you *want* from me? What does it mean that you haunt me? I've no reason to remember you."

The gray lowered his head as he listened to her words. He tipped his head slightly and looked back behind him, then he trained on Addie again. "I don't want to see you anymore. You bring with you *such* feeling. So go, let me be."

The clouds sailed on again and left an open piece of blue sky. The light hit the horse with concentration, the sleekness of his gray and black hide shining in the golden light. He raised his head and stepped confidently to her, this time not stopping to ward off her running. He came to stand a mere two feet before her, his nostrils large and round as he took in her scent.

He was magnificent. The likes of horseflesh Addie had never seen. He was larger and taller than any she had ever been close to. His thick muscles ripped beneath the gray with each movement. Again he lowered his head and tipped his nose around to see her out of one eye briefly before looking at her straight on.

Then he was gone. All of it was gone. Addie lay on the hard floor in the sitting room before the fire that was nearly out. The dog still lay pressed to her back, but the ache in her body as it contested the hard floor made the urge to move too great. Rolling onto her back, she saw the room was nearly dark from the death of the fire. She rose with popping and snapping joints to fuel it again.

The dog thumped her tail on the floor as she watched Addie.

Taking the poker, she roused the embers, then placed the kindling where it would catch easily. As the small embers grew, she fed in larger pieces of wood until the room was light again with the roaring flames. Addie rubbed her cold arms as she stood there watching the flame grow.

"Best lie down again awhile."

Addie turned sharply at the sound of Tom Brady's quiet voice.

"Still snowin'. Won't do chores before the sun comes up and lights the way some."

He stood in the doorway in his clothes, his hair tousled from sleep, or perhaps, from tossing all night, sleepless. His shoulders were drooping in the light as he looked at Addie straight on. Although she had been before, this was the most alone Addie had ever been with Tom Brady.

"You cry in your sleep."

The statement made Addie's heart stop. Her grief was personal. She wanted no one to hear it or see it. At least not Tom Brady. She wrapped her arms tighter around herself and looked into the fire. She locked her inner thoughts away from the view of anyone.

"Sleep awhile." He was gone.

Addie was done with sleeping.

The weather turned mild and stayed that way for more than a week. Although bitterly cold, the sky shone with blue radiance. The wind too fled, and it was easier to keep the house warm without the rush of air threading through any cracks and seams it could find. The blizzard had lasted a full day leaving in its wake a good two feet of snow. Tom Brady and his boys took shovels to the feed grounds to dig through drifts to get the sleigh through. It was a long, hard day.

Then the weather changed and eased the burden of feeding. The boys could sit on the bed of the sleigh and warm in the sun as the day went along. Matters in their minds turned from the agonizing thought of feeding in the cold, to the inkling of Christmas close at hand.

While each well understood their father wasn't a gift giver, they knew that Addie Loveland was an excellent baker. It had been since their mother that they had Christmas goodies to fill stockings by the fire on Christmas morning. But, Luke knew he'd have to ask his father to tell Addie to bake for them. That was the trouble. His brothers were giddy with the prospect and spoke of the treats long into the night in the dark. But Luke was practical enough to realize he'd have to convince his pa.

There lay the problem.

He'd dreaded it. Examined it. Practiced his speech. It all came down to one thing. He was too scared to do it. Luke knew if he asked Addie directly, she'd do it. But, then she'd get into trouble with his pa for not asking and taking liberties with the boys.

Luke had to ask, but he couldn't think of a way to do it.

In the end, he was spared in an unusual way.

For Addie, things were difficult. Not just for the obvious reasons, not because Christmas was approaching and Fett wouldn't be tricking her into believing mistletoe was made of juniper boughs. No, Addie was fighting a whole new battle, something beyond the basic, all the way back to the primitive.

It all started several mornings before that particular day. Charlie had stumbled out of his pa's bedroom, soaked beyond soaked, and Addie knew the bedsheets must be that way too. Ordinarily she would have just overlooked it, had she not washed them the day before, tying up the entire kitchen with the process of drying them.

The bitter cold froze her hands instantly when she had to plunge them into the water to scrub the blankets. It wasn't as if she washed the bedding each week anymore due to the cold, but each time the boy soiled a set of blankets, she had to do the washing. Twice since she'd come Luke had to refill straw beds in the loft. It was never ending.

So, Addie spent the day, a particularly cold one, scrubbing Tom Brady's blankets; again.

The next morning, same story. The morning after that, Charlie really did it. Not only had he peed his own bed, he cried for his nightly meal, then fell asleep with his pa downstairs and peed the bed again just before dawn. Before noon, he'd soaked through several cloth diapers and drenched his pants. She'd hung them by the fire to dry, but by afternoon he was out of pants to wear, and so he wore semi-wet ones while Addie heated water, then scrubbed away at the wash tub.

The cloth diapers on hand were no longer adequate to cover the small boy who should have been trained more than a year before. Some children were able to be trained before their first birthday. Addie doubted Tom Brady had much experience training up a child in the manner of urination, nor would he bother to try.

When Charlie up and decided to poop his pants each day about noon meal time, Addie had enough. She realized it wasn't fair to the little man to be angry with him, but it must have shone in her eyes no matter how deep she tried to bury her animosity. When she would change his pants and then scrub the few diapers that hadn't been thrown out into the desert on the trek from Tuscarora, Charlie would watch from hunched shoulders as he peeked around Spoony.

At one point, Addie looked up from the scrub board to see Charlie watching from the window as he stood on a chair she'd placed there. His pants were completely soaked. Why, did it seem, that the problem was compounding? Maybe because he was now being seen to in a manner in which his body was actually receiving proper nourishment, and of course, that leads to natural ends. And in this case, those ends weren't in the outhouse.

Addie bent over the wash tub and cried for a minute or two.

It kept her awake late that night, thinking on it, wondering. She had watched her mama train her younger brothers, but Charlie was no ordinary boy. It wasn't as if he could listen to and then understand reasoning. He'd hear it; he just wouldn't bother with it. Addie spoke to him all day long in hopes he would eventually try to speak. About the closest he ever got was to mimic her lip movements. She had no idea what it would take to break the strange wall around Charlie's mind.

Addie considered consulting Tom Brady about the problem, but decided he'd addressed the problem already, by not addressing it. He just avoided it. A few times she'd left the soiled blankets on his bed to prove a point. He merely commanded her to wash the blankets. They were soiled. He must have pretended not to notice when she threw a pot at the door he'd just walked out of.

No, Tom Brady clearly had no say in this one.

So, she began just as she'd seen her mother do. She stoked the fire to a roar, got it so stinkin' hot in the kitchen she nearly ran herself out, then she took Charlie's pants and cloth away. He was a sight, standing there, his little thin legs bare, his shirt all that he wore. His dark hair fell endearingly across his forehead as he looked at Addie like she'd finally had it with him.

Addie smiled happily at him. He stood there long after she had gone about her work. Then, Addie started pouring the liquids to him. She snuck a can of evaporated milk out of Tom Brady's cache in the cellar and opened it. She made a wonderful concoction of sugary, milky coffee and fed it to him in small portions all morning. She fed him bread and water, and, just as any good coffee should, it started to flush out that water in record time.

Addie had to hover. She realized he was very capable of holding his urine. It wasn't a matter of can't or won't, but when you have no reason to hold it, why do so? Now Charlie was realizing he'd never peed anywhere but into fabric. He wasn't quite sure what to think about peeing all willy nilly on the floor. So, he held it until he couldn't stand still anymore. Then he wiggled in place. He took to walking small circles, all the while his dark eyes pleaded with Addie for something, *anything* to pee in.

It finally came down to a breach. First it was a few drops, then a weak trickle, then the flood. Addie reached for the bed pan she'd taken from Tom Brady's bedroom and placed it under the flood to collect it. Charlie watched with wide eyes. He was shocked, stunned, amused maybe? When he was done, he looked down at the puddle he'd created in the bed pan and blinked. Addie scooped him up and hugged him tight and smiled at him boldly. She reiterated what a good and wonderful boy he was. She kissed his cheek, something she'd never done, then fixed him another cup of candied coffee. Liking it so much he gulped it down in an instant.

So began the process.

Of course this wouldn't solve the night time issue straightaway, but at least she was headed in the right direction. As he'd never been taught to do anything before, Charlie was a slow learner. He seemed to understand the concept alright, but he wouldn't take himself to the pan when he needed to go. Although Addie kept it in the same place every day, Charlie would wait until he couldn't stand still anymore to signal Addie he had to go. He had accident after accident on the floor if Addie was distracted and couldn't get to him fast enough. It was wearying.

So, she decided to try a new tactic. About a week into the training, when she knew he had to go, she'd go stand next to the pan and look at him. Then she would beckon to him, the whole time he was pinching up his face in an effort to hold it. This new idea went over poorly. She spent several days going backward, thinking she'd lost the ground she'd made. Then it became a near fact that when Charlie had to go, he would just pee on the floor. Almost as if he thought that was what she wanted.

Addie started at the beginning again. She tried taking him to the pan each time he had to go. That way, the pan was in the same place every time. That soon proved difficult in the evening hours when Tom Brady and the boys were home. Charlie was now used to never having wet pants. Not to mention, not having pants at all. And on more than one occasion, Tom Brady commented on the use of wood being up, and the house being particularly hot, which he saw no reason for.

Addie replied nothing.

Finally, a week before Christmas, Addie stood at the workbench kneading a batch of dough, when out of the corner of her eye she saw Charlie dash across the room. When she turned, there he was, in the corner by the door, peeing into the pan. She'd won. How many times she'd scrubbed the floor, carried him to the pan. She'd won. Charlie must have found it invigorating to have total control over something in his wee life, because he took great pride in his ability to pee in that pan. He never peed on the floor. He did not pee his pants when Addie put them back on. Only once did he, until Addie showed him how to pull down his trousers without her help. That took a few tries, but he was too proud in his new ability to give up on it over a pair of trousers. He still had his nightly troubles, but that was mostly due to Tom Brady's lack of understanding. It was difficult to understand why the boy took to fighting him over the cloths. Charlie just wouldn't let him put one on.

Now Addie had to address the second, solid call of nature.

Roy Albert rode up on the feed grounds at a brisk trot. He raised his gloved hand and waved when Luke straightened from where he was bent forking hay and looked at the approaching rider.

"Pa, Roy's comin'."

Tom Brady also straightened from where he pitched hay, as did Andrew. Tom hollered at Frankie to stop the team, and they all stood watching him ride up.

"Oh, don't stop on account of me. I'd hate to be the cause of these boys missin' milk 'n' cookies at the house." Roy side passed to the sleigh and reached his right hand over the saddle horn to shake Tom Brady's, emphasized with a nod of his head.

"What brings you out and about?" Tom Brady asked.

"Oh, I'm on the hunt. Damn gray stud wandered off. Seems I can't keep him content at home these days."

Tom Brady wrinkled a brow. "Your good stud?"

Roy looked off toward the mountains that glistened in the afternoon sun. The brightness of the light reflecting off the snow made it hard to see. His daddy had called it "snow blind".

"Yeah. I took to riding him harder to give him a little somethin' to occupy his time. But, for some reason it didn't change his mind. Now he just jumps out of the corral by the barn and leaves."

Tom Brady cocked his head. "The corral by the barn? That fence must be damn near seven feet tall," he replied with doubt.

Roy shook his head, his thick, dark green sock hat hiding some of the movement. "I know. I have my doubts about it every time I go out and see his tracks. He starts running over by the barn, clears the fence, then you can see where he lights on the other side."

"I ain't heard of the likes of that. I mean I've heard horses clearing lesser fences, but certainly not after a hard day of workin'. You got mares up by the house?" Tom Brady asked.

Roy again shook his head and pursed his lips. "Nah. And anyway

179

he's got no interest in them. His tracks go in the opposite direction."

"What?" Tom Brady asked incredulously. "Where's he goin'?"

Roy leaned forward and rested his right elbow on his saddle horn. The sorrel he sat upon cocked his head to look back at Roy. He was a tall beast, solid red, no white on him. Roy looked briefly at Luke. "He's comin' to your place."

"Bullshit! Why would he bail over a near seven foot fence just to run seventeen miles to challenge my studs for a bunch of mares when he could just stay home and enjoy his own ladies? Besides, I have never seen him."

Roy shrugged deeply. "Perhaps he's comin' for other reasons."

Tom Brady shook his head, his fuzzy, wiry beard catching on his coat as he did so. "What other reasons does a stud have than the call of duty?"

Roy raised his eyebrows and shook his head. He then looked at the boys who stood silently, pitchforks in hand, Frankie with the lines to the work team steady in his little bitty hands. It was a man's job, and as Roy noted, Frankie took it seriously.

"Well, boys. 'Bout time to gorge yourselves on fancy Christmas goodies." Two of the three boys grinned like giddy coyotes. Luke just looked troubled. Roy tilted his head and looked at the eldest in consideration.

He looked back at Tom Brady. "What about you? You ready for some Christmas goodies?"

Tom Brady raised an eyebrow at his friend. "No. I have no intention of enjoying any goodies," he replied firmly.

Roy tried not to grin, his cheek twitching with the effort. "What a pity. Seems to me, you ought to at least try some. Might be better than any goodie you ever tried." At this point Roy cleared his throat. "I mean, Mrs. Loveland is an excellent baker."

Tom Brady sagged his shoulders and closed his eyes, shaking his head in clear disgust.

"Well hell, seems to me, you should at least invite me to Christmas dinner. You know all I got at home is a bag uh beans and really bad

180

biscuits. It would be neighborly to invite me to enjoy some of thy bounty." Roy gave Luke a very quick wink before Tom Brady opened his eyes and looked at him straight on.

"I believe like that damn gray stud of yours, you got other reasons for jumpin' that fence and wandering *seventeen* miles to the neighbor's place. Goodies got nothin' to do with it," Tom Brady sarcastically stated.

Roy grinned. "I believe the goodies got everything to do with it."

"Well, then I guess you best clear the fence come Christmas Day and run those seventeen miles to our place."

Roy sat up straight and glared down at Tom Brady. "I won't do any such thing. My ma taught me never to invite myself in such a rude manner. You want me over, you best ask me. I ain't gonna rudely show up on Christmas Day."

Tom Brady let out a laugh. "Alright. Fine. Royce Albert, we would greatly enjoy your sarcastically enduring humor, rude belching, gas passing presence at our delightfully laden Christmas table."

Roy raise a brow. Tom Brady added, "Please."

"I suppose. I mean, it's a long ride. In the cold. Possibly snow. And I fear you might not be genuine in your invitation. But, I suppose, I can try to make it. It's a lot to ask of a man. In the winter. Bein' cold and all." He paused to watch Tom roll his eyes.

"Shall I leave one of my stockings now? I'd hate to miss out on the…goodies."

Tom Brady turned serious. "It seems a bit of a chance. Risking frostbite just to leave behind a stocking that will no doubt corrode the contents placed in it on Christmas Eve. Seeing as you have the foot rot. Why waste goods on a festering stocking? You can eat them off the plate like a grown-up."

Roy laughed loudly. "Maybe you could hang one of Frankie's for me. Charlie's is too small to hold much." Roy lifted his reins. "Thank you for the gracious invitation," Roy said with a sweeping arm. "I will see you on Christmas morning." He turned his horse and as he rode away said, "If you see the gray, run him towards home."

Tom Brady cupped his ear mockingly. "What? If I see the gray, shoot him? Got it. Will do!"

Roy turned again in his saddle to swipe an arm in the air as if to say, *forget you.* Then he kicked his horse into a trot and was quickly away.

Luke felt a smile form in his chest. It spread a relieving warmth that heated him all the way to the tips of his toes. He looked over at Andrew and they both grinned at each other. Things were looking up.

"We'll have a guest for Christmas dinner."

Addie paused where she held her spoon on its journey to her mouth, filled with broth, beans, and chunks of meat. Tom Brady had spoken into the air, and for a moment she wondered if he were speaking to her. But he'd been talking to his sons in a familiar tone, then changed it to one of indifference when he addressed her.

Addie looked to the opposite end of the table where he sat.

"Roy will be coming to dinner." Tom Brady's dark eyes watched her closely.

Addie blinked a few times. In truth, she had hoped he would treat the day as he had Thanksgiving. She was avoiding the Holy Day with all the strength she could muster to ignore it. "What should I make?"

When she looked back at him she realized he had quit chewing his food, his spoon held loosely in his hands as he looked at her. When her eyes met his, he looked down and began to chew again. "Well, I 'spect the usual trimmin's."

Addie flashed back to the Christmas previous. She clenched her jaw a moment. "I...I haven't had a Christmas with the 'usual trimmin's' for a few years. What do you have in mind?"

"Do you not believe in the birth of the Christ Child?" Tom Brady asked with an arrogant tip to his head.

Luke squirmed. Just when he thought things were gonna go his way...

Addie swallowed hard. "I wasn't suggestin' lack of belief, just the lack of trimmin's. Last year we ate roasted ground squirrel. The year before that we were in Mexico. To tell the truth, Fett never did say what the meat was we ate that year, and I still don't care to know. The year before that we was holed up in a leaky cabin out in New Mexico territory somewheres. Yours was the first sugar I'd seen since we spent a brief spring in Colorado near two years ago. So, I guess if lack of trimmin's leads to a lack of faith, I'm in sore need of a preacher."

Addie looked at him square on. Tom Brady studied her a moment, then looked down at his plate. The boys watched silently as they listened to Addie's statement. It was the first time the thought crossed their minds that their Mrs. Loveland had adventures before she became the hollow housekeeper who sat at their table. Andrew was transfixed on her. He was a dreamer at heart and wondered about places far away from his chores at home.

"We butchered hogs with Roy last October just before you came. We cured hams, so I guess we best have one of those. And I guess whatever sweet treats you know how to make would work fine."

Luke turned to Addie with a look of pleading in his eyes. She wrinkled her brow a moment in question to his meaning. Perhaps he longed for her to forgive the ignorance of his pa, or perhaps he had a special request in mind.

Addie glanced back down the table at Tom Brady. His head was down, his spoon mining restlessly in his bowl of broth and beans. He raised a spoonful to his mouth, but he didn't look up. His thick brows were furrowed in a solid considering line.

"What was it like?"

The whole of the table stopped their eating, with the exception of Charlie who kept fishing out one bean at a time with his pointer and thumb then eating it. Addie watched as Tom Brady rained down a look of consternation on Andrew.

The silence was deafening.

Addie considered Andrew who looked at her over his spoon with regret in his eyes. "What was what like?"

"Mexico," Andrew replied then ducked self-consciously.

Addie raised her eyebrows as she swallowed what was remaining in her mouth. She rested her spoon-holding hand on the table. "Well, I can't really say. The time we spent there was fast. Not that we weren't there awhile, just we was moving fast."

"What do you mean by movin' fast?" asked Luke who was now giving full attention to the detail of the story.

Addie again glanced at Tom Brady who watched her from beneath that same line of dark brow. He said nothing to stop her answering Luke's posed question.

She thought a moment. "Well," she began, then stopped to let out a chuckle. Addie raised up her head and looked at Luke square on, her eyes reflecting the chuckle. "See, Fett, that's my husband, and Pete, his partner, kept hearin' that those ranchers down in Mexico rode just the most awful junk to get by. They'd get whatever skinny-necked, pop-kneed, flat-withered nag they could get a rope around and go to ridin'. So, they cooked up this scheme to take a whole passel of ponies down there and just, I don't know, light their way of thinkin' to a new breed of horse.

"So, we spent about seven months gathering and breaking about forty head of good horses. Which, we later figured out, had all come across the line, from Mexico." She paused to laugh. "We go ridin' high down into Mexico, with each of the four of us that made that trip leadin' a string of ten head apiece.

"First town we come to, we can't get one interested buyer. So we move on farther south. Well, about that time, somebody figures we must have stolen those horses. Now, mind you, it isn't easy to make a run for it leading a ten-head string. They get to running and like to pass you up. Then pretty quick, you're at the end of the string holding on for dear life, trying to gain the lead again, which is near impossible 'cause a mounted horse can't run as fast as an empty one.

"Took those boys the better part of the day to catch up to me." Addie looked down and smiled, then looked straight at Andrew. "But I held on to my string. Didn't lose even one. Fett was pretty proud of that."

After looking down for a moment, she continued. "Well, after that, we were on the run all the time. Pete asked around the few places we stopped and heard about a big place south of where we were, and we might be able to sell our goods there. So, off we ran. When we got there, we were met with one of the most beautiful spreads I had ever seen. Old place, big, with lots of cows and horses all runnin' as far as the eye could see. We are greeted and welcomed. Pete and Fett taking time to meet the owner of this ranch that was passed down generation to generation for I don't know how many hundreds of years."

Addie started laughing here. "He was a fine gentleman. Very fine. His wife was a very fine lady. He looked our horses over. Scrutinized every one. Then politely told Fett and Pete that all the horses he raised and found of lesser quality, he sold up in Texas."

Luke and Andrew started sputtering and laughing, the mirth boiling out cautiously at first, then with confidence. Addie started to laugh too, seeing their appreciation for the irony of the situation.

"Being as it was near Christmas, they felt charitable and bought, what could have in some way, been their own horses back. They paid next to nothing, but we figured that was better than making a mad dash back to Texas at the end of a string, or getting caught and thrown in a Mexican prison."

Addie smiled softly at the two boys who were enjoying the plight of the quartet of Texas horsemen who dared to dream a lucrative dream. "I guess I realize now the value lay in the experience and memory, not in the price of the horses. And, after a peaceful Christmas in Mexico, it was a faster run back to Texas without a string of ten."

It felt good. To sit with those two young boys and laugh about an adventure. Addie could still feel her little bay beneath her, running with all he had, jumping brush and rock piles as he tried in vain to get that string behind him again. He was fast, and Addie still didn't know why the poor little devil never gave up. She guessed because his desire to keep up with the running bunch overcame his need to rest. She smiled at the boys, and resumed eating her soup.

As she dipped her spoon into the broth, Addie looked out of the corner of her eye to the head of the table. Tom Brady had his head bent, his forearms resting on the table, his eyes looking into his bowl of soup. Just before Addie looked away, he glanced up and caught her looking at him. He said nothing.

Addie spent the days leading up to Christmas without much ado. She kept up with Charlie's training, and it was starting to take root. She doubted it would really be possible to teach the boy to answer the second call of nature until the weather broke and they could spend time in the outhouse. Despite the sun, the air was frozen and the icicles that hung from the eaves of the main house never dripped or dropped throughout the day. Even those in the sun.

However, it was enough that the wind wasn't howling.

Addie kept quiet about things, although the boys grew in raucous anticipation. Why, she couldn't fathom. It wasn't as if they were in for a day off from the feeding or stall cleaning. Their stoic father had no intentions of brightening the season with an unexpected visit from human charity.

But just the same, they danced around the kitchen, played games of chase and practical joking all through chores, and counted off another day on Frankie's little fingers each morning at the breakfast table. It was amusing to watch them, for in all honesty, it was Luke who was the most giddy. He'd watch Andrew count out the days remaining on Frankie's fingers, then put one back down to show another day gone by, and then Luke would look to Addie and smile. It was much over a few baked goods in her way of thinking.

Addie started baking two days before Christmas. Although her heart wasn't really in it, she knew the surmounting disappointment that would stem from her picketing the Holy Day would be enough to bring down the beams in the house. At first she had no idea what to make. She stood in the cellar and stared for what felt like an eternity. Her mind wandered to Texas and her ma, and she thought of anything but Christmas. Then, just as Addie remembered the way her ma looked as she brushed out her long hair, humming, in the lamplight, she saw it. A very small jar of strawberry jam. It hid back among the dust and empty jars of meals past. She took it in her hands and looked at it. It was indeed old, but still well sealed, so she tucked it into her apron pocket.

She grabbed a few other items as well. Then, she slipped out of the

186

cellar and closed the door. She trudged up the walk back to the house, looking up at the brilliantly blue sky. When she stepped up onto the porch, she saw Charlie standing on his chair and watching out the window. It was his custom now, to stand and watch out the window any time Addie had to go outside. His anxious little face would watch her go, then wait in silence for her to reappear, clutching his loyal friend Spoony.

Addie liked not to think of what would happen when he climbed up on that chair and watched out the window as she went for the last time, never to reappear. Perhaps she placed too much value in her position in his life. At times she prayed so.

There would come a time for her to leave.

Christmas Eve came and the weather held, no wind to spell ill intentions, so Tom Brady figured there would be no reason for Roy not to come the following day. Addie had diligently prepared, and like a wise woman would, hid her wares from the drooling mouths of the boys in the dugout. Only Charlie got to taste test the goodies, and he kept his secrets like a vault.

It took a fair amount of prodding and cajoling to get the boys into working order on Christmas Eve morning. Tom Brady ruled with an iron fist, but on that particular day even the iron fist wasn't helping. They laughed and wrestled, teased and hollered. It made Addie smile when her back was turned, remembering her own brothers and how hard they were to control in similar circumstances.

Tom Brady went to smacking heads. It worked, but it didn't kill the spirit.

Addie spent the day baking and cleaning, trying to convince her own spirit to rise. She found she was grateful that Roy was coming, for he would offer a soft place to keep the occupants of the Brady homestead distracted. And maybe with his direct way, he would bring strength to the dinner table.

Thinking of Roy always made Addie's heart call out in search of a letter he sent to Texas. She wondered where it was. If it would make it. If there would be an answer before she set out on a long journey home.

Would her mama know, just from the strange hand the letter was composed in, that her girl met with great misfortune? Would she have already guessed based on her mother's intuition? Addie had known it done. Women out on the plains knew one of their own was lost and hurting, or, been killed, just by the cord of communion that stretched the miles between mother and child. It gave Addie courage to know that perhaps her mother wasn't as far as she thought, in way of the spirit.

Looking out the window at the bright world, lit by the afternoon sun, it seemed a promise was lurking in the golden light of the day. It was sweet and comforting, and it took Addie to a place in her spirit, a place she had seen before, had touched before, but was no longer where she dwelled. She would again. How long it would take before she lived in the serene light, she cared not to know. Her road was hard and impassable now, and the thought of another stone in her path, striking against her bruised feet was unbearable. If only she could be carried.

The evening passed with little or nothing said by either Addie or Tom Brady. It would have been hard to be heard over the boys anyway. When at last they had gone to bed, but could still be heard laughing and talking from the loft, Addie put on her coat and took the lantern from the table. Tom Brady was in the sitting room stoking the great fire. When she stepped from the porch, Addie stopped and stared in wonder at the steep mountains to the west. The bright round moon cast a silvery glow down on them, and the snow offered that silver light back up to the sky. Everything was illuminated, reflecting that soft light, the crispness of the air only served to magnify it. The stars twinkled in the sky, happy and content to look down on a world they didn't have to live in.

Addie looked around for a moment, taking it all in, then she walked on to the dugout and started bringing her goods to the house. Little by little she placed it on the table. Loaves of fresh bread, two pies, out of dried apples, tiny tart cookies with little dollops of jam in the center, bread with cinnamon swirled in the middle for a breakfast treat. And, just in case stockings made the fireplace, cookies, little bitty circles dipped in glaze, and hard candies, clear and simple for the lack of coloring, but cinnamon speckles spoke for the flavoring.

Addie placed it all where Tom Brady could see it on the big table. That way, it was his choice for stockings, and, if he chose against it, the boys would have something to ease the disappointment. She arranged it then stood, tightening her huge coat around her. Looking up, Addie found Tom Brady leaning in the doorway to the sitting room. His hands hung loosely in his pockets, his wiry beard hiding the expression his mouth might offer. His dark eyes were hard and unreadable.

They stood for several moments like that, Addie swaddled tightly in Fett's coat, Tom Brady hidden in his own features.

"I apologize." It was a very quiet statement, made nearly, to not be detected.

Addie stood and stared at him. Had she actually heard it? She felt she would look a fool to acknowledge something that wasn't there. She looked away and then back to him, his dark eyes the same. "Beg pardon?"

"I didn't mean to suggest you have no God. I've heard you shout at Him enough to know you carry Him with you," he said flatly.

Her mind went back to the dinner conversation. Suddenly it hit her that she had let a piece of herself, and more importantly, Fett, go. Something of herself had flowed out of her mouth and drifted about the room in aimless search for understanding. Addie wanted it back. If one piece went, then the whole of her soul might be exposed. This man, whose observations made her look to the world like a mad woman, knew something deeply personal about Fett's feeling for her. She had been speaking to those boys. Not to Tom Brady. In her storytelling she forgot he was listening. Addie stood still while the stinging in her chest cavity burned like acid. She looked at the table of Christmas goodies.

She was the worst kind of traitor. She'd made a feast for a man who she was not pledged to. For children not born of her womb. The stinging turned to torrid guilt. When Addie looked back up at Tom Brady, his dark eyes were piercing, and in that moment she read his thoughts. He saw her in the same way, the same traitorous way that she felt about herself.

Tom Brady was very adept at making his own soul known without using his voice.

Addie backed away from the table. She left the main house without looking back, looking only to the sky through the tears in her eyes. She moved out across the snow, and without bothering with the log bridge, plunged across the ice of the creek. She didn't stop to pet the dog who waited for her on the porch of the dugout.

She was becoming numb.

Addie didn't notice how she was quietly being lulled into a life she didn't want. How being a prisoner of routine was starting to suit the passage of time. She spent too much time finding ways to encourage Charlie. Took too much enjoyment in telling Luke and Andrew stories. Relied on the dog for comfort.

She didn't bother to stoke the fire again, merely closed the door behind herself, noting the dog had hurried in, almost as if she knew the woman was treading a line of rejecting her company. Addie went straight to her trunk and lay down over it. She cried as she hadn't in days, the deadened nerves in her body finally registering the pain in her soul. When her back ached and creaked, she hobbled to the bed and lay down under the quilt she and Fett had shared. She drew herself into a ball, the dog pressed tightly to her back.

Shaking and shivering, Addie cried on into the night, long before sleep anesthetized all emotion.

It was very rare that Addie ever rode Buck. She had her own little bay who served her quite well, near to the point of death on a few occasions. Fett kept Buck for himself, as Buck was a bigger horse, a faster horse, and he knew how to work a rope, not to mention he just seemed to read Fett's mind about what he needed done. Even when Fett wasn't astride.

So, it seemed a rare day in the sun to find herself riding Buck up and over a grassy slope. He was saddled in Fett's bigger saddle, as Addie had to point her toes down to have any placement in the stirrup, and then she was on tiptoes. The get-down was looped around her saddle horn, the coarseness of the tail hair it was braided from scratching the back of her

hand as Addie brushed against it. Buck's long, straight black mane
fanned out in the breeze as he topped the ridge, ears forward, eyes alert
for what might be at the top, just out of sight. His head was raised and his
paces quickened, but it remained smooth and easy beneath Addie.

There was nothing waiting at the top that took bodily form, just an
endless grassy prairie, bright and green in what seemed like a warm
spring day. The prairie stretched into forever, the grass waving and
reflecting the bright sun as the air moved along and teased it. With
anticipation, Buck moved into a lope, the even beats of his gait
displaying the strength in his muscles, held deep within his body.

Addie didn't know where Buck was headed, but he was sure to get
there the way he traveled with intent. Addie inhaled deeply and closed
her eyes, feeling nothing but the movement of the body below her, the
bridle reins resting loosely in her hands. She could smell the soft, mellow
scent of horse.

"Baby girl..."

Buck loped on, the sound of the voice crossing the expanse of the
prairie on the wind.

"My sweet baby girl, I hold you in my heart, right in my heart."

Buck hurried headlong into the wind, running faster to catch the
sound of the voice as it came.

"I'm here. I'm always here."

"Mama!" Addie yelled out, spurring Buck to an all-out run. "Mama!
Mama, wait for me! I'm coming!"

*"Sweet Addie, I can feel you hurting. I can feel you breaking. Don't
break. Hold on.....hold on for me!"*

Buck could run no faster. He was moving at a speed that made the
tears roll out of Addie's eyes and back into her hair. But he fired again,
trying to give more, his front legs breaking over and then stretching out
with repetitiveness.

"Mama!"

"God, watch over my sweet baby. Hold her. Carry her. Help her."

"Mrs. Loveland!" Tom Brady shook her violently now, trying to
rouse her out of whatever pit she lay in. "Come on, girl."

When Addie opened her tear-soaked eyes and heard her own voice calling out for her mama, she choked on the sound.

"Good Lord, woman, I thought somebody had ahold of you in here. I could hear you clear down in the barn!" Tom Brady shouted at her.

Addie sucked in air and came back to a physical reality. It was real. She had been there, running free with Buck, pursuing her mother. And her mother's voice, it was as real as Tom Brady's. She wiped at her tears and breathed deeply for a moment. She opened her eyes to find that Tom Brady was standing there, looking down at her where she thought he had left.

Addie could not read his expression in the pale light. After sighing, Tom Brady turned and opened the wood stove to see the embers barely enough to glow when the rush of air hit them. He again sighed and turned to the table. He moved to the rocker that sat empty and took hold of it at the top. In the near darkness, he drug it over to Addie who still rubbed her face. He lowered himself into the chair and leaned forward on his knees. He pressed his lips together tightly as he looked at Addie who stared back with trepidation.

"Woman, you gotta see your way through it. Or else you're gonna lose your mind. You are damn near there as I see it," he stated.

Addie covered her face and felt Buck beneath her again. Only this time, he was a memory, not Buck in the flesh. But the sound of her mama's voice echoed in her ears, fresh and new, a renewal of unblemished remembrance.

"I'm not sure you are any better off than me."

"No, perhaps not. But, I get up each day and keep moving."

"Ain't I moving? Each day?" Addie spat.

"Yeah. You move. That's about it." He paused here, just sat silently and watched her still form. "What happened to your mama?"

At this she raised her head and looked at him straight on. "What?"

Tom Brady sat back in the rocker. "In the few times I've heard you cry in your sleep, I've only ever heard you say two names. Fett, which I know is your husband, and Mama."

"Nothin'. 'Least, not that I know of," Addie whispered.

"When was the last time you saw her?"

Addie exhaled a rough sigh. "Four years."

"Hm. That made you just a babe. And I'm sure your mind has a hard time thinkin' through all you've seen since then."

"What's that mean?" Addie growled.

Tom Brady let out a sarcastic chuckle. "Easy. All I meant was, takin' a farm girl, at least I figure that's what you were, and showing her nothin' but miles and adventure, lovin' for the first time, and the inhospitality of the world was a bit much for you to sort out in short time."

Addie flushed a deep scarlet. She knew that Tom Brady was a man, and in the making of four sons, had enjoyed his manhood. But for him to look at her in a way that suggested he knew of her coming into womanhood made her feel like a childish girl. He was looking at it from a man's perspective, and unlike a woman, saw only the act, not the love that went with it.

Tom Brady leaned forward again in the soft light of the embers. "And I see I am right. Some parts of it you still haven't worked out."

With eyes flashing fire, she looked at him. "And I see that some parts are none of your business!"

Something in his eyes changed, almost softened. "It took my wife awhile to quit blushing, too."

Addie ground her teeth and turned her head. Molly looked up at her and pressed her ears to her head, her dark eyes reflecting the ember light. She attempted to wag her tail.

"Addie, I simply meant there is more to being a grown woman than the lovin' between husband and wife. It takes time to figure that." He looked down at his hands. "The hardest lesson of womanhood, the one that teaches the most, the man set to hold you through it, isn't here to do so."

She looked over at him. His face was still as he looked at her straight on. For the first time, Addie realized they were learning the same lesson. That Tom Brady had already had the time to figure out that the growing between a man and woman happens during the trials of life.

And his greatest trial, he faced alone.

"Come on. It's Christmas, and those boys will be awful disappointed come dinnertime if we have no feast."

Addie remained still even after he stood and walked to the door. "I can't," she whispered.

Tom Brady turned around and looked at her as if he already knew what she was going to say. That he'd already thought his way through the moment.

"It ain't a sin. To look after some boys who got no ma. I doubt even Fett would rather you spend a horrible Christmas alone than spend it with four grateful boys. Well," he corrected, "five, counting Roy."

After he had gone, she still sat on the bed and pressed her cheek to Molly's head. It took her a moment to realize what bothered her most about his words. It really wasn't his observations on her position in womanhood. It wasn't that he lowered himself to tell her he understood why she called out for her mama. And it wasn't that he agreed they were learning the very same terrible life lesson.

No, it was none of those things. It was that he called her Addie.

The boys were indeed beyond excited. By the time Addie had brushed her hair and dressed herself, Luke had the kitchen fire going and coffee on. Anxious faces turned to her when she came in the door to the main house. Luke rose from the table and poured Addie a cup of black coffee.

When he handed it to her he said, "We thought we should wait for you. Since you made it all."

Addie noticed for the first time none of the things she'd brought in the night before were on the table. "Don't wait. Go on."

The boys tore from the table, pushing and shoving, making their way to be the first through the sitting room door. When Addie saw the way was clear, she stepped to the doorway and saw that Tom Brady had filled stockings, and now they dangled from nails in the mantle.

By far, Charlie's was fullest, but only because his sock was so small compared to the other boys'. Luke lifted him so he could pull his own stocking down, then set him in one of the armchairs to look through his stash. Spoony rested with a big grin next to his leg.

Addie hadn't drawn a grin on the spoon. She guessed Luke had, but for some reason, it struck her odd. Spoony seemed to be taking on a life of his own the longer he played friend to the silent boy.

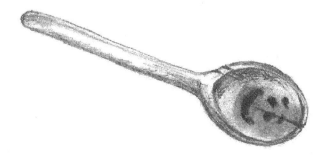

Andrew pulled a jam-filled shortbread from his stocking first. "Ah!" he cried as he popped it into his mouth.

Luke licked a cinnamon candy and closed his eyes in paradise. Frank watched his brothers, unsure of looking into his own stocking. He wanted to know what the others had before he looked into his own. They danced and laughed, fussed over their stockings, teased each other, pretended to steal when another wasn't looking. The sound they made brought a smile to Addie. She hid it behind her hand.

Luke looked to her with a shining look in his eyes, so bright it brought tears into Addie's. "Thank you, Miss Addie," he said in a low voice.

Addie nodded and turned to the kitchen. *Miss Addie.*

As she reached the worktable, Tom Brady opened the door and stepped in from the bright light of early morning stretching across the sky. He stomped the snow from his feet before he crossed the threshhold. Addie uncovered the smoked ham and reached for the dutch. As she started the makings of a small Christmas feast, she also made a light breakfast. It would take meat to undo what those boys were eating in baked goods.

She found where Tom Brady stashed the rest of the goodies in the pie safe. In that way, whether he knew it or not, he had actually made the stockings that much more exciting. Maybe he planned it that way. Addie had no way of knowing.

Midmorning, Tom Brady rose from where he sat in the sitting room and moved to the front door in the kitchen. From where she stood putting potatoes into the oven, Addie looked out the window to see Roy swinging down off his horse at the barn. Tom Brady grabbed his coat and left the house to walk through the snow to greet a good friend. The two men hollered out to each other.

By the time they put Roy's horse in a stall with feed, Addie had a fresh pot of coffee on and near ready. She could hear their voices as they stepped up on the porch, Roy laughing about something. The boys hopped around the kitchen in anticipation of their guest. When at last Roy did come through the door, the smell of a fine meal met his nose and before he greeted anyone who clamored for his attention, he looked for Addie. He smiled a warm greeting, then looked to Frank who bounded before him like a leaping deer.

"Hey, boy, have you been driving this good woman mad with your bouncing?" He raised Frank up into his strong arms and took a moment to tickle the boy's underarms. "Hold still, quit twitching like you got ants in your pants!" Frankie laughed and jerked again with another poke to the underarm.

Roy hoisted him high on his shoulder and turned to give both Luke and Andrew handshakes. Charlie held back near Addie, hiding as much in her skirt as he could. Roy walked to him and ran his fingers through dark hair that fell across his forehead.

"Mrs. Loveland," Roy nodded as he spoke. "Merry Christmas."

"Merry Christmas," Addie replied before looking away. She handed Roy a mug of hot coffee.

Tom Brady stood back by the table, and as Roy greeted Addie he looked down at the goods that lay across it. He chose a cookie without much consideration and took a big bite. From his perch on Roy's shoulder, Frankie took notice, and as Roy raised the hot liquid to his mouth, made mention of it.

"Pa, I thought you wasn't gonna enjoy Addie's goodies?"

Roy made a gurgling sound as he spit hot coffee back into his mug, then politely tried to choke. Tom Brady didn't fair as well, choking on inhaled shortbread, coughing and sputtering, trying to dislodge it. Addie looked from one gagging man to another and pieced things together, then flushed deeply. Again, men she didn't know contemplating her womanhood. She turned back to the bread before her.

Roy's choking turned to suppressed laughter. "I believe you're right, Frankie. He did say that."

Tom Brady cleared his throat. "Why don't we sit in here by the fire." Then he made a quick departure.

Roy set his coffee down on the table a moment, long enough to squeeze Addie's shoulder in understanding. Then he retrieved his coffee and carried both the mug and Frankie into the sitting room.

Charlie pulled on Addie's skirt, demanding her attention. When she looked down at him, his dark eyes searched hers. She made no move to smile at him, so he buried his face into the folds of her dress. It occurred to Addie he was a sensitive boy for all his dull appearance. Perhaps he thought he had in some way upset her. So, to reassure him, she rubbed his head. He pulled his face away to look at her again. This time she smiled at him as best she could. He did not return the smile, but his eyes changed, and he stood and traced Spoony's face.

Addie though back to the wagon ride from the junction to Tuscarora. She could still see the empty eyes that stared at her from under the wagon seat, bundled in blankets. Charlie had changed greatly in a few months. She looked down at him as he again clutched the folds of her skirt with one hand and pressed Spoony to his heart with the other.

Time would come for her to go back to Texas, and it would be Tom Brady's fault the hurt the boy felt at her going. He shouldn't have left him in her care. But her mind flashed to the terrible wind and snow that blew and swirled endlessly at times. Charlie wouldn't survive that kind of weather, buried under loose hay on the sleigh.

The sound of Roy's laughter rang from the sitting room. She could also hear one of the boys laughing with him. It made the image of her father and brothers rise up before her. No doubt one of the boys was taking a ribbing just as her brothers had each in turn endured. They would tease and rile, all the while, her pa just laughed and encouraged. On Christmas especially, since they were held up in the house with idle hands, something they rarely had the chance to enjoy.

When the meal was done, Addie set the plates and cutlery, then placed the food on the big wood table and stood back to look at it. It had been many years since she'd seen that kind of layout at Christmas. Ham, roasted potatoes, fresh bread, pies, bread stuffing. She never enjoyed such a feast when she was married to Fett, but she would trade all her Christmases with all the trimmings to have just one day of him back.

When she called the menfolk to the table, Roy made a fuss over all she'd done. He came through the door and whistled long and low. The boys skipped happily to places at the table.

"My, my, Mrs. Loveland. You sure do know how to fix a spread, don't ya?" Roy drawled out.

When Addie set down the coffee pot next to Tom Brady's spot, she glanced up to see Roy standing and looking at Charlie, who clung to her skirt, with a funny little half-smile. Addie stopped and looked down, a frown upon her face. Charlie peeked shyly at Roy.

"What a difference a woman makes," Roy said softly. He then moved to his seat on the opposite side of the table from Addie, between Andrew and Luke. Addie was at the end of the table across from Luke, beside Frankie. Tom Brady took hold of Charlie and placed him in his seat beside his father.

"Best we thank God for this bounty and the little woman who made it," Roy said.

Tom Brady nodded and the table bowed their heads. He paused a moment before he spoke. "Lord, we thank you for this meal, and we thank you for this important day. We thank you for a good friend to share our table, and we thank you for our good health. Bless all who sit at this table today. Amen."

As they began to dish up and pass the bowls and plates around, Roy looked at Tom Brady harshly. Tom pretended not to notice. "This is a fine meal. 'Preciate the invitation to share it with you." Roy spoke to Addie first, then to the whole table.

"You didn't leave us any choice," Tom Brady muttered.

Roy grinned, "Well, if I've learned anything about you, Tom, it's don't wait for you to do the polite thing. Just go on and muscle your way into whatever it is you want."

A small tater escaped from under Frankie's fork and skittered across the table to hit Andrew's plate. He picked it up and threw it back to Frankie.

Tom Brady paused before putting a forkful of potato and ham into his mouth to ask, "Did you find that gray stud of yours?"

Roy let out a groan. "Yeah, I found him. Right back in that corral next to the barn. Like he never left! He come right to the fence and nickered for dinner like he'd just been waitin' for me."

"What?" Tom Brady drawled out doubtfully.

"Maybe he's a phantom horse," Andrew stated.

"You don't even know what a phantom is," Luke retorted.

Seeing an ensuing argument, Roy interrupted. "Well, he sure seems to be able to fly. I 'xpect he's got his reasons for flying over that fence. What they are we will undoubtedly never know." He stopped speaking there and looked at Addie.

Feeling like she'd been caught stealing the gray beast, she looked startled. "What?"

"Nothing." Roy paused a moment. "Do you ever see him over here?"

She didn't know how to respond. Course she'd seen him. But never at the Brady homestead. He visited her constantly in Texas. He practically lived down there. See him at the Brady's though? No.

"N-no," she replied awkwardly, "no, I don't. But I guess I don't go out much."

"Oh, I think you'd see him, even if you don't go out much."

Turning back to her plate she whispered, "I hope not."

Tom Brady stopped eating to look at her quizzically. Addie ignored him. Roy cleared his throat.

"So, I was in Charleston last week."

"Oh yeah? That gray stud make his way over there, too?" Tom Brady asked sarcastically.

"No, there are no pretty ladies over there with which he would like to consort," he firmly answered. "I had some business. And, as that was the case, I stopped in at the mercantile."

Tom Brady put his fork down and reached for the coffee pot and refilled Roy's cup, then his own. "What's going on in the big town of Charleston?"

Roy nodded his thanks before continuing. "Oh, big news. Seems the wife of Mr. Gibbs," he looked at Addie, "the Gibbs owning the mercantile." Addie nodded her understanding. "Well," Roy continued, "seems Mrs. Gibbs is enjoying the pleasure of the company of her sister, who has come all the way out here from St. Louis."

"St. Louis!" Andrew exclaimed.

Tom Brady raised a cynical brow. Roy grinned at him. "Yes, St. Louis. And, it just so happens that Miz Blanchard would like to make this her home. Assuming, of course, that she can find a suitable, how would we say properly, situation."

"And I'm sure Mrs. Gibbs was just so happy to see you come along," Tom Brady said with great sarcasm.

"Well, I assured her that I am quite happy in my bachelorhood. But," he now looked at Tom Brady with an evil gleam in his eyes, "I sure put in a good word for you, brother."

Tom lay his fork down and glared at Roy. "You didn't mention my name."

"Oh, but I did. And I explained your circumstances rather well. I believe she might have been interested. Uh, Mrs. Gibbs, not Miz Blanchard."

"Well?" Tom Brady demanded.

"Well what?" Roy replied innocently.

"How big of a horseface is she?"

At this point the boys erupted into giggles, and Roy's hold on his facial features faltered with a near-grin. "Oh, she's a...a...a handsome woman. Real handsome woman."

Tom Brady frowned. "Do you mean handsome in the womanly way, or in more a manly way?"

More giggling bubbled up. Addie sat still with her fork resting on her plate, a look of surprise in her face.

"Well," Roy started, his big shoulders shrugging as he spoke, "I'm sure you'll find out. That's the second half of the news I'm bringing. Charleston is hosting a New Year's Eve dance."

At this comment, Luke stopped giggling and picked up his fork and resumed eating, keeping his head down. Addie noted his abrupt change, but the men seemed not to notice.

"It's one of those newfangled things. You know, where the gal asks the fellow." Roy gulped another swallow of coffee and set his mug down.

"What? The gal asks the fellow? What the heck kinda thing is that?" Tom Brady countered.

Again, Roy shrugged. "I'm sure you can guess, can't you? You know, who came up with the idea? It came all the way from St. Louis."

"Right. St. Louis. Well, I doubt we have any reasons, or invites, to go."

The sound of quiet snickering resounded through the room. "Sure we do, Pa," Andrew stated.

Tom Brady paused in his eating. "What reason?"

"Shut up, Andrew," Luke muttered.

Andrew leaned forward to glimpse past Roy at his silent brother down the bench from him. "Luke got asked."

With a startled expression, Tom Brady gazed to the opposite end of the table to Luke whose head was bent as he picked away at his potatoes. He didn't make eye contact with anyone, but Addie had seen him bicker with Andrew enough to know the boy would get a good punching in the upper arm at some point.

"Luke?" Tom Brady asked.

When he didn't reply, Roy elbowed the boy in the ribs. "Come on, don't keep us hangin'."

"Who asked you?" Tom Brady pried.

Luke shook his head. "N-nobody. Just a girl at school."

"A girl at school? You haven't been to school in weeks." Tom bent his head as he queried his eldest son.

Luke shrugged his shoulders. "It don't matter."

Roy laughed. "I'd say it matters. Here are three grown up folks sittin' at this table, not a drop of romance in sight, and you're hidin' yours in your heart. It matters."

"Luke! Who is it?" Tom Brady again asked as he leaned forward to concentrate his glare on Luke, who refused to look up.

"Cat's outta the bag. Best you tell us what you're keeping tied up before that cat does its business in one of the corners of this room." Roy nudged Luke gently this time.

"Anna. Anna Clements," Luke shot out, then resumed picking at his vegetables.

Roy let out a long and low whistle. Tom Brady raised his eyebrows to a sharp peak. Addie just looked between the three men, the smallest of them picking away at his food, avoiding any and all eyes.

Andrew snickered loudly again. "Yeah, and she's older than 'im too!"

Tom Brady lowered his brows and looked concerned. "By how much?"

Luke ground his teeth together and squirmed under the scrutiny of so many. "Ain't by much!" He shot a dark glare to Andrew. "Just two years," he finished in a low voice.

Roy patted Luke on the back and squeezed his shoulder. "Well done, boy. Well done."

"Ain't by much! You're twelve! She's fourteen!" Tom Brady said in an accusing tone.

"Pa, he's near thirteen," Andrew argued.

"Stay out of it. First you throw him to the wolves, then you try to save him. What did you tell her?" Tom Brady moved his glare to Andrew, then shifted it back to Luke as he spoke.

202

Luke again shrugged. "Just told her I'd try, but that I doubted we'd make it." He bent back down to his plate in a sign of obvious disappointment.

"What? Doubt you'd go! This is a big thing in a young man's life. You have to go!" Roy demanded first of Luke, then of his father.

"I'm not sure how bad we need to go encouraging that. In two years that girl will be of marrying age. Luke will be fourteen," Tom countered.

"Near fifteen, Pa."

"Andrew, butt out of it!" Tom Brady scolded. "Either way, too damn young!"

"Oh, for shitsakes, Brady. He isn't gonna marry her, just take her to a dance. What made you jump that far into the friendship?"

Tom Brady scrunched his forehead and cut a sharp look at Roy. "She's a girl, ain't she? Isn't that what they all work at?"

Roy rolled his eyes and leaned back away from the table. "What have you got against fun? I think you're just afraid to go and find Horseface Blanchard is just the kinda woman you've been waiting for."

"This has nothing to do with me! Don't put it on me!"

Roy let Tom simmer a moment. "It's just a dance, Brady. No giving of the Brady name will take place there. No promises. And seeing as Gerald Clements is her papa, I doubt there will even be a kiss on the cheek."

"Well, it isn't exactly realistic. All these chores to do, stock to feed. That stuff isn't gonna do itself," Tom stated.

"Well, no, but…" Roy was cut off.

"I'll do the chores." Everyone at the table looked to Addie who in the building moments had been forgotten about. "I'll take care of the barn chores and house chores. Feed in the meadows 'fore you go, feed again when you get back. I figure you'll be gone all night."

Roy smiled at her. "Well, that seems a fine idea. Unless, of course, you had intentions of asking a fuzzy-faced widower with four boys to the dance yourself."

It was Addie's turn to deeply furrow her brows. "No, I do not. I'm not even sure that's a man under that fur."

Tom Brady rolled his eyes when Roy looked at him with a barely suppressed grin. "Nobody leaves a woman alone in the winter. What if a storm hits and we can't get back?"

"Then you are a day late," Roy said flatly.

As eating resumed, it was obvious Tom Brady had not yet accepted the idea of going, and he hadn't yet accepted the idea of Luke attending with an older girl. He brooded at the head of the table, muttering replies to questions asked, but he was too troubled to really talk for a few minutes. It wasn't until Roy just started openly laughing at him that he was drawn out with agitation enough to move past his stumbling block.

It was a question that had been haunting Addie for some time. She was afraid to ask Roy, afraid of what he'd tell her, but she'd considered it over and over in the dark. "Roy, where'd you get your gray stud?"

Roy stopped eating and raised his head to look at Addie after the quietly spoken words left her lips. He seemed surprised. He swallowed his bite, his blue eyes holding some consideration in them as he put his fork down and rested his hand on his leg below the table out of sight.

"Well, he come from the desert south of here. I caught him when he was about four, probably closer to five." When he finished speaking he lowered his head a bit and looked at her questioningly. Luke sat with his fork on his plate, his quiet eyes searching Addie's face.

Addie nodded her head and lowered it.

"He was something else, that one." Roy shook his head. "I got him run down and roped out of this big bunch, big ol' bunch, and I thought, 'Hey, now, that's a real fine one.' He had the size and conformation to keep a stud, but I wanted to ride him first and see if he had any brains or cow before I put him on any of my mares." Roy looked closely at Addie and shook his head. "He started out willingly enough, scared like you rarely see them, but he clearly wanted to do the right thing. He'd always hunt the answer for you. Work to find what you wanted and give it to you.

"He'd be jumpin' and blowin' sideways from something he caught out of the corner of his eye, then lock on to a cow in the same breath and go to work like the devil hisself could come set on his hip and he wouldn't notice. Push through a bunch of runaway cows with his shoulders and teeth to get to the lead and turn 'em. But he never would get comfortable when he had no job to do. He'd spook at blades of grass, or the wind escaping his be-hind." The boys chuckled at this. Tom Brady even let out a snort.

Roy released a deep breath here. He pressed his lips together before he went on. "Then, about eight months ago, he went rogue. He'd still work, but all the time, if he wasn't busy, he'd be looking to the south. Ears up, head up, eyes wide. All the time. I'd step off and he would leave. Just head south. Not at a run, just in a determined walk. Got to where I had to keep him penned either in the barn or next to it. If he had any way, he'd head south.

"He'd dig trenches in the corrals along the south fence where he would pace constantly, always looking to the south. He'd blow and toss his head, buck and trot back and forth along that fence. When I'd come to get him to do a job, he'd have dried sweat from the night before. I thought he'd lost his mind. Turning him loose wasn't an option, he wouldn't stay with the mares."

Addie didn't know what to think. Eight months ago. Eight months ago Addie was living with the family who looked after her when Fett died. Far to the south....

"Then, a few months ago he quit. Just up and quit. He'd stand in the center of the corral, absolutely still, head up, ears forward, waiting. But now, he wasn't looking to the south anymore." Roy paused and let it sink in. "The fall wind began to fill his trenches with blow sand, and he would try to smell something on that same wind." Roy sighed heavily as he rubbed the back of his neck. "Now, guaranteed, when I would go out to catch him, he'd be covered in dry sweat, like he'd run forty miles the night before. And finally, when snow fell, I could see his tracks in it. Tracks where he jumped the fence to get out, and tracks where he'd jumped the fence to get back in.

"He doesn't pace the south fence anymore, and when he leaves he doesn't go south either. Now when he leaves, he runs west," Roy finished quietly.

Addie sat shaking. She blinked back what was the start of tears based in fear and confusion. She had no idea what it meant. No horse had the ability to think like that. None she'd ever heard of. She knew of horses that had run hundreds of miles to get back to their home range, but never after a person. And what was she thinking anyway? That he was after her? That was absurd.

"The only time I ever saw him certain about anyone, was the day he tried to come to you," Roy stated softly.

"Well," Addie replied, "he's just a horse."

Rather than ride the seventeen miles home that night, Roy stayed up at the main house. By the time they had visited all afternoon, enjoyed pie, and finished chores, it was easy to convince him to stay. Addie made him a soft pallet in the sitting room by the fire, and he went on and on about feeling like an honored guest. Conversation had not returned to the gray.

Addie made her way out in the brilliantly lit night to her dugout, again admiring the silvery moonlight and brightest of the stars. The air was very cold, freezing inside her nose and on her lips. She was tired beyond tired, her sleepless night previous, then the emotion of the day, all compounded with the work of Christmas dinner. Her body was calling out for the comfort of a warm fire and a soft bed.

She'd stoked her fire several hours before, so it would have time to warm some in the dugout. And although she needed the relief sleep brought, she had one last thing to do.

Molly entered the dugout on the heels of Addie, and lowered herself down beside the warm fire as if she could read the woman's thoughts, and there she found Addie unready to go to bed just yet. She watched out of kind eyes as Addie closed the door and moved to the table where her trunk sat.

It was a noble purpose. The sacrifice would be worth it, for the use of it would never come around again for Addie. Opening the lid and hearing the familiar soft squeak of the rusty hinge, Addie inhaled the scent of cherished memories. It was like running a dagger into her own heart, for she could already feel the bleeding from it. But, she pressed on.

It took a moment to find them, and she rummaged with infinite gentleness. Pulling the item out, her eyes misted as she recalled the one and only time she'd used such a fine article.

It touched Addie that Luke was asked to attend a dance by a young girl. And, it'd also touched her that he refused to speak of it, knowing his father wouldn't be willing. She thought back to the dinnertime conversation, realizing how awkward it would have been to voice his desire to go without Roy there to guilt, tease, and torment his father into agreeing.

She instantly recognized the look in Luke's eyes. She'd seen it in Fett's eyes the very first time he'd come to take her to a dance. He came with wildflowers in one hand, and a dirty hat in the other. In his face was a look of apprehension visible enough they must have seen it all the way up in heaven. He stuttered and fumbled, twitched and mumbled. Fett tried hard to be proper in his speech when he addressed her mama, and manly when he addressed her pa.

With Addie he was just tongue-tied.

The first time they saw each other was at a neighbor's branding. Fett wasn't from where Addie's family lived. He came from farther south in Texas. Her older brother, Jim, had left home and roamed to the south taking jobs starting horses on ranches where he went. Soon he was asked by the bigger places, and he spent his time going only to those. At one of those outfits, he met a young horseman named Fett Loveland. They became good friends, and for about a year or so they traveled together.

When Jim made his way home to see family and help out for day wages at a few of the nearby ranches, Fett came along too. He had plans to meet up with a partner, Pete, come late summer that year. Fett figured it wouldn't hurt to make a little extra money before he headed off after more horses to the west.

Then everything changed.

One look was all it took. Fett saw Addie when she drove the team that pulled her mama and a few of her younger brothers out onto the flat

where the cattle were rodeared. The sun shone off the brightness of
Addie's being like an orb. Fett couldn't speak, couldn't move, and
ignored Buck's attempt to keep the herd gathered and from breaking
away.

After he'd watched her all day, Fett finally got the chance to meet
her at meal time. He'd tried to come up with words as he roped, but for
some reason, no matter what he conjured, it just sounded stupid. And so,
when Addie reached out to hand him a tin plate from the wood crate on
the back of the wagon box, Fett just stared like he had no idea what to do
with it. Addie smiled a soft, questioning smile.

The corner of his mouth twitched as he took it from her.

"Nice day," Addie commented as she shielded her eyes from the
sun. Wisps of hair teased at her face in the breeze.

"Uhumph." The sound wasn't words, nor was it coherent.

Addie laughed quietly as she handed Jim a plate. "Let's go, brother,
'fore the magpies get it all!" Jim pushed Fett with his shoulder. Fett
stumbled on. But, even as he held out his plate for his stew, his head was
turned back to Addie. With his inability to focus, most of his stew ended
up on the toe of his boot. Sitting down with his meager dinner amidst the
bawling of calves and mother cows looking to reunite, Fett didn't notice
the hardness of the ground, nor the dust that rose from the moving of a
thousand impatient feet.

Her face was so bright and clear, her nose small and with only the
slightest point to the end. Addie's smile was intoxicating even when she
flashed it at someone else. But it was her eyes, the sparkling green of
them, the way they looked right through him that captured his attention.
And the sun glinting off her auburn hair made her appear to be sent from
God Himself. Her dark brown dress had little tan flowers on it, scattered
in a maze of pattern.

Fett worked at gathering his courage to speak to her.

When, just before evening settled in, the branding was done, cow-
calf pairs were again united, Addie loaded the family wagon with all she
and her mama contributed. Tired brothers were lifted into the box, and
Addie climbed up next to her mother, taking hold of the lines. She raised

a hand to her forehead, shading her eyes as her father spoke to her from the back of his horse. Fett could not hear what was said.

He'd roped calves and drug them to the fire all day. Buck was tired, but Fett abandoned his post where he pushed pairs back out into open country with the other men. He kicked Buck into a high lope to catch the wagon as it moved out over the grassland in the direction of home. Buck sped towards them, and slowed as he reached the wagon.

In surprise, Addie pulled up a reluctant team. A sparkle of uncertainty shimmered in her eyes in the golden light of late day. Fett removed his hat and pressed it with his right hand to his heart, then he stilled a fidgeting Buck with a leg.

"I would like to know your name," Fett stated with clarity.

Addie's ma raised a brow. Addie smiled softly, then said, "My name is Addie."

Fett shifted his hat from his right hand to his left as he passed his horse close to the wagon to take Addie's slender hand into his big one. His eyes lingered on hers a moment. Then, he looked to her ma and extended his hand farther to her.

"Clara Halstead."

He nodded and replied, "Fett Loveland, ma'am."

"Pleased to meet ya," Clara said to the blue eyed-boy who stole glances at her daughter. "Where do you call home?"

Fett rested his right hand on the saddle horn. "South of here. I actually came up with Jim. Been making the rounds startin' horses." Fett turned slightly in his saddle to gesture at Jim who moved with the herd over the hill and was soon to be out of sight.

"I see. Where ya'll working now? Jim hasn't said much about where he'll go when he finishes at Kendrick's."

"Oh, I think we are bound for Marshall's."

"I see," Clara said as she looked over at Addie who listened quietly.

Fett looked for the herd that had gone over the rise. "Well, I guess I best press on." Replacing the hat onto his head, he tipped the brim at Clara in polite respect, then looked to Addie and tipped it again, this time lingering on the word, "miss."

Then he was gone, riding fast away to catch up with the other men. He'd neglected his duties to meet Addie, and both she and her ma turned in the wagon seat to watch him go. Addie with a deep look of amusement and curiosity, Clara with apprehension. She knew nothing of this man. He was no boy. He was far too old and wise to be considered a boy. Clara judged him to be near twenty-four. For some men, by age twenty-four they'd been on their own making their way for ten years. Maybe more.

Addie smiled in the silence of the dugout. Molly lay sleeping in warmth and comfort by the popping stove. She ran her hands down the smoothness of the fabric. The white of it gleamed brightly in the dim light of the lantern she'd taken from the wood table in the main house. She would need light to accomplish what she planned.

Looking back over the years again, Addie thought of the dance Fett took her to. It was small, just a little gathering at the church, but that spring evening was the best of her life. Fett had no buckboard, so Addie rode her father's gelding. They were allowed to ride ahead alone, but Allen and Clara followed behind in the wagon. Addie had taken a white sprig of flowers and placed them in her hair before leaving the others in a cup on the table.

On the ride to the gathering, each time she glanced over to Fett, he was already looking at her. It took her breath away each time to see the expression on his face, so awestruck, yet so sure of whatever it was he was thinking behind his bright blue eyes.

"I don't have much," he'd said unapologetically when Addie asked about his home.

He'd offered the crook of his arm and kept her hand tucked in it all evening when they weren't dancing. He spoke to people, but always in a manner that kept the conversation short so he could get back to talking with Addie. He made it obvious where his attentions lie. Her pa kept a close eye on his only girl, but already in his heart he could feel her slipping away. By the end of the evening, the young couple took a seat on the outskirts of the party and spoke quietly to each other, but Fett made it obvious he wanted to be proper with Allen's girl. That really scared him. A man with honorable intentions was hard to beat. Time taken to show respect meant this wasn't a one-time dance.

It was deep into the night when Addie finally put away her project and lay herself down to sleep. Molly jumped up onto the bed beside her and pressed in close. She made no sound, just lay still and listened to Addie's breathing. The woman had no tears left, just the sweet aching of precious memories.

The week between Christmas and New Year's passed quickly. The wind up for the boys was excruciating, the very thought of the fun to be had in Charleston was more than they could endure. For Addie, it was passed with evenings spent by her little stove in the dugout working by lamplight, delicately stitching away. It gave her mind something to focus on, and in that there was a great amount of solace. It brought back happy memories of times gone, and that was where her heart rested.

It was worked out, eventually, to the satisfaction of Tom Brady how the chores would be done, how they would care for the horses on the meadow before and after the festivities. His dark eyes still registered the lack of desire to participate, but, he'd given his word to Luke at Christmas, so he intended to keep it. And, truth was, Luke was becoming a young man. If Tom made no effort now, well, he doubted Luke would stick around long.

Tom Brady decided about midweek to feed early on New Year's Eve and head over to Charleston so he could go pick up a few goods at the mercantile. At dinner the night before, he'd gone over Addie's list of chores and what-to-do's and do-nots about five times. Truly Addie was just ready to have some peace. The boys were sent to bed promptly after dinner for early morning feeding, then Tom Brady disappeared.

Addie stood washing the dishes in the soft light of the lamp, listening to the popping of the fire in the wood stove. The house was quiet in the slumber of the boys. Even Charlie was going to make the trip to Charleston and enjoy himself some fun. Addie considered how she would tell Tom Brady she'd trained his son to pee in a bowl rather than in his pants, but she decided not to. She figured she'd just let Charlie divulge his secret on his own. It struck her as funny. All through Christmas Day the boy used the bowl, never once did Tom Brady catch him at it.

Addie smiled to herself. What an accomplishment Charlie would have to disclose. She prayed a short prayer for the weather to hold.

Behind her the door opened and closed, and in her peripheral vision Addie saw Tom Brady come in and set a box on the table along with a lantern. He took off his coats and hung them on their peg. He moved back to the table and stood patiently facing Addie. She didn't notice for quite some time, just kept up with drying the dishes and placing them on the shelf. Then she wiped the splashes of water off the workbench. When a feeling of being stared at crept in, she cast a glance at Tom Brady over her shoulder.

She stopped and turned her head to look at him, her arm freezing in movement as she wiped up water. She saw him, and try as she might she was too surprised to look away from him.

Tom Brady stood before her in human form. His face was fully revealed to her, all his features. In his little wood crate was a pair of scissors and a comb, which he had diligently used to trim his long fuzzy beard close to his skin. His hair was neatly trimmed back to show his face clearly. His jawline was firm and strong, shaded by the well-trimmed facial hair. A symmetrical nose stood out from the smoothness of flesh that was naturally an olive color, and for some reason not having all that hair made Tom Brady a bigger built man. The width of his chest and the muscles in his shoulders actually tied in with something other than hair.

He arched a brow, and instantly the quirking of the corner of his mouth told Addie just how amused he was at her staring. Addie wasn't sure she liked having his thoughts easily exposed to her. She looked back to her wiping and waited for him to move off.

"I 'spose this means I best start looking for another job." She paused as she looked back at him again, a lock of auburn hair falling over her eye. "You know, in case she isn't a real horseface."

"I look that nice," he stated in mock surprise.

"Well, at least we can tell what kinda animal you are."

Tom Brady shook his head and let out a snort. "I guess if that's the best compliment you got, it'll have to do."

"I don't think compliments have ever been a thing between us," Addie replied.

After several moments Tom Brady said, "Alright. I like your biscuits. How's that?" Tom Brady raised his chin and looked at her defiantly.

"What? You're lookin' for me to tell you I think you're handsome and you go fishin' with, 'I like your biscuits'." Addie shook her head this time and went back to wiping up.

There was silence behind her for a time, then came, "Then I like the color of your hair, the way the sun hits it and lights it up."

Addie stopped and stood a moment before turning to him. This time his chin wasn't up in defiance, and his dark eyes held a patient look in them. Addie pressed her lips together and slipped her hands into her apron pockets. "Then I think, Mr. Brady," she spoke slowly, "that you look very fine for meeting the horseface."

Addie's face crinkled into a grin as Tom Brady groaned and shrugged his shoulders and gestured at her with his hand. "I paid you a fine compliment, woman!"

Addie's face lit as she stood up straighter. "I paid you one, too!" she playfully argued.

Tom Brady snatched the box and lantern off the table one hand at a time. "That's what you get when you ask a woman for a genuine opinion."

"It was a genuine opinion! And for landsakes, that's the reason for it. So you can meet Horseface!" Addie clapped a hand to her mouth to stifle a laugh.

He jabbed the box in her direction, the corners of his mouth tugging hard. For once Addie could see this. "Ah hell. I might just marry Horseface and bring her on home. Then where'd you be?"

Addie chuckled softly as he retreated down the hall with his box and lantern. It came to Addie that showing anything of himself was very hard

213

for Tom Brady to do. She understood that very feeling. Once it was out, there was no getting it back.

Addie chuckled again as she headed to the dugout.

The day dawned bright and clear, but very frigid. By now the feed crew of the Brady homestead was used to it, not that it made the task any more passable. It was early in winter to get up hopes the major snow of the year was gone and warmer weather was following. But, the fact that in a few hours they would be riding the thirty-some miles to Charleston warmed the boys enough to get them out and on the sleigh two hours earlier than usual.

Addie rose when Tom Brady pounded on the dugout door early. It was easy to do so, knowing she was about to be free for a day and night. She could lie next to the fire in the main house and sleep the duration if she chose to do so. Or, she could stay in the dugout and avoid the house where she devoted so much time and work altogether.

The past few days were spent washing and drying clothes, mending and starching, pressing and re-sizing. Some clothes were handed down to younger brothers, and Luke's nice clothes had to be taken out as much as possible, but even when Addie was done with them, they were small for his frame. It was obvious it'd been some time since the Bradys had attended any functions in town, regardless of the size of the town.

Charlie watched in fascination as Addie worked, at times holding on to Addie's skirt, and other times standing on a chair where he could see her press the clothes with the heavy iron. She'd dip her fingers in a bowl of water and flick drops over the piece of cloth she needed to press, then she would step to the stove and with a rag, pick up the iron. Charlie's eyes would light to see the effect the cast iron had on the fabric. It was smooth and fresh, like it was new again. Charlie never reached for anything, but he ran his little hands over that crisp fabric each time Addie finished pressing it. For some reason, the contrast of old and new caught his attention. What *was*, didn't have to *be*.

When the feed crew came in, Addie had their party clothes pressed, neatly folded, and tied with string into individual bundles. She packed

214

them neatly into a flour sack, then set them into Tom Brady's saddle bag. Everything she did, she was careful not to smash or kink the clothes. She lay the saddle bag out onto the table for the menfolk to take with them when they left. It was worse than packing fine china into that saddle bag, for nobody intended to wear fine china to a dance.

High thin clouds moved in to mar the sun, but no wind forced a storm in with them. They drifted along, benign. The boys saddled horses in the barn while Tom Brady moved about checking things and finishing last minute chores. The boys bathed the evening before as Tom Brady cut his hair in the barn, and when they came in from the barn, it was simply to gather a few belongings.

Addie said nothing to Luke about the dance in the week since Christmas and his invite was revealed. But now she sought an opportunity to speak to him as alone as possible in a full house. It took time, but he came down from the loft and moved into the kitchen carrying his pack slung over his shoulder. He had obviously taken time to wash his face and tame his hair some.

It would need done again after that long ride to Charleston.

"Luke?" Addie asked softly.

He looked up at Addie and smiled kindly. "All ready to go, I think."

Addie brushed some hair that had come loose from her bun back behind her ear. With uncertainty, she reached into her apron pocket. Without looking at Luke who stood next to the table, Addie closed the distance between them.

"Take this," she said as she pulled something out of her apron pocket. "Every girl likes a pretty flower."

Luke's brow wrinkled a moment as he took hold of something white she held out to him in her hand. The softness of it as it was laid in his palm felt cool after it rode in her apron pocket. Addie returned her hand to her pocket as Luke looked down to what she'd handed him.

It was indeed a flower. Addie had intricately stitched around the outside of the petals to keep the fabric cut out of her wedding petticoats from fraying, then layering them together formed a rose. Inside the flower, to hold all the individual petals together, was a single pearl-colored button. She had rolled fabric together to make a stem, and a single pin rested there.

"Pin it along her collar, but be very careful not to stick her with it." Addie gestured on herself where Luke was to place the rose.

"Miss Addie," Luke whispered. He looked up at her and smiled ever so softly. "Thank you."

Addie blinked as she nodded. "Treat her special, don't leave her to sit alone longer than it takes to get her a sip of something. She finds you special enough to buck tradition and ask you, no doubt, against the wishes of her pa."

"Yes, ma'am."

Addie looked at him for a moment and smiled. "I don't think your pa is ready to see how close you are to being a man."

Luke's brows knit together for a moment as his mouth tugged into a line. "No, I 'xpect not."

"Go on. The rest of the boys are already getting horses from the barn."

"Yes, ma'am. Thank you."

Addie reached out and squeezed his shoulder. "Go on."

When all of the Brady men sat atop horses, they rode up to the main house one last time. Addie stepped out the door to watch them go, but instead watched them ride up to the porch. Tom Brady looked over at her from the little red filly.

"Now, don't you forget. If it goes to snowin', don't go out. Just set up tight in the house."

"I know," Addie answered.

"You sure you can handle watering the team?"

"Yes. I just have to walk them to the creek twice a day. Nothing to it."

"Well, those boys are big and can get rough when they are thirsty. Turn 'em loose one at a time if you have to."

Addie folded her arms across her chest. "I've handled teams before."

"Well, I don't want to get home to find you lost them and now they

216

are running out on the desert."

"I won't lose them."

"Keep that lantern up off the straw if you use it. In fact, just go out in the daylight. Don't use a lantern. That's all I need is to find out you burned my damn barn down."

Addie rolled her eyes, gritting her teeth.

"The stock in the meadows is good 'til…"

"I plan on eating all your sugar," Addie interrupted.

"What?" Tom Brady stopped abruptly.

"What I don't eat, I will drink in all your coffee."

Tom Brady narrowed his eyes.

"And I intend on sleeping in that big fancy bed of yours. All day," she finished with a taunting tone. "So, seein' as that is my intention, you best get on your way since that sugar sack is plumb full and this talk is cutting into my snoozin' time."

With a look of shocked disgust, Tom Brady looked to the sons on his right and left. He leaned forward in his saddle and again narrowed his eyes at Addie. "You look here, woman. It isn't proper or fitting to go talking about sleeping in someone else's bed, let alone a man's. It's an abomination."

Addie's mouth crinkled at the corners. "Well, now you won't worry about the stock and barn anymore, will you?"

Tom Brady straightened and looked at her, his dark eyes flashing. His jaw ticked and he picked up his reins. He pressed his lips tightly together as he turned his horse. He never took his disturbed eyes off Addie as he said to his sons, "Let's go, boys."

As they rode out of the yard, Tom Brady turned in his saddle to glare at Addie who laughed behind her hand. As he continued on, she raised her hand and gave him a little sarcastic wave. "Bye," she mouthed.

The boys rode off with their father, Luke grinning and Andrew full of the task at hand. Charlie was bundled up on the saddle in front of Tom Brady, and Frankie proudly sat Mare. Addie watched them go for a while, then she turned and went back in to listen to the still silence of the cabin.

The going was easier than Tom Brady would have predicted. There was near a foot of snow in some places still, and drifts stood close to six feet below the crests of hills, but they were able to make way through shallower hills. The horses all traveled well and they took time to move along easy.

When they hit a game trail they were able to move into a trot. Tom Brady began to wonder if they would actually make it in time for the festivities. Then about midafternoon, just as he was starting to feel they might have a chance, Charlie began to get restless pressed firmly between his father and the saddle horn. At first, Tom was able to still the boy, but as the minutes passed, he grew wiggly again. Tom Brady shifted him and tried to reposition him where he could make the last few miles comfortably enough, but the boy had no intention of setting still. When last they'd stopped to relieve Frankie's call of nature, Tom checked Charlie's cloth to see if it were wet. It wasn't, so they pressed on. Now he figured surely the boy had wet himself.

It had been a while since he had to deal with such matters, and he recalled just how inconvenient such a situation was about to be. The only dry trousers Charlie had were intended for the party. And, when he checked, Addie hadn't bothered to send but one extra rag to diaper the boy with. Tom silently cursed her stupidity, and then in the same breath prayed Charlie could make it closer to Charleston where he could pick up more cloths.

Charlie was all-out bucking now, and Tom Brady thought of how cold that soaked cloth must be. He called the boys to a stop and halted his own horse. Before he could make a move, Charlie vaulted himself from his perch in front of his father. He stumbled in the snow as Tom Brady fumbled to get down and assist.

Charlie waded through the deep snow to stand just below the red filly's neck where the snow wasn't deep. She arched her neck to get a good sniff out of his sock hat, the moisture from her nostrils tickling the part of Charlie's face not covered by a scarf. Charlie wiggled and danced awkwardly as he hiked up his coat.

Tom Brady stood above him in stunned silence. His boy was mad. Madder than he had ever seen the silent creature. At first he thought perhaps the boy had a bug? That was dumb. Nothing could live in cold like what bit into his cheeks. Tom near ran when Charlie shoved his trousers down and revealed two pale bum cheeks that clenched with the freezing air.

"Pa?" Luke asked from the line of brothers who watched, stricken silent by what they saw.

"Charlie!" he yelled as he made a grab for the child who was stripping himself shamefully in the frigid temperature. Could he have gotten so cold he lost feeling and thought he was hot? It happened.

Then, a curious thing happened before the eyes of Tom Brady, and Charlie's three brothers.

Charlie sprung a leak.

It arched high into the air at first, then zipped and zagged and splattered the white snow with yellow as Charlie turned in place to make a boy's art work. The red filly lowered her head to smell the scent of fresh urine from an unfamiliar source. Her ice-laden whiskers brushed his face and he scrunched his shoulders to hide his face the best he could.

Nothing but the sound of wind passing through the sagebrush was audible as Charlie pulled his own trousers back up and settled his shirt and sweater, along with his heavy coat back over his exposed belly. Then putting a steadying hand on the shoulder of Red, he made his way in the snow to stand below his father and look up at him in desire to get moving along.

Tom Brady just looked down at his son. With a small hand he reached up and took hold of his father's pocket and just waited as he looked down at the snow.

"Charlie?" Tom Brady whispered. Bending slowly over, he took hold of his boy under the arms and lifted him up and against his chest. "Charlie?" he spoke again low, moisture pooling in his eyes.

Charlie said nothing. He merely looked down at his father from his vantage point. He tugged his hand free where it was wedged between his own leg and his father's arm. He laid the freed hand on Tom's neck and looked deep into his father's eyes. Still he held no expression, but the depths of his eyes reflected something alive.

"Dear God," Tom clutched the boy to him. "My son," he said in a low voice. "How?"

Then it struck him. It was obvious how. Charlie had been in the company of Addie Loveland for weeks. He had no idea how they spent their time alone together. Now he knew. Since he was an infant, Tom had borne a silent burden of fear for his youngest. The boy was strange. He was off. He was…perhaps not as hopeless as Tom Brady originally felt he was. In all the nights he'd held his son and tried to console him as he cried violently, Tom Brady shed silent tears for the life he was in charge of. The boy would never be right, he'd told himself. He'd be thirty-five still needing a fresh cloth multiple times a day. He'd sit alone in the sunlight and play with finger shadows when he was an old man wearing a long white beard. By then, no doubt, Tom Brady would be dead and gone. Who would tend the man then? People weren't terrible fond of caring for a mindless soul who offered no returns in work or otherwise.

Tom pressed his face to Charlie's. The boy had learned to do something he *never* thought would happen. Tom Brady shook as he held the boy closer to him. He looked again at the new person in his arms. For the first time since Charlie was born, Tom Brady beheld his son. And in doing so, saw the life within him.

The truth of it was, she wasn't a horseface. Far from it, in fact. Tom Brady stood in the big open hall and held Charlie close to his chest as he watched the people around him. The crowd was large, and he began to wonder where all the people had come from. Was the area as settled as this? Certainly not his neck of the woods.

Luke waited awkwardly for his young lady, pressed against a beam near the front door. Each time Tom looked at him something in his heart pinched. The emotion on his son's face was a dead giveaway as to how much this dance meant to him. He'd never said a word until Christmas dinner. And really, even then he'd said little, just let Andrew and Roy do all the talking for him.

He tenderly held a piece of white cloth in his hand, and when curiosity got the better of him, Tom asked to see what it was. Luke held up the intricately made rose for his father to see. Tom Brady didn't have to touch it to know where the fabric came from. He looked down at the pure white of it, and for a very brief moment an image floated through his mind of just what the yard goods had covered in its day of use. He shoved it aside. He chose months ago never to contemplate what moved and breathed beneath the rags of woman's clothing as she stoked the fire in the kitchen.

Seeing Horseface made it easier.

It was one of those times when everything happens at once. Luke stood against his beam, eyes glued to the door and the folks that passed through it. Then he caught sight of her. She came in with her family, a large family. When they saw one another, Luke straightened slowly, and Tom could see his son clear his throat. His hand went to his collar to assure it was neat, then to his hair, then he glanced down at his rose. He walked boldly forward.

In the low light of the lanterns around the log room, Luke stuck his hand out and introduced himself to Anna's father. The man kept a stern face as he gripped Luke's hand, who returned the shake with firmness, just like a man would. Gerald Clements looked down at Luke silently for a second, then presented Luke to his wife.

When at last he stepped aside and let Luke take his daughter, Luke greeted her as she smiled happily at him in relieved surprise that her date had shown. She traced her finger along the soft petals of her rose and stood patiently as Luke pinned it to her collar with very careful fingers.

"I had no idea the fur trade was back on in these parts."

Tom Brady turned to see Roy Albert walking to him from near the entrance. He wore a great big grin and his blue eyes sparkled with mischief.

"I was headed over here to introduce myself to the newcomer, then I realized that was Charlie. I had no idea there was a face under all that."

Tom snorted. "Not one person here has said anything about the way I look. Only figures you would."

221

"Well, it's surprising when sound passes through that thick skull of yours and you take something said to heart."

"Said about what?" Tom snapped.

"I believe it was Addie who brought to your attention the beastly look you had, what with all that hair. And, she was right. Can't show up to a dance looking like a crazed buffalo. Especially since you so desperately need a woman."

Tom Brady laughed at that. "I have more to deal with than my lack of a wife."

Roy nodded in agreement as they both looked to Luke.

Roy and Tom watched young Luke take his older partner's hand. They took to the dance floor and instantly became all arms and feet. Tom Brady met Gerald Clements' eyes across the hall and nodded to him in acknowledgement.

About that time, Roy nudged Tom and when Tom looked at him, Roy pointed toward to the entry with a tip of his head. Tom took the directive and looked for himself.

She was dressed in a dark green dress, and it struck Tom Brady how long it had been since he had seen an available woman, for it was the figure radiating out from that dark green dress that made him furrow his brow and mash his mouth together. Her hair was dark and swept back in a manner he had never seen the wives of his neighbors use. It was rolled up behind her ears, and gathered into a bun on the back of her head. It made no sense to Tom, and he didn't bother to study it for more than a second.

She was a tall woman, comparable to his own height. She was still shorter than himself, but he wouldn't have to look too far down to speak with her. A group of boys ran past and Frankie caught his attention for a moment. But the group moved on, and Tom went back to studying the woman.

Roy stood with his arms across his chest, a thumb pressed to his lips. He glanced from the handsome woman to his friend.

"I thought you said she was a horseface," Tom Brady mused.

"I never said that," Roy retorted. "You assumed it."

Tom looked at Roy. "Well, you sure never did deny it."

"Tell me friend. Have you actually looked at her face yet?"

Tom shot him a look of disgust. Roy just laughed. She looked to be friendly and her smile came easily enough to all she spoke to. Beside her, Mrs. Gibbs, her sister, introduced her to all they passed. Their wraps were taken at the door by the ladies from the Ladies Aid who volunteered to do so. The Gibbses proceeded into the room, and at once all available bachelors were discreetly pointed out by Mrs. Gibbs.

To Tom Brady's horror, Mrs. Gibbs, who looked rather like a scarecrow in her blue gingham dress with its high white lace collar pressed and starched to a piercing crisp, pointed in his direction with a glance of her eyes. The severe pull back of her graying hair only accentuated the sharp point of her nose. When the horseface looked at him, a slow, but genuine smile spread across her face. A few words were exchanged between the two sisters, then they turned away.

Tom looked to Roy who shrugged at him. "All well at home? Addie still alright with staying alone?"

It was Tom's turn to shrug. "She did it. Guess she musta been alright with it still." The memory of her last remarks again perturbed him.

"Well, Addie's a tough girl. I doubt much could happen she can't get a handle on," Roy replied.

Tom took a moment to find his boys among the crowd. Frankie was down on the floor in one corner of the hall playing Jacks with the group of boys he'd been running with. Andrew stood by the punch table with Bill Bushing's boy, Todd, and the two of them were smirking at Luke out on the floor with his girl. The two of them danced a little smoother now, and Luke laughed at something Anna said. And little Charlie lay his head in the crook of Tom's neck and continued to watch the goings on. His brown eyes searched the crowd while his empty hand that longed for Spoony grasped tightly to Tom's pocket in the need to hold something.

"Your boy is fast going to become a young man, Brady," Roy stated softly.

"Yeah," Tom sighed out.

"He turned out a lot like his ma. Same big ol' heart." Roy's face went sad for a moment.

Tom blinked and looked down at Charlie's smooth hair. "I," Tom began. When he didn't continue Roy looked at him. "I wish I'd done better, after their ma passed."

Roy shook his head. "You did what any man is capable of in the same circumstance. But, now you have Addie to help out."

"Remember, she'll go home come spring. But by then, I should have it handled myself again."

Roy didn't answer. A look of deep contemplation set into his face. He looked back out onto the dance floor at the smiling Luke. Tom Brady didn't understand. Life was running in a new current now. By the time Tom had it "handled", all four of his boys would be grown and gone, and he would spend the rest of his life adjusting to that. There was no time to handle anything. Just deal with it as it came.

"Roy, it's…" Tom started, but wasn't able to finish his thought. Roy looked up and welcomed someone into the conversation.

"Well, nice to see you again, Miss Blanchard," he said in a gracious tone.

Charlie moved his head to look at the woman who'd come into his line of sight. Tom Brady looked over to see Henry Gibbs in the company of his wife and sister-in-law. Henry held out a hand to Tom, and he shifted Charlie over to his left arm so he could clasp Henry's right hand firmly.

"Henry," Tom greeted.

"Tom, how are ya?"

"Doing well," Tom returned.

"Tom, I know you have already met my wife, but this is her sister, Mildred." Henry Gibbs gestured to Mildred in her dark green dress. The rich color of her dark brown hair complimented the choice of color on Mildred's part.

Tom had, like all the men in the hall, removed his hat and left it resting on its crown on a shelf at the door stacked with dozens of others. It was a conscious thought to remember it wasn't on his head where it usually was. He tipped his head respectfully at Mildred and Mrs. Gibbs both. Charlie raised his head to look at the newcomers.

"And who is this young man?" asked Mildred as she reached up and touched Charlie's arm. Charlie just stared at her with flat eyes.

"This is my boy, Charlie."

"I understand you have other children as well?"

"Yes, ma'am. I have three other boys. All here somewhere."

Roy slid his hands into his pockets and looked at Henry. Henry raised a brow at Roy.

"I'm surprised you braved the weather, Mr. Brady," Mrs. Gibbs interjected.

"Well, I guess the boys needed a night away from the place."

Mrs. Gibbs turned slightly to look at the dance floor where Luke was offering his date a chair. "I see your oldest seems to be having a fine time. And what a gentleman too!"

"Thank you, ma'am." Tom replied.

"How are things out your way, Tom?" Henry inquired. "Much snow?"

Tom nodded. " 'Bout the same you got. Lot of drifting. But I guess the same problem is here, too."

Henry looked grim for a second. "Yes, winter came in early and bitter this year. Seems a bit more wind than what we're used to, but, I swear I say that every year!"

Roy nodded his head in agreement. "It seems no matter how I prepare, I'm never ready. Guess I just don't want to admit it's coming."

Tom glanced to Mildred to see she wasn't following the conversation, but rather studying him. He gave her a polite smile and noticed her cheeks didn't flush at being caught staring. He turned back to Henry Gibbs who was saying something about business going well.

"We'll enter the slow months now. Anyone who needs goods will just wait 'til spring. They won't chance coming in and getting caught in a storm."

"Ah, this time of year passes slowly. The hungry time, old timers called it. Cow's dry, anything from the garden has been eaten, and the game is scarce. Chickens won't lay." Roy shook his head. "A man lays down at night and dreams of only one thing. Green grass time."

Henry Gibbs shook his head fervently. "Yessir, you got that right."

At a lull in the conversation, Mildred took her opportunity to speak. "Mr. Brady, since the ladies do forgo tradition in this instance, I wonder if I might have the pleasure of a dance?"

Tom Brady met Mildred Blanchard's eyes and found assurance in them. She waited patiently for him to agree to it, so certain he would now that she'd put him on the spot. Tom looked to Roy, but nothing jovial reflected in his friend's face. Roy reached out and took hold of little Charlie, who looked even smaller resting against the chest of such a big man.

Tom Brady offered Mildred his arm. "Miss Blanchard," he invited.

She gave him a satisfied smile and slipped her arm into the crook of his. Guiding her onto the floor, he held her at a polite distance as he placed the palm of his hand just below her shoulder blade. He could feel the warmth of her hand as she rested it on his shoulder, the distance between himself and her breasts less than twelve inches. She smelled like soft lavender and soap, the texture of her skin was without blemish and the pale color of a woman who spent little time in the garden or doing chores. She was young at a spinster's age.

Tom Brady fought the urge to move closer. It was a natural thing, to crave the closeness of a woman, and one so inviting in all the right places, who wasn't afraid to leave an opening for the obviousness of invitation. Mildred Blanchard hadn't danced with anyone else at the party as yet that evening, she'd tallied scores and picked her winner. Now he awkwardly stared down at her face and attempted to stay sober.

"You don't say much, Mr. Brady."

Tom clenched his jaw for a moment, then answered, "To tell the truth, ma'am, I'm trying real hard right now to remember my steps."

Mildred Blanchard released a dazzling smile. "Oh, on the contrary, Mr. Brady! You are a lovely dancer."

Tom again clenched his jaw. "It's been a long while, Miss Blanchard."

"I can't tell. I'm glad you made it here tonight."

Tom looked into her brown eyes and forgot himself for a moment. "I'm glad I made it here too." They danced for a time, Tom Brady looking into the eyes of this newcomer who caught him unawares. "How are you adjusting to winter in this country?"

"Oh, I am well adjusted. I've actually spent time out here, in the west."

Tom raised a surprised eyebrow. "You have?"

"Yes. I'm a school teacher. I spent four years teaching in Indian Territory of Oklahoma. Then I came out here for a year and taught in a small school east of Charleston about two hundred miles."

"I was under the impression you just came here from St. Louis."

"Well," she countered, "I did just come from St. Louis. I went home for two years to care for my mother when she became ill. After she passed I came out to spend time with my sister."

"I see. You must forgive us. We all assumed you were a tenderfoot."

She smiled a dismissing smile at his statement. "I will admit Mr. Brady, I've been anxious to meet you. My sister has told me much about you and your family. She has painted a very intriguing picture."

Tom Brady made no reply. Something inside twinged. He clenched his jaw at the memory of Edith, then at the thought she was being spoken about. Not in a way that was favorable, but more of in a way that said, 'too bad she's dead, but what luck for me'.

"My sister enlightened me to your troubles with your boy. What did you say his name was? Charlie?"

"What about him?" Tom asked in a low and defensive voice.

"Well," she started, "I know it's none of my business, but I really feel I might be able to help you. I've been around children that have problems, and I've found ways to help them. And really, I think I have something to offer all the Bradys. Including you, sir."

Tom wrinkled a brow. "Oh?"

"You see, with your young Charlie, it might just be a lack of encouraged discipline." She took a moment to let out an apologetic laugh, "I know you have much on your mind and hands to keep you occupied. It must be so difficult to manage your time in a way that, allows, for you to provide Charlie with the steady discipline a boy like him needs."

"A boy like him?" It was said with a sharp edge to it. Tom Brady's back went a little rigid.

"Oh, yes. One with complications of the brain," she answered with certainty.

For Tom Brady, the music could no longer be heard. He just stared at the woman in his arms. Luke waltzed by with his Anna, only to openly gape at his father with a disgusted look. Tom took note of this, but did not return the favor.

"Just what kind of discipline do you think 'complications of the brain' call for?"

"A firm hand," Mildred was quick to reply. "All children require reinforced boundaries. If they cannot produce a set response to a request, then comes the firm hand. I have found even the hardest of disabilities flourish when they understand a determined response is necessary after a command is given. Even your Charlie could learn to respond when he realizes there will be a consequence for not doing so."

"I bet the Indians thought a lot of you," Tom said flatly.

"Oh, yes! I made much progress there. Of course there were days I spent the time switching each of my students to condition them, but I felt the benefit far and again outweighed the damage it did to my heart to discipline those children."

"And you think Charlie requires the same amount of, what did you call it? Conditioning?"

"I believe I could help the boy, yes. Now I'm not saying he could ever be considered normal, and responsible for his own care in any way, but at least he could take verbal commands."

All Tom could see was Charlie standing in the snow, making his own form of art while Red caressed his face with frozen whiskers. Animals were always a great judge of character. The softness in that mare's eyes as she looked Charlie over was all the judgement Tom needed to know the boy was full of good. And, try as he might, he could not conger the image of Addie Loveland standing over Charlie with a switch and welting up his tiny bottom until he somehow figured out to pee in a pot. It was so painful for him to attempt to bring the image to life that he quit trying. Instead, he glanced to Roy who held Charlie tenderly and looked over at Tom with a concealed look.

Perhaps Tom Brady was a man a little slow on the uptake, but even in the most horrific times after his wife died, the longest of the nights with an inconsolable infant, he never once thought of carving up a willow to whip him with. Even when he found Charlie hopeless, he never thought of disciplining him, just wondered how he would make it work for the entirety of his life.

Much had changed for Tom in the course of a ride to Charleston. What he thought was hopeless, was indeed not. Addie Loveland trained his son to pee in a pot. She never said a word about it, just did it. She never thought for a moment he couldn't do it. Just worked at it till it was done. To his new way of thinking, Charlie didn't need whipped to learn a command, he needed persistence, and the belief it could be taught. *Without* a switch.

"Mr. Brady, my sister and I have talked it over, and we would be willing to come out your way and spend some time helping out. I could work with the children while my sister helps to get the household in order. We figure it would take a few weeks, but this is the time of year easiest for Mrs. Gibbs to get away."

Tom Brady stopped moving and looked harshly at Mildred Blanchard. "I have a housekeeper."

This took her by surprise. This was the only answer she had not rehearsed. "Oh, I see. A family member?"

"No. A young widow. A very young widow," Tom firmly replied.

This struck Mildred with shock. "With no chaperone? Where does this young widow come from?"

"All the way from Texas. In my opinion, Texas is the place to get willing young widows," Tom Brady smugly answered.

Mildred's eyes popped. "Now, Miss Blanchard, I best check on my sons."

Before the music came to an end, Tom Brady left Mildred standing on the dance floor gaping at his retreating back. Roy wore a satisfied half-smile when Tom looked at him. As he gently handed Charlie back to his father, both men shook their heads.

"Horseface," was spoken by both at the same time.

The next morning, the Bradys were up and moving early. In times of celebration, barns were opened up for sleeping quarters, and once the dance had died down, which wasn't until around six, the hall was filled with bedrolls and sleeping bodies. The wood floor was not a comfortable place to get some rest. So when Tom Brady's back could take no more, he woke the boys, and they gathered their things to ready for the ride home.

Getting into Charleston late the day previous, the mercantile had been closed. Tom had intentions of stopping in for a few items he figured he best get, as it would be a while before he had the opportunity again.

So he did his purchasing, then they left town, riding for the homestead and something besides cold biscuits and a few slices of yesterday's bacon to warm them. Tom wanted coffee more than anything, but it would be a long ride before he had any.

Roy rode with them most of the way, until they reached a deep ravine that led up to his place five miles beyond. They parted with a handshake, and Tom telling Roy not to be a stranger.

Roy looked back as he trotted away and said, "Don't worry. Addie's coffee is too good for being a stranger."

Tom shook his head before setting his red filly into a trot again. Luke was aglow even in the cold air. Tom had no idea what was the final outcome of the dance the previous night. He didn't know what the young pair's parting words to each other were. All he knew was the memory of a feeling he'd had once himself as a young boy. Luke hadn't spoken much, not even to answer Andrew's merciless teasing. Frankie spent the ride rubbing his tired eyes, while Charlie was the least affected of all. He curled into the comfort of his father's strong chest and slept a good

230

portion of the way.

As the miles wore on, Tom felt increasingly more concerned about getting to the home place. Being away from it without any real confidence in the person left to take care of it encouraged him to push his crew to the sweating point. The horses were wet with lather and still they moved across the snow-swept ground briskly.

When at last they topped the hill above the homestead, Tom Brady let out a long exhale to see his home and barn were standing just as he left them. A thin wisp of smoke trailed from the chimney of the main house, and at the sight of them, Molly immediately let out an excited bark, bounded off the porch and up the long slope to them. She couldn't have been more pleased with a rabbit than she was to see her boys.

Addie opened the door and stepped out onto the porch when she heard Molly raise up an excited ruckus. She watched the Bradys ride down the slope to the house. She took note of the state of each: Luke clearly too elated to be tired, Frankie barely able to hang on to Mare's mane, Andrew, whose face was pinched up from the saddle sores, and Charlie who looked at Addie and saw nothing else.

Tom Brady's face was a mixture of relief and determination, and he clearly was ready for the task of feeding ahead. He pulled up at the porch and looked down at Addie. "I believe Charlie needs a good fire."

Addie said nothing, just reached up to take Charlie from the saddle. He reached his little arms out to her, his eyes brightening at the sight of her. She set him down on wobbly legs and steadied him. When she'd straightened and took Charlie's hand to head for the door, she turned to look back at Tom Brady.

Tom watched her with dark eyes, concealed in hardness, and he looked away when she saw him watching. She stopped and asked, "You want somethin' to eat now?"

Tom Brady shook his head. "Nah, we'll get the feedin' done first. It's gettin' late."

Addie nodded.

"Frankie, you get barn chores done. Andrew and Luke, let's get horses on the meadow fed."

Addie didn't think she'd seen more discouragement than she did in those boys. Luke said nothing, well prepared to pay the price for his fun, but Andrew and Frankie nearly cried at the thought of the work ahead.

"Hold up a minute," Addie said, then went into the cabin. She returned a moment later, something in her hands. Moving to the boys, she handed up to them each a slice of cornbread. That brightened eyes, and while nobody but Luke said thank you, it was etched clearly on their faces. Stepping back up onto the porch, Addie held out one last piece to Tom Brady.

He looked down at it and then at Addie's face. "I thought you was gonna sleep the time away. In my great big fancy bed."

Addie scoffed and shook her head. "I don't set foot in that room."

Contemplating her with knowing eyes, he slowly reached out and took the cornbread she offered, then he turned his horse and headed to the barn. The boys followed as they made short work of the cornbread. Addie turned and went back into the cabin to get Charlie his own sustenance.

When she had him settled with it and Spoony, she put on her coat and headed to the barn to help Frankie. She'd already cleaned all the stalls, and pitched hay, but she figured she could help him with the saddle horses. Tom, Luke and Andrew headed out with the team and sleigh to the stack, and the late afternoon sun crept a little lower in the sky towards its resting place below the mountain.

Addie ran the brush through her long hair in preparation for bed. Molly lay by the fire, and watched as Addie pulled the wood-handled brush stroke after stroke. She was making an attempt to keep herself a little better, and it made early morning preparations easier if the tangles in her hair weren't left over from the day previous.

The little stove crackled and popped away happily. The night wasn't as cold as usual with the cloud cover thickening above. It meant surely their streak of calm weather was over. No doubt by morning the wind would be whistling around the corners of all the buildings on the homestead.

Addie had never been one to brave the wind.

As a child, the wind had scared her beyond reasoning. It stemmed from the one tornado she'd experienced. That was enough to spook her for life. When strong wind howled around her, she remembered in her soul that one time long ago. The memory of fear rose without encouragement.

Addie thought of Luke. She had the chance to ask him quietly how things went. He smiled a big smile and nodded his head. He spoke low of how much Anna liked the rose. It warmed Addie's heart to hear it and see the obvious pleasure in his face as he spoke of it.

A soft knock sounded on the weathered door of the dugout. Addie stopped mid-stroke and looked at Molly. The dog lowered her head and thumped the tip of her tail on the dirt floor. In a surge of panic, Addie realized it wouldn't be one of the boys as they were asleep before she left the main house. Could it be a stranger out on the desert seeking shelter from a coming storm?

But then again, Molly clearly knew who it was, or she would have been upset long before the knock sounded. Addie wished she'd bolted the door when she came in.

"Who's there?" she called out in a low voice.

"It's Tom," came the reply.

Addie wrinkled her nose at the dog who gave her a look of undisclosed understanding. "Just a moment."

She briefly wondered if she could just tell him to get lost. What could he possibly need to brave the out-of-doors in the late hour as it was? Her hair was free from its pins, and it was impolite for a man to see a woman's hair loose.

"What do you need?" she called out.

There was an irritated pause. "Just open the door, Mrs. Loveland."

Addie closed her eyes and sighed out a long breath. Pulling her hair behind her shoulders she moved to the door, and after thinking about it for a moment, pulled the door open a narrow slit. It was just enough to reveal her face and nothing more.

Tom Brady stood in the darkness of the porch. The candlelight from the table behind her was hardly enough to light his features, but merely make out his outline. "Yeah?"

Tom Brady studied her face a moment. She could read nothing in his expression before he slowly reached down and opened his coat. He slipped his right hand inside and took hold of something that crackled when he did so. Tom Brady pulled it out slowly before he held it out to her. For an insane second, hope flared in Addie that it might be a letter from her ma. But reality said there was no way for that to be true.

Instead, Addie could make out a small package, wrapped in brown paper and tied with common brown string. She studied a while before Tom Brady held it out closer to her. He said nothing, just watched as wavy hair fell over her shoulder and reached down past her elbow.

With great reluctance, Addie grasped the package and felt the paper in her hand. As soon as she took hold of it, Tom Brady left the porch and made no sound as he moved back to the main house. Addie opened the door and stuck her head out to look after him, but she could see nothing. She closed the door behind herself and looked to the dog that hadn't moved during the exchange of the package. Dark eyes glittered in the low light. Stepping to the table, Addie held up the package to study it in the yellow candlelight. It was simple enough, nothing fancy about it. No doubt wrapped in a simple shop. She longed to know what it was, but a deep burning resentment flourished in her soul. Whatever it was, meant Tom Brady paid attention enough to pick something up about her.

A low growling sound from Addie made the dog rise and come to stand next to her and study the package as well. Addie looked down at Molly. "What's that old goat up to now?"

Addie frowned deeply before pulling the string around the package. She couldn't remember when the last time was she opened a package like the one she held in her hand. When the string was gone, she stared at the brown paper, the tension building in Molly until she wagged her tail in an attempt to spur the woman on and satisfy curiosity.

Unfolding the paper on one side, Addie could see the edge of the contents. With two fingers, she pulled gently on soft contents. As it came out, something fell and hung free apart from what she still held between her two fingers. Holding them up, Addie studied them a moment.

Wool stockings.

Addie just stared. How on earth had he known her desperate need for new stockings? She'd mended hers time and time again, but there wasn't much left to mend. And while she was making do out of lack of any other option, she certainly had never spoke of this. When would Tom Brady have ever known she needed them? When would that old goat have seen hers in such a terrible state?! And why was he looking?!

Then she remembered. The night she and Luke nearly perished in the blizzard. Tom Brady helped her when they got into the house. He would have surely seen her sorry stockings then. Addie's face went still and sad. She laid the stockings gently out on the table and looked at them. Then she looked over at her trunk. It was rare in life a body found itself getting what it needed.

The gray stood on the ridgeline and looked down below. The night air was still, but it carried a certain weight to it, like the pressure was changing. The starlight that filtered through the clouds wasn't enough to light up the earth. The smell of cold was sharp and lingering at the end of an inhalation.

The weather was changing again.

He raised his head high in the air, widening his nostrils to breathe deep of the air. The land around him lay quiet in winter's sleep. He was willing to stand patiently, watching down over that little valley, seeking the coming of the sun that would rise up behind him. And when it did, he'd be long gone, seventeen miles gone, but he would have stood watch all night.

The weather was changing, and this time, it brought isolation.

The skies went from a bright and cheerful blue to a solemn gray. No longer did the sun beam through the kitchen window in the morning, now only a dull light lit the world outside, which wasn't enough to brighten the kitchen where Addie spent most of her time.

She stopped scrubbing the floors, for it took so much heat from the stove to get them to dry. When laundry day came round, she had to stoke the fires in the main house and keep them at a roar or the clothes strung on the pegs and lines in the kitchen took three days to dry. As it was, it took at least two. The air was so damp outside, it refused to soak up the moisture from the laundry.

She felt like she were on her way to being completely mad. The main house was swept and dusted to a high shine. Dishes and dutches scrubbed and polished. There was no butter to churn as the cow was dry, but Addie would have welcomed the distraction. But then again, she would surely have chaffed at the monotony of it. All of it had turned menial, and despite the promise of pay at the end, she could hardly force herself to complete each task. She found her mind wandering each day back to her childhood, to her ma, to her brothers. She avoided Fett, for she found the wretched twisting he caused her insides nearly pushed her over the edge of sanity.

The month of January proceeded on this way. Endless hours filled with housework she'd done the day before. Ears void of any kind of sound. She'd tried to sing, but honestly found that much time spent with her own voice was irritating.

The Brady men weren't much better off. While Addie's day was spent inside slowly grating hours off the clock repetitively going through her chores, they spent their time in the same fashion outside. Groggy boys parked themselves at the breakfast table each morning, only to growl at one another, then rise to answer the call to the feed sleigh, leaving behind them dirty dishes. They'd come in after a long, cold, boring day of feeding and chores only to drop wet clothing, gloves and boots in a heap by the door. By the time Addie had it all picked up and hanging where it could dry in the heat of the stove, she had a floor in bad need of cleaning again. She tried waiting by to help them hang their things as they took it off, but she found the three of them discarded faster than she could collect.

If there had been before, there certainly wasn't anything cheerful about Addie now.

She found herself wondering how her ma had done it with even more boys to handle. Then she recalled it. A wood paddle by the door to get her point across. Addie's ma never endured this kind of rubbish as she could enforce her own rules. Addie couldn't, and it was starting to get very difficult to stay silent with another man's children. One very dark look set Luke to straights, but the others weren't so easy to tame. Tom Brady was always the last to come in, so he never saw the mess Addie dealt with.

And then, long about the first part of February, little Charlie decided to heap on his own brand of misery. For some reason, which Addie couldn't fathom, he took sick. Nothing in the home had changed, no visitors to bring about new sickness, and no one else was touched by it, or at least none of the other boys admitted to it. It lasted three miserable days, with Charlie soiling his britches with the foulest smelling crude any child could muster up. And, as nothing seemed to get a handle on it, Addie was boiling water constantly and scrubbing clothes that hung permanently over the cook stove in the kitchen. Charlie still wore a cloth to catch the solid masses despite his peeing in a pot. Addie figured in the spring when it wasn't so devastating to sit in an outhouse all day training a child, she'd go to work on that portion of things.

That was not to be.

It was a horrible thing to see. Nothing stopped it, and it caused a burning on his wee little behind that ate the skin away and drew blood in places, no matter how quickly she cleaned him up. When she was out of the few meager cloths she still had, she wrapped rags around his bottom and pinned them. Addie had never really heard Charlie cry, but he cried, plenty. She would rush to him when she heard his whimpering, wait till the storm passed, then set to scrubbing him up as gently as possible. Had it been a warmer time of year, she would have just set him in a tub of bath water. But it wasn't a good time to set a child to soaking every few hours.

And in all that hurricane, Charlie decided something for himself. He wasn't gonna wear that around anymore. So, after it passed, and Addie had all the cloths scrubbed down to little more than fibers, and his delicate skin had begun to heal, he made his own resolution; he just wasn't going to go anymore.

It took a day or two to for his system to set to straights and function properly again, and when he felt nature's call, he bore down holding it with all he had. At first Addie didn't realize what was happening, and she worried about his not getting going again. But as she watched him a day or so, she figured on his holding it. By then, of course, he couldn't go. His little belly ached and bloated, but still, nothing would come. And when it finally did move, there again he'd fight with his whole body to hold it back.

Addie begged Charlie, pleaded with him, promised him she'd clean him up before it burnt him again. He would hear none of it, he'd turn his face away from her and wiggle and fight to avoid the acid he was just sure would eat him alive. His belly hurt so bad he would just lay still.

And in all of this, she could think of only one thing. Charlie was not her son. She was not responsible for helping him. It was Tom Brady's problem, and so, she took it to him. One night after dinner she hit him with it as the boys were readying for bed. Tom Brady noticed Charlie was off, and made mention of it.

He'd known of the bout with diarrhea, and he had been concerned. But now as he listened to Addie, he slipped his hands into his pockets and looked at the floor. His face was drawn and he made no remarks until she was done. He licked his lips slowly before he spoke.

"He ain't gonna die over it. The boy's body won't stand for it. He'll go without any say so on his part when the time is right."

Addie blinked at him. It was just the kind of reassurance a man would give. *Don't worry. The boy will poop himself when the time is right.* Like when? Like when his belly popped and he had nothing left to hold on with? The advice was so practical, so reasonable, so judiciously given, Addie wanted to strangle him. If it were that simple, would she really be panicking? Of course not!

Addie pursed her lips as she looked at Tom Brady. He had listened to her accusation of responsibility, he had accepted it, and… tabled it. So, having heard her out, he confessed to no ability to change anything

238

about the situation. It would take care of itself. She put on her coat and left him standing there.

A heavy fog had settled in the valley below the high mountains and taken up residence for several weeks. It held a damp cold that cut through any amount of layers the feed crew put on. Fingers stung and tingled throughout the day, only when hands were tucked close to the body did the burning stop and feeling come back.

Addie waited by the window in the afternoons for the sun to come back. Even the wind, for it would push out the nasty cold that made the soul cry out for relief. The days passed until Charlie did indeed come to the crossroads Tom Brady had spoken of. When all was said and done, Addie started over with a little pot and a makeshift seat attached to it.

Charlie proved to be an impossible student.

With the utmost tenderness she could muster, Addie spent her day by the boy, coaxing and encouraging. But it was no use. To make matters even more difficult, Charlie liked to spend his free time near the fire playing with Spoony. While that wasn't the end of the world, he was not the easiest to work around come meal times. She scolded and told him to move, but Charlie merely looked at her. She needed to talk with someone, tell of her troubles, but she was on her own.

When the burden of training Charlie proved to be fruitless, and the fog refused to lift, Addie lost any desire to press on into the afternoon. There would be no relief when Charlie's pa came home, and the endless winter days surely stretched on into eternity. Addie's was a voice that floated out from her body and fell upon Charlie who wouldn't listen to her reasoning, and found the process confusing.

So, Addie left her bread dough sitting atop the workbench dredged in flour, and little Charlie parked near the cook stove. She wandered into the sitting room and pulled a chair to the window and sat in it, looking out at the gray that engulfed everything. She was tired in her soul, with a fatigue that weighed her down until all her movement stopped.

She pressed her face into her hands and cried. There was nothing left to do, and the nightmare that was her life would still be waiting for her to pull herself together when she stopped. Again, the very thought of how she'd come to be where she was, pulled her backwards until the remaining fight she might have drained out of her.

Addie felt something lightly brush her hair and she raised her face to look up. There before her was Charlie, his dark eyes vibrant with hurt as he looked at her tear-soaked face. His little body trembled as he waited for the reassuring smile he sought, that told him she was still there for him, still strong, despite whatever it was troubling her. It didn't come. The hope of spring had gone from Addie and instead she was replaced with the fog of winter. Her face was wrinkled and red, and nothing came out of her mouth to encourage him further.

Charlie reached out and pressed a finger to her cheek, feeling the dampness on his flesh. He lowered his hand to his side and looked blankly at Addie. Then, seeing that her smile wasn't going to come, the corners of his mouth twitched and stretched. He stood before Addie, so very small in stature, with as close to a smile extended across his face as he knew how to use. While it was not a warm and well-used smile, he used it to offer the same reassurance she'd so often given him. He returned it to her, not sure it would work, but he had to try for his Addie.

The gesture so deeply touched Addie she reached out to him and pulled him into her arms. She raised him onto her lap, Charlie burrowing into the comfort of her arms. He pressed close against her chest, tucking his head next to her heart. They sat like that, Charlie a tight ball against Addie, and Addie finding comfort in the root of her current burdens, for what seemed like the duration of the afternoon. They slept in warmth and comfort for a while, and when it was time for Addie to rise with the jingling of sleigh harness, it felt as though she had left the main house for a time.

When Tom Brady came in the house, Addie stood over the cook stove and didn't bother to look his way. Charlie played at her feet despite the heat coming from the stove. He watched as Spoony "hopped" across the floor. Tom could hear the elder three boys talking from the sitting room where they warmed themselves by the fire. Around his feet was a scattering of wet clothing making it very difficult to get through the door. Although, Luke's was hung very nicely from the pegs.

240

Tom took his things off and hung them, then stepped over the soaked clothes of his sons. He moved to Charlie and reached down for him. "Come boy, let's leave Addie to herself awhile."

He moved off through the sitting room door with Charlie high on his shoulder. Addie watched in stunned silence for a moment as they went. Then from the sitting room she heard him say, "You boys gather up your mess and hang it up. Ain't gonna dry on the floor in a heap."

"But the peg's too high...," Frankie started.

"I don't give a damn. Get to it," Tom scolded.

Addie observed as Frankie drug his father's chair over and stood on it to reach the pegs above his head. When they'd finished, Frank and Andrew's things were hung in an orderly fashion where the warm air would reach them and dry them overnight. Then the sitting room was silent after they retreated back to it.

Addie worked at getting a meal on the table. She was never late with a meal, and in her heart she felt guilty since she had been resting when she should have been working. She pulled bread from the box above the stove. The smell of fresh baked bread filled the kitchen and sent fingers of comfort to the occupants. With quick steps she grabbed deep dishes to scoop boiled taters and meat gravy into. Turning to the wood table she shuffled them into place with spoons accompanying. She lifted the heavy dutch filled with supper from the stove top and put it in the center of the table.

Then she heard something. It was very low, resonating from the sitting room. She listened carefully for a moment and heard it again. Before she called the Brady men to come to the table, she walked softly to the door and looked through. The room was lit only with the light from the fire that cast a bright orange glow. There she saw the boys standing close to the flames, their backsides no doubt smoldering, looking over at Tom Brady who sat in a chair at an angle facing the fire. On his lap was little Charlie, who faced Tom with a raised finger. His little face was so full of expectancy, alight with curiosity.

Slowly, Charlie raised his finger to Tom's face. With each inch the anticipation growing in him until his pointer hovered just beyond his father's lips. His little arm trembled as his eyes focused on Tom's mouth. Tom held absolutely still. Then in a burst of speed, he opened his mouth and took hold of Charlie's little finger with his teeth, but clearly he put no pressure on the delicate flesh for Charlie was able to pull his finger back out without resistance.

Charlie's face widened in astonishment. His eyes reflected great surprise at the quickness of his father. All he really wanted to do was dig around and discover a little more about teeth and tongue, but Tom was too quick to let that happen. At Charlie's look, Tom Brady let out a deep chuckle that rumbled into another. He then stilled himself and waited for Charlie to try again. This time the boy knit his eyebrows together in an attempt to determine a better way to best his father. After a few more tries he realized it didn't matter how fast or slow he went, he was going to get ahold of his finger. Then the goal of the game changed. Charlie was starting to realize the fun of it was in the anticipation. The boys, Luke, Andrew and Frankie, gathered closer to watch and Tom's chuckling grew to include that of his three other sons.

Addie had never seen Tom Brady take such an earnest interest in his youngest son. He provided for him, perhaps not in depth and with as much attention as Charlie's mother probably would have liked, but he was alive. Never had Tom Brady taken the time to play a game with Charlie.

But, Addie thought, to Tom's benefit, Charlie never reflected any kind of liveliness or curiosity before. He was a lifeless lump of demanding flesh that made no move to interact with the world around him. Not even with his brothers who made up his world. And something in Tom Brady looked different. His smile smoothed out all the worry lines etched deeply in his face.

Addie backed away.

When she returned to the table, she waited a moment before calling out to the men that supper was ready. When they came, she waited silently, and then ate without looking at anyone.

It seemed so unfair. So unbalanced. How could it be that one person had so many to look out for them? To comfort them, regardless of whether or not they made use of it.

Addie stood on the porch of the dugout and looked back at the main house. The lamp in the kitchen still burned, so Addie returned to the lantern in her own hand. She moved slowly to the door and pushed her way through. After she'd closed the door behind her, she stood and stared down at Molly who returned the gaze with indulgent eyes. When a skittering in the corner sounded, Molly turned abruptly to inspect.

Moving to the table, Addie opened the lid to her trunk. She peered into it without penetrating the darkness. When the springtime came, and the grass grew tall, the creeks flowed free, and the sun warmed the earth, Addie would venture out into the world alone. She'd travel back to her mama and papa with no one but herself to care much about her well-being. But Tom Brady, he wasn't alone. Never would he be. No matter what, even when his boys were gone, there would be someone that belonged to him and him alone in the great wide world. Addie would never have that. She no longer had ties to anyone but her folks, and when they passed, her brothers would be of a self-created existence with families of their own.

Addie would still be alone.

The pressing weight of imminent solitude bore heavily on the soul of a young woman with a long life ahead. Not for the first or last time Addie began to contemplate the purpose of life and death. If life were meant to be lived, then what was the point of spoiling it with death? And not the death of one's self, but the death of those who made it worth the living part? Addie had no answers.

She dug down to the bottom of her trunk and fished for a little canvas bag. She hooked her fingers on the string that kept the top drawn closed and pulled it out. She held it in her hands and studied the rectangular shape of it and laughed a bitter laugh.

It was of no use to her. Even if she wanted it to, it would not give her the comfort she desperately sought. Jerking the string tie loose, she grasped the leather cover and pulled the book free.

It was her Grandfather Halstead's Bible, and when she married Fett, her mother insisted they take it. While obviously Addie would make no use of it, her mother felt sure in times of trouble Fett could read it to her. While Clara never once doubted the strength of her daughter's faith, she greatly doubted Fett Loveland's as she had no idea of his raising nor the depth of his belief. She knew he acknowledged God, but to what point she had no idea.

So, she sent the heirloom with Addie, with strict instructions as to making Fett read it once in a while. Addie had done so only a few times thinking there would be a lifetime of opportunity for it. Now she regretted it.

She held it up in the lantern light and looked at the words etched in gold on the cover. Holy Bible. She knew that's what it said only because she heard it referred to many times in her life. She didn't bother to open the cover, for the words listed there might as well have been Chinese symbols for all she knew of them.

"It's meant to give comfort. It's meant to bring hope to the hopeless. All I see is a locked box with no key for me. I am shut out. I am denied the promises within these pages," Addie's voice trembled with anger, "because I can't read."

"I seek Your face just like my mama said to. I call out just like she said to. Where are You?"

Addie lay the Bible against her heart. "If You are my inheritance, then what do I do in the meantime? What do I do before I inherit?"

Edging slowly to the rocker, she sat in it, defeated by the challenges of her life she could not conquer, the troubles and foibles that plagued and tormented. Addie lay her head in her hands and rested her elbows on her knees. The desire to be heard and understood burned inside her and beckoned to find a place of comprehension. Looking at that Bible was like watching lips move with no sound.

"If You can hear my thoughts, Lord, then why would You assume I would not long to hear Yours? Why would You shut me out from hearing Your words? Your grace? And most of all, receiving just one ounce of mercy? I am alone. Let me hear You!" she cried out amidst the falling of bitter tears born of feelings of abandonment. "Open my door to understanding!"

Addie again lay her head in her hands. She fell silent from her rantings and just hung her head, hollow and empty, void of any answering voice. She thought again of the Bible and whispered, "I can't even hear Your thoughts…"

Addie cried, tears seeping out from between her fingers and dripping down onto her lap, soaking up her apron. She dared not raise up and look at that Bible.

I can't hear your thoughts…

It echoed and rolled around in her mind. It tumbled and shouted at her. Each time she said it to herself it caused a burning in her stomach. She listened to the words again and again, only to be driven to say it, the image of little Charlie hunched over clutching Spoony to his chest rising repeatedly in her mind.

Then, ever so slowly, Addie raised up her face to look straight at the Bible. Gone were the tears in her eyes, although still present on her cheeks. The feeling of isolation had receded and in its place came the dawning of bright realization. With loud interpretation she again repeated it vehemently and felt the understanding take root.

"I can't hear your thoughts!"

Andrew lay in the dark and stared up at the ceiling. His arm was folded back under his head while thoughts ran through his mind. The sound of Frankie's heavy breathing sounded beside him. Frankie always fell asleep first. The boy never had anything on his mind that would keep sleep away. It seemed he never *had* anything on his mind.

Charlie was asleep in the bed next to Luke, but he was as silent when he was sleeping as he was when he was awake. Andrew considered his youngest brother. "Hey, Luke, you awake?"

After a moment came the quiet reply, "Yeah, I'm awake."

Andrew said, "That was somethin', wasn't it? Seein' Charlie play with Pa like that."

"Huh. What I thought was more miraculous was hearing Pa laugh. I can't remember when he laughed at all, let alone with Charlie."

Andrew pursed his lips in consideration. "Yeah, I guess you're right. What do you 'spose is different about Charlie? I mean, he does seem different these days. Lot less like a nutter."

Andrew could hear Luke raise his head off the pillow to look in his direction in the dark. "Andrew! Charlie ain't crazy, he's just... well he's... he's just different. That's all."

Andrew nodded his head, justified. "Nutter," he whispered.

"You know," Luke started. "I think all this time Pa just figured Charlie was gonna die."

The smugness about Andrew disappeared. "Yeah, I've thought that too. Can't says what convinced Charlie to do otherwise."

"Well, that's obvious, stupid," Luke spat.

Andrew raised up onto an elbow and glared into the darkness in Luke's general direction. "Who you callin' stupid, stupid? And besides it isn't obvious to me seein' as I'm too busy ridin' feed wagon to be around to notice anything!" Andrew bitterly railed. He flopped angrily back down onto his pillow, shaking the whole bed.

"It's Miss Addie. She's what's different," Luke replied, ignoring Andrew's rant. "Charlie's never had no ma to help him along. You seen the way he clings to her skirts, just like any baby does to their ma. And she did the impossible trainin' him to pee outside his pants."

"Yeah, well, she isn't his ma, and what's gonna happen when she goes back to Texas in the spring?"

Luke fell silent then. He had wondered this himself many times. But in his wonderings he wasn't considering Charlie, just himself. "Well, I for one am praying she doesn't go back to Texas in the spring."

Andrew clicked his tongue impatiently. "Grow up. She hates it here. And more importantly she hates Pa. Don't matter how she feels about Charlie, she won't stay here with Pa." Andrew hitched his arm up under his head again as he saw images in the dark play before his eyes. "I wish I could go with her. I'd like to see it."

"See what?" Luke asked.

Andrew sighed. "Texas. I'd like to see Texas."

It was Luke's turn to click his tongue impatiently as he rolled onto

.

his side. "You just want off the feed sleigh. Come summer you'll be just as happy to run horses as you always are."

"I'd like to ask her about it. Runnin' horses with her man, I mean."

"Miss Addie? I wouldn't do that if I were you," Luke warned.

"Why not? She liked tellin' us about Mexico."

"'Cause. I think she'll talk when she's ready. If you go to pryin', it might not go as well as when she told us about Mexico."

Andrew rolled his eyes. "You go to one dance with Anna Clements and suddenly you think you're a man of women. Like you know all about 'em or something."

"I didn't have to go to the dance with Anna Clements to see Addie Loveland is hurtin' some kind of crazy bad inside. All I had to do was look at her with my eyes open!"

Ignoring Luke's counsel, Andrew formulated questions in his mind. "I'm gonna ask anyway."

"Don't do it, Jughead."

"I'm doin' it," Andrew stated with finality as he rolled toward the wall and burrowed deep into the blankets, blocking out all protests his older brother might make.

"I don't know, Addie. I think he's kinda pretty." Fett stood at the end of a long reata and tried not to move much. The reata was wound around a stout pinion tree twice to help Fett keep ahold.

Addie smirked. "You always find something redeeming in all of 'em. Even the ugly ones."

Fett shrugged, the off-white of his sweat-soaked shirt clinging to his skin. His hat rested on the back of his head so air could cool his sweat-drenched hair. "I really can see some little girl just thinkin' he's the purdiest beast alive. Kissin' his sun burnt nose. Rubbin' his painted neck, scratchin' behind his really tall, pink ears… sittin' atop them mutton withers…" as Fett inspected the paint's possible attributes his voice died away.

Addie looked on from the back of her bay, Paddy, in doubt.

Fett cocked his head. "Well, the withers would be good. I mean what girl wants to go ridin' bareback on some sharp-withered old pony anyway?"

Addie laughed at the image she knew Fett had drawn up in his mind about girls riding sharp-withered ponies. "I for one think he's ugly. And seeing as I'm the closest thing you got to a 'girl', well I think you best turn that one back out. *After* you geld him."

Fett couldn't contain a small chuckle as he looked at his recently captured prospect. "Addie, you got no eye for potential. This might just be the gentlest pony you ever saw."

"He's tried to strike you twice already!" Addie argued pointing at the beast in question.

"Come on, Addie. He might be a little rough on the edges, but that'll polish right off. He'll make a little girl pony in no time. He'll figure eatin' all the carrots he can stand is way better than roughing it."

Addie shook her head. "He isn't worth the time. He might gentle down, but you'd have to ride that no-withered shitter until he was. I can hear you ranting now about how he won't hold up your saddle. And forget ropin' off 'im." Addie leaned over to get a closer look at something. "Is that a blue eye?" she ask incredulously.

"Oh, I wasn't gonna be the one to gentle him down. You're better at it than me." Fett gave Addie a sly look. "And you don't rope as often as I do."

Addie shot Fett a look of pure shock and disgust.

"He'll gentle down easy. You'll see." Fett winked at her in reassurance. Just then the gray and pink paint horse blew up and reared backward as far as he could until the rope went tight. Then he took to striking the air with his right front leg. Fett looked over to Addie.

"He'll gentle right down, love."

Addie leaned forward and rested her elbow on the saddle horn and placed her head in her hand. She glared at Fett.

He looked back to the paint. "Alright, but I still think you shouldn't judge him 'til you know his story. Hell, it might just be he needs a little understanding."

"I don't care to understand anything about that."

Fett grinned. "Well, I guess then we best get Pete to help us get this beast gelded and turned loose."

Addie held the chunk of Fett's reata that she'd cut off his saddle the day Pete rode out to head farther west without her. It was dry and withered with no care or oiling. She ran the intricate braiding through her fingers. It was a shame to see such craftsmanship withering away. But seeing as it was only a chunk of the rope meant for nostalgia anyway, it seemed silly to care for it so carefully.

Fett always found the good in everyone and everything.

Addie sighed as she put the Bible and the chunk of reata back into the trunk. Perhaps she was not as dedicated to the 'good in everybody' part, but it might help to see things a little differently.

Tom Brady stood on the sleigh behind the team and looked back at his three sons sitting on the empty bed. He clicked to the horses who started off away from the barn in the direction of the hay stacks and the meadows. The longs puffs of steam that streamed out from their nostrils trailed back behind them in the early morning cold.

The boys were silent as they moved towards the stack under the tightly controlled speed of Tom, who held the stout work horses under his hand. They were anxious to work out some of the previous night's energy in the cold. Matching step for step, the impressive beasts trotted along with arched necks, snow and ice crunching loudly beneath massive hooves.

The sky was a dark blue color, mottled with streaks of orange to the east and black to the west. The air pierced the skin wherever it was bare, numbing hands and feet with lack of movement. Luke and Andrew sat with Frankie between them, legs folded Indian style. They might have spoken, but their faces were covered completely with scarves, all but slits for their eyes to see out of. The humidity from his own breath was soaking Luke's scarf. He thought of the conversation between himself and Andrew the evening previous. Addie had no idea how she lit his day, just by standing in the kitchen every morning when he rose.

Luke prayed for her. Well, maybe not specifically her, but for someone who could help them. As he cried for his mama, he'd prayed. As he watched his father hurt and die inside, he'd prayed. As he held his baby brother who was clearly not right, he'd prayed. He'd prayed till he knew for sure God wasn't listening. Then he prayed anyway, just because it was a habit.

Then they got Addie. The poor ragged figure, not in much better shape than any of the Bradys, hurtin' and dyin' inside just like the rest of them. But unlike the Bradys, she still felt and lived inside enough to cry. She still felt enough to try, to work, to love. And, just like Roy said, responded greatly to the power of just one embrace. Her simple and infrequent smile made his mama live inside him again, for each time Addie smiled, he remembered his mama and the way she had smiled.

He looked again to Andrew. That butt head would never say it out loud, but Luke knew it was the same for him. He'd seen his brother look for her each time the team and sleigh pulled into the barnyard. Andrew would study the house and watch for her, and his eyes always lit on her when he came into the kitchen each morning. Andrew was just as hooked on Addie as the rest of the boys. Frankie accepted her as part of his life with gratitude, but he wasn't one to read too much into things.

And Charlie, well, he was alive. That spoke mountains.

They reached the stack, and Luke rose to open the gate as Tom turned the team and pulled the sleigh up to it. Andrew scurried up the loaf-shaped stack to start sawing through the snow and ice crust that had formed on the top of it. Luke grabbed the opposite end of the saw and together they cut into the stack.

It was a life spent forking hay. In the long, hot summer days, they mowed the meadows and forked the dried hay onto the wagon. Then they forked it off into great loaves where it would wait until the winter's bitter cold to be forked back onto the sleigh and again forked off onto the meadow where it came from to feed hungry stock. How many tons of hay Andrew had forked in his life he cared not to know.

Tom Brady drove his pitchfork into the slice with all the strength his lean body possessed and pulled down a huge chunk of hay that hit the sleigh bed and broke loose and scattered. The team started forward at the feel of the weight, but Frankie's determination held them steady. His little body bore down on the lines and produced just enough strength to hold them. Luke did the same as his father, but he didn't get as much hay as his stronger father. Andrew, now with an ax, chipped away at the crust to free more hay. The ax sent shards of ice flying in every direction.

The sun topped the horizon and bright light hit Andrew's eyes. He stopped his task to look in the direction of the beautiful light that would bring warmth to the day. The rays touched his face and even as he closed his eyes, the vivid color filtered through his eyelids and shone deep into his mind. Something about the dawning of a new day whispered hope to a young boy. And although he had no way of knowing it, his life would venture on past the hay meadows, past the loss of his mother, past the grieving of his father, out into a world unimaginable to his inexperienced mind. His life would go on. It would hold treasures of immeasurable value. And, other sorrows, but that was not to be outweighed by the beauty of the sunrise.

Andrew looked down at his father and brothers, each struggling in their own task, and realized, he would remember that moment all of his life. The beauty mixed with the toil, the heartache blended perfectly with the rejoicing of the coming of the sun, and, the promise of another day, one in time, with better things to offer.

Tom Brady stopped to look up at Andrew who studied him. When he was caught looking, he immediately started to swing his ax again. Tom Brady took a moment to look at the dawning sun. In it, the painful twist in his heart found a moment of relief. It unwound and relaxed, while the sun warmed the bleeding wound and caressed the scars. He closed his eyes and just felt the comfort of it.

When Tom opened his eyes again, he found the world had stopped to watch the coming sun. The boys all stood in rapt attention, looking to the light. The team held ears forward and stamping feet still. The skittering sparrows stilled flight and held on for the coming warmth of the day.

When the moment passed, and the first load of the day was on the sleigh, Frankie moved the team away from the stack. Tom stood behind the boy in case he was needed, but the sleigh was heavy now and the team had to work at just keeping it moving. Andrew and Luke sat on the top of the loose hay and warmed their hands before they had to start forking hay again.

As Frankie drove the team through the gate Tom opened, horses on the far end of the hay meadow picked up the sound of jingling harness. From across the way, horses gathered in bunches and began streaking across the meadow. The thundering sound of so many hooves echoed in the quiet morning. At the coming of comrades, the team lifted feet higher and pulled harder on the burden that slowed progress. Yearlings came running ahead of the mares. The lead mare broke free, and the rest figured they'd follow suit. It would be the same in the next meadow over, when they fed the next bunch.

As was the custom of well-bred and well-kept horses, Tom Brady pulled his studs out of the bunches in the early fall. He ran them all together in their own pastures south of the homestead with all the saddle geldings. He kept no mares in that bunch to keep peace among the sires. They were a complacent lot when they had no ladies to bicker over and got on with the geldings easily.

At the sight of a black stud, Tom hurried to get his pitchfork and walk beside the team in readiness. Despite the obvious encumbrance, the stud would not hesitate to charge the team. The heavy horses, burdened as they were, could neither fight nor run from the swift studs who struck and tore hide with their teeth in defense of the coveted mares.

"Pa?" Luke hollered.

"Yeah, I see 'im. Must've bailed the fence last night and went wandering," Tom answered. "We'll have to get him roped and back with the geldings."

The black lay his ears against his neck and charged from a quarter mile back, baring his teeth and flashing his dark eyes. Tom raised his pitchfork over his shoulder, sharp tines pointed at the stud. The black knew better, he'd been stabbed many times before, his flesh pierced with the tines of the fork, and he kept the lessons tucked in his mind. About twenty yards away, he slid to a stop on the ice and reared his insults. The rest of the band charged the sleigh, unconcerned for they had no reason to fear the tines.

When they reached the meadow bottom, Tom jumped up on the sleigh and he, Luke, and Andrew began forking hay into piles as the team moved the sleigh along. Horses gathered alongside the sleigh to snatch mouthfuls of hay. They held no fear of the feed crew, despite the fact that come summer they would be wild again, and completely untouchable. Andrew reached out and rubbed the neck of a brave filly who was willing to bear the fear to get a bite. She was a fine little thing, her rich red coat full of promise of the mare she would become.

Frankie held the team steady as the load lightened along the way. The team walked faster with each forkful tossed away. It had been so long since the sun was visible through the fog, Luke stood to look at it and feel it on his face. Tom and Andrew kept up with the work.

"Hey, boy. Get that girl off your mind and get the horses fed."

Luke looked at his father in surprise and fear of his anger. But, Tom Brady's eyes were lit with mischief despite his ability to keep his face stern. Luke tried to hide a smile as he bent back to his pitching. Tom playfully nudged his shoulder.

"Huh? You dreamin' 'bout her again?"

"What girl?" Luke asked.

"What girl. You know what girl. Don't give me that 'what girl' story."

"I'm not dreamin' about a girl. Just appreciatin' the sun." Luke forked hay for a minute or so, then looked at his father seriously and said, "What about you? Are you thinkin' about that woman you danced with?"

Caught off guard by the seriousness of the question, Tom Brady looked at his eldest son. Then he chuckled at the expression on Luke's face. "Well, she was a mighty fine built woman. That I had not expected."

Luke looked perplexed a moment, then went back to forking hay.

Andrew stood and looked at the sun where it climbed higher in the sky. "I can tell you. I'm thinkin' about a woman."

253

The shock of the statement nearly made Tom Brady fall from his position on the edge of the sleigh. He looked at Andrew with dismay in his face. Andrew tried not to grin at the disturbing looks he was getting from the rest of the feed crew.

"Yep. Can't get her off my mind," he drawled out. "But mostly, I just can't stop thinkin' about what she's makin' for dinner!"

Luke burst out laughing as he looked at his brother. The sound of it echoed up the meadow. Andrew broke into a wicked grin as he looked back at Luke. Before long Frankie's little laugh sounded as well. Tom Brady stood and balanced on the moving sleigh as he looked at his sons. He grinned himself and chuckled at the pride in Andrew's face at having made such a good laugh. Luke threw hay at him, but Andrew ducked before it worked its way down his shirt. Andrew threw a forkful back at him.

"It's true, ain't it? That's all I ever think about! Mrs. Loveland bent over that stove, makin' something wonderful!" Andrew joyously shouted in the morning air.

Luke laughed harder. The horses beside the sleigh shying away from the feed crew that made uncommon noises in the morning air. Tom Brady stopped chuckling. His brow raised as he looked at Andrew.

"Don't say, 'bent over the stove'," he stated.

Andrew looked at his father questioningly. Luke slowed his laughing only slightly.

"Why not?" Andrew asked.

Tom Brady went back to laughing a deep and rich sound that came from somewhere deep inside his chest. He shook his head. "Someday you'll understand."

Addie didn't bother chattering away anymore. She still spoke, but only when it would do the most good. The silence within the main house was enough to drive anyone mad, but she realized that it wasn't the spoken word which would be the form of conversation anymore. That in truth, now she knew it never had been.

It took a better part of the morning for Charlie to really catch on.

254

Addie looked back on all the times she'd interacted with Charlie and came to understand she was only giving him portions of the story. Each time she would begin to explain something, she'd move where he could no longer see her face, watch her eyes, and see her mouth moving to know she was in some way trying to engage him in something.

She tested her theory that morning just after the Bradys left to feed. She set Charlie on the floor next to the wood stove where it was warm, drew Spoony a new face, then went to making noise. First, she crept up behind him and clapped just behind his head. He made no move to acknowledge the sound, but when the floorboard she stood on gave a little under her weight, he immediately turned to look at her.

So she tried something else.

She stood back at the workbench and banged away on an enamel pot with a spoon, making enough noise surely the milk cow could hear her from behind the barn. Charlie didn't turn to look at her, nor did he even stop Spoony's "hopping". Charlie heard nothing from the pot and spoon.

Then Addie screamed.

She let out with the most blood curdling howl any woman could put together. Charlie merely reached for a tiny piece of wood that had fallen from the wood box. But, as soon as Addie shifted her weight and Charlie could feel the difference in the floorboards, he turned to see where she was moving to. Seeing her look at him, he stayed twisted around to watch her face.

Was she leaving? Should he go too? No. She gave him that soft, reassuring smile that told him all was well. He turned back to Spoony.

Addie clamped a hand over her mouth. Suddenly, as his tiny frame sat cross-legged on the floor, Addie could see just how little bitty Charlie was. How very alone he must have been from the time he was born. How very vulnerable his insides must be. How very clearly he could see the rest of the world going on about the day, communicating between themselves, including everyone but him. He was shut out from life, left to dwell in his own prison with nothing and no one to hear his thoughts, nor return the favor of expressing their own.

Addie was crushed inside. She was no better, and although she hadn't meant to, it must have been so devastating to realize she wanted something from him in training him to use the pot, but he only got snippets of what she was imparting to him. Then, to see her discouragement at him. How cruel to know you have upset someone, with no hope of learning how you did it. What if she never figured it out? Would he have watched her go to Texas thinking he had so badly discouraged her she left? He had no way to understand what was going on around him, that very little of it had anything to do with him. That the pain and suffering he read clearly in Addie's eyes was caused by the death of a man he never met.

All he could account for was his own actions. He had no idea a whole world revolved out there with other people and tragedies beyond his own mind.

Addie didn't want him to see her cry anymore. No more tears in front of Charlie. Each one that fell was another one his little heart bore with guilt. Addie took a deep breath and fortified her feelings with solid rock.

Today is a new day, Charlie.

If Charlie couldn't hear, Addie would have to do things differently. She put on the brightest smile she could find. She stoked the kitchen fire so it would be ready come meal-making time. She turned to Charlie and held out her arms to him. He scrambled to get up with Spoony in his hand. He reached back and Addie lifted him up into her arms and close to her chest.

She carried him into the sitting room and pulled a chair over into the beautiful sunlight streaming through the window. She sat down and cuddled him close to her for a moment. When he raised his head to look at her questioningly, she smiled at him again, looking deep into his brown eyes.

Taking his little hand, she pressed his open palm to her throat. Then she spoke. "Addie." She repeated herself over and over while he felt the vibrations in her throat and watched her mouth moving. She said it slowly so he could memorize the movements of her lips and tongue, and

256

waited for him to piece together that the vibration meant something in her throat was moving.

After a time, she pressed his palm to his own throat and repeated herself. He didn't catch on he could make his own vibrations, but she hadn't expected him to. It would take time for him to realize he held the same possibility as everyone else.

Addie found Charlie held no limitations for concentration. That was a great surprise. Most likely because he had never held such rapt attention before. She held him and spoke to him for a long while, Charlie studying her every move. She kept nothing but a smile on her face and light in her eyes.

It was the first time since Fett's death she'd bothered to do that for anybody.

Carrying a heavy bucket filled with dirty dish water, Addie stepped out onto the porch. She needed to haul more wood for the stove. The fog lifted, and it was odd to see the contours of the land around her, the colors of the sage against the white of the snow. The world was still sleeping. Spring had not yet come. The clouds hovering over the peaks of the white mountains to the west spoke of what the next day might bring.

Molly walked with Addie to the edge of the porch and raised her head into the air to sniff what was on the breeze. She snorted to clear her nostrils, then kept sniffing. Addie threw the contents of her bucket far away from the house, watching as the warm water soaked into the snow to make an ice spot by morning. A trail of smoke rose from the dugout, and Addie was relieved the fire hadn't died during the afternoon.

Taking a moment to smell the freshness of the coming evening, Addie held the wooden bucket at her side. Much like the dog, she inhaled deeply with her chin raised into the breeze. It was cold, but the stale air of the house was hot and smelled of wood smoke and grease. The feel of the cold was a relief.

Molly jumped from the porch and ran down across the barnyard, sailing over the nearly frozen creek at the sound of Luke's voice coming from the barn. He appeared leading the two great horses that pulled the feed sleigh and walked them to the creek to drink their fill for the night.

Addie turned back to the sunset. Just above a flat bench that ran between two sharp peaks, the sun burst through the clouds. Bright orange stained the western sky, beaming down on all of creation. The intensity of the light caused Addie to raise her hand to shield her eyes. She looked on into that February sky, taking in the beauty of it.

Down at the creek, Luke looked too, studying the outline of the mountains highlighted by the light of the sun. The sky to the east was a darkening blue that would transition over to purple, then blackness. No stars were yet visible, but they would be soon. The bitterness of the winter air was real, but the sunlight made it bearable.

In the barn, just out of sight of the main house, Tom Brady stood leaning against the rail of a stall. From his vantage point he could not see the setting sun, but rather his focus was on something else. He slid his hands into the pockets of his coat, and let out a slow breath. Tom watched Addie as she stood admiring the sun, the reflection off her hair like a glow.

When she turned and walked back into the house, Tom remained where he was. He looked at the closed door for a time, then he inhaled deeply and looked down at the straw-strewn floor. Slowly exhaling, Tom lifted himself off the rail and went about his way.

"Didn't you want children?"

The whole of the table stopped chewing, stopped scooping, stopped swallowing. All eyes went to Andrew who wore an earnest look on his face, like the question had been burning a hole in his pocket where he carried it. If the table were not so wide, Luke would have kicked his brother in the shin. As it was, he tried anyway but missed entirely.

"Andrew," came the dark and stern voice of his father.

Andrew shrugged and looked back down at his supper, stabbing at a dumpling like it was the unfairness of the world in a biscuit. Stab it and get some revenge. He kept his focus on his plate as he chewed, irritated. It was just a simple question.

While the rest of the table resumed scrapping and clanking, Addie looked down into her plate and swallowed hard. She wondered if there would come a time when simple questions weren't a sucker-punch to the gut.

Say it out. Let it go.

With a blank face, Addie looked up at Andrew and stared at him until he noticed. Then, his eyes widened with surprise and dread. Tom Brady stopped eating and watched Addie closely. Whatever was about to come out of her mouth was no doubt going to teach Andrew to keep those questions in his pocket.

"Yes," came the ragged reply. "Yes, I wanted to have children. I came close once, but I lost it early on. Not long after I saw Mexico on the back of a running horse."

Addie looked back down at her lap, and all assumed she was finished speaking. The corner of Andrew's mouth twitched, but the lesson was no doubt far too soft for him to have learned from it.

"I.. I wa…," Addie tried to get something out, but it wouldn't come. Still looking at her lap, she took a deep breath and started again. "I wanted a little girl," came a very low spoken statement. "I… I wanted to name her Rose." She clenched her jaw. "I always thought that was pretty," she whispered.

After pressing her lips together, Addie looked up at Andrew. "Does that answer your question?" she quietly asked.

"Well, sure," he answered. "but, why a girl?"

"Andrew," Tom Brady growled as he rubbed his forehead.

Addie let out a very small smile. "You want to know why?" she asked.

Andrew nodded.

Addie straightened, raising her head high as she looked at him to give an honest answer. "So I could brush her hair."

Andrew just looked at her for a moment, then let out a laugh when he saw she was serious. With tears shimmering in her eyes, Addie laughed with him. "That's silly," he stated.

Addie smiled, "It is silly, isn't it?"

A small giggle erupted from Frankie when the tension of the

moment passed. "Who'd want a girl when you could have boys?" His little hand gestured around the table.

Addie looked at him and said, "'Cause you won't let me brush your hair!"

That made Andrew and Frankie laugh louder. It evoked a small smile from Luke. Charlie watched in wonder at his laughing siblings.

Andrew lay his fork on his plate and held his face in his hands as he shook his head. When he looked at Addie again, he asked, "Why would brushing her hair be so important?"

"Because, smarty-pants, I was the only girl out of eight kids. All I ever wanted was a sister to play with. When all I got was more brothers, I figured I'd just have to come up with my own girl. Now look at me. Still stuck with a buncha boys!"

"Girls cry all the time!" Frankie shouted. "Like that time Katie Newberry fell off the footbridge into the creek over by Johnstones. She cried like a baby just 'cause she was wet!"

Andrew laughed. "Or like that time I put a snake in the outhouse and Sally White sat on it!" Andrew bellowed out with a wicked laugh, then felt the scalding look of his father upon him. Andrew cleared his throat and looked back down at his plate.

Beside her, Luke snorted out a laugh although he tried desperately to hold on to it. In fear of letting out more dastardly information on themselves, the boys settled into a barely controlled silence for the remainder of the meal. But as they headed with a candle up the loft ladder, the sound of their snickering and laughing told that the conversation had resumed out of earshot of their father.

Addie smiled to herself. Boys had their good attributes. Even if Sally White had the fright of her life sitting on that snake. The joy of it lit a February day.

And a good snake in the outhouse story made for good diversion from a sad subject.

Addie reached for an enamel platter to dry. The water droplets splattered on the counter as her heart froze. At the time when she lost the baby, Fett had said little about it. He held her tightly and whispered that there would be a chance for another. That God had His own time for doing things.

She hated the way it left her empty inside. The way Pete left them behind and headed up the country to give them a few days to work out their sorrows alone. Fett never did say he felt guilty making her ride all that way, but she closed off any talk of it. In time, there was enough to keep her occupied when they hit Santa Fe. She locked that experience away in her heart.

Then Andrew pulled it out.

It struck Addie as odd, how looking back now, her married life to Fett had been hard. While she was in it, she wouldn't have thought it, but to count back through all the sorrows that pierced her heart, she'd survived all of it by not considering any of it.

Just like Tom Brady said.

He'd said it Christmas morning, right after she'd dreamed of her mother. At the time, she thought he was mad, that she'd dealt with all the new experiences and tragedies just fine. Like a grown woman would. She'd put all those memories into a box and tucked them away, fully sorted and examined. But Tom Brady was right. It wasn't until a quiet winter's day on the Brady homestead that the boxes scattered their own contents out to be cried over. Just like the first experience she didn't want to face; leaving her mama, knowing full-well she'd likely never see her again. Addie just didn't think about how bad that would hurt later.

If Fett had lived, and they'd been married until they were old, would she have found she resented him for any of it? Or would she look at it all as she did at that moment with a dish rag in her hand, as an incredible adventure cut short by tragedy. She had no idea. Only age would tell her that.

The confusion at her circumstance hit her once more. To look back on her journey to the very moment she stood in, she found all of it such a dream. Was that what memories were like? A dream you spent the rest of your life trying to determine as to its authenticity? All Addie loved was past and gone. The future was full of dark uncertainty. The only thing she knew for sure was the bread box was nearly empty, and coffee beans needed ground. Luke's toes had ate another hole in his stockings, and Charlie couldn't hear.

Addie put her dishes away and set her yeast cakes to soaking. Tom Brady sat at the table and sharpened several knives on a whetstone. In her thoughts Addie felt like she was far away, but Tom had watched her as he worked. When she moved to the door to put on her coat, Tom spoke quietly.

"Thank you, for going easy on the boy."

Addie looked at him in surprise. She shrugged as she took Fett's coat off the peg. "He's just a boy. He has no way of knowing what you and I do."

Tom's hand stilled. The swirling of the knife on stone stopped. He looked straight at Addie. "Well, he could at least learn to keep his mouth shut."

Addie looked down at the floor and licked her lips. "I suppose you were right. When you said I really hadn't sorted it all out. I see that now."

Glancing at him, Addie saw the clean-cut of his beard and hair. His dark eyes leveled at her in understanding. He pressed his lips together for a moment, then looked back to his knives. "Addie, I'm a good ten years ahead of you, and I haven't got any of it sorted out yet. But, I guess, it doesn't hurt to cry over it sometimes, and just when you think you might have a lid on it, some kid brings up the darkest part of it all."

"Goodnight, Mr. Brady."

"Goodnight, Mrs. Loveland."

"There he is, Addie."

Addie toddled and wobbled through the high grass as it waved in the wind, clutching to her mama's hand. Clara Halstead wore a brown gingham dress that trailed behind her where it caught on the grass. Her blonde hair was rolled neatly into a bun behind her head, the late evening sun shimmering off of the strands. Addie had to look way up to see the smile on her mother's face.

Clara bent over and looked at Addie. *"He's comin', little one."*

On wobbly little legs, Addie looked where her mama pointed down the slope to the river. The blue and purple melted with the orange as the sun rested on the horizon only briefly. She could hardly see over the top of the tall grass.

Clara extended her arm to point. *"There."*

He *was* coming. Far across the river, on the opposite hill, he came swiftly. He was moving along as fast as his legs would carry him, his black mane flowing behind him, his tail straight out in his self-made wind. His black etched ears lay pressed against his neck, and the tips came close to touching the horse hair get-down looped around his neck firmly and tied in a knot at his throatlatch. The sun caught the silverwork on the bit in his mouth. The rein chains brought communion between the bit and the rawhide reins that were draped around the saddle horn. The monnel stirrups swung in time with the movement of the gray.

He hit the river and didn't slow, crossing from one bank to another in a spray of water. It took him five strides to do so, the water never reaching past his knees. The gray of his hide turned nearly black where the splashes hit high up on his neck and hindquarters.

The gray started up the slope on Addie's side of the river, the empty saddle the color of new leather, but it made no creaking or popping as the gray exploded into new speed. Clara looked down at Addie with great reassurance.

"Here he is," Clara spoke as if she had been waiting for him a great while and found relief in seeing the gray come up the slope.

Clara moved around behind Addie, but she placed a reassuring hand on her head, pressing auburn curls to her temple. The feel of her mama's skirt billowing around her in the breeze comforted the child, as if protection enfolded her. The gray kept up his speed, until he crested the hill. He gathered underneath himself and slowed to a walk. He trained his ears forward on the woman who stood with her child, looking on in awe.

"Go on," Clara said as she softly nudged Addie forward.

Fear struck into the girl's heart at feeling her mother go from her, the safety of her skirt gone from Addie's skin where the wind brushed it against her bare arms. The gray lowered his head and walked to her, until he was just out of reach. The cricket worked in his mouth as he moved his tongue back and forth.

Tears filled little Addie's eyes as she looked at the giant that stood saddled and waiting before her. "Mama!" she cried.

She turned to look for her mother. She was there, a ways back, smiling a sad smile. Her blue eyes were filled with sympathy.

"Addie, sweet little Addie, we all go forward in uncertainty."

Then Clara turned and walked away down the slope, not turning to the sound of Addie's small voice calling for her. The sway of Clara's skirts making soft rustling sounds as she went. The sun had gone down, and only bright orange streaked the sky.

Addie turned back to the gray when she felt the warmth of his breath on her face. His dark eyes were soft and gentle as he lowered his head to look at her. The cricket played away in his mouth, the steady puffing of his breath warming the skin Addie hadn't realized was cold. She was held fast by fear, the kindness radiating from the gray not enough to help her over the mountain of uncertainty. Tipping his head, he softly smelled the scent of her skin, his breath drying the tears on little Addie's face.

"I want my mama," she cried.

The gray raised and shook his head and neck, mane flying with the movement, the rein chains singing a soft song as they jingled together. Addie cried harder.

Lowering his head before her, the flatness of his forehead level with her face, he stepped forward again. This time, through her tears, little Addie didn't move away. Instead, she lay her face against the gray's, the feel of his soft, warm hair caressing her cheek. The tears melted into the fibers of his coat.

Addie Loveland woke with a great shudder. She lay in bed on her back, Molly pressed tightly to her, the dog's eyes bright with an innate knowledge, as if she well knew where Addie had been.

The tears on Addie's face were dry, simply crusted streaks that flowed out of her eyes and down her temples into her hair. It was few the times she'd woke up after crying, not during.

"I want my mama," she whispered.

Addie took the handful of forks and turned to face Charlie. She smiled at him with the utmost confidence, then she held out the forks. With great uncertainty, he looked from the forks to Addie's face. She kept up her smile and nodded.

He'd already put the mugs on the table, in a somewhat haphazard manner, but each of the Bradys had a mug to use during supper. Charlie furrowed his brow before taking the forks from Addie. She had engaged him in doing simple things, things she showed him all day, things he could do all by himself. He didn't need anyone to help him with them, but it gave him a feeling of belonging in the family, even if in a small way.

He, too, could help out.

And he did so, with trepidation, but as the days went by, it was nothing for him to set the table in his own way, carry folded clothes up the loft ladder, feed scraps to Molly, despite the barrage of face licking he got for doing so. Each afternoon, Addie sat in the chair by the window and spoke to Charlie, pressing his tiny hand firmly to her throat. She'd take the tintype of his mother off the shelf and show it to him, repeating over and over, "Mama".

Charlie was completely engaged now. He rose knowing the purpose of his day was to learn everything he could, to watch and be inspired. He spent his time at the meal table watching everything his father and brothers did. He couldn't quite master the fork yet, the spoon being easier for him to scoop with, but he tried to use something besides his fingers.

One evening when Tom came in from chores, he took Charlie into the sitting room and sat with him on his lap. Charlie looked at him in great expectancy. Tom was so amused by the expression on Charlie's face he chuckled, then asked, "Just what are you waiting for?"

A small hand reached out and pressed against the side of Tom's neck, the look of expectancy turning to wonder. His father could make the vibrations, too. Tom was taken by surprise, not having any idea what the action was founded in. When he spoke more, Charlie also pressed his free hand to Tom's throat. He was completely fascinated by the same feeling that came from his father as it did from Addie.

Addie watched from back in the kitchen, a soft twitch at the corner of her mouth to see it. Charlie held his father's attention, his gaze, his joy. The laughter that rumbled out of Tom Brady's chest was an unfamiliar sound to all in a sorrowing house. But to behold a son he thought he had lost long before he'd gained, woke a piece of Tom that had given up when Edith died. Granted she'd been given no choice and Tom had. It was far easier to lay his heart in the ground next to her than fight.

Fighting took strength he just didn't have.

For Addie, it gave her hope life could come back around. It would never be what it was, but it could in some way take a livable shape.

The next day, the sun shone down bright and promising. By ten in the morning, drops of melting snow dripped steadily off the eaves of the main house. The frozen crust on the top of the snow went from nearly unbreakable to soft and heavy. Little birds skittered and fluttered around, landing on the corral fences, fluffing their feathers repeatedly, chirping out gay salutations to a waking world.

Charlie was captivated.

He stood like a statue on his chair at the window, watching blissfully. By eleven, Addie relented and bundled him up and turned him loose on the porch. Within minutes he was knee deep in rotting snow. While Addie sighed at herself for having let him do it, she watched with a smile as he threw handfuls of snow into the air.

When Tom and the boys came in for dinner, their voices rang with a note of excitement. Luke said he saw a bare strip of ground up on a ridge above the meadows. While it wasn't much and certainly not a spring thaw, it gave the body hope for one.

The boys chattered away through the noon meal. Tom Brady ate his dinner in silence, watching his sons. Addie didn't sit down to eat, but rather started another round of laundry water.

"I wish we could make a sled run off the big hill. That way when it comes back in and freezes up, we'll have a real fast one," Andrew plotted out.

"Yeah! We could get the toboggan up it, then I could drag you with a rope down, so we don't leave prints in the track," Luke contributed.

"We could take your brown horse up there to pull it down."

"Nah. Take one of the work horses. They pull it faster," Luke reasoned. "We'd just leave the harness on and dally up to that. I'll just jump up on Fred when we're done with the feedin'."

Addie turned to the boys. "They have names?"

Frankie spoke through a mouth full of food, "Yep. Fred and Freddie."

Addie furrowed her brow. "Fred and Freddie?"

"Uh huh," Andrew answered.

"We may not be a creative outfit, but we see everyone gets named proper," Tom Brady explained.

"I see."

"Can we, Pa? Take Fred and make a run?" Luke requested.

Tom Brady pursed his lips together as he set his coffee down. He thought a moment, then answered, "Well, that team will be tired after a day of feedin'."

"We won't need him but for a minute. Then we'll bring him right back," Luke proposed.

"When will you even have time to go tobogganing?" Tom reasoned.

Luke looked at Andrew. "Well, tomorrow. We quit early on Sunday."

Tom Brady sighed deeply. "Alright. We get the feeding done, and if Fred isn't over-tired, you can make your sled run."

The boys, who were serious as they waited for their father's decision, broke into grins and returned to their meal. Tom Brady looked at them with a particular light in his eyes, perhaps a light that suggested a memory of his own boyhood.

Addie lifted a bucket full of water and poured it into the big pot to heat. She used her apron to pad the metal handle. As she set the bucket back down onto the workbench, Addie wiped the sweat from her brow with the back of her hand.

"Do Texans know what a toboggan is?" Tom Brady's voice came.

Addie looked at him. "Well, I guess there isn't much call for one in Texas."

"You ever been on one?"

Addie put a hand on the well-worn fabric of the dress covering her hip. "No."

Tom Brady stood and gathered up his dishes. "I 'xpect you best try, 'fore you go back to Texas. That way you can say you got some enjoyment out of this winter."

Tom put his dishes on the worktable, then turned to his sons. "You boys come along after you clear the table."

Addie watched as the boys finished eating what was on their plates, then rose to start picking up plates and mugs. They left the dutch and what remained of its contents, but the rest they stacked neatly. Tom Brady had put on his winter gear and left the house, the boys followed not long after.

After the door closed behind Frankie, the last to wander out, Addie looked to little Charlie who watched her confused expression. "What just happened?"

The next afternoon's sun was bright and clear. The icicles that hung down from the house let off steady drips of water that turned into pools beneath them, that by nightfall would be ice slicks. The intensity of the sun's rays reflected off the snow and brought about squinting.

The boys were near uncontrollable. They had taken time to feed double to the farthest meadow the day previous, just so they could have the entire afternoon to enjoy their tobogganing. Tom Brady had sent the boys on to feed the first meadow alone that morning, and he rode out on a saddle horse to check the bunch they wouldn't be feeding.

By the time he rode back over the three meadows, the boys had finished the first round and were loading for the second. Tom hobbled and left the red filly at the hay stack to keep herself occupied cleaning up scraps. Then they headed out to finish up with the second meadow.

Meanwhile, Addie fixed a good meal to help fuel the boys who would no doubt need the energy. She planned on a stew for supper, but for dinner she made a ham and boiled potatoes. She rolled out cookies and cut them with a biscuit cutter. The house was filled full of a beautiful mixture of meat and sugar. The smell greeted the hungry with cheerfulness.

When the men returned, boastful and light of spirit, Addie had the meal set out for them. It brought a smile to her lips to watch them, so lively and full of excitement brought on by the prospect of the afternoon's fun.

When he'd finished, Tom Brady asked, "Are you ready, Mrs. Loveland?"

She looked over at him, where he sat at the head of the table, and said, "I don't think I'll be going. You boys will have enough fun without me tagging along."

Tom leaned back in his chair. "Well, I think you best come along. Might be you have some fun."

Addie rose from her place at the table and gathered up dishes. "I think I'll have plenty of fun here keeping ahead of things."

"Aw, come on, Addie." Luke groaned.

She set down a plate and looked at him. "Don't you, 'Aw come on Addie' me, boy."

"Come with us," Frankie added.

Tom Brady leaned forward and watched her from where his head rested in his hand.

Andrew spoke up, "Leave her alone, fellas."

Addie turned to look at him with a pleasant expression. "Why, thank.."

Andrew cut her short. "She can't help it she's just a scared girl. What else is a girl supposed to be? Chicken. That's what all of 'em are."

Addie's pleasant expression turned to one of indignation. "What?"

"Chickens. Feather fluffin' chickens." Andrew's eyes had an ornery glint as he stabbed another piece of ham from his plate. Just before he put it in his mouth, he said, "Bok, bok, bok."

Frankie giggled behind his hand.

"Chickens?" Addie answered incredulously.

"Yep," Andrew drawled out. "Chickens."

She glanced to Tom Brady who watched her with a raised brow, as if to ask if Andrew was right. His eyes held a light in them that twinkled with something akin to boyhood mischief.

Putting her hands on her hips, she leveled a gaze at Tom. "I am not a chicken. I have things to do!"

"Of course, Mrs. Loveland."

"Bok, bok," came the low reply from Andrew who looked down at his plate.

Frankie giggled harder behind that little hand. Luke joined Andrew in his goading with chicken clucking of his own.

"Luke!" Addie cried with surprise.

Tom Brady lowered his hand from his chin and began to gather up his dishes. "Alright boys, that's enough. Let Mrs. Loveland be." He stood and looked at Andrew with a steady eye. "We need not pester her. And, we don't need to state the obvious that there is poultry among us."

Indignation again flared in Addie's eyes as she heard his final declaration. "Poultry! Chicken! Are we talking farm animals or what you'd like for supper? I've never been chicken in my life!"

Shrugging with exaggeration, Tom replied, "Well, I guess you'll have to prove it."

Addie set down the dishes she was holding and marched to the door. She snatched her coat from a peg, then turned to glare at the room full of boys. When she looked at Tom, she raised her chin and shot him a piercing look, then she pulled the latch on the door and walked out.

The boys all collectively shoved and rushed to the windows to watch her go, Tom holding little Charlie up so he could see too. Addie walked down to the dugout, the sun shining brightly off her auburn hair.

"Alright, boys. Get your gear on," Tom commanded.

In a burst of energy the boys scrambled to get ready.

By the time the boys were ready, Tom Brady had the team hooked again to the sleigh after he'd given them time to eat and rest in stalls.

Luke divvied up gloves and hats so Addie could have mittens and a stocking hat, then dressed Charlie warmly. The boys stoked the kitchen fire and left the house to see Tom just emerging with the sleigh. Before Andrew stepped off the porch, he went back into the house and retrieved a little canvas sack from under the workbench and filled it with fresh cookies. Then he headed out to the sleigh.

Tom took Charlie from Luke and settled him on a comfortable seating of loose hay. When the other three had settled themselves in, the toboggan riding awkwardly on the back, Tom set the team to motion, rounding up the incline to the dugout. Stopping just beyond the porch, the boys hollered out impatiently.

Addie opened the door to the dugout and stepped out. The passengers of the sleigh fell silent. Where she had been wearing a worn and torn, faded and tired dress before, Addie now stood before the Brady menfolk wearing.... pants. They were a simple canvas work pant, big and baggy to allow for room to work freely, simple pockets on the front of the leg, but they completely changed her image. They made her look smaller, more delicate. They defined her legs and hips to a point she could have been Tom Brady's fifth son, no older than Luke. The biggest thing on her was her determination.

And yet, even though her skirts left a man to guessing what size of woman hid beneath, the pants took much of the guessing away and replaced it with a surge of femininity more defining than the dress had been. Addie had covered her worn-out stockings with the wool ones Tom gave her New Year's Day. She'd concealed her simple blouse with Fett's coat, and now she stood ready to step from the porch to the sleigh. She did so with ease, noting the silent stares from the boys, but she made no mention of it.

Standing behind Tom Brady at the helm, she put her shoulders back and raised a defiant look to him. His face was still, no twitching at the corners of his mouth, no changing of his eyes. Luke stood there, still clutching the hat and mittens. Looking to Luke and not catching any of his concentration, Tom reached down and pulled the hat from his grasp. Addie watched him with a raised brow. Taking the stocking cap in both

271

hands, Tom raised it up and crammed it down over Addie's head.

Her hair, caught by the cap, was pressed against her forehead and tickled her eyes. "There now. All my boys are ready to go," Tom stated.

Addie frowned. "I'm *not* wearin' a dress to play in the snow."

Tom turned serious. "Yeah, I see your point. All that sledding and speed, sure would hate for that skirt to come up over your head again."

At her murderous look, Tom tried to suppress a laugh and turned his attention back to the team and hollered out, "Up fellas, before she changes her mind!"

Fred and Freddie surged forward and set themselves into a trot back down the incline and to the road leading from the barn to the meadows. Little Charlie came forward and took hold of Addie's pant leg and looked up at her as if in question as to her true identity. She smiled down at him.

They wound up the meadow in the same tracks they used each day, the snow high on each side of the sleigh. The sun was warm, and Addie doubted it would take much for the boys to shuck coats and play in the warm sun without them. She didn't have much for shoes, just the same tired ones she used each day, so she had no alternative.

The striking white of the peaks above against the deep blue of the sky was mesmerizing. High up there, the evergreens were all that stood bare of the snow they held before the warm sun melted it over the previous few days. The air was crisp and clean, and for the first time in a long time, didn't freeze the lungs with each inhalation.

The strong horses labored to drag the sleigh through the deep snow when Tom Brady directed them off the track. They plunged and pulled with their great strength to the base of a tall hill. Addie shielded her eyes with her hand as she looked up to the top of the run Luke and Andrew carved out with the help of Fred.

"You best get to trudgin' up that hill," Tom said as he stepped off the sleigh. He unhooked the team and pulled off the rigging that allowed them to pull. He hobbled them and set them to eating what hay was on the sleigh. They were content to do so, grateful their portion of work didn't include carrying anyone up the steep slope.

Addie walked up the hill, holding one of Charlie's hands while Luke held the other. The boys used Fred to bust out a trail to the top that ran next to the sled track where he'd pulled Luke down on the toboggan. That made it easier to climb to the top of the hill. Once at the top, Addie stood and looked out over all there was to see. She looked to the east. She could make out the barn and corrals, and the meadow beyond. A hill blocked all but the roof of the main house. The country to the north was vast, empty, and a great, sharp mountain chain ran in steep and frozen crags. In that direction, the trees could not be seen easily through the snow.

To the west, towards the mountains Addie was familiar with, the meadow continued. In the bottom of the meadow, a creek meandered like a twisting snake. At the head of it was a moving mass. Dots ran on the outskirts of it, reared and played, bucked and rolled. These were Tom Brady's horses. She could make out different colors, and a few of the younger ones. The size of the bunch was impressive.

Andrew and Frankie had struggled up the slope with the toboggan, and now they stood at the top looking down the long track. Little Charlie clung still to Addie's hand as he watched them. Tom Brady now made his way up the hill on the path cut by Fred.

"Come on. All three of us can go." Andrew sat at the helm, and encouraged Frankie to sit behind him. Luke sat on the back and anchored the sled until all occupants were ready for the ride.

"Miss Addie, would you give us a shove? That way we can get goin' real fast," Luke asked.

Addie nodded and let go of Charlie's hand. Crouching, she put her hands on Luke's shoulder. "On three," she said.

The giggles of anticipation sounded. "One, two, three!" Addie shoved with all her might, then stood to watch the toboggan carrying the three Brady boys sail down the hill. The boys hollered as the sled gained speed as it went. Addie smiled at their fun, then looked back to see Tom, who finally made the top of the hill, had bent and picked Charlie up. He now stood holding his son, watching as the toboggan flew down the hill.

"It gets goin' a little," Addie said as she watched.

"Well, that's the fun of it," Tom replied.

Addie laughed as the boys up-ended at the bottom, sending arms and legs flailing in all directions. Frankie landed on Andrew and drove him head first into the wet snow. Luke's head was all that was visible where he landed on his side in the deep snow. The work horses raised their heads and looked at the struggling, laughing boys. They deemed the situation regular shenanigans and went back to eating.

Shielding her eyes, Addie looked out over the land again. "On a day like today, this country seems almost bearable."

Tom looked over at Addie. "When the spring comes, this will be a whole different place."

Addie looked back to the herd of horses at the head of the meadow. She stood there, silent, watching them. She folded her arms across her chest and sighed. "How many are there?"

Tom stepped next to her and looked in the same direction. "There's this meadow, and two more like it."

Addie looked at him in surprise. "Two more?"

Tom's brown eyes settled on her face. "Two more."

"What do you do with all of them?" she asked as she marveled at the horses.

Tom chuckled. "I can't ride all those myself, can I?"

Addie looked up at him. "Well, I assume Luke helps, but still..."

Charlie squirmed in his father's arms to better see his brothers who had collected themselves and the toboggan and were making way back to the track up the hill. Tom shifted Charlie to a better vantage point and looked again to the horses.

"Army remounts."

Addie looked sharply at him again. "What?"

Tom pointed to the horses with his chin. "Up until now, there has been no actual remount buying program. And there still isn't, but four years ago I met a Lieutenant Baldwick. When the army allocates the funds, he comes to me for horses. That isn't real regular, but what with the Indian Wars, they need more horseflesh." Tom paused a moment. "But, most of them end up on ranches, some back east."

274

Addie inhaled deeply and looked again to the horses below and to the west.

"Those that don't make the army or ranches, and the fillies that don't get chosen for broodmare stock, get shipped back east where they need horses."

Addie pursed her lips together for a moment. Then in a quiet voice she said, "Fett and I had heard of places like yours. Never dreamed I'd see one." She paused a moment, then asked, "How do you get them all started?"

"I have a crew. Same group of men come every spring in late April. We gather, we sort, then we spend the next month or so starting horses."

Tom Brady looked down the slope at the three boys coming up the hill, struggling as they laughed, pushing each other down into the white snow.

Addie looked up at Tom, who sighed. "I haven't told him just yet, but Luke gets to be part of the crew this year. When his brothers go back to school in the spring, Luke will stay home and help with the horses. "

Addie too looked down at the tall young man who hefted Frankie up on his back, then started again up the trail. Andrew drug the toboggan.

"He's near grown. Guess I best treat him like it, or one day he'll just go, and I'll live out my days wishin' I could have him back." Tom Brady's voice turned regretful, and his eyes held the memory of the feeling of total loss.

Looking down that hill, Addie was hit again with the great wealth Tom Brady had. His future was before him, climbing that hill, hers was lost in time somewhere. She looked back up the valley to the band of horses that frolicked in the afternoon sun.

What a shame. Nobody ever got what they wanted. Tom lost his wife, but gained his sons. Addie lost Fett, and gained nothing of it. Now she considered what was once Fett's dream, only to find it belonged to someone else.

"He'll be good at it. I can see," Tom glanced at Addie. "He has the makings of a horseman."

Addie smiled softly at Luke. "Yes, he will. Though I doubt Andrew will think it's fair."

Tom Brady raised his eyebrows as he looked at his son. "No, I don't think he will, either."

"Alright, Miss Addie! Your turn!" Luke yelled as he neared the top of the run.

"Oh, no. That's tempting, but it looks like work to me."

"You came all the way out here, best you try it once," Luke replied.

"I am happy to stand in the sun."

Andrew, breathing heavily, flopped the toboggan down in the sled track. He straightened the sled and looked back at Addie while he held it in place. "You can't go back to Texas without trying it once."

"He's right, Addie," Tom agreed.

"It'll be alright," Luke encouraged.

"Don't make us shame you again," Tom stated, his brown eyes serious under his brown hat.

"Shame me! Is that what you call it? Taunting a woman 'til she gives in and does what you want?"

"Yes, ma'am. It worked, didn't it? You're out here where you said you wouldn't go," Tom stated matter-of-factly.

From somewhere near the toboggan came the soft sounds of a chicken clucking. That traitorous little hand was again over Frankie's mouth. Luke merely gave Addie a discerning look.

Already her feet were starting to get numb, but Addie stepped forward towards the toboggan. Tom set Charlie down and moved to the sled. He and Andrew held it steady while Luke sat in the front.

"Where do I sit?" Addie asked as she stood watching.

"You ride on back. You land on Luke if you spill. Sound reasonable?" Tom asked.

"No. Not at all," Addie replied as she sat down behind Luke.

"Alright, then the real reason is so when the snow flies up over Luke, you get it in the face," Tom countered.

"What?" Addie shouted. As she settled her legs cross-wise in front of her, Tom's strong hands pressed down on her shoulders. Luke looked back at her grinning mercilessly. "No! Not a hard shove!"

"Alright, alright. Not a hard shove," Tom reassured as he patted her shoulder. He looked comfortingly down at Addie's stricken face. "Instead I'll give you a *really hard shove!*"

With that he pushed with all the strength his lean body contained, sending the toboggan and its riders down the slope with great speed. Addie let out a scream as the wooden sled flew down the steep incline. The wind rushed past her face into the hair concealed in the stocking cap, loosening it slightly. The tickling of the rapid decent in her belly was a feeling she hadn't felt since she was a kid, and it brought with it a surging of excitement. What snow the sled did send flying up turned to water droplets of her bare face.

The feel of all control left Addie, and just as Blue's speed had done, the toboggan reminded her of something she'd forgotten. There was a place in her soul that was free of all belonging, free of all that weighed her down and existed only for the moment. She could let that part of her soul soar with the feel of the wind, the feel of the warm sun, the feel of complete freedom to move rapidly and in an uncertain direction. Holding it all together wasn't an option, and in these circumstances, she didn't want to. She was void of the entanglements of emotion. Freedom to just be was hers.

Addie could feel them again, hear them, smell them. She closed her eyes, and saw them. They moved freely, manes flying out behind them, tails raised as they ran. The faster the sled went, the faster those horses in her soul flew. They carried her senses away until all she could feel was the movement of them beneath her. The wind in her face was combined with the wisps of mane tickling her cheeks. On and on they ran, taking her with them, horses of all colors, all sizes, a running mass moving together as one. Then she could see him, the gray...

The sled left the track as it cleared the mound of snow set at the bottom of the run to keep the toboggan from sliding way out onto the meadow. Addie and Luke were airborn for the briefest of moments, and when the sled hit the deep snow, the gray was gone. Addie saw white just before she was engulfed in it. Snow made its way down the back of her neck and into her shirt.

When she finally came to a rest, she could hear the toboggan slide on over the top of the ice crusted snow. With her face up towards the sky, Addie slowly opened her eyes. The bright blue of the heavens made her squint. The golden sun beamed down a warmth that dried the moisture on her face. Addie lay there for a time, just feeling the comfort of it. She breathed in heavily the scent of a fresh day, dry despite the snow on the ground. It was full of a promise she hadn't felt in a very long time.

"Miss Addie? Are you alright?" Luke asked in a cautious voice.

Addie didn't reply right away, not wanting to break the beauty of the moment. "I'm alright," she paused to inhale deeply. "Just look at it."

Luke looked up at what she was seeing. "That is something, isn't it?"

"Hey!" came a yell from the top of the hill. "Did you kill the housekeeper?"

Luke looked up at his father. "No, she's alright!"

"Then get her up and bring the toboggan back!" Tom hollered again.

Luke stood and held out a hand to Addie to help her up. When he'd pulled her to her feet, Addie tried to clear some of the snow from her collar.

"Well," Luke questioned, "what did you think of it?"

Addie looked over at him and smiled. "It was unlike anything I'd tried before."

"Now you can say you've had some real snow fun," Luke said proudly.

Addie laughed at his tone. "Yes, I can say that." She looked back up at the sky. "And as for You, it nearly worked. You nearly convinced me to forgive them."

She closed her eyes as Luke stared at her in utter confusion. "Forgive who?"

With her eyes closed, face tilted to the warmth of the sun, and the memory of the gray in her mind, Addie stated, "Those damn horses."

The sun was down below the mountains casting an orange glow

when Addie entered the house to make supper. The Bradys, with the exception of Charlie, rode the sleigh down to the barn to do chores. Despite the bag of cookies Andrew had thoughtfully taken along, bellies were empty and supper was much anticipated after an afternoon of expending energy.

Luke climbed up into the loft with Frankie and started to pitch hay. Andrew stayed below and helped pull the harness off of Freddie. Steam rose off the hot horses as the atmosphere turned suddenly cold with the setting of the sun.

After Luke pitched the hay, he climbed down and took up a manure fork from the post by the big double doors. As he grabbed it, he looked up towards the house and saw Addie tossing dishwater from the porch. He paused and watched her as she did so, resting his hands on the top of the fork. Even after Addie had gone back into the house, Luke stood there contemplating.

"What's the matter?" Tom Brady asked as he came out of Fred's stall. He'd caught sight of Luke standing and watching.

Luke turned to look at his father. "Nothin'. Just thinkin'."

Tom reached up to hang the harness on the peg in the post at the corner of Fred's stall. Luke now focused on his father's actions. Tom methodically hung each piece to keep it from bending or becoming entangled.

"Pa?"

"Yeah?" Tom responded without looking at Luke.

"Mrs. Loveland ..well.. she said something. Something I didn't understand."

Tom now looked over to his son who stood in the alley of the barn leaning on the manure fork. "What did she say?"

Luke shrugged. "She said it after we rode the toboggan down the hill. She said something about the sky bein' real pretty, then.... then she said somethin' else 'bout almost forgivin' horses. What do you 'spose she meant?"

Tom looked back to the harness he'd just hung. He fiddled with it as if to rearrange it, but he wasn't really accomplishing anything. Then he sighed. "Well, from what little we've seen, and what little she's told us, I think we know horses used to be a big part of her life. And now, for whatever reason, she has chosen to shut them out."

"That doesn't make sense. Can't get anything done without 'em," Luke stated.

Tom nodded his agreement. "That's so. But, maybe they're all tangled up with what's hurtin' her on the inside. And, whether or not she chooses to admit it, they are more important than she knows."

"How do you mean?"

Tom wandered to the big double doors and looked up at the house where lamplight now burned. "Maybe God wasn't preparing her man Fett for a lifetime with horses, but maybe it was Addie He was teaching with a purpose."

"Teaching for what purpose?" Luke asked, startled.

"I guess she'll never know the intended purpose if she doesn't forgive them." Tom then turned and walked back into the barn.

Tom opened the bread box on the workbench. Within the wooden container were several loaves of bread. Tom took out one. In the soft light of the lantern he unwrapped the bread from the cheesecloth it was enshrouded in and sliced a piece. Then he replaced everything.

He turned to Charlie, who sat atop the eating table, and walked to him with the slice of bread held out. Charlie didn't notice for a moment, he was rubbing his eyes so hard in an attempt to get the sleep from them. The boy no longer fussed at night, but, as he had that morning, rose early, just before Tom's normal get-up time to ask for something to fill his belly. And, now instead of crying incessantly, he softly woke Tom with a nudge, then would take his hand and lead him to the bread box.

The days of a mug of milk passed with the severity of winter and the drying up of the milk cow, but Charlie was perfectly happy to eat a slice of soft bread. Somewhere along the lines, Charlie realized he could make his needs understood. Tom thought back to the horrible nights they'd passed together and then looked at the little child who sat quietly eating a slice of bread.

Charlie was inside that shell, working his way out.

Tom moved in the chill of the dark air and stoked the kitchen fire. As the embers glowed brightly from the breath Tom blew at them, small flames formed and reached higher for more kindling. Addie made a habit of filling the coffee pot before her departure to the dugout each night, now Tom Brady took hold of it and moved it from the workbench and placed it on the stove. Flames were now rolling out of the warm stove. Tom closed the door and listened as the fire popped softly.

He felt a tugging at his arm.

Charlie stood there, holding on to the sleeve of his nightshirt. His bright brown eyes were large and expectant as he tugged. "What little man? More bread?" Tom asked.

Charlie mouthed something. No sound came with it, just the formation of his lips around a word that wouldn't come. *M..m..muh,* came the movements while little puffs of breath accompanied each effort. Tom shook his head in lack of understanding.

Charlie tugged harder at his sleeve. Tom took a step and Charlie moved with him, pulling him away from the kitchen fire and across the floor. They stood in the doorway of the sitting room and Tom peered into the darkness beyond.

He looked down and shook his head at Charlie. "It's dark in there, boy. I can't see anything." Again Tom shook his head. "It's dark."

Charlie let go of Tom's sleeve and disappeared into the black. "Charlie! What are you doin'?" Tom called in a hoarse whisper.

When Charlie did not reappear, Tom went back to the table and took up the lamp. When he stepped into the sitting room, he couldn't see Charlie. Then after searching the room, he found Charlie looking at him with expectancy from beneath the shelf. He was firmer in his mouthing the *m..muh* now. When Tom came to stand beside him, Charlie looked away from his father and up at something on the shelf. He looked back up at his father and reached for something he could not grasp way above his head.

"What is it you want, huh? Spoony isn't up there." Tom softly replied as he set the lamp on the desk and picked Charlie up into his

281

arms. "What is it?"

In a movement that caught Tom Brady completely unaware, so unprepared to protect his heart, Charlie took hold of Edith's picture and showed it to Tom.

M..m..muh.. m..muh...

Charlie watched as his father's face went from complete misunderstanding to stricken grief. His little brows knit together, causing great furrows in his forehead.

"Oh," said Tom in a choked voice. Tom never expected this. He'd explained it so many times, to friends and neighbors, letters back home to Edith's family, to his own. He never thought he'd have to explain it one more time, to his own son.

But now he clutched the tintype with a tiny hand and kept making the efforts to form a word he'd never heard before. A word he never knew until... Tom didn't know when. Tom shuddered and looked at the tintype.

"Mama," he whispered.

Charlie looked at him in great excitement. He'd made his father speak the word! His little face beamed despite the disturbed look on his father's. Charlie held up the tintype and looked at his father expectantly again.

"Mama," Tom again whispered, only this time clenching his jaw tightly after the word was spoken. He took the picture in his hand and peered down at her lovely face. It was taken a few days before their wedding. Tom closed his eyes.

He'd kept himself busy over the last few weeks, kept his mind on other things, let her go to the edges of his consciousness. But now here she was, looking out at him from that tintype, suppressing that all-consuming smile. And worst of all, his son was asking about her.

Charlie touched Tom's cheek with the palm of his hand. When Tom opened his eyes and looked at the boy, his expectant face had turned to sadness. Looking at him, Tom watched Charlie stretch his mouth into a rehearsed smile. It was flat and emotionless, but the boy had somehow come to understand the importance of reassurance.

Tom let out a low chuckle, one fraught with misery. "Yes, mama. Your mama." Tom looked deeply into Charlie's eyes. "Her name is Edith."

Charlie looked back down to the tintype. *M..m..muh..*

"I miss her very much, boy. Sometimes I don't think I'll make it without her," Tom whispered in Charlie's ear. Charlie wasn't looking at Tom, but at his mama, repeating the beginning sound to her name. "Other times, I know I won't."

As the tears pooled in his eyes, Tom bravely looked back down at Edith's face. "I wish you could have known your boys as they are now."

It was true. They were growing into fine young men without their mother. But she left a hole in their life void of any comfort. Tom looked over at Charlie. Something inside him stung deeply. It burned and oozed as he looked at that boy. Perhaps Edith wasn't able to know her sons as they were now, but time had been taken so that Charlie knew *something* of his mother. Even if it was only her name, which was all Addie Loveland knew anyway. A generic piece of information, but a very vital one.

It struck Tom with great force. All this time he'd assumed differently. Now he knew the truth of the matter. Addie Loveland had absolutely no intentions of taking the place of Edith Brady. Her heart lie in the ground, buried beside the man she called Fett. And come spring, Addie was headed back to Texas.

As the first of March came, the weather began to change. The gray sky laden with snow turned black, laden with rain. It poured down in warmer torrents and rotted the snow, turning it to mush. Water filtered down through the snow and pooled beneath it several inches deep. The wind blew the droplets sideways and splattered them against the windows of the main house, leaving everything with a deeply dampened feeling.

The hours of sunlight slowly lengthened, until finally it was light near to suppertime in the evening. Then, with all the assured confidence of spring, Tom Brady came into the house after early morning chores to announce to Addie the milk cow had calved during the night.

For Addie, it was like hearing God had closed the gates of heaven, and all who weren't already there couldn't go. She asked God silently to open them up again by bloating that cow. But, by afternoon, she carried Charlie to the barn through the rain and deepening mush to see the new arrival. It was just as she expected, wobbly and soft, peering at them from underneath its mama in the barn stall. It was the same red color as its mama, but the innocence shining in the calf's eyes made Addie smile some. For once, Red Beast seemed content to show off her accomplishment and chew her cud.

When the cow tired of standing, she lay down, leaving her calf to its own devices. The little creature wandered over to them on shaky legs, sniffing Charlie's little hand that Addie held out to it. When the calf spooked and turned away, Addie was able to see the calf was a little heifer.

When Charlie looked at Addie, she said very clearly, "Calf." She repeated herself many times while Charlie looked. When he looked back to the calf, he worked over the "c" formation. He struggled down out of her arms when the calf came close to the poles that made up her enclosure. He held out his hand for the calf again.

Addie looked at Red Beast and remembered the night she'd saved her and Luke from freezing to death. She reminded herself that even the things that look to be void of any good, often hold what you need to survive. That when you least expect it, the key to hope lie in unexpected places.

Just like her time with the Bradys.

When she came, Addie wasn't ready to stand by herself yet. She had no place to hide, no secret place to mourn. Not that she was done with her mourning, but she did have reasons to get up every morning. And those reasons helped her to get through a miserable winter that was now waning. It hadn't occurred to Addie until that rain started falling and the snow started melting, but spring was arriving. The snows were going, the roads would dry, and the stage would resume its trek to Texas.

Looking down at Red Beast and her calf was solid proof. Spring was coming. Addie looked to Charlie who gently touched the calf's wet nose. She helped him get the attention of his father, now he could go on and continue to grow with his father's guidance. But would it be that easy? Would she just walk away without looking back? Yes, she felt she could. She had no ties here. She had no reasons to stay. And, Tom Brady would be just as glad to see her go as she would be to leave.

It was as if the whole world felt it. That night at the supper table, the boys must have seen something glowing inside Addie, for they were contemplative and quiet. Until Andrew spoke up. His father had been talking about the horses, and the weather. It was a comment out of the air, with no real root or purpose, and he spoke it mostly to himself.

"What's so great about Texas?"

The silence that ensued around the table left an opening for the pattering of rain on the house to fill. It was like a clock, slowly pattering away the moments until the road was clear. A steady reminder life was waking, and soon Addie would be free to go.

"Well, it's my home," Addie replied softly. "All my heart is there. My family, my memories, what's left of my life."

Looking to Tom for some kind of reinforcement on a difficult subject, she found him watching her from below his brows, his dark eyes full of something she couldn't read. He licked his lips and looked back down at his plate. He lowered the hand that hovered between plate and mouth, then stabbed at another piece of stew meat.

That one comment changed the mood of everything. Addie broke from her tasks each day to look out the window in silent anticipation, waiting, watching, hoping. That rain just kept on coming, to a point where on a Friday, Tom and the boys couldn't get the feed sleigh to the meadows. The team bogged down in slush and mud, and the sleigh would sink with just the weight of the boys. So, the Brady men drove the horses to the stacks in the meadows.

Mares were getting heavy with foal. Soon the ground would be bare, and the meadow would waken. The creek that wound like a snake through the bottom of the meadow was swollen and eroded all in its path, the water on its way in a hurry to places unknown. It filled the reservoirs out on the desert, pooled under sagebrush, and swept away the steep sides of washes.

Tom Brady watched it all in wonder. It was as if the earth was feeling the rage of torment within him and reflected it back in a rush of angry torrents, taking its own sorrow out on the land in a way that hadn't happened in all the years he'd lived there.

Tom caught Addie at the window many times, but he spoke nothing. He could feel the change in her. He watched her look at the sky, and feel the rejoicing in each drop. Despite the tattered dresses she wore, Addie looked new again.

After breakfast one morning on a particularly wet day, the boys drug about getting out of the house, reluctant to spend a soggy day feeding horses. She herself had to start her day at the milk cow and had gotten plenty wet in the process of getting to and from the barn.

She'd used that calf to her advantage. Once Red Beast was in the milking stall, Addie put the calf on its mama's off side, and knowing the old sow wouldn't kick her own baby, went to milking the near side. Addie was right. That old beast stood like a champion and gave Addie no guff, let down her milk happily, and didn't take the risk of kicking her own baby in an effort to best Addie.

She'd come out of that stall smiling, surprising Tom Brady who was barely leading the work team out of stalls. Red Beast ambled back down to her own stall home past him, looking back to make sure her babe followed. Tom looked to Addie to see if she had just given up getting anything from the old fart. She was already covering her head with a scarf and heading out into the rain. The milk could not be kept for the first few days, as it was full of colostrum and would taste very poor, but the cow had to be milked for comfort and supply's sake.

Once in the house, Addie set to making breakfast. It was then the boys made their appearances one by one, and yawned and stretched into a new day at the table. Tom returned to the house, silent and thoughtful, but Addie didn't make it any of her affair to ask over what. When the first meal of the day was over, Tom sent the boys out to the barn to begin harnessing the team while he finished his coffee.

Taking his mug to the window, Tom looked out into the gray morning. The rain drizzled down from the sky in steady fashion. He held the curtain aside for a long while staring out into it. Then in a peculiar voice slowly said, "Look at the weather change. Our weather is changin'. Just look at that weather change."

Addie stopped. She looked at him from where she stood over the lamp refilling it. She set the oil can down on the workbench and stared at him. In her mind she went back to the last time she'd heard such an ominous statement and saw Fett's face. Fett had predicted it absolutely the night the first storm of winter blew in and trapped her on the Brady homestead. It was a dream, wasn't it?

Tom looked back at her. He said no more.

As he set to gathering up his coat, gloves, and hat, Addie went back to work. It took him what seemed like an hour to put all of his things on, and Addie looked at him several times to see if he were having problems. All seemed well. Then, just before he pulled on the door handle in his hand, he said, "Addie."

Her hands stilled at their work as she looked up at him. His brown eyes were full of something she couldn't read as they looked at her from under his stained brown hat. His mouth was drawn into a grim line, the set of his jaw ticking as he looked at her, then down to Charlie who played with Spoony.

He swallowed hard before he said, "There's a trunk at the foot of my bed. In it might be some things of use to you."

Addie's heart contracted and squeezed all the blood out of itself at once. She looked at him and shook her head. "No."

Tom looked down at the floor, then back at her. He took a deep breath before continuing. "She's gone, Addie. She don't need them anymore."

"No," she stated again.

"Perhaps you should look at yourself, Addie. I think you've passed the rags of mourning." With that he was gone, out the door into the light drizzle of the day, the steady and constant melting of the snows.

Addie just stood in silence.

She looked over to Charlie. He was playing so contentedly, she doubted he saw anything transpire between herself and his father. She had no intentions of ever going through that trunk, but his words bothered her.

The day progressed, and as the hours of quiet passed with only the sound of the rain, his words repeated themselves to her over and over. What he'd meant by them, she couldn't say. But, the truth was, Addie hadn't seen herself in some time. She had no desire to look now. What Tom Brady picked to make a point of was beyond her.

You've passed the rags of mourning.

The rain paused a bit several days later. The water still ran over the surface, and the mud grew deeper each day as the ground thawed. The sound of pattering rain on the roof was replaced by the wind coming round the corner of the buildings. The warmth it carried only hastened the melting snow and thickening sludge.

The house was damp, and that made it feel cold, but the start of a roaring fire did little to dry the air. Everything just felt wet. The ground held huge strips of bare earth, but the great drifts formed in the winds of winter still held strong. Addie watched from the confines of the house with impatience. She went about her chores with irritation.

Just when she thought nothing would break the monotony, she heard a long silent voice call out from the desert, then the happy bark of Molly who wagged her tail as she stared at the door.

"Hello the house!"

Going to the window, she pulled back the curtains to peer outside. "Roy!"

Dropping the curtain, her hand immediately went to her hair in self-conscious effort to not appear tired. It occurred to Addie she hadn't bothered to look in the mirror before. Why would she worry about her looks now? She wiped her face with her apron and smoothed out her skirt. Charlie watched her in curiosity, then followed her to the door.

Before she opened it, she ran a hand over the worn-out dress she wore, wiping off flour that clung to the fabric. It was a mess of threadbare seams and torn hem, but she had nothing else and no time to put it on anyway. She smiled at Charlie, then opened the door.

He rode in on a little roan, whose ears pricked forward at the opening of the door. While it was not a tall horse, he was wide in stature. For a fleeting moment Addie pictured the gray. The wind teased the hairs at the back of her neck that had come loose from her bun. It tickled her skin as it prickled with the cold of the swift-moving air.

Roy rode the roan to the porch and looked straight at Addie. "Good Lord girl, if you aren't a sight for sore eyes." With that he swung down from his horse, his eyes never leaving Addie.

"Hello, Roy!" Addie exclaimed as she folded her arms across her chest self-consciously. Tom Brady's words from several days before echoed in her mind. She tucked a wayward strand of hair behind an ear.

Roy draped his get-down over the railing of the porch, then reached back into his saddle bag. He pulled out a bundle of what appeared to be newspapers and a few catalogs held together with string. He stood before Addie and smiled down at her. He took her in and then smiled broader.

"Where's those Brady boys? Don't they have sense enough to leave one among them behind as to watch over the only woman they got?" Roy asked in his strong voice.

"Well, they left little Charlie," Addie answered as she looked down to the boy who clung to her skirt. He peeked up at Roy, then at Addie.

"Ah, I see. Leave the one you are most likely to fall in love with. Then you won't stray too far. Clever." Roy grinned as he spoke.

Addie flushed some as she looked up at him. He was very tall, and it seemed strange after the months gone by to look at a new face. Roy removed his hat in one motion and held it close to his belt. His blue eyes sparkled and his short graying hair had recently been cut.

"You look good, Addie," he said in a soft tone.

"Well, maybe not good," she returned in uncertainty.

Roy's smile returned. "Any of those young cowboys come to pay Tom a random visit yet?"

Addie couldn't help but laugh softly. "No. No, I don't believe so."

Roy raised his eyebrows quickly and lowered them again. "I guess Tom's just lucky the mud's so deep."

"Speakin' of Tom, he's out in the meadows, if you are lookin' for him."

Roy shook his head. "Not just yet. I'll see him 'fore I go, but not just yet. I'm afraid I come bearing some very bad news."

"Oh, dear. What is it?" Addie asked with great concern.

Roy was very serious as he said, "The schoolmarm has declared lessons will resume March twentieth, seven-thirty in the morning."

"How dreadful. The boys will collapse in weeping and sorrow," Addie said as somberly as she could. "Would you like to come in? I can put some coffee on."

"Addie, I haven't thought of anything but your coffee since I saddled up."

Addie took hold of Charlie's hand and led him into the house. Once there, he clung to her skirt and watched Roy with something close to distrust. Roy tried to make friends as he took off his coat and hung it on the peg, but the boy just buried himself deeper into the folds of Addie's skirt. She kept up with putting the coffee makings together.

Roy took up the bundle of reading material and put it in the middle of the table. It caught Charlie's eye and he tried to decipher what the bundle was from his comfort zone inside the fabric of Addie's skirt. When Addie turned to offer Roy a seat at the table, Charlie followed her with Spoony clutched in one hand, Addie's skirt in the other. When Roy again smiled at him from where he sat at the table, Charlie didn't shy away.

"Been too long. The boy's all but forgot me." Roy reached to the center of the table and took hold of a cookie off a plate that sat there. He held it out to Charlie who reluctantly took it. After he had done so, Addie set him on the bench next to where she intended to sit. The water in the coffee pot started to hiss as the heat of the stove crept into it.

"How was the winter, Addie?"

Addie sighed. "Well, it's close to over now."

"Yeah, what's left of the snow will be gone 'fore too long. Once that happens, why, I guess we can deal with the tempers of spring pretty easy."

"Sometimes I think back and I can't believe it's almost over." Addie paused a moment to look down at Charlie. "When do you think the stage will run again?"

"That's hard to say. With all the mud this rain and melting snow is causing, could be awhile."

"What about you? How did your winter pass?"

"Oh, well enough I suppose. I ended up having to hire a couple guys to help me with the feedin', but all in all that just gave me somebody to visit with all through the slow months. My stock came through alright, didn't lose but a few to the cold, and they were fairly old anyway. I guess I'm pretty lucky."

Charlie was still eyeing the bundle of reading material and when he'd finished his cookie, all of his concentration went there. Smiling softly, Roy untied the string and placed a thick catalog on the table in front of Charlie. His eyes lit with astonishment.

"That boy is a changed little man. Even from when I saw him at Christmas," Roy said softly.

Addie opened the catalog for Charlie and pointed to a picture of a coffee grinder. After that Charlie entertained his own curiosities with the pictures in the book.

"He really is intelligent. He just couldn't get it out."

The coffee water on the stove began to sputter as it boiled, so Addie rose and finished making the hot drink. She placed three mugs on the table, one for Roy, a milk mug for Charlie, and one for herself. She poured out the milk and coffee, then handed the cookie plate to Roy. She retrieved the sugar and a little cream, as an extra treat, then sat down to enjoy her own coffee.

"The ol' cow must be back in working order," Roy remarked.

Addie let out a low laugh. "Yes, she calved. I near cried when Tom came in and said she had. That is the meanest old beast I ever had to milk."

Roy began to laugh. "You know, that's the same cow he had when

Edith was alive. But, he never made Edith milk her 'cause she was so mean. Edith plain refused."

"I don't blame her!" Adie cried out.

"I think it's great you've taken all the hard things Tom has thrown at you and put it right back in his face. He needed that. Somebody to come along and make the world for somebody else, instead of himself."

"It hasn't been easy to do," Addie replied.

"No, I'm sure not. You carry plenty of courage, Addie Loveland."

Addie was quiet a moment, then start to laugh. "You know, when the boys all went to the New Year's dance, Tom got himself all cleaned up, trimmed up, and stood here in this kitchen and waited for me to tell him I thought he was handsome. Tried to encourage me along with, 'I like your biscuits.' Like that compliment would just give me the world."

Roy laughed out loud. "Yeah, he got what he deserved too, from that woman."

Addie looked at Roy, amused. "How so?"

"Well, he gets there, all prettied up, and sure 'nough, here comes the country's most available woman. Lookin' real smart herself, with a tailor-made dress, hair fancy too." At this point Roy put his hands behind his head to emphasize the audacity of her hair, "Her hair was all, twisted and knotty at the back of her neck. Literally scoping out the prospects with her sister in tow. Pointing! Pointing out the available men!" Roy exaggeratedly pointed across the kitchen at an imaginary man.

Addie giggled.

"Then she lights on Tom. And I am not joshing when I say, she nods her head in approval. Comes over like he's a horse at auction or something." A twinkle came to Roy's eye at that point. "Now, you can tell she's made an impression on ol' Tommy. He clearly likes what he's seein'. And in truth she's," Roy stopped himself as he brought his hands, both cupped to his chest. He cleared his throat. Addie laughed harder.

Roy looked at her from the corner of his eye and grinned. "I apologize. I've spent the winter in the company of men."

Addie just laughed harder at his embarrassment.

"Anyway," he began again, "she is a beautiful woman, built to catch the fancy of the opposite gender. And she clearly has caught Tom's fancy. So over they come, the Gibbses, and Miss Mildred Blanchard. They introduce themselves, and all Mildred can do is give Tom the look-over.

"They get out on the floor to dance, and you can just see his face turning from agreement to complete mortification. Now, I don't know what she said to him, but he didn't even bother finishing the dance. He left her right there in the middle of the floor!"

Addie tipped her head back and laughed. "Oh, that was worth the chores. He gave me such a hard time about not losing his team, not burning down the house. So I got even with him and told him I was gonna eat all his sugar and drink all his coffee. Then to really make him squirm, I told him I was gonna sleep in his bed."

Roy really cut loose then with a laugh that shook the beams of the rafters as it left his big frame. "Addie, I don't know how God picked you, but He sent the only person in the world big enough to best 'im."

"Was he always this cantankerous, or was it just a treat he saved for me?"

Roy slowed in his laughing fit. His face became somber and he looked thoughtful. "Well, he's always seen things his own way, but he was always real good to Edith. She wasn't like you, she was very meek. I think she got away with being treated like a queen 'cause he brought her out here to a life she didn't necessarily want to live so far from her folks. So, Tom worked hard to make it up to her. There were times she struggled out here."

Addie took a sip of coffee. "I see. I can understand her feelings. This is a long way from family." Then she looked straight at Roy. "And what about you? What is your story?"

Roy smiled softly at Addie as she rested her head in her hand. "I'm every bit as cantankerous. I just go about it in a nicer fashion."

Addie chuckled. "The beautiful Miss Blanchard held no fascination for you?"

Roy smiled and looked down into his coffee cup. "No. I've met plenty of Miss Blanchards in my life. Very lovely to look at, then they open their know-it-all mouth. I can spot 'em a mile away. And usually the first clue is they aren't young girls anymore, and still not married.

"Now take you, for instance. Addie, if I weren't twice your age, I'd think about making you my girl." He leaned forward on his elbows and gave her a flashing smile. "My age and the fact I think Charlie here would chew my legs off at the ankles if I tried to take you away!" he finished with sarcasm.

Addie laughed and looked down at Charlie who was completely immersed in the catalog. She smoothed his hair down and he looked up at her with brown eyes.

"What a difference a woman makes…," Roy said quietly as he watched. Then he cleared his throat and looked at Addie. "You know, I had a very special reason for coming here today."

"What?" Addie asked.

Roy smiled and replied, "I really came to bring you something." He reached into his shirt pocket and pulled out a folded envelope. With a grin, he unfolded it and handed it to an astonished Addie.

"One of my hands rode into Charleston a few days ago, and he brought back this."

Taking hold of the envelope, she looked at the writing on the front of it. While she had no idea what it said, she recognized her father's handwriting. She smoothed the paper between her thumbs. An emotion in her heart took all the power from her. She couldn't read it, but she could clearly hear his voice as he spoke to her.

"Would you like me to read it to you?" Roy asked in an understanding voice.

She wasn't ready to turn loose of the envelope. They had touched it, held it just the way she was. Her mother was next to her father as he wrote it, watching as his hand made marks on paper that would carry a message to her, words that her father had put together in his mind.

With tear-filled eyes, she nodded, and handed it back to Roy. He took gentle hold of it and exercised care as he pulled up the back flap. Casting her a reassuring smile, he pulled out two slips of paper.

Lightly clearing his voice, Roy held up the letter. "They addressed this to me, but they must have known I could get this to you as the heading says your name."

Dear Addie ~

With months of no word, we were grateful to get a letter. Mr. Albert has told you are safe, but he didn't say as to how you are making out. We fear not well. We got a letter from way out west somewheres, but it was so rane-ruint we culdn't make out what it said. Holding it made your Ma's hart fearful. We don't know what bad thing has hapend, but we will pray. Take hart girl, your home is here. Return to us. If you canot- send word. We are hopeful Mr. Albert is a man of good charcter and will help you if you are in need. We know you work now, and that can only mean Fett is no longer able to care for you. We pray tragdy has not come to him. We fear the worst. Our love comes to you, where ever you are, and wait to hear from you. At best now we pray. You have our love and comfort, and until we can hold you, we pray. We will rite agin, we fear this leter may not find you before you move on. With love from your famly~

Your Pa

Sitting there, Addie made no comment. Quiet tears fell down her face. *They knew.* She had no idea what the rain-ruined letter might have said, nor where it might have come from. Perhaps the family she'd stayed with? They knew where she came from, so it would have been easy for them to send word. They'd been so apprehensive about her taking work with a man she'd never met. Might have been they sent word to tell her folks she was possibly in danger.

Roy looked across the table at her. "Sounds like they already have a pretty good idea what's going on in your life. They're ready for you to come home." He looked over at Charlie. "Will you be ready to go?" he asked with doubt.

Addie was about to assure him she was when the door to the house opened and Frankie stood there, cheeks flushed from his run up from the

295

barn. His face sought Roy, and when he found him sitting at the table, he smiled. "Roy!"

Addie reached for her letter and envelope, then tucked them safely into her apron pocket.

"Hey, boy!" Roy said boisterously as he stood and untangled his large frame from the bench seat. He took hold of Frankie and lifted him high off the ground with a bear hug. "Ah!" he growled as he pretended to crush Frankie.

Frankie squealed with delight.

"Where's the rest of 'em?" Roy asked as he set the wobbly, giggling boy back on his feet.

"Comin'. Unhitching the team. Whatcha doin'?"

"I figured I hadn't seen the Bradys in a long while, and I'd better come see what you was up to," Roy answered.

Frankie's eyes set on the opened bundle of reading material. He made a dash for it, but Roy stopped him. "Hold on now. Best you let your pa see that before you scatter it all about the house, and he can't get articles finished for the newspaper being lost."

"Here, Frank. Have a cookie instead." Addie held out the plate to him and his face lit with just as much delight at the cookie as it did at the bundle. He took one and relished a big bite.

"I better get supper going. The boys are back early, but I'm sure Mr. Brady will want you to stay," Addie stated.

"Well, I might wander on down to the barn and see if I can't make myself useful. That way Tom will feel I earned it." Roy gave Addie a wink as he put his coat back on. Closing the door behind him, Addie was left to wonder why he doubted her readiness to leave.

The break in storms passed, and the wind and rain resumed. It pounded and howled, taking very little reprieve between them. The creek in the meadow was slowly seeping out across the flat, and the ground could hold no more. Even the little spring that ran from the rocks up behind the house was full, the melting snows and constant rain filling it up with runoff. The bridge was now just a log in the middle of a pond, floating there, it seemed, although it was anchored and not going anywhere. The spring had to be crossed up behind the house in order to get to the barn. Tom placed a narrow board across it for a crossing spot.

For Addie, it was a long walk from the dugout each morning to the barn for milking chores, and once there, it was treacherous navigating the deep mud. Water pooled on top of the ground when it could no longer take in the moisture, and it was deceiving which step would be firmer, or plunge the leg deep into the mud. The early light of day made it harder to pick her way.

The cow and her calf never left the barn in the storms, and the boys had to work hard to keep the stalls cleaned. The alley had to be mucked as well, since the animals tracked in as much filth as they dropped. It seemed the land would never again be dry, and the brown color of the desert turned to a gray as it took on more and more water.

Addie turned Red Beast out after milking and followed her back to her stall with the calf in tow. She closed the pole gate that kept the cow in, but the calf was able to slip underneath and wander the alleyway during the day. For the moment, however, the little red heifer was content to lay in the dry hay in the corner of her mama's stall.

Covering her head with a shawl, Addie looked up at the sky before she set out. She'd covered the milk bucket with a cloth to keep some of the rain out, but as she looked at the sky, she saw it had all but stopped raining, and the wind had not yet wakened for the day. Picking up her bucket, Addie stepped out into the saturated mess, trying to pick her way carefully.

The mud sucked at her shoes as she went, pulling her ever deeper into the mire. Each step was worse, and she toddled some, nearly tipping her bucket. She righted herself and took another step. Her right foot plunged deep into a puddle, then as she extended her knee, into a bottomless muck. Addie tried to pull her foot back, and as she did, she felt water and mud seeping into her shoe. The wool stockings Tom Brady gave her were now soaked nearly up to the knee. She held her skirt up high, but it did no good, the entire hem was wet and caked with mud.

It took Addie a moment to steady herself, the full milk bucket in her right hand offsetting her balance. At all cost, the milk must be saved. It was a precious commodity, not to be tossed away for the sake of a tattered dress. Her foot was stuck. She pulled and pulled, but all it did was pry her shoe closer to off than on.

"Are you stuck?" came Tom Brady's questioning voice from behind her.

Addie sighed heavily and turned slightly to look at him from around the shawl that covered her head. "It seems so. Can you take the milk, please?"

Tom Brady moved to where he could reach the bucket, picking his own way very carefully. When he could reach the bucket, he came no further, but extended out a leather-gloved hand for the handle of the bucket. Addie leaned part of the way to pass off the bucket. Once Tom Brady had a hold on it, she went back to work in trying to get her foot and her shoe out together.

Losing her footing again, Addie fell forward, catching herself with her hands, but not before she dunked the front of her skirt in the mire. Even the tips of her shawl were now muddied.

"Hold on, I'm comin'," Tom Brady said as he again made his way to her cautiously.

"I don't think you want to help me now. My hands are covered in it, Mr. Brady."

When Addie looked in his direction, he stood with his hand out, his well-trimmed beard unable to hide the soft look on his face. She was surprised to see he held no mockery in his gaze as he looked at her, his brown eyes didn't twinkle with suppressed laughter at her expense.

"It's Tom, Addie."

Addie didn't take his hand right away. She didn't take hold of the solid line he was offering. Instead, she watched his face and waited for his usual countenance to make use of a laughable situation. He didn't.

She reached out a dirtied hand. Tom took hold of it and gave her a firm grasp. When she tried again to dislodge her foot, he pulled, but nothing gave. He held out his free hand to her.

"You better give me both of your hands."

"It's got my shoe. My shoe doesn't want to come," Addie said.

"Well, maybe you should let it go. There isn't much left of it anyway," Tom replied in an easy voice.

"Is spring always like this here?" Addie asked as she pulled again, Tom's strength lending to her force.

"No, I'm guessing you brought this with you."

Addie felt the mud give, and with her foot all bunched up, she pulled her shoe out with it. Tom kept hold of her hands until she'd made somewhat firm ground. He released her and looked at her from underneath his brown hat. Then he bent and picked up the milk bucket.

As he handed it to her he said, "I guess now would be a good time to look through that trunk."

With pain in her eyes, Addie said in a desolate voice, "I won't go through that trunk."

There was no clenching in Tom's jaw as he replied, "Addie, that dress won't survive the scrubbing it will take to get it clean. I'm not sure what's keeping it together now. The time has come." He gave her a moment, then in a gentler voice said, "I'm not saying you gotta throw it out, you can hold on to it."

Soft rain began to fall on Addie's upturned face as she looked at him, stricken. "I can't," she whispered. "I can't go in that room. I can't tell you why, I just can't."

"Then I'll do it for you," Tom reassured.

The rain came down faster, but still no wind blew drops into Addie's tear-filled eyes. "What would they think of us? Just goin' through memories like that. Like they didn't mean anything?"

Tom tried to smile as he said, "I doubt they'll say much about it."

Tom held the milk bucket as they picked their way through the mud and standing water to the upper bridge. Tom stood aside to let Addie cross first, then made his own way over it. When it came time to go into the cabin, he had to crowd her through the door. Once inside, he handed her the milk bucket and asked her to tend to it. He lit the lamp on the table and then disappeared down the hall.

Addie did tend the milk, and her ears listened intently for the moment Tom would come back and agree with her that the whole thing was just too much to take, that going through those clothes to give to another woman was harder than he anticipated. But when she heard his footsteps coming back up the short hall, then stop directly behind her, she turned to see he actually held fabric in his hands, and despite his coat and hat, his face didn't hold the panic-stricken look hers did.

His brown eyes searched her face as he whispered, "I think these will suit you."

She wasn't sure if he whispered because the boys were still sleeping, or if that was all the volume he could muster within himself. He waited patiently for her to take the dress from him, and when she finally did, she couldn't say anything as she looked down at the soft blue.

"Don't trudge back through that mud to the dugout. I'll go finish chores, and if you're quick about it, you can change before the boys wake up." With that, Tom turned and left the room, closing the door on her, leaving her standing there holding the crisp fabric of a dress that wasn't yet well-worn.

She set it aside, and washed her hands, carefully trying to clean the dried mud from them. She washed her face, in case mud splattered there, too. Then she turned back to the pile of clothes. She took her time unbuttoning the dress her mama had so carefully stitched, for what Addie knew was the last time. All the life and adventure she'd seen in that dress was over. The different lifetimes she'd lived in it were gone, worn into the fabric like paint on canvas. It seemed a last injustice to know its last use covered it in mud.

Addie gently folded it and lay it on the floor, with the intention of washing it anyway. It was as Tom said. She wasn't expected to throw it away, and she could keep it locked safely away in her trunk of memories.

Then she reached for the dress Tom found for her.

It was indeed a simple work dress, but it was so clean and unused. The buttons down the front were a dark brown, and they were small and functional, but something in the color of that dress caught Addie in the soul. It was the color of Texas wildflowers in the spring, when life was coursing back through the earth, and time was soft and kind. That dress felt like spring to Addie, even though her soul was far from the warmth and life of it.

It was almost an agreement. To put on the dress, something dark and unfeeling inside her would have to fall away. The drab of mourning in her used brown dress would have to loosen its hold, and in that thought she remembered Tom's words.

I think you've past the rags of mourning.

He'd included soft underthings, and used but usable stockings as well. And while Edith Brady was larger than Addie only slightly, the clothes fit. Partway through the debating process she'd heard somebody stirring upstairs and in a panic hastily put the underthings and dress on.

As the boys all appeared one by one, Addie kept her back turned and her hands busy at her work to avoid their looks of undoubted surprise. She said her good mornings, and tried hard not to cry, for she knew the older boys would recognize Edith's things. She greatly feared they would judge her for attempting to take Edith's place. And then the sound she dreaded most of all came as the scrape of the door met her ears.

She refused to turn around. She avoided looks as she set out the breakfast makings. She tried to ignore the stone silence of the usually vibrant boys. She could feel their eyes moving up and down the length of her, taking in her auburn hair shining in agreement with the light blue dress.

Little Charlie was the last to wander in, rubbing sleepy eyes, padding softly in his bare feet and nightshirt. By now Tom sat in his usual place at the head of the table, sipping hot coffee, waiting for the rest of his meal and saying nothing. He lifted the boy onto his lap and held him close. When at last Charlie could see, he sat up straight and pointed a small finger in Addie's direction.

"A..a..aaa," he tried to sound her name.

"Yes," came Tom's low answer as he spoke very slowly so Charlie could see the movement of his mouth. "Addie looks very pretty."

Addie turned slightly from where she stood at the stove stirring cinnamon and sugar into the morning's mush. Tom's face was unreadable as she found he was already watching her. When their eyes met, he held hers only briefly before he looked back down into Charlie's face.

"Pretty Addie."

The weeks of mud and rain passed slowly, and the intermittent days of sun and wind began to work their magic, drying the face of the earth where rain had run in torrents and pooled in great stretches of water. The air held a subtle warmth now, not that the threat of a late snowstorm wasn't possible, but the fact was, it wouldn't last this time.

The roads were passable, and despite the deep moanings of the boys, school was to resume, a week later than originally intended. It had to be delayed a week after the mud kept the school teacher from coming up from Elko when she had planned. When she did arrive, she needed a few days to get her classroom in order. That put the start of school well into April. By then, the hint of green around the hills wasn't just something to rub eyes at. It was there, and real.

The landscape had changed drastically. The high country was still draped in white, the tops of the peaks still suffering what looked like the throes of winter. And when a heavy rainstorm passed in the night, the trees wore a fresh layer of snow in the morning. The low country, however, was freed from the heavy blanket it wore through the winter. The rushing gullies and watersheds still ran, but the great force of it was over.

The vibrancy of a rough country going from brown to white, then the ebbing of the gray into slow coming green was mesmerizing. For Addie, it was like waking each day in a whole new world. What she had grown accustomed to over the winter was now gone. She could make out landmarks, hear the soft calling of the meadowlarks, and see the robins about their work.

Molly spent her time outside. She never strayed far from Addie, but she chose to sit outside the open door of the house, the tips of her paws hanging off the edge of the porch, watching and smelling as the world came back to life. She was faithful, keeping Addie company in all things, leaving her only when her boys needed tending.

Sunday afternoons were spent around the cabin now, as more of the horses were turned out to scrap for themselves with the greening of the grass. The winter supply of hay was near to gone now anyway, and even Fred and Freddie spent free time out in the pasture close to the barn. During the day, the chickens were turned out, free to scrabble over what buds of green and little bugs they could find, and they darted about happily hunting, the rooster calling frequently in effort to keep his girls in order.

On the Saturday before the start of school for the boys, Tom stood up behind the house chopping wood for the kitchen stove. The long winter cut a chunk out of reserves, but with less feeding, Tom had more time to tend to such things. In his mind, he thought about a wood cutting expedition that would need to take place soon. He worked with Luke and Andrew to help him. As he swung his maul, Molly appeared around the side of the house, head up and scruffy ears forward. She let out a low growl and the hair on her neck stood up. Letting out a deep bark, she moved forward to look at something in the east.

It wasn't Roy. Tom knew that much. Molly knew him and greeted him differently. Whoever this was, was foreign to Molly. He walked to the edge of the house and saw nothing had come into sight yet. Walking back past the wood pile where the boys were still stacking, Tom moved to where Addie hung wash on the line.

"Somebody's comin'," Tom called to her. Looking from him up the country, Addie turned and slowly picked up another sheet from the basket.

Tom watched her for a moment, the blue of the dress she wore fitting well with the white of her apron. He'd given her the rest of Edith's work things, not making a display over it, just placing them on the table of the dugout when Addie wasn't around. She'd made use of only two of the four he'd given her. In his mind he knew time would be what made those clothes usable to Addie.

Addie stopped to raise a hand to shield the bright morning sun from her eyes, pausing in pinning the sheet to the line. She looked so clean and crisp amongst her laundry, past the tired and hopeless she'd looked back in the autumn. Tom looked away and back to the east where three riders outlined the horizon in the bright light of a near cloudless day. He heard water splashing down at the spring where Frankie and Charlie were floating sticks Frankie called boats.

With hands stilled, Addie looked to Tom. He still held the maul in his strong hand, the muscles in his arm and shoulder flexing with the weight of it. He wore no coat with the warmth of the morning, and no wind brought about a chill. Addie hadn't bothered with a shawl, and the sun on her face whispered a promise of greener grass by the end of the day. Tom's hair and beard were still trimmed neatly, and while Addie never saw him do it, she knew he must have been keeping up with it. His neck was shaved cleanly every few days as well.

From across the brief distance, Addie heard Tom sigh. Addie looked back to the riders and saw clearly now that two of them were women. He rubbed the back of his neck with his free hand, then lowered it to his hip where it stayed. When Addie looked back to the riders she saw that one of the women raised her hand high in an exaggerated wave.

"Luke, Andrew, wash up. We have visitors," Tom hollered to the boys. "You too, Frankie. Help your brother."

Then Tom moved to the front porch and watched as the boys headed to the spring to wash up. Addie took the time to hang her wash, thinking it wasn't worth souring her hard work. By now the riders were near to the house and Tom stepped off the porch to greet them.

Luke watched from the spring where he and Andrew plunged hands into the water and splashed it on their faces. He had a full view of what was going on, and he growled at the sight of the guests.

"It's that damn Blanchard lady. What do 'spose she wants?" Luke scowled as he spoke.

Andrew let out a high-pitched sarcastic laugh. "She wants to be your new mama!"

"Shut up!" Luke spat as he gave his brother a hard shove. Andrew merely laughed at his older brother.

Andrew stood and rolled his shirt sleeves back down from where he'd rolled them out of the way of the water. He watched with his brother, and just as intently as Tom Brady held out a hand to help Miss Mildred Blanchard off her horse. Luke felt she leaned into his pa a little more than necessary as she slid to the ground. Her loud voice carried and echoed off the buildings.

"Ah, what a fine spring morning!" she drawled out.

Tom moved around the front of her horse to take hold of Henry Gibbs' hand. "Mornin', Tom. This is a fine morning."

"Nice after a winter like the one we just passed," Tom agreed.

Henry Gibbs moved around to assist his wife off her horse, then turned to ask Tom, "I hope we aren't interrupting anything?"

"No," Tom said slowly. "Just the usual work. But that will still be there tomorrow no matter what I accomplish today."

"Ain't that the truth!" Henry returned with a big smile.

"We've been waiting for the weather to clear to pay you a visit, Mr. Brady," Mrs. Gibbs spoke up.

"Have you?" Tom replied flatly. He caught the sight of a raised eyebrow from Henry Gibbs, and an equally flat look that spoke to Tom about the conspiracy of it all. Henry tied horses to the rail.

"Have you time for a visit, Mr. Brady?" Mildred Blanchard asked sweetly.

Tom hesitated for a moment, then said, "Of course. Won't you come in?" He extended his arm towards the house, encompassing his guests.

Mildred smiled broadly, as if she were working things just as she'd hoped, which was a miracle to even find Tom at home.

"Boys, come and say hello," Tom called.

From her hesitant location by the clothesline, Addie watched as the boys trudged up the hill from the spring like it was a glacier or something. She raised an eyebrow at Luke who cast her a sideward glance. He refused to take the hint and pick up his feet. Charlie bypassed the whole scenario and came to Addie and buried himself in her skirt. Tom looked back for him, and not seeing him searched until his eyes rested on Addie.

Just before the party reached the steps of the porch, Tom stopped them. "Mr. and Mrs. Gibbs, Miss Blanchard, I would like you to meet my housekeeper, Addie Loveland." Holding out a hand that requested Addie to move forward, she reluctantly did so, surprised at how quickly that slight incline became a glacier.

"Addie, this is Henry Gibbs and his wife, and her sister Miss Blanchard," Tom finished off the introductions.

"How do?" Addie nodded to each politely.

"So this is the young housekeeper? Well! Nice to meet you, girl," Miss Blanchard said in a raised voice. She stepped forward to take Addie's hand, her black riding hat tipped at an ignorant angle, the deep red of her riding dress accenting the dark brown hair rolled into a bun just below her hat. Addie took her hand reluctantly as sweat-loosened hair tickled her face.

"I am so glad to meet you. Mr. Brady spoke of you before. I think it's simply wonderful what he's done. Taken in a young and desperate woman and offered her a place to earn honest, clean money." Mildred turned to look at Tom. "You are a saint, Mr. Brady. What a chance you've given this child."

Addie squinted as she looked over to Luke and Andrew who stood just to the right of her. Luke pressed his mouth into a crooked line and shook his head ever so slightly at Addie. Pasting on a fake smile, Addie looked back to Mildred.

"She's hardly a child, Mildred," Henry Gibbs chided.

"Well, I suppose twelve or fifteen years is a bit of difference in age, Mr. Gibbs," Addie muttered.

Piercing brown eyes were on Addie's face only briefly before they locked on to Charlie who stood clinging to Addie's skirt. "Oh, my! We meet again, young man! I think you've grown since last I saw you." Mildred leaned forward and walked to where Charlie burrowed deeper into the folds of Addie's skirt. "Come now, don't be shy," came the lilting voice once again.

Addie reached a hand down and took hold of his, which he clung to with all his might.

"Come now. We'll be friends."

To Addie's astonishment, Mildred took hold of Charlie and pulled him away from her. "I," she started to protest, then realizing Charlie was not her son, and she had no say in anything that happened to him, closed her mouth.

Frantically Charlie reached for Addie, but Mildred got in his face and took his focus away. He went limp in her arms, too fearful of what was happening to keep on struggling. Mildred triumphantly walked to Tom.

"See, we're gonna be great friends. Even Charlie knows it. Don't you?" she asked him as she looked at his stricken face.

Tom clenched his jaw. Then she started up the steps into the house.

Addie looked over to Luke, Andrew and Frankie. Luke held his head in his hands, Andrew offered Addie a crooked smile, and Frankie came to take hold of Addie's hand. Addie avoided looking at Tom.

Addie smiled down at Frankie. "Best you boys go on in and visit with your company."

The sound of Tom clearing his throat was heard. "Boys, Addie." He stood at the bottom of the steps and gestured for all to retreat to the inside of the house and leave the brilliance of the morning.

Mrs. Gibbs cast a justified smile down on Addie before she entered the house. Luke and Andrew crowded Addie up the steps and blocked her retreat to the dugout. As soon as she crossed the threshold and her eyes focused, Addie could see Charlie struggling to free himself. Tom again rubbed the back of his neck in some kind of effort to restrain himself. Whether that was from hitting or claiming a beautiful woman, Addie had no idea.

"Ah, girl. There you are. Since you are a widow and housekeeping will no doubt be your mainstay from here on out, it would suit you to know that when company is visible on the road, you immediately set coffee or tea water to boiling. For feminine company, usually the proper thing is tea," Mildred reassured her with a depreciating smile, then turned back to Tom who was engaged in general small talk with Henry

Gibbs and hadn't heard Mildred.

Addie just blinked at Mildred. So this was her. The woman Tom had so meticulously groomed himself for. The one he'd ridden across the desert for in the dead of winter. The woman she herself had stayed alone to do chores so Tom could meet her. Addie pressed her lips together. That wasn't true, she told herself. She'd done it for Luke. Tom had done it for Luke also, meeting this woman was just a side benefit.

Knowing her mama would be greatly displeased to know Addie hadn't treated company properly, Addie set about making coffee, no tea since Tom didn't have any, and putting the cookies she'd intended for the boys onto a plate. She'd hear about it from Andrew later, about how she'd given away cookies meant for him.

She carefully placed everything on the table as Tom visited with the company, quietly answering questions from Mildred, and talking business with Mr. Gibbs. Mrs. Gibbs, on the other hand, spent her time talking with the boys, asking about school starting back up, the state of winter affairs, and general small talk held between an adult and children.

Although, Luke was hardly a child.

"Who's minding the store today?" Tom asked Mr. Gibbs.

"Matt Torrey's wife. She works the post office for me sometimes. She's good help."

"I see. Things picking up a bit now that the weather is cooperating some?"

Henry nodded. "Yeah, you know how it is. Mud or no mud, folks are coming in to replace the stuff they've been living without since February. That's a long time without a good cup of coffee!" He laughed. "What about you? It's near time for your crew to be comin' in."

"Yes. Hard to believe. I was just thinkin' that this mornin'. I need to get your way soon to get a few things myself."

"If you have a list ready, you can send it. I'll have the order done and ready for you when you come. If you can't get away, send Luke for it." Henry Gibbs shut his eyes, his high forehead wrinkling beneath graying brown hair. "Oh, I forgot. All the school kids are back at it come Monday."

Addie poured cold water into the coffee to settle the grounds. Then carefully as to not shake them up again, filled mugs at the workbench and handed them out, immediately rinsing and starting another pot of coffee water to boil. She set the plate of cookies in the center of the table and waited for one of the boys to reach for them. Frankie took the bait and Addie stopped him.

"Guests first," she informed him. Andrew scrunched up his face and looked to the empty space before him. The coffee also went to guests first.

Addie herself didn't take any coffee.

"School," Mildred spoke as if she'd been reminded of something important. "I was going to speak with you on that very topic, Mr. Brady. I know your boys quit early to help out here at home, and the school teacher is getting a ridiculously late start this spring, I was thinking you might like me to tutor your boys some."

Charlie had resorted to kicking and fighting shortly after Mildred sat down and placed him on her lap. Tom rescued the boy immediately, and he now held his youngest son on his own lap. Without comment, he reached forward and took a cookie off the blue enamel plate. He handed it to Charlie who rested his head back on his father's chest, comforted in the strength he found there.

In a quiet, but firm voice, Tom Brady replied, "I don't think that will be necessary. We are not the easiest family to work around, but Miss Carthridge has always done an exceptional job teaching my boys when she has them. Even if it is only a few months out of the year. I see no reason to undermine her work."

Without looking at anyone, Addie sat down in her usual place at the end of the table. On the opposite side the three boys were sitting, jammed together so that Mildred could have the seat on the bench next to their father. Beside Addie sat Mrs. Gibbs, and next to her was Henry. Looking across the table to the boys, Addie saw their looks as they stared at the table.

"Well, it wouldn't be undermining, Mr. Brady. Just a simple solution to the problem of wasted time catching them up. It must be dreadful covering lessons already taught in an effort to get the boys back up to speed. I would simply be eliminating that step for Miss Carthridge. Luke, for example, is nearing an age where lessons taught really have to go the distance. He will be completing school soon," Mildred countered.

Tom took a long sip of hot coffee and set his mug down on the table. He looked up to Luke and his eyes went soft. "Luke doesn't know just yet, but he won't be going back to school come Monday."

Luke looked up at his father in surprise.

"He'll be thirteen in a week or so, and the fact is he can read and write, work his numbers better than most grown men I know. So, since Miss Carthridge has done her job quite well, I think it's time Luke stay home and work with the crew this year. Learn what it is to make his livin' with the horses."

"But what of education? What if he yearns for more?" Mildred asked in disbelief.

Tom looked straight at her. "Well, that's up to the boy. If he hankers for more, then so be it."

Addie looked over to Luke who was aglow. He tried to hold his delight in, but his mouth refused to do anything but smile. His eyes twinkled and his containment was barely held. He looked over to Addie, and she met his eyes with returned happiness. Luke sat up straighter, put his shoulders back, and in that moment decided to leave whatever boyhood he had left behind. It didn't matter what the guests spoke of now, Luke's mind was already horseback.

Andrew, on the other hand, was another matter. His shoulders slumped and his head drooped. He gave Luke no reassuring smile.

Mildred, despite her distaste, decided to drop the subject matter.

"These cookies are wonderful," Mr. Gibbs said as he leaned forward to look past his wife at Addie.

Addie smiled slightly and said, "Thank you."

"Tell me, where do you come from?" asked Mrs. Gibbs.

"Texas."

"My goodness! Such a long way for a young girl! How on earth did you get way out here?" Mildred drawled out. Addie looked at her and realized dramatics weren't just in the theater for Mildred.

"The orphan wagon. You know, the ones preachers drive from place to place giving away kids. Mr. Brady adopted me off one."

Next to Mildred who was aghast, Tom closed his eyes to stave off a chuckle. Henry Gibbs didn't bother to suppress his.

Addie looked straight at Mildred. "I came out here with my husband." Struggling to remain polite, Addie knew that Tom Brady might well have an interest in this woman. And despite what she knew would be a horrible marriage, she had no way of knowing if Tom were intent on pursuing what was available.

Like the boys, Addie kept her eyes on the table in front of her. She knew Tom was a man. And men had different needs when it came to marrying. It might just be he was tired of sleeping in that big bed alone at night. Perhaps he wanted to feel the warmth of bare skin against his, to enjoy the night again, as he did when his wife was alive. Mildred was a very beautiful woman on the outside. She held appeal, and even though no man had bothered to possess her body and deal with her mind, Tom might be lonely enough to do it.

Addie knew what it was to hunger alone in the dark. To feel her body cry out for a man who was gone. To burn with desire and have only memories to placate. In those times she'd resorted to tears, which were a very lame comfort. She didn't know when Tom's wife died, but she knew he'd been at widowing far longer than herself. His hunger must have reached an intolerable rise.

Addie felt ashamed. Here he was, probably trying his best to impress Mildred, and she was making snide remarks. For some reason that filled her with regret. She looked across the table at the three boys who listened to the conversation that had moved on to matters she was no longer paying attention to.

To think of them as hers was wrong. She couldn't do so with the intent of leaving them for Texas. What kind of feeling was that? When again Mildred spoke, Addie kept her head tipped forward and looked at her out of the corner of her eyes. While she couldn't imagine Mildred at the washboard, nor the stove for that matter, she could envision her in

Tom's bed. She hated herself for doing it, but she could well imagine Tom's pleasure at Mildred's naked presence.

It made a burning in Addie's gut that she'd never felt before. Her cheeks flushed as she realized what she'd just done. She'd never really contemplated Tom in such matters before. He was a man, yes, and it was obvious he had the desire to exercise his manhood. But why she was picturing it, Addie didn't know. She closed her eyes and tried to picture Texas. That was where her heart was. The pleasure *she'd* know in seeing it again was all that mattered. To see her mama, just like she'd been longing to do.

Addie opened her eyes, and slowly, she turned her head to look up the table, past Mrs. Gibbs who was saying something about the cost of good fabric, around Mr. Gibbs who rested his thin arms on the table, to Tom.

Addie's heart stopped.

While his head was tipped to Mrs. Gibbs who spoke, Tom's soft brown eyes were looking right at her. His right arm rested on the table, his fingers barely holding his mug. His shirt was pressed to his shoulders where he'd moistened them with sweat while chopping wood. His dark brown beard made him seem much more mature than she, having nearly raised his eldest son, lost his wife, and made a homestead, all in one life. She had accomplished little but seeing the country on the back of a little bay horse.

Tom held her gaze for what seemed like an hour, his eyes keeping that same look, his features holding no formidability, his son, Charlie resting easily against him. Something in that look replaced the longing she had for Texas with regret. Addie looked away from him and out the open door.

Far to the south, clouds gathered. The sun was still bright as afternoon came, but, the dark of those clouds held the promise of rain. A slight breeze stirred up the short blades of grass on the hill. Addie moved slightly.

She stood and fixed the coffee that was now boiling, silently placing the pot on the table where mugs could be refilled. Then she said, "I'm sorry, ladies. I see the wind is picking up. I best get my wash off the line. Excuse me."

With that she was gone, out the door and down the porch steps. She made her way slowly to the wash line, realizing for the first time, there would come a day in the near future the wash line would no longer be her problem. She'd no longer look up at the mountains as she strung her wash and pinned it. There would be no little Charlie to cling tightly to her skirt as she did it. There would be no Luke at the kitchen stove in the dark of early morning to hold her tight when he sensed she needed something. No more Andrew to throw dead rats into the flour bin.

Addie covered her face with her hands.

Back inside, Charlie squirmed on his father's lap until he released him. Charlie looked up at his pa, then slipped away after his Addie. He made no sound as he went, just passed through the room.

Luke sat patiently for only a few minutes more, then he stood politely and said, "Pa, I best see to Mr. Gibbs' horses. They've come a fair way today." He waited for his father to nod, then left. Andrew wasn't as diplomatic, but rather blurted something about helping Luke and shot from the table.

That left Frankie.

While he didn't rudely bolt from the table, he fidgeted and wiggled as he changed position constantly to get a look at what his brothers were up to. Tom tried to keep track of the conversation, but he found Frankie and his antics amusing. He watched his boy with understanding, knowing what it was like to be trapped at the table with guests when the world held all the possibility outside the house. There was exploring to do, his brothers to follow, and Addie to find.

After several minutes, Tom said, "Frankie." With a guilty look, Frankie stilled his movements and looked at his father. "Go on, boy." Tom pointed to the door with his head.

A smile burst forth from Frankie just before he excitedly left the table.

"What sweet boys you have," Mrs. Gibbs remarked as she watched Frankie go.

"Not always sweet, Mrs. Gibbs, but they are doing better now," Tom said.

"Well, who could blame them? Losing their mother at such tender ages," Mrs. Gibbs lamented.

"The girl, she probably made things easier for you. You know, helping out in the house. I think…" Mildred was cut short.

"Mrs. Loveland," Tom stated.

"Beg pardon?" Mildred asked.

"Her name is Mrs. Loveland. She's not a girl. She's a grown woman, and her name is Mrs. Loveland. Do not belittle her station. She's stronger than any four men put together."

Henry Gibbs smiled smugly at Mildred. "And Mildred, boy, can she clear a table."

Outside, Luke hastily went about tying three horses into the saddling stall in the barn. He forked them a little hay, hoping with all his heart they'd have to turn around and walk the distance back home in the same day. Not that he held it against those horses, but he'd sure hate to endure more of Miss Mildred.

When he'd finished with the horses, he left the barn and wandered up past the wash line to the little meadow beyond. Andrew was throwing sticks for Molly to ignore retrieving. Frankie was attempting to teach Charlie to wrestle since his older brothers were too much for him. Charlie appeared to be highly amused at Frankie who lay on the green shoots of grass and pulled him down on top of him and mauled him gently.

Addie stood back from both activities and laughed. Molly kept looking back at Addie and smiling, wagging her tail. Then Andrew would reroute her attention, and she'd take an easy hold of the stick Andrew offered to her. Andrew would slap his knees and she'd drop it at his feet. Andrew would growl and start all over again.

"How'd you boys escape?" Luke asked.

"I'm 'sposed to be helpin' you," Andrew answered.

Luke shot him a sarcastic look. "Thanks for all your help, Numbskull."

Andrew answered the name calling with a laugh, then threw the stick for Molly who in return left to greet Luke.

"Pa told me I could leave," Frankie said from where he sat on the grass.

Luke looked to Addie and shook his head as he chuckled, "Orphan wagon…"

Addie looked stern in reply. "I shouldn't have said that. That was disrespectful to your pa. People might've took me serious. They would think he was some kind of queer, takin' in a mostly-grown orphan girl."

Luke laughed as he watched Addie. "Nobody would think that. All they'd have to do is look at you to see you weren't an orphaned girl. You're a woman."

Sighing, she said, "Just the same, Luke. I shouldn't have said it."

"How come you don't do what she does?" Andrew asked.

In confusion Addie looked over at him. "Do what?"

"You know, when she's talkin' to Pa. She puts her, you know… those," at a loss for an appropriate name, he reached up and gestured at Addie's chest, "those, lady things, on the table, kind of."

Addie covered her face with her hand. "Andrew!" she muttered. After a moment, she said, "If a woman uses those when she's speakin' to you, she isn't playing fair, you hear? Steer clear of those women. They'll get what they want out of you without your consent. Got it?"

Furrowing his brows and scratching his head, Andrew answered, "Alright, I guess."

Luke smiled and looked out at the mountains. "Clouds are comin' up. Sure is pretty when the sky changes."

"You shouldn't have put their horses in the barn. Now they'll never leave, and we'll have to sit out here in the rain," Frankie fussed.

"I guess I best get my wash off the line for real," Addie said as she turned to walk back to the wash line.

About that time she heard Tom call from the porch, "Luke! Horses!"

He jumped up and jogged down to the barn, Molly following closely behind. The three visitors appeared with Tom on the porch, and while she couldn't hear what was being said, Addie could see that they were still chatting. The wind was starting to pick up now, and the laundry waved gently in time with it. Frankie and Charlie wove their way through the moving fabric, Frankie laughing, Charlie wearing as close to a smile as he ever got. Andrew sat at the base of the post that held the wash line, picking bark off the willow stick he'd been using in an attempt to convince Molly to do something she would not.

As Luke approached with the horses, Mrs. Gibbs hollered at the boys, "Bye, children!" She added a small wave.

Mildred said nothing nor did she look in their direction. She accepted a hand from Tom as she mounted her horse, this time bestowing a lavish smile on him when she'd settled herself in the saddle. Tom stepped back as he looked up at her and nodded.

Addie sighed and looked away. Men were such uncomplicated creatures. She doubted, like his father obviously hadn't listened to his mother, that Andrew would develop any defenses against women like Mildred Blanchard. They always spoke well of holding strong, but they always forgot themselves when "lady things" were present and on the table.

"It was nice meeting you, Mrs. Loveland," Henry Gibbs called.

She raised a hand and waved, with the other hand still holding a wash rag. Neither woman said anything in polite departing words. It was just as well. Addie was in the way.

Looking down at the boys who stood in a group by the post where Andrew sat, Addie said, "Best you boys go see if they left you any cookies."

They were off like a shot, each boy taking one of Charlie's hands to help him along. With that, Addie moved to the far side of the wash line, out of the view of the house and the leaving guests. The wind was stronger now, still holding no threats, but merely causing the sheets to press against Addie as they waved. The sun went behind a huge cloud, blocking out the sun, but painting a masterpiece across the sky. Addie pulled another blanket off the line and commenced to folding it.

All was quiet with nothing but the sound of the wind in the wash, and the sweet smell of rain. Addie kept up her work until something caught her eye. With the retreat of a gust of wind, the sheets lowered enough for her to see the outline of something near the wash line. When she looked, it was Tom leaning against the same post Andrew had leaned against a few minutes before. His hands rested in his pockets as he watched her go about her work, a look of deep contemplation in his dark eyes.

"You abandoned me in there."

Addie looked back to her folding. "I had work."

"I know. What with the blasting winds scattering your wash over the desert, you musta been awful busy chasing it all down."

With an annoyed look, she said, "I think we both know they weren't here to see me."

"Oh, come now. They were just paying a respectful visit to see how my latest adoption was working out."

Addie held back a smile and focused on a pin she was pulling off the line. "I'm sorry. That was rude."

"No trouble. I did, however, set you up for some tutoring with Mildred. That way you're ready to head to school come Monday."

"You wouldn't dare!" Addie shot.

Tom laughed, the sound coming from deep within him. "No, I didn't, but only 'cause I think you'd never be able to overcome that temper of yours, and Mildred would get a punch in the face."

"I wouldn't do that!"

Tom turned serious. "Yes, you would," he said with certainty. At her look he laughed again.

"Well, maybe next time she comes for a visit, I'll be gone, back to Texas where I belong."

Tom's face went hard and he stood up straight. "I don't think she'll be coming back. And if she does, I guess the boys and I will get a little more pointed with her."

Avoiding looking at him and discovering whatever might be written on his face, Addie kept up with her folding. "I don't suppose Mr. Gibbs knew when the stage would start up again?"

Tom clenched his jaw. He didn't have the heart to tell her the stage out of Elko no doubt started several weeks ago. Elko was farther past the cut off to Tuscarora, and he had his own reasons for not wanting to make such a long trip.

"He didn't say."

Addie pulled the last of the sheets off the line and folded it, then tossed it into the basket at her feet. "Well, I best get dinner going. I'm sure the boys are hungry."

Another week passed, and with it came the true emergence of spring. The sun shone with intensity, and although storms gathered and rolled in the late afternoons, the combination of sun and water caused green to burst forth until it hurt the eyes. Even the crags and slopes of the mountains above began to show pieces of bare ground. Little wildflowers dotted the landscape and the once depressing place where Addie hoped to leave was living and almost spiritual.

Tom was making preparations for the crew that would be arriving in a week or so, and the real work of sorting and starting young horses would begin. He and Luke spent the day making repairs to the barn and corrals, and getting the loft of the barn ready for men to sleep there. They put in a wood stove to heat the boarded in space. There would be branding to tend to as well, and Luke bubbled with anticipation. Each morning his two younger brothers made their way to the schoolhouse, and Luke stayed to help his father. Addie watched it all and realized if she were going to make her getaway, she'd better get it done.

When she brought the subject up to Tom on Saturday evening, he looked grim. She said she guessed the stage must be running, since the land around them had firmed up despite the great holds of water still out in low spots on the desert. Addie stated her case, said she'd best get on down the line if she were to get going before the colt starting crew arrived. Once that happened, she'd be stuck a long while.

Tom said nothing, just looked down at his folded hands where they rested on the top of the table, glad she'd waited to say it after the boys had gone to bed. Now she stood at the workbench, her arms folded across her chest, the light blue of the dress he'd given her softening her features.

Addie waited for him to speak.

Tom bowed his head and moistened his lips. "Addie," he began. "Luke's birthday is next week, on Sunday, I believe. I'd hoped you'd stay that long, but seein' your intent to go, well, maybe you'd humor us with a picnic tomorrow to celebrate the occasion."

"I guess I don't see why not."

Standing, Tom looked at her and nodded his thanks. Then he moved to the door and left without another word. Addie watched him go, anxious as he never said he'd take her to Tuscarora, but he didn't say he wouldn't either. They'd both known that spring would come, and she'd go. They each looked forward to it all winter. Addie knew life would be hard again for the Bradys when she left, but she'd gotten things in order beyond what the original agreement was.

Now Texas called.

Addie lay in bed that night, thinking, and wondered what Tom Brady would do when she was gone. He'd indicated Mildred would not return, but perhaps desperation would settle in and he'd change his mind. Or, maybe he'd wander and find himself another woman, a widow, who needed a place as badly as he needed a woman.

He seemed different the past few days, quieter, more thoughtful. It may have just been that he had lots on his mind, what with the colt starting crew coming shortly. Addie herself was far away, thinking of Texas and the journey she would make. When she dreamed at night, she saw nothing but the empty prairie, the gray leaving her alone, the running horses not to be seen.

All these thoughts were really just a distraction from the truth. What was she really going to do with herself once she got back to Texas? Addie held the letter from her father up in the dark. Just holding it was promising enough. It was proof that somewhere out there, they were thinking of her. They had not forgotten their daughter. They were waiting for her.

She put the letter back under her pillow. Her family was waiting anxiously to hear from her. She wouldn't send word, she'd just be there.

And, instead of words written in a stranger's hand, they'd have her to hold. She'd waited so long to feel her mother's comfort, and now, in a mere matter of days, she would. Addie planned to insist on the picnic the next day that Tom take her to the stage come Monday.

The following morning, Addie rose early, something keeping her from sleeping like she normally would, the heavy weight of exhaustion removing itself. She dressed, brushed and pinned her hair, then went to the main house in the dark, the east showing sign the sun was considering rising for the day. The air was cool, but clean and dry. When she entered the house to retrieve her milking bucket, Tom was already sitting at the table pulling his boots on. He looked up, startled.

"You're up and about early."

Addie looked at him. "I couldn't sleep."

Tom looked back down at his boots. "Gonna be a fine day. The sky is clear."

Addie nodded as she stoked the fire. Embers shot up as she raked the coals. She placed small pieces of wood in to coax it back to life. She took her white apron off the peg near the door and tied it on herself. She thought a moment about asking Tom to take her to Tuscarora the next day, but, for some reason held back. She figured if he were anything like Fett, early morning before he'd had his coffee wasn't the best time to address a subject that would take a lot of effort on his part. It was a sure way to set him against it from the start.

"While this fire gets going, I'll go get the milkin' done," Addie said.

"I'll come with you," he said as he stood and tucked his shirt in.

Addie looked away from seeing him finishing his dressing and said, "I didn't meant to hurry you. Come when you're ready."

Taking her bucket from the workbench, Addie moved to the door and pulled the handle. Tom was close behind her as she walked to the barn, and while he said nothing, Addie could feel the pressure of things needing said. She needed to tell him she was ready to go. He no doubt needed to tell her he was ready to have her go.

Nothing was said.

Accomplishing her milking gave Addie quiet time to think as the sky started to declare the emergence of the sun. It was barely light enough to see in the barn, but Addie had done this chore enough to do it in the dark. Red Beast's calf was growing, and when she'd finished sucking what she wanted, she took time to come and inspect Addie, licking at her hair and clothes. When Addie gently shoved her away, she walked up behind her and pressed her forehead against Addie's back. Red Beast let out a low moan as she looked back at her calf.

When Addie completed the job, she stood and scratched Little Red Beast behind the ears. The calf threw her head and sniffed at the milk bucket. "I sincerely hope you turn out better than your ma."

Addie returned to the house to start breakfast and try to prepare a meal for a birthday picnic. She tended to her milk, and washed out her bucket. Since it was Sunday, she cut pieces of cured ham and fried them, and with the humble beginnings of a flock starting to lay again, scrambled eggs to go with the ham.

By the time breakfast was ready, the Bradys were gathered around the kitchen table and anxious to eat. Eating her meal very quickly, Addie began to get things ready for the day. She decided to make meat sandwiches with strips of ham. By now the sun was up and shining brilliantly. When Tom informed the boys of the day's activity, they were only too happy to get going and get the wagon rolled out of the lean-to next to the barn and in using shape. It hadn't moved since the trip to collect Addie from the stage the fall previous.

Tom took Charlie with him out to the barn, leaving Addie to attempt a cake. It had been a very long time, but she remembered enough to get started on. She made a simple white cake, and a thin layer of frosting to go with it. It took time to complete, and she hovered over the box in the stove to keep watch as it baked, afraid in her inexperience she'd burn the thing. She still struggled with bread at times in that oven.

When it was done, frosted and sitting pretty on the table, Addie went to work on the sandwiches, reluctant to start early and have the bread be dried out. She fried potatoes in a skillet and put them in the dutch when they were done, putting the lid on top. Not having seen nor heard from any of the boys in some time, Addie looked out the window to see where all the menfolk had gotten off to.

They were there, all of them together. The boys were perched on the top railing of the corral fence adjacent to the barn, little Charlie in Tom's arms where he stood below them, speaking very seriously to the four of them. The boys were still, their faces holding no expression. Andrew nodded slowly, then when Tom looked at Luke, his agreement came readily. Frankie responded with his usual smile.

Addie's brows knit at the curious scene. But with work to do, she turned away and went back to it. When things were about finished, Tom came into the house and asked Addie if she were ready. She agreed she was, and he went down to get the team and wagon that was all hitched.

The boys came and helped carry everything out, even coming up with a quilt to lay on the ground. They climbed up into the wagon box with Molly among them, leaving the seat next to their pa open. Tom climbed up first as Addie took off her apron in the house and hung it on a peg. She closed the door behind her and stepped off the porch. Shielding her eyes from the sun, she looked at the closed wagon box. Then she looked to Tom who held out his hand to pull her up. Reluctantly she took it, taking a handful of skirt and placing a careful foot on the spoke of the wheel to step up.

Gathering her skirt, she sat down. Tom released the brake and set Fred and Freddie into motion. Thinking on the names of the team, Addie turned a curious face to Tom.

"Does the milk cow have a name?" she asked in a dawning tone.

Tom glanced at her from under his brown hat. "Yes, ma'am."

In suspicion, Addie asked, "What is it?"

Trying to remain serious, he looked straight at her and replied, "Sweet Belle."

Throwing her head back, Addie let out a loud and skeptical laugh.

"As I said before, woman. We may not be real creative, nor accurate for that matter, but we see that everything that needs a name, gets one."

Stopping her laughter, Addie raised a brow as she looked over at Tom. "Would you like to know what I call her?"

Tom let out a deep and full-bodied laugh. "No, ma'am, I would not!" he shouted as he sent the team into a trot up the meadow.

The gate was open and they moved through easily with only a few of the older mares remaining in the meadow to wait their turn to foal. It was a big part of Tom and Luke's day, riding out over the country checking on their mares. One mare in the meadow had foaled during the night, and now the spindly-legged little fellow wobbled along next to his mother away from the rumbling wagon as it came up the two-track.

Fred let out a nicker to mother and baby, and the little bitty foal answered in a high-pitched tone. The mare stopped abruptly and turned to pin her ears at Fred for being so forward with her babe. Fred kept an ear on the pair as they passed.

"It's funny how some geldings love a baby," Tom remarked.

Addie looked back at the little black foal and smiled. "Life just keeps on going. No matter what."

Tom looked at Addie from where he sat, leaning forward on his legs. "Yes. Yes, it does."

The meadow was beautiful. It was green and growing, blades of shining grass shimmering in the bright light of the sun. A cool breeze offset the heat of the sun as Addie watched mares who lazed in the warmth of it, bellies heavy with foal. Puffy white clouds floated above the peaks, patches of blue behind them. After what seemed to take a long while, Tom brought them near to the base of the mountain. Just as the land started to rise with hills, he stopped the team and jumped down from the seat.

"We'll leave the wagon here. Andrew and Frank, help Addie get the goods down by the creek and pick us a nice spot. Luke and I will bring the horses down."

Molly didn't wait for the gate to be lowered, but bounded over the side and made her way to explore the creek. She let out a bark when she saw the folks weren't following as quickly as she would have liked. Frank took off after her with sandwiches in hand.

Andrew took the dutch full of potatoes, and that left the cake and Charlie for Addie. She picked their way down the slope slowly, not wanting to slip and drop Luke's birthday cake, Charlie holding tightly to her skirt. It was beautiful by the creek. The sound of the water rushing by was comforting. Frank and Andrew spread the quilt out in the soft green grass on the bank, then set the food next to it. Then Andrew headed back up the hill to get the utensil box.

Frankie wandered off to follow Molly. Tom and Luke hobbled the horses down the creek a ways where the grazing was good. When they finished, Andrew and Luke came back to the quilt to pick up Charlie. Luke hefted him up on his shoulders. They turned in the direction Frank had gone.

"Aren't you hungry?" Addie asked.

Luke turned and smiled at her. "Not yet," he replied in a voice clinging to the edge of changing to the deep sound of manhood. Then they were gone up the creek to throw stones where the horses grazed.

Addie watched them with a perplexed look. She noticed Luke and Andrew were careful to keep Charlie occupied. Each time he turned to search for Addie, they distracted him with something else. Before too long, the boys were taking shoes off and wading on a shallow sandbar.

"Would you like a fire for coffee?" Tom asked.

"I packed the fixin's if you want them," Addie replied.

Tom nodded and went about putting kindling together he'd brought in the wagon. Addie sat down on the quilt and folded her legs behind her. She watched the boys up the creek as the splashing commenced. Shocked screaming and hollering ensued with the feel of icy water running straight off the peaks.

Tom filled the pot from the stream and set it next to the flames of the small fire.

"Those boys are gonna be sick tomorrow. That water has to be freezing."

Tom chuckled as he sat down on the quilt and stretched out to lean back on his elbow. He was careful to keep his muddied feet off of it. "They'll be alright. Just be glad they aren't here where you'll get wet."

Looking at him she saw a dark and mischievous gleam in his eye. "You wouldn't dare."

His mouth broke into a wicked half-grin. "I'll try hard to keep the urge away."

"You better," she stated cautiously.

Tom looked away and up the creek where Andrew was kicking water at Luke. "Kids don't care about the cold. Don't even notice."

Addie smiled as she recalled her brothers. "Girls grow outta that faster, it seems." Her eyes wandered down the creek and through the willows, then up to the clear sky. Where the creek ran past them and away from the mountains, willows grew thick along the banks. When Addie looked back, Tom was watching her. He plucked a twig off the quilt and turned it between two fingers.

"Addie," he began as he looked down at the twig. "I," he stumbled over his start. He swallowed hard and tried to gather thoughts.

"I thought I was Mrs. Loveland?" Addie asked quietly.

"You were," he said.

In frustration Tom sat up and looked across the creek to the buttes beyond. "Addie," he said pointedly, but for what reason she couldn't tell. "I'm… sorry…I never asked… about him." He paused as he broke the twig between his fingers. "I could see…you needed help. But, I…" Tom shook his head and rubbed the bridge of his nose with his thumb.

Addie looked away, fear and anguish at what he might say next forcing her to draw her knees up to her chest. She held them tightly there. She didn't want to hear it. He was struggling over something hard, and hard was not something she wanted to deal with.

"When Edith...," he sighed impatiently with himself. Gritting his teeth he started again with determination. "That night. That night Charlie was born, Edith had nobody but me to tend her. I..," he stopped again. "How do I say this? I can't get the right words." Tom looked over at Addie who was looking for all the world like she was trying to protect herself. He turned back to the creek.

"She didn't think she needed help, having birthed three before Charlie. And I, well, I figured she could handle it. I tended her when she had Frankie and Andrew both. Neither of us figured things would go any different." Tom watched as Charlie threw a rock into the creek, his little arm barely throwing it far enough to hit the edge of the water lapping on the bank.

"She said she'd be fine, and truth told there wasn't anybody close enough to get anyway. It took her a long time. She labored most of the day, walking around the kitchen, then when the night came and the pains were desperate, she lay down. I shoulda known then somethin' was wrong, 'cause it had never taken that long before. I could see it...in her eyes. She was scared.

"I held her hand, and I kept Luke outta bed, so he could help, maybe fetch things, bring blankets, I dunno. Maybe the truth was I just didn't want to be alone." Tom was quiet a long time before he went on. Addie waited, her heart racing, knowing the feeling Tom was about to explain. "She worked and pushed, and worked and pushed, and finally, a very bruised and weakened Charlie was born, feet first, his little lips blue. Edith started crying as soon as she saw him, she figured he was dead. I...I turned him upside down and slapped his bottom, for no good reason, I just heard once folks did that when babies weren't breathin'. He sucked in air an' started a weak cry."

Tom found a small stone among the grass he picked at, and threw it into the creek. "She was so relieved he was alive, she took him and

326

immediately put him on the breast. He was so limp he could hardly take hold, but he finally did. 'Bout that time I noticed Edith couldn't really hold him up anymore. So I looked down at her legs an' saw a great big ol' puddle of blood soaking up the blankets."

Frankie splashed Luke in the face. Luke retaliated by throwing a big rock into the water next to him. Water sprayed Frankie. Luke cheered at his own victory. Molly barked as she bounded through the water after Andrew.

"Then she looked at me…she looked at me and I knew. I knew what Edith already did. I panicked. I looked at Luke who stood in the doorway, his face all white. He was starin' at his mama for the last time. So, I stood and said, 'Stay with her, boy.' I figured I could ride for help." Tom clenched his eyes shut and shook his head. Then he looked up at the sky. "God help me for bein' a coward. I knew she'd be gone long before I got a horse saddled, much less gone and gotten help. I just didn't want to sit there and watch her die. And in my selfishness, I was gonna leave Luke to do it for me."

Tears came into Addie's eyes when she looked at the tall young man who carried Charlie on his shoulders as he waded through the creek.

"Time just stopped. I looked at her, the light goin' from her, to Luke. I realized the burden me leavin' would place on his shoulders. How, for the rest of his life, he'd think he couldn't save his ma. That had he been able to think straight, he coulda stopped the bleedin'. But there was no way a man and a boy could know how to do that. And that wasn't a burden a young man should shoulder."

Tom rubbed his face. "We buried her, Roy and I, after I sent Luke on Mare to get him. That boy was cryin' so hard by the time he got to Roy, Roy figured the whole clan was dead in a house fire or something. I have never needed another person the way I needed Roy to step in and tell me what to do."

Horrible images of Addie's own memories flooded her mind. She wanted to run from Tom, tell him to stop talking about it. It awakened her own nightmare.

"I am so ashamed, Addie," he said as he turned to look at her. "I'm ashamed because I just waited for him to die. I waited for Charlie to die. I even hoped for it, 'cause only God knew how I was ever gonna keep him alive, weak and tiny as he was, with no mama to tend him and feed him proper. How could I, a man alone, ever tend him and his brothers? And the truth is, when you came, Addie, I was still waitin' for him to die."

Addie tipped her head back and closed her eyes. She didn't know what to say to him. She didn't know why he was telling her these things. Was this his way of explaining himself before she left? Justifying his reasons so she didn't spend the rest of her life thinking of him as the man he was when she first came?

"Life for us stopped the day Edith passed. It made me numb. I couldn't help my boys; I couldn't even help myself." Watching the boys send sparkling drops of water up high into the air as they played, Tom studied each boy, recognizing their mother in each of them: Luke's heart, Andrew's wit, Frank's inability to see the bad in anyone. And little Charlie, well, he looked so much like her. Edith lived on in her sons.

Tom turned his dark eyes back to Addie. He said softly, "I understand what you've been through. I just didn't want to admit it."

Addie stood and walked away from him. This wasn't what they did. They shared no feelings between them. Why now? Addie's stomach flipped. She stopped next to the creek and turned to see he'd followed her. His brows knit together in anxiousness.

"Addie, I.."

Addie gathered her skirt and brushed past him. "I best feed those boys. It's well past noon mealtime. They gotta be hungry."

Tom gently caught her arm. "Addie," he began.

Just as he spoke a loud crack split the sky. Addie looked up to see the mountains above them had been engulfed in a shroud of black clouds. Already a sheet of white blocked the view of the highest peaks, and a look further to the south spoke of the duration of the storm. It was moving in, and fast.

Tom still held Addie's arm as he read the sky. He looked over at her in complete disappointment. "I guess the picnic is cut a little short."

"Mr. Brady," Addie addressed him.

He looked down at her, the wind ruffling his dark brown hair as he removed his hat.

"Mr. Brady, will you take me to the stage tomorrow?" she said in a rush of desperation. The hammering in her chest sending apprehension shooting throughout her body.

Tom's face was creased with desolation as he shook his head. "Listen to me," he commanded.

"It's time. It's time, Mr. Brady. We've waited all winter for this day to come."

"Addie." He gripped her arm firmly to catch her attention. She looked deep into his face and waited. "There is gonna come a day. When..," he shook his head and sighed in aggravation. "Back home, there's gonna be other men, young men who see you and appreciate you, for all that you are... just...Can I write to you? Can I send you letters?" He finally cut to a question and left out all the reasoning he'd planned to go with it.

"Why?" Addie whispered. As the wind kicked up with greater force, it pressed Tom in closer to her, his leg touching hers.

"Because..."

"Oh, it doesn't matter why!" Addie was close to hysteria inside. Her eyes welled up and she tried to take her arm back. He held it with a gentler hand. "It doesn't matter," she said in a quiet voice. "You may write all you want. You can write a hundred of them. But," she looked into his brown eyes, full of an emotion Addie could only determine to be anguish. "I can't read," she breathed.

Another loud boom split the sky. A flash of light lit the creek as the clouds consumed the sun. Addie jumped in alarm as her attention was snatched away from Tom. He continued to look down at her as the boys ran to them, Luke carrying Charlie. As soon as Luke set him on the ground he rushed to Addie and reached up for her to hold him. While he couldn't hear the intensity of the electrical storm on the mountain above him, he could feel it in every fiber of his being. Seeing the boy's need, Tom released Addie. She swept him up in her arms and he buried his face in her neck.

"Gather up the goods, Luke and I will hitch the team," Tom said to Addie just before he lunged away.

Lifting the cake, Addie handed it to Andrew along with the utensil box. It was no use to worry about the cake now, in a few minutes it would be completely ruined anyway. She handed Frankie the sandwiches, then rolled up the quilt hastily and tucked it under her arm. She hoisted Charlie onto her back who was now crying silently. She snatched up the dutch and held it in the same hand as the quilt. With her other arm she held Charlie and started at a jog up the slope, Molly close behind as the dog made sure all left the creek.

Tom and Luke were already there, hitching the team who stood with heads high. When Tom turned and saw her coming, he quit what he was doing to help her get everything in the wagon.

"Climb in the back and cover yourself and the boys with the quilt." Without looking into his face, Addie nodded.

She helped Frank in the wagon bed, then climbed in as the rain began to pelt down on everything. Reaching down, she gave Andrew a hand, pulling him up. She grabbed the quilt and settled the boys in a bunch behind the wagon seat and covered them with the quilt as Tom and Luke scrambled up onto the seat.

The sky let loose in great thundering torrents that came down with big, fat drops soaking everything within a matter of seconds. Drops bounced up off of the backs of the horses, then ran in rivulets off the rocks on the ground.

"Sit," Tom said in a voice near to begging. Addie looked at him through the rain and tried to read his expression. Rain ran down his face and filtered through his beard, his shirt was pressed against his chest and shoulders. He bent and held up the quilt for her to hide under. After she'd sat, and he'd arranged the quilt to shield her, he set the team into an immediate lope. Addie held Charlie close to her on one side, while Frank pressed in close on the other, squeezed between her and the seat. Andrew packed in close to Charlie.

The ride was rough.

The wagon bounced out across the meadow, not even on the road, as the tracks were already filled with water. Tom directed them out for surer footing, but it wasn't as even as the two-track. Addie wondered if the team would run away, but she figured it wouldn't matter. They had so far to go. They were tossed about inside that wagon box, the rain soaking through their quilt, dripping down on them in steady fashion. Molly ran the distance home beside the wagon, her legs carrying her swiftly across the meadows.

When they arrived at the homestead, Addie was surprised to see Tom didn't take her and the children to the house. Instead he pulled the wagon straight through the double doors of the barn and into the alley. When they came to a stop, the horses heaved and stamped their feet. Addie threw the quilt off and helped Charlie and Frankie to stand. Tom untied the gate and let it drop.

"Come on, boys," he said when Andrew bent to gather the picnic supplies. Luke jumped down from the seat and headed to the back of the wagon. Tom took hold of Charlie and handed him to Luke, then set Frank down. He looked at Luke. "Take them to the house."

Without any question, Luke set off in the rain, his younger brothers running ahead of him.

Addie folded the soaked quilt in a haphazard way, then bent to pick up the cake. It was wet, but some might be salvaged. "You should have sent some of this with them," Addie said as she picked up the dutch.

"Addie," Tom said softly.

When she looked at him, he had his hand held out to her, ready to help her down. "Let me bring this."

"Leave it." His firm voice stated. "Come, Addie."

She looked at him for a moment, then walked to him. He took the wet quilt from her and lay it aside on the edge of the wagon box. Reaching up with both hands, he waited for her to crouch. Her breath caught and her heart raced as she looked down at him. His eyes were seeking, but behind them was great patience. He'd wait.

Slowly, Addie knelt down, her throat already on fire, her mind trying to decide on standing and climbing over the side of the box on her own, or allowing him to take hold of her. Tom decided for her by tenderly taking hold of her rib cage, well below her breasts and drawing her to him. He took all her weight against his chest as he lowered her to the barn floor.

Her hair was saturated and lying flat against her head. She looked at him and droplets rolled off his hair where the water gathered it in bunches and stuck it together. The contours of his chest were visible through his wet shirt.

He didn't release her once she was on her own feet, but instead opened his hand as he moved it across her back, drawing her to him. With his free hand he lifted a lock of hair off her face and lightly pressed it behind her ear. Then, without allowing her time to think of a way to escape him, he pressed his lips to hers, ever so softly. Addie's hands were locked between her chest and his, and he kept her pressed tightly to him so she could not free them. With his hand tracing her cheek lightly, he deepened his kiss, knowing Addie was not inexperienced.

He explored the surface of her lips with the tip of his tongue. Addie was frozen there, feeling what should have been nothing but cold from the drenching rain, but instead found the warmth of life, coursing just below the surface of Tom's skin. His heartbeat was rapid and hammering through his chest and shirt where Addie's hands rested. Tom was warm and welcoming, as opposed to the cold she'd felt for the duration of the winter.

Tom took the hand that caressed her face and ran it down her shoulder, then her arm, down the curve of her side, and brought it to a stop just above her buttocks. He pressed in closer to her, bringing with him the welcoming feel of heat against her wet body.

Lightning flashed wildly above, and Addie broke away from him as thunder sounded within seconds. Tom glanced away from her up to the sky, and she took the opportunity to move away from him. When he looked back, she'd put the wagon between them, and watched him cautiously. He looked at her knowingly, and she was well aware of what lay behind that look.

"Don't," she whispered to him.

He moved around the edge of the wagon, reaching out for her. "Why, Addie? Why not? I wasn't sure before, if you felt it, but now I think I am."

Addie's face crumbled as she backed away from him, a sob crawled up out of her throat. "Feel what?" she trembled out. He followed her slowly as she reached out and felt the warmth of the hide on Freddie. He tipped his head to her to watch her come. Freddie rounded his nostrils to take in her smell, then reached around to nuzzle her arm. Tom kept coming, slowly, easy as he went.

"Addie, I'm in love with you. I've been in love with you since the first time I laid eyes on you in a man's coat, clinging to that trunk. I won't fight it anymore. Come to me."

Addie shook her head and darted around the front of the patient team. Tom looked at her over the backs of the horses, the sound of the rain beating on the roof as it came down harder. "Listen to me. I can't let you go back to Texas. I can't. I can't lie in bed every night thinkin' about all the young men who are gonna ask for your hand."

"Young men! You say young men! Like you know we got a world of age and livin' between us and you don't care!" Addie shouted.

Tom remained rooted. He shook his head and water trailed down his cheek into his beard. "Age ain't much between a man and woman who love each other."

"I'm not much older than Luke! How can you say that?"

"You're a woman, Addie. A good woman. And I know I was rough to you. I know I was as unfeelin' as a man could ever try to be. I was a fool, Addie. I know it and I admit it. I treated you poor, and now I will do whatever it takes to make it up to you." He moved around the front of the team to bridge the distance, but Addie took the chance to run. When he saw her bolt, he pursued out into the rain. He caught up to her and took hold of her arm.

"Why?" she screamed up at his face. "Why now? Are you realizing the hardship you'll face without me? Are you so desperate to hold on to your housekeeper you'd marry the woman you hate to keep your house in order? Is that it?"

"I don't hate you, Addie," he said as he shook his head again, the rain running down his chest and into the hair at the base of his throat. "I tried to convince myself to hate you. I tried. But you aren't the kind of woman a man learns to hate."

"No. I don't believe you," she shouted through the rain stinging her face.

Tom took hold of her by the shoulders. "Addie, you tell me what you want. I'll do it. If you want Texas, I'll give it to you. I'll leave here with you first thing in the morning and never look back. I'll take you and the boys to Texas. Leave all these horses to the wind, the house and everything in it. If that's what you want, I'll do it." He tried to draw her close again but she pushed off his chest.

"No! No, you don't mean that."

"Yes, I do. You say the word."

"I won't live like that again. I won't!"

"Live like what? With no home, no house, on the range? Traveling place to place with never a roof over your head?" Tom asked.

Addie broke then. She started to cry in deep sobs and racking noises. She pushed away from him, trying to run, but the tears made her weak. The feel of his strength beckoned to her and lured her into his arms, to lay her heart upon him and trust what he said, to let him carry her burden for her. She fought it, barely winning the war within herself.

"I'll provide for you. I'll care for you. You won't be left alone anymore."

"It's not that!"

"Then what is it?" He took a stronger hold on her, pulling her closer, her hands pressed against him in defense.

"I won't...," she cried out. "I don't want to lose like that again. I won't live through it a second time... To be alone..." Addie bent over, the tears she sobbed making Tom's eyes well. He understood what she meant.

Tom pressed close to her ear. "You won't be alone again. Never again."

"You can't say you'd never die! You can't promise that!"

"No," Tom said as he looked gently down into her face and the emotion that raged there. "I can't promise you I won't die. But I promise you that if I do, you'll have my boys. They will be yours. They will watch over you. Them, and whoever we create between us."

Addie fell in his arms. He held her there, trying to draw her near to him, offering his strength. "Come to me, Addie. Please."

Thunder shattered all thought as it ripped through the atmosphere. Addie jerked from him and tore away. She raised her skirt and dashed to the dugout, Tom close behind. She made it in and slammed the door, lowering the latch behind her. She stood staring at the closed door. She backed slowly away from it as Tom knocked.

"Addie, Addie just let me talk to you. That's all I ask."

"No," she said to herself. She backed to the wall and slunk down it, covering her ears and burying her face in her knees. Tom kept knocking for a while.

"Please, just let me hold you. Let me show you. Let me hold you," he begged through the door.

Tom sat on the porch of the dugout long after the rain passed, long after the sun sat on the mountains, poised for the rapid fall to the other side of the world. He watched the clouds leave, the blue sky dominate once again. Then, he slowly stood and walked to the barn, to tend the team who still stood patiently. But when he stepped into the barn, the team was gone, already eating their evening meal.

Luke walked into the alley, holding a manure fork in his hand. His eyes shone hopefully at his father. Tom looked to his eldest son, and shook his head.

Addie lay still in the dark, huddled under her blankets, the quilt she'd shared with Fett on top of the heap. She didn't leave the dugout, she didn't start a fire. She simply crawled into bed and cried. There was nothing left to do. She didn't want to be strong anymore, and she didn't want to give what was left of her heart to anyone.

She wanted to hoard it like gold.

Her mama would have known what to tell her. What to say to help her along, help her make the choices as an adult that she needed to. But in her heart Addie suspected she already knew what her mama would say. She'd be practical, just like she was with everything else. Clara would tell Addie that life was awful long, and being alone would just make it longer.

Addie wasn't ready to feel the burning in her stomach that Tom Brady caused when he held her and kissed her. She didn't want the womanly response to the feel of his strong body as it held her tightly to him. He weakened her, took all the fight right out of her. It didn't seem right for a grown woman to want to fall into his comfort. To willingly allow him to take her up into his arms and carry her wherever he chose, and as a grown woman know what he'd do when she gave into him, and not bother to fight the sinfulness of it all.

Her mama had warned her about it. She'd remained steadfast when she was engaged to Fett. True, her folks, including her brothers, had watched her like hawks, but she had no intentions of losing her virtue before her wedding night. Now right and wrong seemed less obvious.

She never figured herself for wanting Tom Brady. It would be a kinder cut to go back to Texas, to leave him free to find someone else. Addie just didn't think it possible for her to love another with all the zeal she'd had for Fett. Being left broken and bleeding, alone and homeless was an experience she couldn't take any more of.

Grief is the consequence of love.

She'd withstood the pain of it. Now she just wanted to be comforted, to be like a child again, her mother's hands taking gentle hold of her face. The comfort of a loving mother who loved her children with all of her mother's heart. She wanted to lay her head on her mother's lap like she did when she was near thirteen, to feel her mother run her fingers through her auburn curls and explain the complexities of the heart.

When at last she drifted into an uneasy sleep, Addie dreamt of nothing but the vast, empty prairie. No horses ran free, no prayers from her mother were carried on the wind. It was endless, and hopeless.

"Why you 'spose she told Pa no?" Luke whispered into the dark.

It took Andrew time to answer, and Luke began to think that he'd gone to sleep. "I told you a long time ago she hated him. Don't know why you got your hopes up."

"I got my hopes up 'cause life is gonna go back to bein' real hard once she leaves," Luke answered condescendingly.

"I know that!" Andrew spat. "But," he started softer, "did you know how... how Pa felt about her?"

Luke pursed his lips. "Well, I'd seen the way he was always lookin' at her. And, he did seem to change the way he was toward her. I dunno."

He thought back to the conversation on the fence. Tom had gathered the boys together that morning before the picnic and said he'd needed to talk to them about something serious. It was hard for him to say it, and he kept saying that Addie wasn't taking the place of their mother. That Edith would always be their ma, no matter if he married Addie or not.

But, he said he needed her.

Tom looked to Andrew and Luke and said, "The day is comin' when you boys are grown, and you'll want to go off and make your own life. Maybe you'll stay here and work this place with me, but even if you do, you'll have homes of your own, and maybe you'll marry. As for me, one by one I'll watch you go, until I'm sittin' in an empty house." He sighed before he went on.

"I miss your ma. She was my first love, and the mother of my children. That is a very important place in my heart that nobody can take. But the truth is," he paused a moment. "The truth is, I love Addie. The very thought she'd go off to Texas and leave me here to think of her the rest of my days is agony for me. Now, I'm not so stupid as to think I won't have to do a fair amount of begging," he laughed at himself. "At this point, I'll do whatever she asks. I need her in many ways you boys just don't understand yet."

He looked to each of the boys for their approval, and only Andrew hesitated. Tom looked at him. "It's not like you'll have to adjust, Andrew. You already know what kind of woman she is."

Andrew nodded slowly.

"Luke?" Andrew asked from across the room where he lay in bed, Frank snoring lightly next to him.

"Yeah?"

"You know, I kinda feel sorry for him."

"Yeah, me too."

When they finished chores and returned to the house, Tom served the sandwiches Addie made for the picnic for dinner, then turned to Luke and Andrew and said in a low voice, "Get your brothers to bed, will you?"

Then he was gone, moving silently down the hall, closing the bedroom door behind himself.

"What now?" Andrew asked.

"I 'spect we best ask God that question," Luke replied.

Addie remained in the dugout until well past the time the boys should've headed off to school. She didn't bother with Red Beast. She left her duties unattended. Tom didn't come to the dugout to tell her to pack her things, that he'd take her to Tuscarora after she'd rejected him and his offer.

Not sure of what step to take next, she just waited. Being on her way was what she preferred. But, the thought of rising and packing her things into the trunk felt odd. The promise of it had carried her through the winter, now it seemed actually doing it was wrong.

If she could wake up in Texas, her world would be right again.

When she came out of the dugout, she set her steps in the direction of the main house. Not exactly sure what she'd say, she just knew it was time to set Tom straight. She was going back to Texas. If he wouldn't take her to the stage, she'd take herself.

When she finally raised her eyes to the main house, he was there, leaning against a pillar next to the steps of the porch. When he met her eyes, he stood up straight. Addie stopped where she was walking and just looked at him. Her mind kept going back to her trunk, to all its contents,

338

the memories they represented. Then to the house, and all the memories it held of a long winter's grief for her. So she remained on neutral ground, where neither could claim her.

She saw Tom Brady sigh, then press his lips together. He knew by the way she walked, she'd made up her mind. "Addie girl," he said softly.

Molly rose from where she was lying next to Tom on the porch and cut loose with a deep warning bark. The hair on the back of her neck stood up, like she'd seen a ghost; like whatever was coming out of the east was coming straight from the dead.

Tom didn't want to look away from Addie.

Molly growled again.

Addie wrinkled her brow and felt the trembling in her chest as she inhaled. Tom could make her change her mind. That she could feel. He could take her in his arms, against her will even, and use her weakness against her. The strength in his arms, her need to be held and comforted, would break her down.

A meadowlark called, not far from her, and the sweet song it sang took Addie right back to the prairie in her dreams. Right back to the feel of the gray's breath on her cheek, leaving a trail of moisture, to the feel of his soft hide. She saw Fett turn in the saddle and look back at her and smile.

Molly became more insistent.

Fearful of what a step in any direction would bring, Addie remained rooted where she was. She covered her face with her hands. Tom called to her again as he stepped off the porch to come to her. Addie raised her head and looked at him, then Molly came between them, the hair on the back of her neck rising even higher.

Looking from the dog to the horizon she was pointed at, Addie saw two riders coming. Watching only for a moment, then crumpling, down to her knees in the moistened earth. Deep sobs escaped her chest as she rocked back and forth, that meadowlark trilling in her ear again.

Tom hurried to her side and touched her shoulder. "Addie?"

When Molly let out what was akin to a howl, Tom looked up at what she was sending out her warning about. He squinted his eyes in the bright morning sun.

He clearly made out Roy, riding his gray stud, whose stride covered ground like he'd never seen the animal do before. His mouth gaped open where Roy held the bridle steady, his head collected, but the gray forcing his speed anyway. Next to Roy rode another fellow, one Tom didn't recognize, but who sat in his saddle like a man who knew how to ride.

And behind him, he led a string of ten.

Luke came out of the barn where he saddled Brown to make rounds without his father that morning. He heard Molly making a ruckus and came to see what she was making the fuss about. It took a moment for him to notice the incoming riders, as his eyes were focused on Addie and his pa, he holding her shoulder, Addie crumpled on the ground, crying into her hands. When Molly began to howl her desperation in obtaining anyone's notice, he walked from the barn and watched the riders come. Such a deep feeling of hopelessness followed what he saw.

"Andrew," Luke called back over his shoulder. It took a moment for him to appear at Luke's side.

"What is it?" Andrew asked in genuine concern.

"Look," Luke said, pointing to the riders.

Andrew looked to the eastern horizon, watching silently for a moment, then he muttered, "Dear God, help us."

"I think this is His answer, Andrew."

Tom took a gentle hold of Addie and helped her up, holding her elbow as they watched the man with the string close the gap between them. Addie wiped her face and took a deep breath, then stepped away from Tom Brady.

The man came within twenty feet of Addie, who walked a few steps and stopped. He wore a gray cowboy hat, stained from the use and the sweat of hotter days. Around his neck was a faded red scarf, flattened and torn with the miles it'd seen, sometimes for the use of warmth, sometimes to soak up sweat. His coat was tied to the back of his saddle, and his once dark blue shirt was bleached from the sun, and his top button remained unaffixed. While he was no older than Roy by any means, his eyes were encircled by crease marks where he'd spent many hours squinting in the sunlight. His chaps were soft and pliable from wear, and the conchos that decorated the side were tarnished. The moustache he wore was speckled with gray and needed trimming, but the hair on his lip was hardly noticeable, for his gray eyes that locked on Addie held something close to   exultation.

"Adelaide," he murmured. Standing gradually in the stirrups, he swung his leg over and lowered himself to the ground without ever taking his eyes off Addie. He hung his rawhide bridle reins over the saddle horn and removed his hat slowly, holding it in his hand unconsciously.

"Adelaide, God knows how I've searched for you," he said as he stepped away from the blood bay he rode. The horses behind that blood bay were quiet and still, and didn't bother the rope that was merely draped over the seat of the saddle.

His face broke into a broad smile as he lunged from where he stood next to the bay. "Adelaide!" he laughed out joyously.

A tear escaped Addie's eye as she smiled in return. "Pete!" she said just before he swept her up into his arms and pulled Addie close to him. Her arms went round his neck and she cried as he rocked her back and forth, swung her around, and clasped the air from her lungs.

"I told you. I told you I'd be back for you." Pete released Addie and gripped her shoulders as he held her away from him. "Ah, let me get a look at you." His grin was blinding as he looked into her face and took in the condition of her body. "Just as purdy as ever!" He hugged her tight again.

"Oh, Pete," Addie released slowly the agony of her heart felt at the sounding of her voice.

Pete clenched his eyes closed and he gripped her tightly, burying her face against his neck. This time he stood still, holding her while she cried deeply, the kind of crying that purged the soul of a woman and demanded the courage of men to just be able to stand and listen.

Tom sighed very heavily and slipped his hands into his pockets.

With a stricken look, he glanced at Roy to see he was watching him, not the scene between Addie and the man who'd rode across the desert. Roy's face was calculating as he looked at Tom, then back to Addie. In his usual way, Roy had already come up with the means to the situation that was in place long before he rode into the middle of it bringing more complication with him.

After a while, when some of her crying ebbed, Pete tenderly said, "I've had hell, girl, looking for you. I've cursed myself a hundred kinds of fool for not taking you with me." Addie drew away from him, her cheeks wet and her eyes full of sadness. "I don't know what scared me worse. Not finding you, or finding you in some terrible place, getting by however you could. Why didn't you wait for me?"

Addie answered with a sob, "I... I didn't think I'd see you again."

Pete took hold of her face in both his hands. "I told you I'd come back for you." Pete smiled again then. "I brought you somethin'."

Charlie bounded off the steps of the porch about then, but Tom caught him up and held him before he could go to Addie. His little red lips kept making the 'a-a-a' motion as he pointed to her. Tom clenched his jaw tightly closed and looked away, down to the barn where the two older boys watched silently. Luke's shoulders dropped and he looked to the ground in front of him.

"Look at that bay," Andrew whispered. "Ain't he fancy?"

"Come on," Pete said as he walked away from Addie, putting his hat back on his head, tilted slightly to one side. He gestured for her to follow. He walked past his bay, who tipped his head in respect to Pete, and walked with purpose past every horse in that line. Each tipped their nose and watched him pass. Pete stopped at the very end and looked back to Addie who hadn't ventured past the blood bay.

Pete reached up and rubbed the neck of the little bay who brought up the last of the string. His dark brown eyes were bright and kind, and his ears were fixed on Addie who came no further. The little bay wore a saddle, unlike any of the others.

Addie covered her mouth.

Looking at that little bay standing there, saddled, ready, casting a patient look at her, completely erased the past winter. The feel of cracked and bleeding hands plunging into wash water was gone. The cold and severe pain she'd felt just before she was sure she'd succumb to the cold of the blizzard as she frantically searched for Luke never happened. The feel of Charlie's soft, warm body curled against her as he slept in the gray of the afternoon light was a pleasant dream. The taste of homemade bread by her own hand, a wish hidden in her heart for more prosperous times.

Focusing only on that bay, Addie went back to other days, happier days. He wore her saddle, ready to find adventure just over the next butte, or valley, or in the vast expanse of the prairie. He'd carry her to Mexico that afternoon if that was where she sent him. He'd willingly run down another string of ten, bounding over cactus and brush, hold a reata tight while Pete and Fett cut a stud.

Bear with fortitude the love between a young man and woman as they lived without fear of dying.

It was possible, looking only at that little bay, and Pete standing beside him, to believe Fett were there as well, just beyond her line of vision, just beyond her focus. As surreal as it was to see Pete coming, the Bradys and the homestead became, in that instant, what was surreal. Fett's laugh was as audible as it was when he was alive, the feel of his skin against hers, his blue eyes looking back at her from where he turned in the saddle.

Suddenly, she had to know.

Addie took her hand away from her mouth. "Buck?" she whispered.

Pete smiled weakly, then shook his head. "He just never was right… again, after that day. I had to put him down, Adelaide."

Addie looked at the ground for a moment. When she looked back up at Pete, she nodded.

"But," Pete said, "I kept Paddy."

Addie let out a sad laugh. "You've been saddlin' him every mornin' and draggin' him everywhere you go?"

Pete smiled and looked over to Paddy and rubbed his neck again. "Ah, wasn't no trouble. He kept the back end of the string movin'. I planned on findin' you sometime, though I near gave up hope."

"Pete?" Roy asked from the back of the gray. "Might I introduce you to a few of these fellas?"

Pete walked away from the little bay and came to stand next to Addie once again. He kept close to her, almost as if she'd ridden in with him, instead of him riding in to find her. Pete gave Tom a wary look, but held out his hand despite it.

Roy swung down off the gray and hung his reins on the saddle horn. Smiling kindly at Addie, he removed his hat and walked to stand near her. "Pete Summers, I'd like you to meet Tom Brady."

The two men shook hands, both eyeing the other with deep suspicion. Addie watched them with dismay, and catching her look Roy laid a comforting hand on her shoulder.

"Boys," Tom called and motioned the boys to come up from the barn. Frank, who'd been watching from the porch came to his father as well. "Boys," he said when they'd all gathered, "this is Pete Summers. Who I can only guess knows Addie in some way."

Pete shook the hand of each boy and smiled. "This might sound a little off, but Addie and I were saddle partners once."

"Women aren't saddle partners," Andrew muttered.

Pete laughed. He put an arm around Addie and pressed her close to his side. Laughing again as he looked down at her doubtful face, he said, "Then you don't know the real Addie very well."

"I'm afraid we must not know that Addie at all," Tom said softly as he looked to her. His eyes were full of something, but Addie looked away from him. She looked up to see Roy watching her reaction.

"What brings you out this way?" Tom asked of Pete.

Pete looked squarely at Tom and said, "I've come to take her back to her mama."

In surprise Addie looked up at Pete. "All the way to Texas?"

"Unless your ma has moved closer," he grinned.

"Well, seein' as it's near noon, maybe you'd like to stay and eat, Mr. Summers." Tom cut in. His look went soft as his eyes fell on Addie. "That is, if it's alright with you?"

"Of course," Addie replied, avoiding him. She looked to Pete who watched her with a raised brow.

"I have to say, Roy," Pete commented, "that gray of yours sure settled right down once he got to where he was goin'."

Roy didn't turn to look at the gray who stood with his ears pricked forward. "He's always like that when he heads west."

Addie cast grief-stricken eyes on Roy. "You couldn't catch any of your other saddle horses?"

Roy shrugged. "I thought he might be pertinent."

Addie looked back over her shoulder at the gray. Dipping his head in a request for permission, he took a step towards her. "I really don't need you in the middle of things," she whispered to him. The gray lowered his head and pointed black etched ears at her.

"Well, where'd you get this bunch of renegades?" Addie asked of Pete as she looked back down the line behind the blood bay.

Pete laughed as he moved away from her. Gesturing to the chestnut in the front of the string he said, "No renegades this time. I hand-picked these myself."

"Where was the fun in that?" she asked.

"This was what Fett and I wanted. To pool our money and buy a string to start out with." Pete looked down the line. "This is them."

"Fett had money?" Addie asked doubtfully.

Pete's expression returned that doubt. "Not exactly. But combined, this is what we got." Pointing to the end of the string, a little buckskin and another chestnut, Pete said, "Those, along with Paddy, of course, are yours, Addie. You can keep 'em for yourself, or you can sell them and keep the profit. Whatever you choose."

"I have money?" Addie asked in disbelief.

"Not paper money, yet, but you've got the start. And from what I understand about Mr. Brady, you might be able to turn them into paper money if he is interested. That of course, is up to him."

Wandering slowly down to the humble beginnings of her own remuda, Addie stopped in front of the buckskin.

"I'm sorry, Adelaide. I wanted to bring Buck back to ya. But, this was as close as I got."

The mare had a kind eye, and she stood patiently. She was smaller than Buck was, but she did bring back memories of him.

"I wish..." Addie began. "Maybe not. Maybe seein' Buck would have been too much for me. Maybe it's best he's gone too."

"Pete," Tom said after a moment of silence. "Why don't you put your string in the pasture next to the barn while Addie makes up some dinner?" Tom asked in an inviting tone.

"I'd appreciate that, if it isn't too much trouble," Pete replied.

"None at all."

Luke came forward and held out his hand. "Can I take your saddle horse? I'll get his gear off."

Pete smiled and nodded. "You bet. Thanks, boy." Looking at Addie he said, "I'll be along in a minute."

Luke led the blood bay away from the gathering, and Pete took the lead of the string and walked them away with Tom towards the pasture gate. Charlie looked back over his pa's shoulder to Addie. Tom didn't say much, but the one thing he did say Addie couldn't hear. Pete replied with a yes and a smile.

It was a fine string Pete led.

When she turned to head to the porch, Roy stood beside the gray, ready to lead him to the barn. In his eyes was something close to understanding.

"It's miserable, ain't it?"

"What?" she asked.

Roy shook his head as he took off his hat and wiped the sweat from his brow with his forearm. "The way life likes to tie itself into great knots and webs with thorns and briars just waiting to tear at our soul."

"You don't think this is good? Now I can get back to Texas. Faster, too."

Roy knocked some of the dust from his hat. "Addie, all I really think is somebody's gonna carry a hell of a heartache away from this tangled wreckage."

"What do you want from me?" Addie half sobbed out. "Why is it all of a sudden the woman who was never meant to stay can't get outta here without everybody fallin' apart? I did what I was supposed to do! Now I want to go home."

Roy pursed his lips together. "Just remember, there is no such thing as going back. I've tried. Even what seems the same doesn't work anymore. What you think will be isn't necessarily what you get."

Addie watched Pete turn the lead horse out into the green grass. "It's like none of it happened. Like I never lost him. He's just in the barn or something." She rubbed her face. "I just know I don't want to be confused anymore. I want to take the one thing I'm sure of and hold on to it. And that one thing is Pete. I've known Pete long enough to understand what his intentions are."

Roy chuckled. "I believe the only intentions you're scared of are your own."

Addie turned her head to look at him, only to find mischief in his blue eyes. "Roy Albert. Don't give grief. I have more than I can take right now."

Looking up at the sky he said, "So now is a bad time to bring up the gray?"

With an ashen face she cast her eyes to the gray, who stood patiently, his ears ticking forward on her when he caught her look. "I'd just as soon he went back to wherever he came from." With that she climbed the porch steps and passed Frankie who bounded off in the direction of the pasture gate. Roy watched Addie go, then he headed to the barn.

"That last bunch we gathered had near thirty in it. Big bunch for one stud that far out on what they call the Black Rock. Not a damn drop of water anywhere for a water trap to run those horses into." Pete shook his head as he took another sip of coffee. "I decided even in the winter, that place is no place for the likes of me."

"That's a hard country. Even for the creatures that call it home," Roy stated.

"How many of those horses would you take out of a bunch?" Tom asked.

"Oh, depends. Back when I had Addie and….," he shrugged his shoulders. "Back when I had a bigger crew," Pete started again, "We'd keep ten or so. Just depends on the quality of the stock. Helps to mind the breeding options. Cut the studs that shouldn't be papas. Find a real bad off mare that is in too poor a shape to slowly starve with a foal on her, put her down so she don't have to suffer her way outta the world. Fett was a hell of a hand. He could start five a day. No fences. No ropes. Just himself sittin' one."

"What if one was too rank for him?" Andrew asked in complete awe.

"Well, he never did find one like that, but if he were tired or burnt out, I'd rope a hind leg so they couldn't run or get too rough. When we had 'em good and gentle," Pete said wryly, "we'd send 'em on to Addie to put the finishing touches on."

Addie scowled at him from the workbench. "Those horses never were gentle. I spent most of the day tryin' not to rustle anything."

Pete reared back and let out a booming laugh. "Ah, hell. You remember the time Fett stuck you on that counterfeit paint?"

Addie turned to face him fully. She dropped her shoulders in disgust as her face went stern. "Do I remember," she said sarcastically. "How could I forget." She shook her head. "Fett tells me not to worry. He'd been rode for a couple days and he had no buck. No buck. He'd trapped him into every tight spot he could, had asked for plenty more than the horse was taught to give. No buck in him. Well, did I learn a very important lesson." Addie turned to stir her stew to Pete's uncontrollable laughter.

She turned to look at the boys who sat in rapt fascination at the table. "You boys remember somethin'. When some horseman tells you 'he's got no buck', what he really means is, it's a runaway. That paint caught sight of a strand of my hair that'd come out of my braid, and he launched himself into a dead run. He had no give in the face, so off we ran. Thinking somebody on a broke horse would come to my aid, I just held on as he catapulted over brush and rocks, looking back at me instead of where he was a goin'!"

Pete gleefully clapped his hands together. "We'd have come after ya, but we was a little too late to get a good start out. We figured he'd get tired and stop at some point, but that bugger was headed for his home range somewhere in south Mexico!"

Addie pointed a finger at Pete. "I woulda bailed if I'd have thought I'd ever see my saddle again. Not to mention I'd have died in the fall at that speed with all the rocks about." Roy started to chuckle at Addie's expense. "I kept lookin' back over my shoulder for the help I just knew was comin'. Never did see 'em."

Tom looked aghast. "How'd you get out of it?"

Addie sighed and went back to slicing bread. "Well, when I finally figured I was on my own, I just kept working him till, at a dead run, he started to give his nose just a little. Then, when he wore himself out just enough, I took his nose and made a wide circle. He caught sight of me up on his back and ran, just as nuts, back toward camp."

"When they got back, that paint was so lathered he had no brown spots left on his renegade hide. But, I have to say, Fett and I both rode him after that, and we both had to whip the dog out of him just to get him to lope. He wasn't gonna make that mistake twice!"

"Yeah, and from then on I was busy at camp until they had a better handle on 'em. And I was wiser in asking if the horse had any *run* in him if he had no buck," Addie finished as she refilled coffee mugs. She held out a plate of sweet cinnamon bread to each of the boys to help themselves to a slice.

"Oh, Adelaide. You had more guts than some men I know. And most of it was born of a very misguided trust in Fett. He had a belief in your ability to learn skills I've never seen. He would just say, 'She'll figure it out.' If he said the horse was good, you took him at his word. That trust gave you a confidence you wouldn't have had if Fett'd told you the truth."

Addie gave him a sad smile. "He was something else. Sometimes I wonder what he would have been like as an old man." Looking back at

349

her ladle, she poured stew into a deep dish plate. "It would have been very hard watching him slowly lose his strength and life. To see him livin' life on the porch, with nothin' but memories of his young days."

Pete looked down at his hands on the table. "I think that might be the first time I ever heard you contemplate old age, Adelaide." Pressing his lips tightly together a moment, he continued. "Don't let death cheat you out of the thrill of that runaway paint."

She didn't know what to say to him. She didn't want to look very deep into her soul and see that maybe he was right. She'd let Fett's death cheat her out of the thrill of living.

"I have to thank you, Mr. Brady," Pete said as he looked over to Tom. "You've taken good care of her. Adelaide looks good. I was very afraid of what kind of shape I'd find her in."

"Thank you, Addie," Tom said in a low voice as she set a plate of stew before him. Then he turned to Pete. "Well, we had a rocky start. But, I'm glad you find her to your liking."

"We would have headed over last evening, but that storm hit," Pete stated.

Roy shook his head. "That was a bad one. Figured we'd sit tight for the night and head over when we weren't gonna get cooked by lightning."

"We was out in it!" Frankie exclaimed.

"We *were* out in it," Luke corrected.

"What was you doin'?" Roy teased. "Don't you know lightning likes to tickle little boys in the armpit?"

Frankie laughed. "No, it doesn't!"

"Yes, it does," Roy replied with wide eyes.

"We went for a picnic up the meadow and it snuck up on us," Andrew said with his mouth full of potato.

"Whoooeee," Roy drawled out. "I bet your undershorts were soaked by the time you got back."

Frankie giggled.

Tom looked at Addie. She kept her eyes on her stew plate as she sat.

Roy looked between them. Pete watched Addie.

After a moment of silence, Pete asked Tom, "Seems like you got yourself a good spread here."

Tom chewed his bite and swallowed before he answered. "Yeah, got a fair amount of horses here abouts. Most of the older mares just came off the meadows from the winter. Still got a few that are waitin' to foal. But the rest we'll start gatherin' this week. Brand any we missed last fall, take the older colts and start them under saddle."

Pete took a sip of coffee. "May I ask where you got the makings of a herd that size?"

Tom shrugged. "Well, for the most part, same as you. The fancier mares I traveled back to Missouri and hand-picked myself. Same with the Thoroughbred studs. I spent time south and west of here gathering horses, bringing them home. I won't complain. They've built us a fine life."

His curiosity piqued, Pete continued. "What do you do with your crop? Where is your market?"

Tom wiped his lip with his thumb. "Most of them go on the train east. I sell plenty to ranchers from here down to Arizona. Last year I sent a small bunch over California way to supply the miners and settlers. But," he added with optimism, "I had a Lieutenant Colonel ride through last June, looking for a few army remounts. I sold him about thirty head. He liked the looks of them, said he'd be back."

"So you do have a somewhat steady market."

"I'd like a steadier one. Trouble with the remounts is, although that would be a constant source of income, the army doesn't allocate funds for the purchase of remounts. The cavalry is only given small sums every few years from Washington to replace what they've lost. So, when they get money together, they'll come to me. Otherwise, the majority of my well-tended herd goes east to become farm workers. And, since that's not what they're bred to be, I see that as a waste. But, a man has to provide for his family."

"At least some of them go on to become ranch horses," Pete reassured.

Tom brightened some. He leaned forward to rest his elbows on the table. "Yeah, more of 'em are spreading out there, making a name for me." He let out a depreciating laugh. "Whether it be a good name or not."

"Hell," Pete said as he folded his arms across his chest. "Must be makin' a good one for the army to travel to you."

Tom nodded, then cast a glance at Addie who had risen from her spot to pick up dishes. Looking down at his hands a moment he said, "Well, boys, we best leave Pete and Addie to visit awhile. I expect they have things to discuss." Tom rose slowly and looked at Roy. "Since you're here, you can saddle up and make yourself useful. Help us gather the geldings off the south piece."

Roy groaned. "You know, that's the trouble with you. I can't eat here without payin' for it."

Tom grinned at Roy. "It's like a stick that I use to beat you. And bein' an old mangy dog, you never have learned to say no to a handout, with all its strings attached."

Roy stood and stretched. "Thank you, Addie, for the fine meal." He cast a wry glance to Tom. "Even if I have to pay for it. It was worth it."

Addie laughed softly. "Any time, Roy."

As Tom and the boys gathered cowboy hats off the shelf by the door where they rested on their crowns, he turned to Addie. "Would you keep an eye on Charlie for me?"

Sending him only a glance, she replied, "Yes. He can stay and play."

Tipping his head to her, Tom said softly, "Thank you."

The three boys wandered out into the pasture to gather their horses, but Tom and Roy's were both in the saddling stall. Tom had plans that day for the red filly, but the original purpose wasn't to gather geldings off the south piece. He grabbed his blankets and saddle, throwing them up on her back with unintentional force.

"Tom?" Roy asked.

"Yeah?" Tom answered without looking at him. The filly's ear jerked at his tone.

"Everything alright?"

"Whatever gave you the idea it wasn't?" Tom harshly replied.

Roy hitched an arm over the gray's hip. He ran a smooth hand over his hide. "Oh, not much. Just the looks you give Addie that she won't return."

"Well, she and I have never been ones to look at each other." Tom jerked his cinch and the filly squared up her feet to brace herself.

Roy nodded solemnly. "That's true." He was quiet a moment, then he continued. "Sure is somethin'. A man just," he gestured widely with his arm, "ridin' in off the desert, lookin' for one widowed woman. He'd been all over lookin' for Addie. Spent most of the winter at it, but the snows kept him from venturing too far, too fast."

Tom's shoulders slumped and he rested his arms on the seat of his saddle. Looking to the rafters of the barn he said, "What are the odds?" In a louder voice he said again, "What are the odds? Who would guess that some man would show up just then. Is my timing bad, or is it his?"

Roy tipped his head as he looked at Tom. "Timing for what?"

Lowering his head, Tom said, "Yesterday," he cut short. "Yesterday I asked Addie to stay with me. Told her I…" With a rough hand Tom wiped his mouth. "And today we get up, and here comes Pete Summers. What are the damn odds?"

"Did she say she'd stay?"

Tom turned and looked at Roy. "No. She didn't. But I really thought with time I could make her see. She belongs here, with me." He shook his head violently. "Not now. She'll be ridin' out of here with him first thing. I left Charlie in hopes she wouldn't leave before we get back from gatherin' geldings."

"She won't leave without sayin' something. She isn't like that. And she won't leave Charlie to his own before we get back with the geldings." Roy assured. "May I ask why she won't stay?"

Tom ran a hand down the red filly's neck. She cocked an ear at him. In a more temperate voice he replied, "She said…she said she couldn't. That the fear of losing like she lost Fett was more than she could live with. And I don't 'xpect it helps I was a miserable ass to her when she first came here." He paused a moment. "Ah, hell. I spent the winter bein' a miserable ass."

Roy chuckled. "No, I doubt that helps."

Tom turned rigid again as he finished cinching up. "Who the hell am I kidding. She's twenty-two years old. No beautiful young woman is gonna burn up her chance at life with a man near twelve years older than her, raisin' four boys that ain't hers. She could have any young man she pointed her finger at."

"It's good you realize that." Roy looked up at the face of the gray, who tipped his eye to look back at him. "But, I don't know how out of time you are. Seems to me you might be holding more aces than you know."

Tom stopped and looked over his shoulder at Roy. "What are you talkin' about?"

"Well, you got a big gather, brandin', and colt startin' to get through. Really, that oughta take some time." Roy leisurely explained. "And seein' as you have what is obviously a horse-hand sittin' at your table right now, and you need hands for the job..." Roy looked expectantly at Tom.

Tom straightened and gave Roy a look of understanding. Roy looked back to the gray who began to work his cricket.

Addie lay alone in the dugout that night and listened to the soft sigh of the wind. Molly was close to her, dreaming her rabbit-chasing dreams, her feet twitching and her ears wiggling. Every so often, she'd let out a tiny squeak from deep in her throat, as though in her dream she barked and whined at something.

It was deep into the night, and she lay there without the hope of sleep. Several times she'd wondered if the day had actually happened. Was Pete really laid up in the barn loft, occupying one of the bunks Tom and Luke set up for the hands coming to start colts? Sitting in the kitchen talking to him, it was like he'd always been there, a part of her winter, her life. He was warm and full of life.

But he brought no Fett with him. Only the memories.

Clenching her eyes against the coming tears, she buried her face in the blankets. She'd thanked God for the gift of the arrival of a good friend, one from her past, who wasn't trying to stake a claim on her future. Pete would take her home to her mama, and to her beloved Texas. Addie just wanted the comfort of another woman to help her through things. To help her sort things with womanly compassion. While men are comforting, at times, they just don't see things with the same intuition.

The pain of it was simple. Women need women.

But there she was, surrounded by men, all with intentions of their own, not a one very compassionate in Addie's way of thinking. Perhaps all willing to help her in what was their own way of solving her problems, but she wasn't sure she was ready for any of those answers.

At the supper table, Tom asked Pete if he'd stay on awhile and help out with the horses. Pete was more than willing, but he'd looked to Addie for her say so. He knew she desired to get back to Texas. They'd spoken of it while the Bradys and Roy were gathering the geldings.

Addie told him of her troubles, of how she'd spent her winter. She'd been honest in the way Tom Brady treated her when late fall brought her to this place. She related the occasion of the dead rat in the flour bin. Pete chuckled, but tried not to laugh too hard. Addie left out the part about her dreams, and about the day previous, when Tom Brady asked her to stay with him.

What would Pete Summers think of her? Staying with a man like Tom after she'd supposedly loved Fett with such devotion. She looked up to Pete, thought the world of his opinions. He would surely scorn her for hastily marrying another. What would he say if he knew that just yesterday she'd kissed Tom?

Addie again hid her face in shame.

She wasn't a loose woman. Not even close. Yet he'd think of her as one. Life was cruel, to make her live with choices like this. To be instilled with the desire to be held and loved, to feel the touch and warmth of another human being. To crave it in the long hours of the night. Then to take the man from her who'd woke those feelings within her.

That was very unkind.

Molly jerked beside her, so much so she woke herself. She looked over to Addie with sleepy eyes, then lay her head on Addie's stomach and fell instantly to sleep again. Addie appreciated the humor of it. In her life, many times she'd been told animals have no soul, no dreams, no ponderings. Whoever said that never slept beside a dreaming dog, nor mounted a young horse who'd spent the winter turned out, only to find it had taken a firm grasp of ideas it hadn't understood the fall previous. Nor seen the devotion of a beloved pet who traveled miles to be with someone they loved.

The gray.

What was he? Why was he? Addie wasn't at a point in her life to contemplate the craziness of it all. The deeply carved lines, all crossing each other in the pathway of life, and just how far back those lines had been moving closer together to cross. What was a gray horse? Flesh and bone. What was his purpose? To carry a man and his burdens. What was his understanding? Nothing. All he knew was what he was commanded. What were his capabilities? Limitless. To haunt innumerous dreams. To cover miles and miles in a single night.

He was an enigma, as was his part in Addie's life.

Just before dawn, Addie drifted into restless dreams that rivaled Molly's. And when she drifted off, Molly woke, and with her head lying on Addie's stomach, she watched. She let soft and low whines and covered Addie's arm with her paw.

For Addie, she saw him there, waiting for her in the golden light. He rose up against the brilliant blue of the sky behind him. The black of his mane fanned out, shimmering in the light as he stood on his hind legs, his ears pressed tightly back on his neck. The emotion flashed in his eyes, as he struck wildly into the air with his front legs. His mouth gaped, teeth bared, and a high pitched squeal came from deep in his soul.

Nothing about the gray was comforting nor welcoming.

Mare worked her way through a dense bunch of brush just below a rimrock. She lowered her head and looked closely at a deep hole that extended back into the rock. There was a smell coming from that hole, but whatever lived within it chose not to show itself. Cocking an ear back at the boy who sat steady on her back, she picked a rocky path over the ridgeline.

Frank was quiet and as still as he could be. He spoke nothing to his horse, nor did he trouble to change Mare's choice of pathway. Mare had done this many times and she understood what was about to happen. They went wide around the meadow below as it wound and hugged its way up a swollen creek. Way across the meadow and riding on the opposite ridge was Andrew, just as quiet and steady, moving along in the camouflage of the brush and rocks, or out of sight over the ridge.

Somewhere, way ahead and out of sight of either boy, was Luke, sneaking slowly as he ventured to put pressure on at the mouth of the greening meadow. Clouds gathered up on the mountain, but they held back, bulging out from the peaks, then fading back to nearly nothing, only to do it again as the wind picked up courage. The bright sun coming from the east was warm, and it wouldn't be very late in the morning before the boys were drenched in sweat.

Tom told them to go easy as long as possible. Work them easy before they hit a run.

They would be feeling good, the first of the stud bunches they'd gather. The foals at the sides of the mares were young, some only a week old or so, but those babies would keep up with their mamas with unbelievable speed. Luke eased Brown off the hill above the bunch at the mouth of the meadow. Below him was a deep cut valley, the best of scenarios, where they'd run those horses on flat ground straight back in the direction of the homestead. As they got closer, the crew of experienced cowboys would be waiting to guide them in on fresh horses.

This would be the easiest of the bunches to gather.

Upon hearing a high-pitched whistle, Luke knew he'd been spotted as the stud blew and snorted through his nostrils at the incoming intruder. The studs were turned out several weeks before with separate bunches to perpetuate the foal crop for the next year. Tom sent Luke with a pistol full of birdshot to help the stud get moving, if need be. Luke also had the hardest of the jobs among the boys; keep the stud from fading away from the bunch of mares. A stud would quit the bunch when he realized he was near trapped. He'd let those mares go on and take whatever was coming alone.

Halfway down the hill, Luke saw that the bunch was standing and looking in his direction. Hoping they'd hold out until he hit the valley floor, he encouraged Brown to walk faster. Already Brown's heart beat fast, and Luke could feel it through his saddle like a hammer that struck against rock.

With a squeal, the big sorrel Thoroughbred stud pranced around to stand between the newcomer and his mares. His tail was raised and his head was high, his ears pressed back against his neck. Brown moved into a trot as the lead mare, a black with a strip face, took her foal and started away from the bunch in the opposite direction of Luke. It took only a second for a few of the other mares to get the same idea, and they took off with incredible speed. The stud called out, but in seeing he wasn't going to win the argument, he turned and made after them. By now the bunch was moving in mass, about twenty-five mares and a few older fillies. Brown cleared the last cluster of brush and was free out on the meadow, charging after the already hard running bunch.

Luke leaned forward and slouched in a lower profile against the wind coming at him. Brown stretched and broke over, increasing his speed until he was giving all his lean runner's body could give. The bunch began to string out some, taking to a barely visible path in the bright green. The lead mare was guiding them to where the path would climb up to the rimrocks, and they'd be free on top in the brush and rock. There it would be easy to lose the horse and rider closing the gap between them. They'd become a circling group, winding and retreating their way to nowhere, but tiring Luke's horse and losing mares and foals along the way as they slipped from the bunch and headed back up towards the mountain. They'd gather together again, standing to watch the lathered horse and rider look at them with defeat.

But not today.

Just as the path cut sharply into the brush on the ascent to the ridgeline, Andrew jumped out at them from a huge cluster of willows and spooked them back to the middle of the meadow. They bunched again, their colors melting together briefly as the lead mare reconsidered her next move. She thundered on, tipping her head to see that her babe was still loping along next to her. Having made up her mind again, she exploded into speed and cut across to the opposite side of the meadow.

For once, Blue succeeded in fulfilling his potential. His build was what made him the tall, lanky and somewhat ugly beast he was. But somewhere in that lank was what made up his incredible speed. His stride was wide, and he could recoil and fire rapidly. They kept on in a straight and strung out bunch for a good two miles, then the lead mare cut sharply again, following an invisible trail up the rocks and sage to the top and freedom.

This time it was Frank who bounded out of the sage at her, his little hands wound and tangled in Mare's long mane. Just like his pa told him to do. Luke used one of his father's, but there was no saddle for the younger boys. They rode bareback.

Frankie, all you have to do is ride. Hold on with your hands in your horse's mane and ride. Don't push 'em, don't try to steer 'em, just ride, boy.

Mare lunged at the lead mare who jumped across a ditch and lengthened out in exasperation down the meadow. She was confused, and turned now to the option of merely running as hard as she could. Mare looked back out of the corner of her eye at Frank who was laid out against her neck, wound tightly into her mane. She saw that he was as firm in his seat as he could get, so she extended her stride as wide as it could go, forcing the lead mare to quicken her pace.

By now the stud had taken in the whole of the operation and the odds of the bunch slipping away. He weighed them out to not be good. So, looking back to Brown who still pounded along behind him, he worked his way back to the right. Seeing his intent, Luke went with him, hoping he could persuade him to rejoin the bunch before he cut up into the brush and away from the group. Once in that brush, Luke would have to let him go as it would be hopeless to abandon the bunch and waste valuable time trying to work him out again. Once Luke was gone from the drag, the mares would gain confidence and fan out, completely uncontrollable for Andrew and Frankie.

Pushing them hard and fast was the only way to pry them from their home ground.

With quick and steady pressure, the stud veered and joined the bunch again, but he wasn't done thinking about it. He tipped his head constantly to look for an opening, so Luke hollered and hoorayed a bit to press a little more speed from the already surging bunch. The lead slowed drastically as it hit a bog and their feet sucked deep down into the mud. They were hit from behind as horses still running full force collided with them. Only the light-weight foals pressed on without trouble. Mare took to the side hill and jumped the source of the bog, a spring running freely out of a crag of lava rock. Frankie's little fanny left his seat for a quarter second, then met with it again with a bounce. He rode part of the time with his eyes closed, but only when he didn't know what Mare would choose to do.

A deep wash cut up the meadow and separated the horses and Andrew, but he kept on with the pressure. About a mile later, the wash jagged suddenly in front of him. Blue shortened his stride, but lost no momentum nor timing as he flew over it, covering the expanse with no difficulty. He lit on the opposite bank and pushed himself hard to catch what minimal speed he'd lost.

Nearing the seventh mile of the journey, the horses bearing riders were drenched with sweat, but still they pressed on. Andrew's pants were sweated through with moisture from Blue, and Frankie's wet butt stuck firmly to whatever dry spot on Mare's back he slid into. The salty smell of horse sweat was heavy in the air. But still, the hearts of those three boys pounded with adrenaline, raging on without fear of falling or failing.

The meadow widened broadly ahead as it leveled out and became open, flat ground. Anticipating it, the mares started to spread out to make a break for it in all directions. Already the stud was trumpeting out his gathering call. With a final burst of energy, Blue and Mare pressed with as much force as they had left to bring them tightly together again. Horses now tried to cut in front of the riders, taking foals with them. With arms waving and dry throats screaming, they warded off the first attempts at break out.

As the lead mare hit open country, two riders came off the desert towards her. One on her right, Tom Brady, and one from her left, Pete Summers. By now she was tired, and her baby heaved in and out with the trial of running. She was leaving the range she was most familiar with, and in desperation she jagged hard to the right in a last attempt to flee back to what she knew. Anticipating her move, the stud prepared to go with her. But, there again was Brown, cutting off his retreat.

As the bunch plunged through a deep ravine and came out the other side, they climbed a steep hill which slowed their speed enough for the boys to catch up again. As they crested the hill, they traveled across the flat top, then descended down into the unknown. They'd left their territory and were now moving along with the prompting of the men at their sides. In the ravine, Roy was waiting to take Luke's place at the drag, as now the stud would be frantic to leave the bunch and go back. It would take a fresh horse to hold him.

As the boys' mounts tired out coming off that butte, they slowed and trotted on together and watched from sweat-drenched horses as the men with experience pressed on towards the trap. Between where they watched and the trap, three more men waited to funnel horses into the enclosure.

Frankie unwound his little fingers from Mare's mane. They were numb and stinging from where the blood was cut off by the severity of his grip. He wiped sweat from his brow. The older boys wore hats, but Frankie was too scared his would fly off and be left behind. Now with the bright sun in his eyes as he watched the running bunch, he wished he had it.

Luke was out of breath as he said, "That went about as good as it coulda." He swallowed hard to wet his dry, burning throat. "I guess that's why we keep that useless blue-eyed bastard around. Damn he's fast."

Andrew, with sweat dripping down his face, looked to Blue who watched the bunch with his head up and ears forward, ready to make another charge. "Yeah. He ain't much good for goin' to school on, but he makes out alright doin' this."

Mare looked back to the boy who sat quietly on her back. She wanted to reassure herself she hadn't lost him at some point, but he was there, shielding his eyes from the sun. Life had gone around for her, near full circle. She'd started out her life at the side of her mama, running hard from skilled riders who worked to edge her own band into a trap. When she was old enough, she was cut out and started under saddle, just as would happen to some of the fillies that she ran today. Then she spent time running with foals at her side. Now, getting on in her years, it was about merely keeping up. That was her source of pride, and in that, the ability to keep her young, inexperienced rider up on her back and in the race.

Mare played all the parts available to play in the lifetime of running horses. She'd done it all, from every angle. Now the little brown mare was wise, and she realized only the strong survived the game as long as she had. With heart and grit, she'd make another run, but the times she'd do so were numbered, until finally, she ran for good with the big bunch in heaven. Every so often those horses ran through her dreams; all the good horses who'd gone before her.

The sweet smell of the sage drifted across the range with the breeze. A stray cloud drifted across the sun, a temporary and welcome offering of shade. Dark patches moved along the contours of the land as the clouds cast shade while moving freely in the sky.

"We best move along. They might need help." Luke picked up into a brisk trot, his brothers following suit.

Roy's red roan was fighting hard to keep the stud going with the bunch. They were now necking down slowly between both natural lava rock barriers and stretches of handmade fences. Moving in a balled mass, the mares in the lead weaved back and forth between the barriers, constantly working to seek an out. Keeping them moving, the barriers were near a quarter mile apart. Across the flat they traveled on, there was a bluff, and below that was the homestead. Far in the distance it could be seen, and now all six of the men took the horses in at an easy lope.

As they came near the trap, the mares attempted to balk, but from the steady pressure, they kept moving between the wide fences, set that way to prevent the braver of the horses from jumping out. The gates to the corral were open wide, and the bunch passed with great uncertainty. They moved into a dead run again, thinking once through they could run free, only to be halted by the high fence on the opposite side of the corral.

General chaos ensued.

Mares ran frantically in a circle, their foals in a tangled bunch beside them, squealing and darting between mares. The huge log gates were shut behind them, and they were successfully trapped. Tom Brady immediately took down his reata and built a loop. The big sorrel gelding he rode was lathered and breathing hard, but he faced the circling bunch, walking just behind them, keeping Tom in position until he found what he was looking for. Tom did not impede the front of the running bunch, for they would proceed, whether that be in attempt to clear the high fence next to them, or over the top of each other and foals to get past him. When the stud placed himself at the rear, Tom's loop sailed out quickly and settled over the stud's neck.

He flung himself and bucked high into the air once, but with a rough jerk from the stout sorrel gelding Tom rode, the stud walked away from the fence to the center of the corral as the mares raced on. All of Tom's studs were started horses, well-educated animals, and the quality of their breeding was obvious. These were well-tended stock.

Without further discussion, Tom handed the stud off to Roy, who lead the beast out of the melee into a corral of his own. Tom and Pete stood at the opposite end of the corral from the mares, allowing them time to settle and rest a moment. They nuzzled their foals and watched with growing suspicion the men across the distance.

By now the boys were trotting in from the desert on tired horses. Luke rode Brown around the corrals and from his horse's back opened and shut several gates. He rode into the barn and pulled his saddle and placed it on the back of another while Andrew and Frankie let their horses go in the meadow. Luke rode out on his fresh mount with tired muscles, but with a spirit of excitement. Frank and Andrew climbed the corral fence and sat on the top rail, waiting for further instructions.

By now, the branding fire built in an adjacent corral was hot and ready as flames sent sparks shooting out when the wood added to it popped and started to burn. Irons were thrown into the base of it and the metal heated and expanded.

"You boys get in there," Tom hollered to the two boys on the fence. They immediately climbed down from their perch and took hold of old reatas handed down to them from their father.

As Frankie and Andrew walked to the center of the corral, the bunch began to move again, shifting restlessly and in anticipation of what was coming. Andrew felt the worn, braided rawhide in his hand and the smoothness of the well-oiled hide was like silk. He swung his loop to warm up his arm as he walked. The mares began to run in a great circle around the enclosure, Frankie too swung his loop. As the mob thinned out to squeeze through the distance between the boys and the fence, Andrew swung harder, waiting for his pick. At the back of the line, two little colts rushed to squirt by before the running bunch left them to circle around again.

Andrew let his loop sail.

It settled down over the head of the one in the back, and he jumped and bucked, his little stub tail wringing in frustration at the tether on his neck that wouldn't release. Andrew braced as the colt hit the end of the reata and fought to keep running. Taking the reata in his right hand, Andrew spread his feet apart to brace his stance, then tucked the rope in his hand behind his right leg. He stood at an angle, the reata across the front of his legs, his body offering all the resistance it could physically give to hold that colt that bobbed and jerked at the end of the line.

Jumping down from his horse, Luke ran across the corral to help his brothers. Frankie was already helping Andrew anchor the fighting colt. While the baby outweighed Andrew, his determination didn't. Luke took hold of the reata, and Andrew was able to move in closer to the colt. By now, all other activity had ceased, the men tending the fire stood out in the open to watch the fight. Pete shouted words of encouragement, but Tom watched with silent pride for his sons as they worked together.

Getting up closer to the colt, Andrew gathered a handful of hide at the apex of leg and flank, then another up by the neck of the colt. With one quick move, Andrew swept the colt off its feet and laid him down on his side. Frankie rushed in to settle on the little colt's neck to keep him from struggling to get up. Luke ran for an iron. One of the hired men met him halfway with it. With long strides, Luke was back at the side of his brothers. They held the foal steady as Luke lowered the hot iron to its hide, just above the stifle. A pretty, clean ~B was fresh on the unblemished hide of the colt when Luke straightened back up. From where he held the foal, Andrew reached up under its belly, feeling for any possible testicles, but the foal was too young for them to have dropped. It was a habit Tom had impressed on his sons. If you had one down, check everything no matter the age of the colt. Tom didn't want the colts roped or laid down any more times than absolutely necessary.

The boys finished checking over the foal, to make sure he was correct and had no abnormalities that needed tending. When the colt checked out, the boys let him back up. He sprang to his feet and bounded, bucking and squealing, back to his mother who stood not far from him watching. She greeted him with a gentle puff of breath as she smelled him over.

It was Frankie's turn. While his reata sailed out a few more times than Andrew's did before it caught on to anything solid, he did finally feel the deep sense of accomplishment as his settled over the neck of a little sorrel. Frankie left trenches dug into the dirt of the corral as the foal pulled him along. It fought with all it had, and as it was bigger than the foal Andrew had caught, Frankie had to work harder to claim his prize.

Pete and Roy yelled and hollered out their appreciation for his effort between fits of uncontrollable laughter. Tom had to restrain himself from rushing in and assisting, but he knew it was better to let the boy sort it out and learn on his own than to have his hard work taken away from him, thus learning when deep in a fight, somebody will do it for you.

Luke hung back, just behind his little brother, as he worked his way up the reata, closer with each step to that rollicking baby. As it broke again, Frankie dug his heels in and went with her, but this time she made it back to the bunch.

Now, Tom did interfere, loping his horse quickly to Frankie's side as the startled bunch began to run again, tripping and tangling themselves in the reata. Tom took it from the boy and dallied, dragging the foal back out into the open, where he handed the reata back to Frankie to finish his fight. Tom side passed out of the action, but stayed closer as the fight raged on. Frankie was now out of breath as he moved up the reata again. Tom nodded to Luke, who anchored the reata, just as Andrew had done. While it bucked and writhed, Frankie slipped up next to it, and with as much speed as his little body could muster against the foal, reached over and took two handfuls of hide. This took several attempts as the foal kept breaking his grip, but finally he was able to get a hold and keep it. By now all bystanders were cheering as loudly as possible to encourage the boy. Despite the fact his feet had been stepped on several times in the process, Frankie kept on. He jerked and pulled with all his might, trying to set it off center and out of balance. After his first try, it got wise to his game, and fought to keep squared up under itself. But, as luck would have it, Frankie pulled just as the foal hopped, and jerked it over. Andrew, hollering his approval, jumped down onto the foal's neck to keep her from rising again.

Luke again ran partway for the branding iron. Laughter and clapping sounded for Frankie from all directions. He was panting, out of breath, but his grin spread from ear to ear.

With his hand full of her skirt, Charlie watched the corral as Addie made her way from the main house to the men. In her arms she carried a large wooden box full of all that was necessary to make coffee, and offer a biscuit or two to the men who'd already spent the morning running horses off the desert. She smiled silently at Frankie as he won his fight against a much bigger and stronger opponent.

When she reached the fence, Tom Brady was there, taking the box from her after he'd swung down from his saddle. He said nothing and kept his eyes away from her. For that, Addie was grateful. He set the box aside, and reached for Charlie. Addie hauled him up and Tom took hold of him from the opposite side of the fence. Tom put Charlie up on his horse, and the boy looked back at Addie for a moment before reaching down to run his hand along the neck of the beast. It watched Charlie out of one eye, but he neither raised his head nor looked concerned.

"Here, Addie," Tom motioned as he spoke to a gate down the fence a ways. They walked to it and he opened it for her, then closed it after she'd passed through it.

All eyes of the men left the efforts of the boys in the center of the corral as they fought to capture another foal, and rested on the form of the young woman who walked awkwardly beside Tom Brady as he carried her wood box of coffee fixin's. She was crisp and clean in the midday sunlight, the white of her apron shining as it ruffled in the breeze against the blue of her skirt. Her auburn hair shone like a crown in the sun.

From beside Roy, Pete chuckled as he leaned forward on his elbow where it rested on his saddle horn. Roy glanced at him in question. Pete then sighed. "He's got it somethin' fierce for that girl, doesn't he?"

Roy clenched his jaw a moment before he nodded his agreement. "I'm 'fraid they all do."

Pete slapped the tail of his romal against his leg softly. The blood bay raised his head and shifted his weight in uncertainty, but when Pete asked for nothing, he relaxed and lowered his head. "Well," Pete started. "There ain't nothin' harder than convincing a woman to change her mind once she's set it." He sighed again. "Especially Addie. She's been through an awful lot."

Roy nodded. "You think she'll be happy in Texas?"

"I think Addie deserves to see her mama once again. Even if she figures out it wasn't what she wanted."

Addie knelt beside the fire and took the huge coffee pot out of the box. She arranged it carefully next to the fire. She shielded her eyes as she looked up at Tom. "You want me to take him?"

"Nah. He can ride with me awhile," Tom answered softly. He turned from Addie and climbed back up into his saddle, lifting Charlie as he did so. When they were both settled, Tom turned his horse and rejoined Pete and Roy. By now, Andrew had another foal down, and Tom and Roy began to collaborate on the older fillies.

"Good afternoon, ma'am," a voice from behind Addie sounded.

She turned to look at the fellow who had spoken.

He removed his hat. "I don't 'spose you remember me. We met some months back. The last time I was here helping Tom in the fall."

Addie really didn't remember him, but she recognized his face some. "Of course. How are you?"

"I'm well, ma'am. How 'bout yourself?"

Addie smiled weakly. "I'm alright."

He replaced his hat on his head, his blue eyes sparkling as they looked at her face. "I'm glad you're still here. I wondered if you would be." He hesitated a moment before adding, "I'm Tate, in case you don't recall."

Addie didn't recall, nor did she care to. She nodded politely, then she walked to the fence and stood next to it, watching as the boys wrestled down another foal. It squealed and protested, but they got it down and held it there tightly as Luke ran for the branding iron. She chuckled softly at the mighty expenditure of effort on Frankie's part. The boy gave everything he had, but it really wasn't quite enough to hold down that foal.

About that time Roy and Pete went to sorting off the older fillies, those that would be coming of breeding age. As they sorted them off, about five of them, Tom saw one had never been branded. Roy easily swung his loop, then watched as it sailed out over the filly's head and settled down on her neck. The roan he rode lunged after her as she started away, but Roy dallied up and pulled her around the corral as Pete stepped up and roped her from the off side, the reata encircling her front legs. As easily as possible, to avoid throwing the filly on her face, the men pulled her off balance and down onto her side. At that point, Tate and another man rushed to the filly who kicked with her hind legs in a struggle to get up.

Tate knelt on her neck to keep her down, while the other man pressed his weight onto her hindquarters. Reaching between her legs, he took hold of her tail and pulled it back up towards her belly. Once that was accomplished, the filly wasn't able to fight. Within moments the ordeal was over, and another fine filly wore the ~B.

She was up with a snort and mad dash, but Tom and Charlie cut her off and sent her back to the small gathering of fillies who stood in a corner watching with bright eyes. The one who'd just been branded shook the dirt from her mane and licked her lips as she processed the proceedings. While her hide was tender, the thickness of it kept any real pain from troubling her.

The older fillies would be kept back and started in a few days after all the bunches were gathered off the range and foals branded. Those in the east meadow would come in and the real work would begin for the cowboys as those horses would be saddled and ridden for the first time in their lives. Tom kept his horses well-tended; therefore, most of his were started by the time they were five. Very few made it past this age as an unstarted beast. This made it easier to get them started under saddle, as the older horses were stronger and held more confidence in themselves and resisted the process.

Addie watched the horses as they were sorted different ways, then her breath caught as a mare came after Luke when he drug her little foal away. Tom was quick to intervene and sent her back a ways. It was over in a short time, and she had her babe back at her side, but she kept a close eye on the littler men who worked afoot in the corral. They were trickier than they appeared.

"Atta boy, Frank!" Roy yelled as Frank again worked at throwing a foal in the middle of the pen. That boy would be tired come evening time.

Charlie sat in front of his father and watched with wide eyes. He wasn't sure where to look as all the excitement was more than he knew how to take in. Tom handed him to Roy at one point when he needed to take a closer look at one of the older mares. She had a deep gash on her shoulder, several days old, that needed cleaning. Tom and Pete roped the old girl and had her down without much fanfare, then addressed the oozing wound. It was packed with dirt and pieces of brush from where she'd laid on it. Addie went to the house for warm water, and Tom sent Luke to the barn for supplies needed to doctor it. When all was said and done, the mare's injury was cleaned and she was let up to find her foal. She did so without any bucking or running, having been laid down a few times in her life.

When Addie had watched a few hours, she wandered up to the house. On the way she thought of Fett and how he'd dreamed of this life, how he'd have his own place and bunch of horses just like Tom Brady's. The fun he would've had working horses with a group of men like these. To watch Pete work again and remember the good days was a double-edged sword. She loved seeing him and remembering sweet memories, but at the same time aching over the passing of those memories. Addie wanted to fall asleep and drift back to those times and remain there forever.

It was late afternoon before the work was done and the men turned to thinking of a meal. They left the mares and foals in the corral to settle a bit before they took them back out to their home country. They'd eat a fast meal and saddle up on fresh horses, those that Tom and Roy had gathered off the south meadow two days previous.

As they came in, Addie was setting the meal of beans and fried bread on the table. She dressed it up with several apple pies made from dried apples Luke brought from the mercantile the day before. The boy had gone with Andrew to fill the order Tom sent with Miss Blanchard's brother-in-law the day she'd come to stake a claim on him. At least one good thing came of that afternoon.

How things had evolved since then.

The men came in and removed their hats and set them up on the shelf, turned over on the crown. Then they took turns at the wash basin, which Addie had to dump and refill with clean water four times. They rolled back their shirt sleeves and washed themselves properly, Tom even going so far as to wash his face to get the dirt off of it. Each man watched Addie when she wasn't looking, all with their own thoughts.

The homestead was filled with the delicious smell of food, and warmed with the presence of a woman. They sat, with Tom at the head of his own table, and began to pass the dishes of food round.

"That old mare was gonna grind Luke into fine dust," Roy remarked as he took a piece of fried bread and passed the plate on. The huge table was full, and it was a sight to see it filled with men and boys of all ages. Addie took a moment to look at them, absorbed in eating and talking of the day's events. They were dirty and tired, but far from done with the day's tasks. They would enjoy their repast, then take to the work again until nightfall and another meal. Smelling of horse and clean air, hair matted with sweat and dust, they embodied the soul of passion lived to its fullest.

"I saw Andy Masters last week," Tate stated.

"Andy? I haven't seen that boy all winter. Where's he been holed up?" Roy asked.

"Oh, he left home and went to the IL to work awhile. Near killed his pa to lose a good hand. He come back to help with branding time at the home place."

"That figures. No doubt spent the winter suffering on a feed crew, which is what he coulda been doing with his pa, then 'bout the time the fun starts he heads home to help out," Roy replied ironically.

Tate laughed. "Well, it was good to see him branch out a little. He wasn't as bent outta shape about missing the fun as he was about that Clements girl."

At this Luke stopped chewing and looked at Tate. His look wasn't returned when Tate grabbed another piece of fry bread.

Tate chuckled. "I guess he rode clear down to the Clements' place to see her and ask if she'd go steady with him. Seein' as she's fifteen now," Tate added.

Tom wrinkled his brow. "How old does Andy gotta be?" he asked in a disbelieving tone.

"Eighteen. Just last month. Anyhow, he rides clear down there to confess his undying love and affection for her and ask if she'll go steady with him. Turns out, as she tells him, she's already got her a steady beau.

He demands to know who it is. She tells him a Mr. Luke Brady."

Roy lets out a whoop and goes to clapping vigorously. Pete joins in no less joyously. "Hell yes, boy!"

The two hands hired along with Tate show their enthusiasm as well. Tom was looking at Luke with a raised brow. Luke's face was beet red and he seemed to be having trouble chewing the large bite he held in his mouth. Addie laughed and clapped too.

"You just bested an eighteen-year-old man!" Roy cried out. "That is damned impressive!"

Tate went to slapping Luke on the back and laughing. Smiling at Luke, Addie cast a glance at Tom. He watched her with dark and contemplative eyes for a moment before looking slowly back to Luke. Addie pressed her lips together and turned back to the workbench and a batch of dough she worked into loaves.

Roy watched her, then looked back to Tom without saying anything. When the table had settled some, Tom stated, "I blame you for this."

Addie turned to see who he was talking to and saw him looking directly at her. His brown eyes were firm as he held her in his glare. "Me?"

"Yes, you."

Addie tipped her head back and laughed. "Roy started it. I think it's his fault."

"Yep," Tom said dryly. "And I distinctly remember Roy sewing up that ornate little flower outta his undergarments, too."

Addie dropped her dough and turned to him. The table of men held their breath in order to keep an outpouring of response from rushing forth. Luke stared at her with wide eyes.

"Well, I'd say that little flower did an awful lot of good, didn't it? Your boy did pretty well for himself. All I did was make him a flower to give to a girl with sense enough to take notice of a good man when she sees one," Addie said gently.

"Yeah, and all you did was bring Charlie to life. All you did was show him how to look out for his own needs. All you did was feed hungry boys and wash their clothes, buck out their rotten horses and see to it they had a cookie every now and then. Yeah, I guess that was all you did. If you don't count the heart that went with it," Tom said softly as his brown eyes looked at her with honesty.

Addie pursed her lips together and turned from Tom and the men who looked on in silence. Pete tried to hide a smile. Knowing Addie as he did, he found it no mystery to see what she had actually spent her winter doing, despite the fact she looked at it differently. What she found as a duration of a stay in hell, was in reality a winter spent saving the lives of four boys.

Even Tom could see that.

Inside, Addie pictured Fett. With each of the things Tom described, she'd held his face in her heart, aching and grieving,. Therefore the quality of the things she'd done weren't what she thought it should've been. The pain of loss was still just as evident, just as raw, just as consuming, but for some reason it was all tangled up inside that homestead. Each time she thought of holding Fett close to her body, she felt Charlie as he clung to her. When she thought of Fett's consolation, she could feel Luke's strong arms around her as she cried by the wood stove on a winter's morn. When she recalled riding a runaway paint as Fett looked on with pride, she could only feel the amazed looks of three boys who watched her buck out a blue-eyed kids' horse.

Nothing made sense anymore. She felt the fervor of anticipation, the feel of a running horse replaced with one who stood at rapt attention, waiting for something big. That gray spent his time running through her thoughts and dreams, and the more the feeling of anticipation built, the more adamant that gray became.

Conversation behind her turned back to the matters of work, and the clanking of cutlery against enamel plates again sounded. Addie kept at her work, not turning to look at the table, just kneading out that dough and rolling it into loaves. As the task was completed, she took the loaves and placed them in the sun to rise before she put them in the little oven.

As the men finished their meal, they rose from the table, gathered up their gear, put hats on their heads and thanked Addie for the fine meal as they sauntered out the door into the afternoon sunshine. Now that the first bunch was gathered and foals branded, older fillies sorted off, and mares looked over closely and doctored if they needed it, they would run them back out onto their home range.

"You care to ride along, Adelaide?" Pete asked from the doorway of the cabin.

Addie looked up at him, surprised. He stood next to Tom, both men with their hats on, ready to walk out the door. Addie wrinkled her brow before answering, "No, I've got work here to tend to."

To Addie the moment felt awkward and out of nowhere. With trepidation, she glanced from Pete, who gave her a look of mild frustration, to Tom. He watched her with soft understanding. In that moment, if he had asked her, she would have gone with Tom. If he had asked, she would have walked away from her bread and out into that brilliant sunshine. About that time, Charlie toddled over and took hold of Addie's skirt.

Tom's eyes changed, from a look of understanding, to one of complete heartbreak. He stepped past Pete and out into the light without saying a word. Addie watched him go, then looked to Pete who regarded her with a raised brow.

"Texas is a long ride from here, Adelaide. Best you make sure you're up for it," Pete said just before he stepped out the door after Tom.

Addie looked down at Charlie who gave her his very best mechanical smile. The edges of it were beginning to soften into something real, like it was becoming more evident the emotions he was supposed to feel when he smiled at someone.

Tears burned deep inside Addie. "You boys!" she scolded softly. "You all make it damn hard on a woman who just wants to stop hurtin'. You push and pull and drag her when all she wants to do is cry a little. You ask for more than she's got to give ya."

Charlie's dark eyes filled with concern. He reached his little arms up to Addie, begging to be held. Addie took him up and pressed him to her heart and felt his breath as he buried his sweet face into her neck.

Addie felt like she was being pushed into squaring up with something she never wanted to look into the face of. If it were a beast of some kind, she would have had courage to spit at it. If it were a mountain, she'd climb it one rock at a time. If it were weather, she'd stand as the wind and rain blasted her. But this wasn't something she could best with physical strength. She would be forced to use the weakest part of herself, the part too broken and bleeding to prove of much use. The nerves were raw and exposed, and each time she tried to use them, they'd scream out in anguish. And in order to use them, she'd have to cut and sever the nerves of those around her. Like a downed horse, she'd have to kick and struggle to rise, tearing at the tender ground at her feet. In order to stand and run free again, she'd have to break away, and in doing so, the hearts of those who stood by waiting for her would be crushed in the struggle.

Addie was ready to crush away.

Tom led the little red filly silently out of the dark barn. It struck him as odd how she made no unnecessary move, and she placed her hooves down silently, almost as if she knew the men above her were sleeping and cared not to be disturbed. But, as she moved in the silvery light of the moon away from her own respite, she still padded along behind Tom without any noise. Each time he slowed or stopped to open a gate or two, she'd gently press her muzzle against his arm, and mostly, Tom didn't notice.

As he left the barnyard, an ember glowed bright from the barn loft where the doors hung open in the night air. Someone watched Tom make his way out past the corrals, then swing up into the saddle and ride away into the sage. Pete made no move as Tom disappeared into the moonlight, blending in with the country around him. He took a long drag off one he'd rolled himself and blew the smoke out of his lungs up at the starry sky. Quietly, as he had for the past nights since he'd ridden up to see Adelaide standing, torn between a dugout and a man, wondered if he should intervene.

No, he thought again. It wasn't time yet.

She'd clung to him and cried, like a woman who'd been strong far long enough. She was like a child, weak from the strength she'd exerted in keeping a straight back, but once a safe harbor showed itself, Addie forgot all about that straight back. Pete had held her so many times while she cried, and if he were honest, hearing those tears bound him to her in a way Pete Summers had never known anyone. He sought to help her, but he could sense she wasn't ready for that yet.

Addie was like water. She'd flow in raging torrents, washing away the steady banks that held her in, collapsing rock and pines as she went. Then, when the rains stopped, and the water slowed, she'd flow into a gentle lake that would look back at where she'd been and regret the damage she'd done.

She'd loved Fett Loveland with fiery intensity. They had been close, living many months of their married life with only each other for company. Her life had been so hard, yet she never seemed to realize it at the time. And just as sure as he felt it the first time he met her, Pete knew that a day would've come when she no longer cared to live a nomadic life riding buckers and runaways. While they were pleasant memories to rock in time with as an old woman, they hardly offered security. Addie had too much to offer an ailing world, too much love and understanding to focus on a bunch of horses nobody wanted to give ten dollars for.

Pete also knew, that while Texas would welcome Addie with great big open arms, she'd find it wasn't the Texas she was searching for. That Texas was gone forever. Even those who lived still, would not be what she thought she'd find. Addie had changed, far too much to return to girlhood, and he knew for certain she'd realize it about a day too late. But Pete cared very deeply for Addie, and if Texas was what she wanted, then that was what he'd give her, knowing it was his duty to see her safe.

Even if Texas grieved her wretchedly to see it.

Tom Brady rode up the well-worn path out to the desert in the light of the full moon, not concerned with the steps his filly took as she went. Her ears worked constantly as she traveled, but she kept her head down and moved with a contented pace. She thought she'd head north from the barn to a secluded spot around the butte behind the cabin. She'd taken Tom there many times, and stood by as he spoke soft words in the moonlight to a wood cross pounded into the earth. When the snow was

376

deep he didn't go there, but he'd gone a few times since the snows had melted. What he said to the wood and rock, she didn't know.

But on that night, he headed south, out into the pasture the geldings ran in. He aimed her steps off the path and straight up the side of a steep hill, climbing with determination to reach the top. Rocks skidded and slid down as her sure feet knocked them loose from their resting place. The breeze was ever so slight and carried on it the scent of life coursing through the desert. The earth had woken from its winter slumber and now regenerated itself into a vibrant green.

As they topped the hill, Tom stopped the filly and stepped out of the saddle, touching down lightly. He took a moment to rub his face before taking one split rein in his hand and walked ahead of the filly to the far edge of the butte where it overlooked a valley and the expanse of the mountains. The breeze stopped its sighing, and the sounds of the night waned.

Tom swore he heard the stars reflecting the awesome light of the sun.

The red filly lowered her head and stood in complete silence. Tom stepped out and away from her, dropping the rein. She made no move to follow him, just watched and waited. Stopping at the edge of the hill before it fell away from him to the valley floor, Tom Brady very slowly removed his hat, and stood holding it in his hands. He traced the brim with work-calloused fingers, trying to remember what he'd come to say. The words wouldn't flow. The night only grew quieter, and he knew creation waited to hear what he struggled to say. A feeling deep inside urged him on, so he began with gentle tones and shaking speech.

"I'm sorry. I guess I don't talk to You much anymore." Tom's shoulders trembled and he couldn't bring himself to raise his head and view the majesty of the moonlit mountains before him. "I 'spose I limit our conversations to begging nowadays." He turned the brim in his hands again as he stood silent a moment. "I beg for You to save somethin', then I beg for You to take it. I guess that kinda conversation isn't real exciting. And, if you take into consideration all the things I've hollered at You to damn, well, I guess I owe You an apology for that too."

Tom shifted his weight from one leg to another several times, then continued. "I am simple, and I can't see Your reasoning. I can't see what You do nor why it's important. All I can see is what's in front of me. And it isn't always good. Sometimes it's downright hell." He inhaled deeply before gathering his courage to look up at the sky. "I don't know why I lost Edith. I don't see what was so damned important she leave those four boys behind for. I've cursed myself for my part in it; I've fought hard against cursing You for Yours."

Tom closed his eyes and clenched a fist inside his hat. "I want to be free of it. I want to let it go. I'm so damned sick of hurtin', so damned tired of weariness. I want to look up and see somethin' joyful, somethin' with life that doesn't cause me regret of things I've done in the past. To look at my boys and not feel the weight of guilt 'cause their ma isn't with them."

With shoulders sagging, Tom looked again to his hat. The aching in his heart swelled to the point he thought it would rupture. "I know she don't want me," he whispered. "I know I don't deserve her. I know she won't stay. But the achin' that the thought of losin' her gives me, I can't see my way to livin' through. I don't want to lose again." He closed his eyes and breathed the smell of the desert.

"I love her, God. I love her. I want her with the desire you put in a man, but not just to relieve the constant wants of a body left alone. But with the want of a man who has found the woman who could be his partner." Pausing as a star shot for the last time across the sky, Tom watched it burn out. "I know she'll go. I know she'll go back to Texas without me, and never think on me again. And I'll spend my life regretting what I did to turn her away. All I ask, is that you take the hurt away from Addie and give her peace. Don't make her finish her days as I will. Give her happiness again. Help her see it when the opportunity comes."

Tom pressed his lips together. "So I guess, really, all I'm doing is asking for something again. Only this time, it's not for me."

As Tom stood silently overlooking that valley, following the stream up to the mountains, he heard the filly shift behind him quickly. Turning to look at her, he saw her head was up and her ears pointed at something across the butte. The moonlight reflected in her eyes, shining as she turned her whole body, focusing on what she looked at.

Tom turned quickly to seek what captured her attention. He was startled to see him there. In the stillness of the night he heard no noise that would have occurred when something climbed the butte. Tom took a step back. The red filly was frozen where she stood.

The gray watched Tom, the nonexistent breeze playing with his tail where it nearly touched the ground. His black etched ears were hardly visible, but the white in his coloring emulated the silver of the moonlight. His attention was for Tom, the strength in his chest and neck obvious as he held his head high. The black of his mane rose and waved, following the teasing of something unfelt.

Tom's breath caught. The filly bobbed her head in uncertainty. The gray's nostrils rounded as he lowered his head slightly. That did nothing to sooth Tom's concern. Just as quickly, the gray raised his head and rotated his ears to take in a sound behind him, tipping his head to look in the same direction out of one eye.

It was as if someone had spoken to him. Told him to move on. The gray calmly turned and walked to the edge of the butte, then with one stride he was gone. And at no point did he make a single sound. The rocks didn't shift under his weight, nor tumble and slide as they had for the filly. Tom felt rooted in his spot, unable to persuade himself to follow, completely unconvinced he'd been with Roy when he'd ridden that horse in his presence.

There was no way it was the same horse.

When Tom coerced his thoughts back to the moonlit night, he found that the red filly was standing quite close to him, tucking her head against his shoulder for comfort. Her ears worked constantly as they searched for a sound, any sound that would indicate a heavy horse made its way down the rocky slope. She could find none.

As for Tom, he'd said his piece. Now, with the sighting of a gray he thought once he knew, he was ready to head in the opposite direction for the homestead. As he swung up into the saddle and the filly warily made her way down the slope, the breeze returned as if on command.

Addie didn't trust Red Beast enough to rest her head against her flank. While she was tired and worn down, she didn't for a second expect Red Beast would allow her to rest her burdens against her strength. As she milked with one hand, the calf nudged from the opposite side and tried to gently pry Addie from the tit she worked. The calf licked and pushed, but to no avail.

Addie smiled to herself. It was more a suggestion from a sweet baby, where her mother would simply kick with rage when she wanted something. Perhaps the calf would grow to be a gentle mother, but more than likely her personality would follow that of Red Beast as time passed.

"Miss Addie?" came a voice from behind her.

In surprise, she nearly fell off the wood bucket she sat on. It was early, very early, and she hadn't heard much from the cowboys in the loft above yet. Turning she saw Luke standing there, next to the post at the corner of the stall where she milked. He looked at her with uncertainty in his eyes.

"What are you doin' out here so early?"

He shrugged his shoulders. With a touch of pride in his face he replied, "My turn to wrangle horses."

"Ah," Addie said as she nodded her understanding and turned back to her milking. "I thought it was awful quiet up there. Guess those boys get to sleep in a bit this morning thanks to you."

Luke wandered in and knelt down beside her to watch her hands work. The calf broke from its breakfast to look at Luke with curiosity. Red Beast gazed back at him, but she resumed her eating without much complaint over the intruder into a morning tradition of silence. She knew Luke well, and his existence meant only that her life was better for the feed he brought with him.

"She seems better," Luke stated as he tipped his head towards Red Beast.

"Well, I don't know if I'd say better, but I guess we've come to an understanding."

Luke sighed. "You've come a long way since you came here."

Addie raised a brow as she looked over at him. "What do you mean?"

He shook his head. "Nothin' really. Just that you came here broken and down. Now you seem to have things together. And I think you look better. Not that you weren't pretty when you came, but you sure was skinny. Now you aren't."

Addie nodded her reluctant agreement. "Don't know about having it together, but yes, I feel better."

"Miss Addie, I," he started in a low voice. In that moment he looked like a very young version of his father. Struggling with what he felt compelled to say, yet stricken with the thought of it. "I need to say I'm sorry."

In shock she stopped her milking and looked at him. "For what?" Of all the Bradys, he had the least to be sorry for.

"I used to pray all the time."

After a moment of silence, Addie said, "That's hardly something to be sorry for."

"No. It's not that. It's just…well I prayed for help. Again and again. You know, after I figured out God wasn't gonna send my mama back to us."

Addie pressed her lips together. "Well, why would you need to apologize to me for it?"

"'Cause. What if I pestered God so much He finally got tired of hearin' me and He took your man, just so's you'd have to come here and help us?"

As Addie turned to face Luke straight on, the calf quietly claimed the tit she'd been milking. Addie let it go. "Luke, I think we like to have reasons for things. Reasons why the sun comes up, reasons why it goes down. Why the flowers grow and foals are born. Why we have to attend to chores and wear clothes. We can find answers for those things. Feel like we have some knowing as we grow older. It's just the things we have no way of reasoning, no way to get answers for, that torment us."

Addie gently squeezed his forearm. "If that's why my man died, then I'm gonna ask you to do all my prayin' for me. I've never gotten that kind of results."

When Luke looked up at her sharply, he was met with a half-smile. After consideration, he smiled as well. "Don't worry, boy. My man isn't gone 'cause you prayed. He's just gone."

Luke looked at her and nodded. "Best you wrangle horses. First time you get the chance to do a man's job, you best do it."

Luke nodded his head as he looked over at Addie. She again smiled and watched as he rose and left the barn. Looking back to see her tit soft and clearly void of any contents, Addie looked down into her bucket.

She guessed if one didn't take advantage of things when they were offered, somebody else would gladly do it for themselves.

Charlie peeked through the poles of the corral fence and was met by a muzzle. He was surprised greatly and leapt back, only to catch the heel of his boot on a rock and topple over backwards. With his brows knitted tightly together, he sat back on his elbows and stared at the fence. Through the poles of the fence the muzzle reappeared, dun in color, and not big.

The nostrils rounded as some kind of creature took in Charlie's scent. The muzzle was pulled from between the poles, and Charlie could see nothing of the owner of the velvet nose. As he gathered himself to rise, the muzzle came again, jammed sideways through the poles, the nostrils rounding again. Charlie fell back a second time, unwilling to see just *who* owned that muzzle.

He'd wandered down the fence from where Addie stood watching the men work when he decided to look through the fence and see what the men were up to. At first he saw nothing, for the corral he looked into was not the one the men worked in. It appeared empty.

Then out of nowhere something thrust itself through the fence and into Charlie's face. That spooked him something terrible. Now, Charlie slowly and easily collected himself off the ground, moving as to not draw more attention to himself. He looked up the fence line to see Addie was still there, watching him, then looking back to the men. Charlie decided whatever was jamming a nose through the poles wasn't probably something he needed to play with. So, with careful steps he started back towards Addie.

He jumped again when something took hold of his shirt sleeve and gave it a firm tug. Jumping sideways away from his accoster, he stumbled again, and as he rose up to his knees, he saw the reason for the firm tug was still jamming its nose through the poles. With a spark of indignation, Charlie stood up and pursed his little lips at it. In anger he started again towards Addie, but this time he kept his shirt sleeve out of reach. The muzzle followed him up the fence line, then disappeared.

Charlie stopped to see where it had gone. He bent low and peered through the poles. He saw nothing, so he crept closer to get a better look. He looked into what appeared to now be an empty corral. Just then the muzzle came out again, quickly, meeting with Charlie's face. The softness of it was pleasant, but the wetness of the lips as they explored his features was not. Charlie reared back and stood glaring at the fence, a few strands of his hair stood up where the wetness stuck them up and held them there.

Not sure if he should cry or run for Addie, Charlie contemplated the audacious beast on the other side of the high fence. As his eyes began to fill with tears of confusion, he saw something approach the fence. A dun colored head lowered, and a large brown eye stared out at Charlie from between the poles. It was a kind eye, although it held a hint of mischief as it considered the little boy outside its enclosure.

Again the muzzle jammed through, and this time Charlie was relieved to realize it was a colt, not a monster that beckoned to him. After a moment of sniffing, the colt again held an eye up to the poles, and looked at Charlie in expectation. Gathering his courage, Charlie took a step closer to the fence. The colt reached for him again, and this time Charlie held out a timid hand, reaching from way back as to not offer more of himself than necessary.

As the softness of hand and muzzle met, the little colt jerked his head away and sucked back before sending himself around the corral, bucking and leaping as he went. When he'd made his round, he came back to Charlie and held out his muzzle again. This time, seeing the sport of it, Charlie quickly caressed the flesh and felt the stubble of whiskers. The colt flung himself in great amusement around the pen again, and Charlie crept close to the fence to watch. Something about the scene tickled Charlie and a small smile formed on the corners of his mouth. The colt took off at top speed and just before sailing into the fence, he tried to drag himself to a stop, but the ground was slick and hard causing his butt to give way out from under him. He fell onto his side, but his embarrassment was short lived, for he bounded to his feet again and charged at Charlie.

This pleased Charlie immensely. Somewhere deep inside a rumbling formed, and while he had no idea what it was, it felt wonderful. The colt jammed his nose out and something burst out of Charlie. He felt it go from his chest, and while he had no idea it came out with sound, it brought him a joy he'd never had. Jumping into a run, Charlie forgot about the security of Addie and ran towards the barn. As he went the rumbling in his chest continued, the colt bucking his way down the fence line with Charlie. When the dun colt hit the end of his line, Charlie turned and they headed back the other way.

The game went on.

Unable to stop herself, Addie climbed up the fence and waved at Tom who stood watching while Tate sorted out a colt to start from the bunch they'd gathered the day before.

Great concern filled Tom's eyes and he kicked his horse into a burst of speed to get to Addie. She smiled broadly at him as he reached her and pointed to where Charlie played with the dun colt. Tom side passed his horse to her, and they sat together, watching as Charlie made his very first friend. Pressing in close, Tom rested a hand just behind Addie on the top rail where she sat, leaning in to watch over the fence. The laughing was coming easy to Charlie now.

Tom smiled softly. "I had to put that colt's mama down last fall," he murmured into Addie's ear.

She looked over at him and was met with tenderness. They were very close. "Oh?" she asked.

Tom's expression went grim. "Yeah. She was in real bad shape. She was down and I couldn't get her up. I brought him home with me, and he spent the winter with the studs and geldings in the south meadow." Tom chuckled as Charlie yanked his hand away from the colt and broke into a run. "Looks to me like Charlie has his very first horse."

Addie smiled and looked over at Tom. His dark eyes locked on hers, holding her gaze. She could feel the heat coming from his arm where it nearly touched her backside. The brightness of the sun was blocked from her face as his hat shaded her, and she could smell the mixture of horse and human sweat on him, mingling together on the breeze. Her breath caught as she thought he'd surely move in closer to her, and she wasn't sure if she was ready or not.

Tom's hand lowered to the saddle horn as he looked over at Addie, his features relaxed into something close to a smile. Then without another word, he tipped his hat and rode back to the bunch where the men were getting ready to saddle a horse for the first time.

Tom returned to let his reata snake out and settle on a little sorrel colt. The horse took off and bucked and jumped against the rope. Tom followed the three-year-old around awhile, allowing him ample time to fuss and fight against the rope. Then when he'd tired himself out some, Tom started to pull the horse around. In this manner he would eventually put it together how to be led and tied. All of them had to be started this way. They were too big to be haltered on the ground, too strong to pull on foot.

Tate was now roped up and flying around the round pen adjacent to the corral Tom broke the sorrel to lead in. Addie watched as Pete rode his big blood bay out in front of the bucking and writhing colt to slow his progress and encourage him to think his way through the process. Tate held on, and without moving nor startling the colt, he rode well and kept a steady seat as the colt figured out the feel of weight and saddle on his back.

It took a while. Pete slowed the horse as best he could, until the colt tired himself out and took to a high lope around the round corral. With that, Tate began to move some, working his legs to let the colt know he was real and alive, but the movement would cause him no harm. This sent the colt hump-backed around the fence again, but sweat was running off his body now, lather showing under the cinches. The colt kept up a fast pace, until, with an ear cocked, he'd thought his way through the man on his back. Now tired, he slowed to a trot. Riding up next to them, Pete put a loop gently over the horse's head and dallied up. When he had him held good, Tate swung off as quietly as possible, to not cause any sort of anxiety in that part of the riding session for the next day when the colt was ridden again.

The saddle was pulled, and the sorrel was let out into another pen where two other horses stood, sweat marked from their own first rides. Now attention was turned to a little black mare, just as pretty as could be, with wild eyes.

"This one's yours, Luke!" Roy hollered.

Luke's face went white for a moment before he swung off his horse and began to undo the cinches. Tom rode over and looked down at his son. "She was rode twice last fall, so she shouldn't be too hard to ride down. Just hang on and let her work out her kinks."

Luke swallowed hard and jerked his saddle. Andrew stepped up and took hold of the bridle reins. He watched as his older brother carried his gear to the gate and walked through it into the round corral. Andrew licked his lips and fought the burning sensation in his stomach. He had no reasons for why he was nervous. He wasn't the one stepping up on that mare.

Addie hadn't been paying much attention. She watched Charlie as he happily played with the dun colt through the fence. Now she looked back to see the black mare was saddled and bucking her way around the pen, making little grunting noises as she went. Pete kept up behind her each time she started into another bucking fit, and after a while she settled and ran to the opposite side and stood, watching him for her next move. He'd kept his reata on her as she'd fought, and now he dallied up to her and held her firm. As he held her there, he twisted one ear in his hand to keep her mind occupied. Roy helped Luke check the cinch as Tom came into the round pen on his own horse, just to help keep her as calm as possible.

Addie watched with something close to terror in her gut. She climbed the fence again to see what was going on. Luke stood next to the mare in readiness, Tom close by, his reata ready for action. In a swift motion Luke was up and on, roped up and prepared to make a ride. Pete released the mare's ear, and instantly she was moving sideways away from him, and looking up on her back to see that the weight there belonged to a body. Squeezing her between the fence and his horse, Pete got the rope from her neck and moved with her as she started around the pen. At first, she made several laps without complaint, Tom remaining out of the way in the middle of the enclosure. However, when Pete allowed her more space, she pressed her advantage.

Luke tried to remain steady, but the sweat in the palm of his hands made it hard to hold on to the reata tied to his saddle, nor the Cheyenne roll at the back of his seat. As the mare lunged away from Pete, Tom moved to cut her off, but not before she got two hard jumps in. Daylight was visible between Luke and the saddle both times, the stretch wider the second time.

Running ahead of her, Tom slowed her bucking, but the black moved with a huge hump in her back. As soon as she saw an opening, she burst again, throwing everything she had into lifting her hindquarters into the air. She was snappy, and Luke didn't have a good enough hold to counteract her force. Making three jumps with her flinging herself as she was, Luke's hands were torn violently from their holds. Luke felt the sensation of flying free before he met with the high impact of ground. His eyes rolled and he watched as the black passed over the top of him in her flight overhead. He felt her well-placed feet as they hit the ground on the left side of his body, then felt dirt cover his face as she made liftoff and launched herself over him, just to land on her hind feet on the right side of him. It all happened quickly, no more than a few heartbeats between, but Luke was aware of everything as she went over. Tom and Roy made a wall to keep her from coming round again in her bucking fit and forget to avoid him the second time. Their voices sounded out loudly, and Luke felt the strong arms of the hands, Amos and Tate, as they gathered him up and pulled him out of harm's way.

Addie covered her mouth in horror, completely unable to stand there and watch to see if Luke was alright. She backed away from the fence, horrible images playing out in her mind as she cowered away. Just before she bolted, she saw Luke shake his head and begin to dust himself off at the urging of Amos. She turned then and ran, her skirt gathered in her hands, not looking back to see if Charlie followed. He was, stunned to see his Addie leaving in short order. He was scared he'd done something wrong.

From the round pen, Pete watched her go, and sighed very heavily. Roy looked from Addie to Pete in confusion, while Tom merely removed his hat and wiped the sweat from his brow. He watched Addie go, unsure of what to say to her if he were to try to console her. Tom looked to Pete for answers, but Pete could only shake his head, then utter the word, *damn.*

Addie flew into the cabin and covered her head with her hands. She wanted no part in this. No part. If God wouldn't take the horses from the earth, then she'd just have to take them from her life. They had already claimed everything she loved anyway, they deserved no part in what was left. She hated them now, with everything she had.

She saw Fett. She sat down on the bench and tucked her head to her chest and cried bitter tears. He was there, so real, so alive. She'd held him in her arms just that morning, waking with the dawning of the sun to make love to him for the last time. The tenderness they'd shared was explicit that morning. Fett had lingered over the breakfast fire, smiling at her with his blue eyes bright. Why he'd been so reluctant to leave her and catch up to Pete was unusual, and looking back Addie knew the reason.

Fett saddled up and rode away into the rising sun, turning not just once but twice to look back at her where she stood over the cook fire. She laughed at him the second time, waving to him as he burst into a captivating smile. He pulled Buck to a stop, then with a low voice said,

"I love you, Ad. Always will."

She had put her hands on her hips and said back to him, "What will Pete say when he knows the reason you're late?"

He grinned and replied, "Best reason for bein' late I can think of."

Then he turned and was gone. The last sight she had of him was Buck moving off into a lope, carrying him into the cedars and out of sight. She stood and listened to his hoofbeats for a moment, before she turned and looked at the unmade bed in the teepee tent they called home.

That was it. There was no more of Fett after that last morning. His soul broke free and went on to better things, better horses, better forevers. He didn't return to his Addie, he didn't say goodbye, didn't hold her as Pete brought a lifeless body back. Fett didn't console her and talk sense to her when she screamed at Buck, cursing him from one end of the earth to the other. He didn't tell her it would be the last time the horse ever reached for her to forgive him.

Fett was just gone.

And now, she'd see it again. She crumpled to the floor and cried, sobbed and wailed, the last of the good days gone. The scourge of the earth still thundered and nickered, still grazed and beget. They would live on past her lifetime, claiming other loves of women to come. Addie was crushed and dying, the blood seeping from her soul as she again saw Fett turn and look at her for the last time before riding off.

Gentle hands took hold of Addie and pulled patiently until she was up and off the floor, and back on the bench from where she'd fallen. Tom gathered her to him and pulled her close to his chest, his arms encompassing the entirety of her body, holding her with the strength of a man who had felt just what she was living. She crushed her face against his chest and wept until the weakness claimed what was left of her senses.

Roy came quietly into the cabin and took hold of Charlie who watched with horrified eyes. He took the boy out silently, closing the cabin door softly behind him. He carried him as he writhed and wiggled back to the corral, back to the silent men who stood in a circle with eyes downcast. Tom's gelding stood still, the bridle reins looped around the saddle horn, waiting patient. Luke wiped tears from his eyes as he watched Roy carry his baby brother from the house his father had gone into.

Addie held on to Tom's neck with one hand, soaking his shirt front in her agony. Pressing his face to her forehead, he bore as much of her burden as he could, knowing the soul was unable to rid itself of the hurt in entirety. And when she was done, she knew one thing.

She couldn't stand by and watch another man die.

"I need to see my mama," she whispered.

Tom was silent awhile. Then he said, "I'll tell Pete."

Roy looked down at Addie and smiled as best he could. It wasn't like him to say goodbyes, and he'd needed to return home and check his own livestock. So, after supper, he went to the barn with Tom to attend chores. He saddled up the gray and caught his roan to take with him as well.

He and Tom spoke for a while in the barn, and when they had concluded their conversation, Roy swung up into the saddle and worked the gray up towards the house. He hollered for Addie, then waited for her by the porch.

"Where you headed?" Addie asked as she dried her hands on her apron.

Roy removed his hat and replied, "I best head homeward for a while. I haven't been there in a few days, so I better check and make sure my stock are all where I left 'em."

"I'm sorry to see you go. I won't..." Addie trailed off. A look of regret passed over her face.

Roy looked down and studied his hat brim for a moment. "The truth is, Addie, I just don't do goodbyes very well. I'd just as soon not be here in the mornin' when you tell those boys so long."

Addie studied the face of the gray. "I understand."

"I'll give 'em a day to cry themselves silly, then I'll come back and, I guess do what I did when Edith died."

"And what was that, Roy?" Addie asked softly.

His blue eyes met hers. "Try to convince them to go on livin'." He swung down from the gray and stepped up on the porch, his spurs making the slightest noise as he did so. "And what of you, Addie? What will become of you?"

Addie stared out across the corrals to the sage beyond. "I don't know. I guess I'll..." Swallowing hard, Addie crossed her arms over her chest. "I have...so much to say to you...Roy. I don't know where to begin."

"I know. You don't need to say anything," Roy replied in a confident tone.

With tears brimming, Addie said, "Yes, I do. You made this place bearable. Just when I thought I wouldn't be able to make it through, you came. You always came."

"It scares me, little Addie. To think of you out there, beyond the reach of us here. I picture you riding all that way, from Texas, a mere girl, right next to your man. You went boldly that time, unaware of the hand you'd be dealt. Now you go a wise woman, despite your age. How will you make the journey a second time?"

Addie gave him a fake smile that didn't reflect in her eyes. "One horse at a time. Just like the first time."

In a quick motion, Roy had a hold of Addie's forearm. "Take him. Take the gray. I get this feeling. You'll make it, *if* you have the gray." It all came out in a rush of near desperation.

"What does he have to do with anything?" Addie cried out in defense.

"I don't know. But I know for sure he's here because of you. And I know, somehow I know, if you ride out of here without him, you just won't make it."

"Paddy will get me there. He got me all the way the first time. The gray is merely a horse. He has nothing special to keep me safe with."

Roy shook his head. "I used to believe that, too. But... there is no way to explain it."

Addie shook her head vehemently. "No. You'll see. Once I'm gone, it will be like I never was. Life for the Bradys *and* the gray will go on as it has. You'll see."

It was as if something occurred to Roy. His face relaxed, and his mouth stretched into a line. Casting a glance at the gray, he saw that the horse's placid brown eyes rested on him. After some contemplation, Roy nodded his head and looked back to Addie's face.

"I won't say goodbye. That just means it's over, and I'll never lay sight on you again this side of eternity. So, I'll reserve my right to hope." With a squeeze, Roy released Addie's arm. He mounted the gray, and with one last look at her, Roy moved off into a lope, the roan following closely behind the gray. Addie watched until he'd disappeared over the rise.

She tried not to cry, but the tears came down anyway. He had been her only friend in an unfamiliar world filled with pain. Roy Albert had taken one look at her and understood the heavy burden of grief she'd carried, even when he had no reason to. Sending that letter to her folks was the kindest thing any human being had ever done for her. Bringing her their reply was a gift from God carried by an angel.

And now, he was gone from her life. And with deep regret, she realized, she hadn't even thanked him. He seemed to know, but that wasn't the same as saying it out loud. The strange way he acted about the gray was confusing, but perhaps he finally understood Addie wanted no part in him. None at all.

Looking out at the evening settling over the desert, Addie saw Pete riding in from the south pasture with the string of horses they'd be taking with them back to Texas come the dawn. They followed obediently behind him, ready, despite the enjoyment they derived from the life of leisure the past week.

It was time to move on. The weather was perfect, and no big storms would come to stop her this time.

Addie made her way slowly to the dugout, looking for the last time at the silhouette of the mountains against the setting sun. It was getting late, and mountains were dark blue and their features impossible to see. The orange of the sky was bright and outlined the white of a few clouds that hung over the peaks.

It was strange, to finally be leaving a place she'd considered her prison for so many winter months. But now, realizing the sun would set on her in a camp many miles south of where the Brady homestead lay by the next evening, Addie was left with a feeling of shock. What felt like an eternity was now over, and she was free to go with Pete who would see her safely back to Texas. She was no longer alone.

But in truth, had she really ever been? She'd had the Bradys through the winter. And although he wasn't very constant in the beginning, Tom had clearly been aware of everything that had gone on with her. Maybe he didn't have the details, but he knew what she was suffering through. He told her that himself.

Horses stood quietly in the corrals. The ones that had been started that day mulled over their experiences, the ones left for the next day mulled over the possibilities. They were still, ears moving ever so slightly to listen to her footsteps, and Addie realized they shared much in common. They stood on the eve of a new day, a day that would end what lay in the past. For the horses, their freedom to roam the ranges was over. Now they would be useful creatures who went on to learn valuable skills and talents, to work beside man in all of his endeavors, to learn to trust and befriend him on his journey through life and work.

For Addie, a beautiful story was ending. It started the day she fell in love with Fett, when she left her mother and father and followed him into the unknown. She clung to him as his wife, his lover and his friend, working beside him through all of his endeavors. Just as the horses had done. But now, he had moved on, to wait for her at the banks of the River Jordan. And Addie, she closed that wonderful time in her life like a story book, going back to the beginning in the end, and rejoining her mother and father. She would not move on like the horses did, to become something valuable, to learn talents and skills, nor work beside a man in all his endeavors.

She would merely be.

As Addie came around the side of the dugout, she caught sight of a horse standing by the porch. She slowed even more when she recognized the red filly Tom always rode. She stood with her right hind leg cocked, her ears relaxed, but moving to pick up sounds out on the desert. She tipped her head and pointed her ears to look at Addie as she approached, shifting her weight. The filly had grown over the winter, and her muscles were firm from working horses all day.

Addie looked to the porch, and there she saw Tom, running the tip of the lead rope through his hand, again and again. He sat on the step, his shoulders slumped, his face hidden by his hat. At the sound of Addie's footsteps, he looked up to see her.

He stood slowly, never taking his eyes off her face, and the filly woke herself and reached the tip of her nose out to touch his arm gently. Tom looked down at the filly out of the corner of his eye, then back to Addie.

"I need to talk to you about your wages, Addie."

Addie pursed her lips and looked away from him. She folded her arms across her chest and stopped walking just out of his reach. "Oh, there's no need for that. I don't need no wages. I had a home for the winter. That's wages enough."

Tom took a step forward, the filly following closely, her broad forehead against his shoulder. Reaching up, Tom tucked a lock of stray hair behind Addie's ear. When he'd finished, he stroked her cheek with the back of his fingers. "Yes, you do need wages, Addie. For all you've done here," he whispered.

Addie covered her mouth with her right hand and looked away from Tom. Seeing her reaction, Tom turned to the red filly. "I know I promised you money, and money was what I intended to give. But things haven't worked out the way I figured they would. I had planned to sell this mare before you left, clear back last fall before the big storm. That was supposed to be your wages home."

With a light hand he stroked the filly's forehead. "She wasn't much last fall, and I didn't need her to bring much. But now she's had a winter of growin' and learnin'. She's worth more." Tom looked from Addie's face to the ground. "Seein' as you're leavin' 'fore I can get anywhere to sell her, I think you best take her. Put her with your other mares, or have

394

Pete sell her for you. Either way, she's yours."

Addie let out a laugh. "For never wanting to own another horse, I sure own a lot of horses."

Tom gave her a look of uncertainty. "I don't expect you to keep her. You can sell her to the first cowboy to come along."

Addie shook her head. "It's not that. It's…" she paused a moment, then shook her head. "I don't know what it is."

Tom turned his gaze far out to the mountains and the peaks looming above. "That isn't all I got to ask of ya, Addie."

With tears already burning, Addie gathered her strength and looked at Tom. His face was full of pleading, hopeful acceptance. She waited for him to state his intentions.

"Take Charlie with you," Tom requested in a low voice. He watched her face for a reaction before he continued. "I know what I'm asking, but the truth is, you're the only mama that boy will ever have. He needs you. More than anything in this world, he needs you. I can't give him what you have."

A tear started down Addie's cheek. It was something she refused to think about, leaving Charlie. All the boys for that matter. She'd closed her heart to it. Inside, Addie knew though, they'd resurface in Texas.

"I don't think…" she began.

Tom cut her off. "Addie, he's my son. And my regrets with that boy run deep. I can't go back and fix that. But," his voice broke, "but, I can do what is best for him now. I can give him what he needs most of all. Even if that something isn't me."

"No! He needs his father! Not me. He needs to be with his brothers. I can't say what I'll find in Texas. Maybe I won't be able to take care of him. Provide for him."

"I'll send you money, Addie. Once I sell this year's horses, I'll have money to send you."

"That isn't really the worst of it. What if… what if…" Addie couldn't finish.

"What, Addie?"

"What if he died?" she blurted out. "What if something terrible happened to him on the way to Texas? How could I live with that? To take him from his home where he's safe, and put him on a trail to Texas that's full of the unknown? Why risk his life?"

"Why risk yours, Addie? Why leave here where you're safe and travel the trail to Texas that's full of the unknown? Why leave me in hopes you can grow old next to your kin? What happens when your mama dies and leaves you completely alone? What then?"

"I can't live waitin' for the next somebody to die. I want to go home."

"Then why live like that? It isn't up to us who lives and dies. That's the plain talk of it," Tom stated.

Addie wiped a tear from her face and avoided looking at Tom. She collected her thoughts for a moment, then whispered, "I can't take him with me. He needs to be here, with you, with his brothers. This is where he belongs."

"I still contend this is where you belong. And I want you to know, I'll be here, Addie. I'll wait here, for all of my life. And if you send for me, I'll come to Texas." Turning, he picked up the get-down he'd tied around the filly's neck. "The mare is yours, Addie, to do with as you see fit."

Leading the filly away back towards the barn, Tom stopped and looked over his shoulder at Addie. "How did you know he was deaf?"

Raising shimmering eyes to Tom, Addie replied, "I guess I just found a moment where I understood exactly what he felt like."

"I'd been living that moment since the day he was born. I never did figure it out, till there was you." He turned then and led the filly away.

When he disappeared from view, Addie looked up to the mountains and let the tears fall freely from her eyes. She had no idea how Tom would deal once she was gone, but the fear of something happening to Charlie was too great for her to consider taking him with her. Addie didn't want to love something so precious and fragile. She just wanted to break away, despite the hurt she was causing.

That night Addie dreamed of empty plains. Nothing filled the vast stretches of prairie, and no horses called out to her as she stood, shading her eyes from the sun. The grass didn't sway with the teasing of the wind, and her skirt didn't catch on the stems as she walked. It wasn't something she could easily understand.

When the gray did appear, he was standing on a high rise far from her. He stood silently and still, his ears trained on her. He made no move to make his way down the hill to her, just watched as she wandered across the prairie. Addie called out for Fett, but he didn't come riding in like he did in dreams past.

When she woke, Molly was by her side, and a look of deep contemplation rested in her eyes as she studied Addie. Instead of lying there and attempting to recover her sleep and dramatic dreams that waited for her there, Addie rose and began to gather her meager things. She would not be able to carry the trunk with her, but she could put all the precious memories into a bag that would ride on the pack horse.

Roy didn't bother going into the house. Riding over the desert, the last of the sun lit his way for most of the ride, then the stars guided him for the last of it. He watched as the moon rose up over the land, big and yellow, and he rode into it as it claimed the sky from the sun.

The heart of the gray was heavy.

Loping along steadily, he looked back over the country they'd crossed with one ear cocked. By the time Roy swung off his back, the gray had no sweat marks on him. It was as if he could go on forever. But as many times as he'd covered that distance, Roy knew he must have been in some kind of good condition.

Not bothering to turn either horse out, he stalled them in the barn, feeding them generously. The roan had no qualms with digging in and filling his belly, but the gray didn't bother with it. He stood in the far corner of the stall with his head lowered, his eyes bright. Hitching one leg up, he appeared to be resting, but as Roy watched, the black etched ears twitched and jerked with very slight movement. Whatever was going on in his mind was far from restful.

Roy sat in the rickety old chair outside his house on the small porch and removed his hat. With silent contemplation he watched as the stars moved infinitely across the sky, the moonlight becoming brighter as the night wore on.

Roy Albert already knew what he was going to do.

When the prelight of dawn showed itself and announced the day was coming and the moon would soon go, Roy rose from the chair and stretched. He shook his head sadly at the barn, and wondered how he could be right.

But it didn't matter if he was right or not.

Roy had spoken with God many times, but he'd never gotten an answer like the one he'd contemplated all night. The last time God sent the storm of the century. This time, He planned on something else. Something He'd been working on for some time.

How much this would take, Roy didn't know.

Walking into the barn, he was met with a nicker from the roan, who was obviously thrilled breakfast was going to be early. Reaching his head towards Roy, he was ignored as Roy moved directly to the gray. He stood with his head up, ears forward, ready. It was like he had been waiting for Roy to come to his conclusion. Now, he was ready. Roy just looked at him for a moment.

Sliding the poles away that served as the stall door, Roy stepped in. The gray brushed Roy's shirt front with his muzzle, then stood still. His bright eyes reflected what little light existed in the early dawn. Reaching up, Roy stroked his keen head. With tears in his eyes, Roy relished the feel of the gray's soft hair.

"Go on," Roy whispered. With both hands, Roy held the gray's jaw. "Go on, sweet Addie. Go on and save yourself."

With one last stroke down the gray's forehead, Roy stood aside. The gray raised his head higher and tipped his nose to Roy, just before he exhaled deeply. With the next inhalation, he was gone. Out the door and away through the barn, his tail nothing but a stream behind him. Roy hurried out the barn door to watch him go, flying across the desert with intense speed. He was nothing but a vision, the sound of the meadowlarks singing beautifully in his wake.

Roy nodded his head as the last of the gray moved over the rise.

Addie emerged out of the dugout just as the light was breaking over the horizon. She didn't bother with breakfast, in fact had refused to go near the main house. Red Beast was left to her calf, and Addie folded the quilts she'd used through the winter and left them on the bed in the dugout.

Molly watched as she collected her things with head hung low. Each time Addie looked the dog's way, she'd wag her tail and dip her head. Pete rapped softly on the door just as the first rays of light appeared to wake Addie. She was already up and answered the door.

"You sure this is what you want?" Pete asked again with doubtful eyes.

"Yes. I'm sure," she answered with as little question as she could muster.

Before leaving he turned to her and said, "You know, Adelaide. You're the only reason I have for going back to Texas. It wouldn't disappoint me to avoid a long ride. But if you're sure, I'll go."

Squaring her shoulders, Addie lifted her chin. "This is what I want. I want to return to my folks."

Pete lingered before he said, "Alright. I'll saddle up."

Addie closed the door and rubbed her hands together as she paced the dugout. She was afraid to leave the confines of the little haven she'd passed the winter in. She looked to the corners and remembered Molly tearing into rats of all sizes, Luke rushing in at the last moment to bring a shovel down on one before it reached the hem of her tattered dress. She recalled the long nights she passed in the rocking chair. Now she carried it back to set it near the little wood stove, just where she'd found it. Turning to look back at the room, Molly nudged her hand. Addie looked down and rubbed her head.

She bent low and whispered, "You, dear friend. You were there the whole time weren't you?"

Molly answered with a soft whine.

Standing there for a long time, Addie reviewed the memories she'd made in that dugout alone. Bracing herself, she heard Pete holler it was leaving time. Addie closed her eyes and grasped her canvas bag that held everything she owned in the world. She took only one of Edith Brady's dresses, just the one that was the most worn. She left the other folded on the bed with the quilts.

Addie wore pants. If she were going to make the long ride to Texas, she'd best be suited for it. Paddy flashed in her mind. Would she actually have the courage to swing a leg up over him? The last time she'd ridden that horse, Fett was alive and riding beside her. And the red filly, well, Addie found she had even less courage to ride her away from the range that raised her.

Keeping her eyes closed, Addie took hold of the handle on the dugout door and left, without looking back. In her mind, she registered it had been far easier to leave Texas over four years ago than it seemed to be to leave Nevada. Inhaling and filling her chest cavity to capacity, Addie walked off the porch. As she rounded the hill that protected the dugout, her knees tried to give way.

Pete stood next to the blood bay, a string of ten behind him, Paddy replaced as drag by the red filly. Paddy now stood abreast with the blood bay, with Pete between them, talking to Tom. Tom wore no hat, and the early morning light was a purple haze behind him. Next to him was little Charlie, who at the sight of Addie tried to run to her. Tom was quick and took hold of his son by the arm. He swept the child up and against him, holding him tightly without ever taking his focus from Pete.

Addie looked down. She couldn't look at them.

Pete walked forward and claimed the canvas bag from Addie. Without further words, he placed it in the pannier of the packhorse behind the bay.

Addie moved quickly to put Paddy between herself and the Bradys. She fiddled with the cinches, checked the stirrup leathers, set the reins around the horn several times. When she looked up, Pete watched her with a scrupulous eye.

"These boys be waitin' to say their goodbyes, Adelaide," Pete urged gently.

Addie swallowed hard and looked back to Paddy. Watching her with tender interest, he bent his head to her. At that moment, he seemed to be her oldest, most unfamiliar friend in the whole world. She had recollections of him, but they weren't of the same lifetime as the one she stood in.

Tom took hold of Paddy's reins and moved him backward, removing the wall of security she'd placed between them. Without moving forward, he looked over to Luke. The boy was trying his damnedest not to cry, but his breath came in little sucking noises. Lacking the need for encouragement, Frankie rushed forward and wrapped his arms around Addie's mid-section tightly. The boy didn't bother to hide his tears. He cried openly, sobbing into her waist. Hugging him, Addie ran a hand through his long hair and held her breath.

"Goodbye, Miss Addie," Luke choked out as he leaned over hastily and placed a kiss on her cheek. He turned and ran back into the house, his long legs covering the distance easily.

Her throat was swollen and aching, Addie could say nothing as he went. She ran her hand over Frankie's hair, smoothing it down. Tom reached out and pried Frank away from Addie by his arm and whispered, "Be strong, boy. Just like I told you."

Without raising his eyes to Addie, he said, "I'm 'fraid Andrew couldn't summon the courage to say his goodbyes. Best you not take hold of Charlie. I don't think his little heart can take that."

A tear fell against sheer will and determination down Addie's cheek. Not raising her eyes to meet Tom's, she could not find words nor sound to voice them with.

Tom set Charlie up on Paddy for a moment and closed the distance between himself and Addie. He clenched his fists, then relaxed them repeatedly, forcing himself to maintain stability. Raising them, he grasped Addie's face and turned it up so she had to look at him. The soft rustling of the early morning breeze played with the collar on his red shirt. The hair of his beard was trimmed close and neat, and Addie could still see the look in his eyes as he fished for her to tell him she thought him handsome. That look was replaced with one of deep regret.

As he lowered his warm and soft lips to hers, she felt the impact of life and longing once again, waking her body to the aches of a lifetime alone. It was quelled with the promise of his touch, his hands claiming her freedom in the power of tenderness. His beard tickled softly against her chin, and as quickly as the sensation came, he removed it from her. Looking deep into her eyes, he whispered, "I'll be here, Addie. I'll wait for you."

Then the warmth of his body was gone. Charlie reached violently for her as Tom pulled him from Paddy, his little fingers spread wide, his palms open and seeking. He cried tears as he looked at Addie over the shoulder of his father who carried him away at a fast pace. A sob came from the boy's throat. In depleting desperation, his voice finally broke free, and the world heard Charlie Brady for the first time.

"Aaaaaiieee!" he wailed. With the next inhalation it came again. "Aaaaaiiieee!" He cried with volume, the sound of his voice trailing out across the sage, clear up the meadows.

Addie listened to the sound of Charlie crying out with his attempt at her name as he was taken into the cabin. The sound of the door closing made her jump, severing the wail of the child who cried out for her, the first of his words *being* for her.

From behind her came a low voice. "If we have to go, best we get to it."

Pete held out a hand to Addie. She took it, gratefully, and moved round to take the saddle horn and reins in her hands. With shaking legs, she swung up on Paddy, the feeling of him beneath her a distant memory brought back to life with the dawning of the sun. Looking to her for permission to move out, Pete waited.

Wiping the tears from her face, Addie nodded to him. With one last look at the homestead, Paddy started forward with the blood bay. It was done. Addie was at last starting on her way to Texas, to her mama, to her precious memories. The feeling was like rocks grinding in her guts. Pete offered a thin smile, then moved the whole line of horses into a trot out of the barnyard. As she passed the corrals, she caught sight of Andrew, with his face tear-streaked as he looked on from the protection of the side of the barn. Tate and Amos waved as she passed the open barn doors.

A deep and horrid howl sounded from somewhere near the porch of the house. Molly stood and raised her face to the sky, and as she did when Blue ran free, Molly cried out with the only tears she had. The lonesome sound echoed off the buildings and penetrated the wood.

Pete covered the country away from the Brady homestead in a brisk pace, like a man with a long journey to make. Paddy fell behind as Addie looked back one last time as they crested the hill. With his eye on her, he moved into a lope, ready to take her where she pointed him, and not one to be left behind. Then it was gone. Swallowed by the range surrounding it, like the homestead tucked safely in the meadow nestled next to the spring was non-existent.

Paddy carried his girl bravely, head up in the smell of the new day coming. His heart was bound for where ever she cared to go. Addie had no idea where she cared to go, but her mama would be waiting. Thanks to Roy, she knew Addie would be coming. Maybe not when, but she knew her girl would.

As the tears ran down her face, the cool wind of the morning made her wet face cold. Addie promised herself she'd forget it. The miles would turn into anticipation. Of what? Of seeing her family, of returning to her home where she belonged. Returning her precious heart to dwell in comfort the rest of her days. One mile rolled into another, and then another.

Addie foolishly refused to look back.

He came with the sun. As the golden rays crept their affectionate fingers over everything, waking the life before it, he came like an orb, streaking across the desert without sound. The light reflected off his gray, shining in a glory Pete had never seen.

Pete twisted in his saddle to look back and over at Addie, who with stubborn determination stared at the ground in front of Paddy's brisk pace. As the light lit the world around her, Addie seemed to retreat within herself, shrinking away from it.

Then the horses in the string saw him.

Heads turned; ears pricked. The red filly near crawled out of her skin. Her head went up and she contemplated running, then hit the end of the rope that tied her to the neck of the horse in front of her. With wide eyes, she watched him come, unable to do anything else.

Pete stood in his stirrups to watch him as he moved through a dip in the landscape. "Uhm…," he started. Looking back at Addie, Pete realized she hadn't noticed him yet.

The gray never broke stride, never faltered, cleared every rock and clump of brush like he had wings. "Whooeee," Pete muttered to himself as he watched with utter fascination.

As he neared the string, about twenty yards out, the gray let loose with some kind of sound from deep within himself. It was not a squeal, but more the announcement of his approach. Pete stopped the string and reached for the rifle that rode beneath his leg in a scabbard. He drew it out quickly and with one movement had it trained on the gray.

Addie heard the sound let by the gray and looked up with horrified eyes to see him there, approaching as he was. By now the string was in near chaos, and Pete had to lower his rifle to steady them. Before he could raise it to the animal again, Addie was off and away from Paddy who spooked sideways at her departure. Seeking comfort in the blood bay, he crowded in close to him, pinching Pete's leg between them.

Without looking, Addie scooped a rock into her hand and hit a running stride as she started across the desert with intentions of meeting the gray head on.

"Adelaide!" Pete yelled, unable to steady the string and level his rifle on the gray.

"Come on, you gray bastard! Come on! I'm done with you haunting my life!" Addie screamed as the gray came within rocking range. She let fly with the lava rock she held in her hands, watching as it flew at him and struck him dead center in the chest. The gray dropped his hind end into the dirt and drug himself to a stop, raising up on hind legs as he did so, reaching and striking at Addie. He was still a good eight yards off, but Addie recoiled with another rock she fished from the ground next to her feet. Aiming for his face, she threw again.

The gray was clever and dropped his head, otherwise her aim would have been true. As she scrounged for another rock, the gray took his chance and moved in closer. Addie screamed up at him in great anger and hit him in the shoulder with a larger stone. With his dark eyes flashing, the gray bared his teeth, pinning his ears flat against his head. Rearing up again, the gray looked as though he would trample the small woman below him who searched fervently for rocks to throw.

"Adelaide! Get out of there! Run!" Pete yelled frantically as he jumped from the bay. The string was now left to their own devices, and they wildly pulled in every direction.

As he was hit repeatedly, the gray ducked the ones he could, jumping hastily to the side to avoid them, taking the ones he couldn't avoid bravely. One struck him dead center in the forehead, and for a split second a look of regret crossed Addie's features. The gray saw his moment and lunged in closer to her. She retreated some of her ground, and as she did so, she realized the gray was merely playing down some of her energy. He rose up again before her on hind legs, striking and biting at her viciously, but never making any contact with Addie's body.

Pete looked away from them for a mere tenth of a second to his rapidly fraying string and pulled the hammer back on his rifle. He was steady now, without the prancing of the horses to knock him off balance. Raising the rifle to his shoulder, he peered down the iron sights…

The gray reared again, broadside, giving Pete a clear shot at his lungs…

Pete started to squeeze the trigger, knowing the blast would scatter the string, some dragging the others along.

The gray pressed his ears back, and his eyes flashed.

Addie screamed out again in anguish as she hurled another porous rock. "Damn you, gray bastard! I hate you!"

Now was the time, Pete had the shot.

Addie flung her rock, and as it left her hands a huge noise sounded. A great explosion filled her ears and traveled through her chest cavity, bouncing off her heart as it beat with insanity. The report was so loud, her ears began to ring and all sound of the morning unfolding around her was gone. With what seemed like slow motion, she turned her head slightly to see the string of ten making way to parts unknown, bursting into a full run up the rutted road, but their retreat made no sound through the ringing in her ears. Looking back to the gray, his high form where he stood on his back legs began to shrivel and he lowered himself slowly down onto four legs again.

Gone was his look of fiery greatness. His flashing eyes changed as he looked away from Addie back out to the desert.

Addie gazed back over her shoulder to Pete, who stood with his rifle still raised to his shoulder, but now instead of looking down the barrel, his line of sight was just to the left of Addie, trained on the gray.

Something big took hold of Addie. It locked her in an iron grip as something else thundered by. Addie was unable to hear it, but she could feel the vibrations in the ground just before she was entrapped. As she snapped her head back to view her captor, a rider-less roan galloped on past. The golden light was now so intense Addie could hardly see.

The iron grip crushed the air from her lungs and she fought wildly to get away. Looking up, Addie saw it was Roy who held her, taking away her ability to lash out and strike at him. With his left hand he threw a rifle away to the ground.

"Addie!" he yelled. "Look at me!"

She did so, but her eyes were wild with tears and the urge to fight her way out of the situation. Not just from Roy, or the gray, or even Pete. But from the junction in which she found herself.

"Addie, you must be some kind of big medicine the way the Lord has to fight to keep you here," Roy said down into her ear. "He has to use tricks I've never even heard of."

"Pete shot him! Pete *shot* him!" Addie cried out from where her face was pressed against Roy's chest.

"By the way you were fighting I have grave doubts as to why that would bother you."

"He knew! He was there, in all of it. The gray was there, with Fett. Many times! Oh, now he's gone! Gone!" Addie wailed out. "It was my fight. I chose to fight him!"

"Addie," Roy gently chided.

"He knew Fett! I know it!" came out with a great sob.

"I know he did," Roy stated matter-of-factly. "Addie, look at me."

Addie shook her head against Roy's chest, burrowing deeper. "The gray is gone. He's gone just like Fett! Buck, the gray, all of the horses that knew him. Not even Paddy knew Fett like they did. The dreams! I saw them in the dreams!"

"Addie," Roy urged.

"Why? Why do they go like that? I'm the only one left!" She never even got to say goodbye to them. She'd raged at them the last time she saw them. Buck who had let her down when Fett needed him most, and the gray. Only moments before she hurled rocks at him and cursed him for all eternity. Now he was gone. Returned to Fett, to run with the big bunch in God's country.

Pete watched as his string fled up the country and sighed. The bay, having been Pete's right hand for months, also watched them go with a raised head. But the bay remained, rooted to the man in whom his confidence lay. Pete put his rifle aside, leaning against a brush, and knelt down beside Roy and Addie.

Addie clung tighter to Roy, her vision clouding and blurring with the tears. "Oh, he's gone! My Fett is gone!"

Roy clenched his jaw and closed his eyes. Pulling her closer to him, he whispered to her, "What happened, Addie? What happened to Fett?"

Pete removed his hat in somber recognition of a time and place he was still haunted by. Making no comments, he let Addie answer Roy, for there was little he could say. What if he'd never asked if Fett wanted to partner up? What if he'd have just ridden on west without him, instead of waiting until Fett could marry Addie and bring her along? Fett would still be alive. But that was useless. Fett could have just as easily died from fever.

"Tell me, Addie."

"The horses…," she moaned. She sucked in a ragged breath and hid her face. "He left me. Just like he always did every mornin'. Then just like that, he was gone. Somethin' so simple. Buck spent every day of his life running something. He never fell, never lost his footing. That's why Fett used him to run horses down. Buck was good." In a fresh bout of anguish, Addie pictured Buck, obviously hurt, unable to walk right as he moved to her, with Fett's body draped across his back. He sought Addie, hung his head like he knew he'd taken the world right from her hands.

She pinched her eyes shut at the sight of that broken horse.

"It was so stupid. Fett ran a stud up over a bluff just for the fun of it. He topped that hill and…" Addie choked. "And Buck hit a hole. A hole in the rocks he couldn't see. It flung Buck forward, and he rolled over on Fett in those terrible rocks."

Pete rubbed his forehead as the image played out in his mind. Fett topped that hill going about as fast as Buck could travel, then it was nothing but tangled horse and sage, and in there he could barely make out the figure of Fett, rolling along with Buck where he was hung up, being crushed between horse and rock. Pete rushed to them, but by the time he got there, Buck was struggling to rise, clearly suffering from injuries on the inside. As for Fett, he still lived, and the panic in his eyes was very hard for Pete to endure. Fett attempted to move.

Pete held him down. Then he clasped his hand and shoulder as blood gurgled up and out of his mouth. Broken in more places than Pete could see or count, Fett met his end with as much courage as he had. His eyes begged something of Pete, and in understanding, Pete said, "I know. I'll watch over her. I'll care for Addie."

Then, as Buck finally rose to his feet, Fett let out one long rasping breath, and was gone. The young man who had laughed and loved only just that morning was gone. Buck hung his head in shame and pain, trying to come to Fett's side.

"Why? Why would God take him from me? What is His answer for all this suffering?" cried out Addie.

Threading his fingers in her hair, Roy answered, "I don't know, Addie. I wish I could tell you, but I can't. All I know is there is a great beyond, and when we get there, Fett will be waiting. Until then, he listens and comforts you the best way he can."

"But what of me? What happens to me?"

Roy shook his head. "I think you already know that. I think God has already stated His piece on the matter. And if you look back, you'll see He has never left you, not even for a moment. And to offer comfort, He has sent many to help you."

"Like who? Who has been here? Huh? Where was my comfort?" she yelled.

"Like your mama," Roy said quietly.

Addie looked up at him sharply. "What?" she asked with intense disbelief.

"All those times you needed her, didn't she come to you? Did her memory carry you through? The times she comforted you as a child rose up and saw you through that horrible moment you were in. And Fett, wasn't he there, each and every night, just like I said, comforting you, letting you see he really wasn't gone, was he?

"And I guarantee, he is standing here right now, comforting you as you seek answers. He already has those answers, and someday you will too."

Roy smoothed back the hair from Addie's face; Pete took her hand in both of his.

"I don't think God ever said He took from us forever. But I do know He clearly says we will all gather together again. And now you ask what of yourself. I think right now, that's what God is trying to tell you.

"Is Texas worth the regret you'll surely feel?"

Huddling closer to Roy, she felt the comfort in Pete's hand. Closing her eyes tightly, she found Fett waiting for her. Buck moved up through the grass just beyond the country where Addie had grown up and was now leaving as a newly married woman. Blond hair curled out from under his hat as his blue eyes sparkled intensely. A mischievous grin spread across his mouth. Against the deep blue of the sky, he was as real as Roy.

"Ah, Addie darlin'. I don't know how I'll swing it, but I'm gonna give you everything you ever dreamed of. We're gonna make love every night and laugh all day. With you, I'll do anything." He slowed Buck so

Paddy could catch up.

Stopping and taking her hand in his, Fett smiled at her confidently. "You're gonna have a good home, someday, Ad. Warm and strong and happy. You'll have strong sons, all around you, driving you crazy with antics." Touching her cheek softly, he continued, "And beautiful curly haired baby girls to help you tend the homestead. I know you're gonna be happy. And God willing, you'll have more horses than you can ride in a month."

How it hurt to hear that, just as she'd heard it on her wedding day. Fett leaned over and kissed her softly. "I love you, Addie. And I'm gonna see to it you're looked after. I swear you'll have a happy life."

He had made a promise he wouldn't fulfill. He'd taken her far from her home, then died, just so she could step into another life, while another man made good on the promises Fett made to her. Fett never did say in those vows they'd be his sons, nor his daughters. But he did say she'd have them. The warm home wasn't one he'd ever step foot into either.

Then Addie realized it. Just as the memories of her mama helped her through, this was Fett's way of showing her what way to go. How he made sure he'd made good on all the things he swore she'd have. He really wasn't gone, merely out of reach. Addie didn't have the courage to lay aside the grief and take his lead.

"Addie," Roy whispered. "Look, Addie."

Prying her away from the security of his chest, Roy raised her head to look at him. "Look."

Opening her eyes to the blinding golden light, Roy tipped her chin. Before her, encased in the light, was the gray. As she looked at him, his ears came forward, and his head lowered. He'd come to stand only a few feet away, and now he reached for her, his neck stretching out.

"I fired that shot just to keep Pete from killing him," Roy assured as he squeezed Addie's arm tenderly.

Rising, Pete helped Addie to her feet. Raising his head, the gray looked at Addie with soft brown eyes, the viciousness of the moments prior now gone. The black etching of his ears were defined against the gold. On shaky legs, Addie stepped toward him.

With caution, she held out a hand to him, which he arched his neck to smell only briefly. Running her palm down the expanse of his forehead, something happened within Addie. All the times the gray had beckoned her, reached for her, sought her out in dreams and reality, all came to this. Taking another step, the gray came closer. As he did, Addie wrapped her arms around his neck and lay her head against it. The feel of the softness in his hide contrasting with the coarseness of his mane beneath her cheek was warm and alive. His black mane soaked up the tears from her face. Embracing him fully, accepting him, was like balm to the soul. Turning his head, the gray cradled Addie against him, tucked safely against his neck.

"Who is he? Why is he?" Addie asked no one in particular.

Pete shook his head in bewilderment. Horses had always been concrete things to him. He appreciated their skills, recognized their ability to understand and learn, but this was never something he fathomed.

"How much of our lives is wasted, Addie?" Roy began. "How much time do we waste, seeking the true purpose of our existence, only to ignore, avoid, hide from, and reject it when it meets us face to face? He's you, Addie. Standing here in the flesh, he's you, and how much time have you spent avoiding him, rejecting him, running from him? Your purpose has its root in horses, among many other things. Accept yourself, embrace your calling, don't hide from it anymore." Roy paused a moment. "And in those dreams of running horses, I think you had a rare glimpse of what will come, as I believe God loves a good horse."

Pete fumbled with his hat. "You have a choice to make, Addie. You make it now. Regret isn't something to carry with you as you go through life."

"They need you, Addie. They need what God gave you. Don't hide from what they can give you in return," Roy said softly.

With a surprised raise of his brow, Roy watched Pete's string come back over a distant hill, trotting evenly, mannerly, back to him. As they made their way to the small group gathered, Addie released the gray's

411

neck and took his face in her hands. The gray raised his head and Addie rested her temple against the bridge of his nose. For a long moment, she was silent. The sound of hooves broke the stillness of the golden light as the string drew closer.

Closing her eyes, Addie whispered, "I wanna see my mama."

Charlie lay curled into a ball on Tom's lap. Sitting on the porch facing the mountains, Tom held watery eyes on them, following their dips and crags. Beside him, Luke sat next to his father on the wooden planks. Andrew sat on the top step and leaned his head against a wood pillar, throwing little pieces of bark as he peeled them away from a small willow branch. Frankie buried his face in Molly's furry neck, the dog looking solemnly across the desert.

"Aaaiiee," came the low wail as Charlie cried into his father's chest. For never having had to comfort the boy in the whole of his life, Tom would be making up for it in spades the next few weeks. Clutching him, Tom kissed the hair on the top of his head.

In the corrals, the hands went about the process of putting second rides on colts from the day before. Only today, they allowed the Bradys space. A late evening meal was all they could expect, and even then it wouldn't be good. Addie was gone, and with her she took her culinary mastery. Now, it would be as it had been in the last few years. Slim on the pickin's.

Despite the glowing sun, and the green mountain's reflection of it, the day was gray. Darkness once again settled on the Brady homestead, only this time it was doubtful God would send a second round of help. No matter how much Luke prayed. And anyhow, no one could top Addie. If Edith was gone, then no one else would do but Addie.

Tom was torn. Should he ride after her? No. She was gone. She made it clear she wanted to go. Begging again would serve little in the way of results. She made her choice. Now he had to live with it.

No meadowlarks sang out in happy tune. Only the occasional shouting of the hands, or the grunting of a horse as it moved around the round corral was heard. The boys sat in unusual stillness, their hands and feet unmoving. The heavy feeling was oppressive, and the sounds of the only word Charlie had uttered in three years of his life was like barbs to an already bleeding heart. Muffled sniffling was hard to trace, as it seemed to come from all directions.

"Come on, boys. We can sit like this all day, and it won't change anything. Let's head down to the corrals, get a few rode," Tom said. "Remember, this is the part I told you to be strong for."

Luke scratched his hairline, then rose slowly. "C'mon, Andrew. Help me wrangle horses."

Andrew threw the stick he'd been peeling the bark off of and followed Luke down towards the barn. Frankie looked at his Father in question. Tom tried to smile. "Maybe we'll get a rope on that dun colt. You can pull him around in that pen he's in. Break him to lead."

Reluctant to leave his chosen place of comfort, Frank buried his face in Molly's neck again. Tom gathered up Charlie and stood, then stooping, he pulled Frankie up. "Come on. Best get after it." Tom's voice didn't reflect his words.

Molly rose, but she didn't follow Frankie as he jumped off the porch. She sniffed on the air and wagged her tail, then gave up on what she thought she heard. Laying back down on the top step, her paws hanging over the edge, she kept patient eyes on the south horizon.

Tom looked down at Charlie. What to do with Charlie. The boy would have no intentions of standing alone. It just might be he really would grow up horseback, seeing as that was the only safe place to put him out of the way of the work, and still have him visible. He couldn't hear shouts of warning when danger was near, and he couldn't hear it coming.

A deep howl followed by a sharp bark sounded as Molly came to her feet in a flash. She raised her nose to the sky and let loose with a long and mournful sound. She followed that with an excited yip. Bounding off the porch, she ran halfway to the barn, stopped and howled again. After the sound dissipated, she was gone, flying out through the sage.

"Where's Molly goin'?" Luke yelled from the barn door.

Tom shrugged and shook his head.

As he watched the brush where he could see Molly bound up every now and then, something on the crest of the ridge caught his eye. At first he thought he was imagining things, so Tom blinked and rubbed his eyes to clear what looked like a white spot from them. When he looked again, it was still there. It was moving steadily, and fast.

Setting Charlie down, Tom called to Frankie. Pausing in his down-headed wander to the barn to fetch a rope, Frankie turned and looked back at his father. "Watch your brother," Tom said as he himself jumped off the porch. He crossed the barnyard at a run and made his way the same as Molly had.

"What the hell?" Andrew asked as he watched his father go. Luke shot him a glare and punched him in the arm.

The gray was coming in with all he had. He ran free, no bridle, no reins, nothing to slow his speed. Vaulting over a cluster of sage and bunch grass, he was then free on the road. Stretching out his legs, he found more momentum, somewhere deep in his already pounding heart. His nostrils were expanding with each breath, the mane on his neck flowing behind him, just as it always had in the dreams he ran in. He was never more magnificent than he was in that moment.

The gray came with all the speed he contained, but he did not come alone. Astride the thundering beast sat a small figure. Entwined in his mane were small hands, delicately made, but never delicately used. The wind tore at the bun she wore, freeing auburn strands to fly out behind her, glinting brightly in the golden sun.

From way back, two lone figures stood on a bluff and watched the gray make his run, streaking across the desert with great clarity, just as he always had. Behind them was a string of horses, gathered and ready to head in whatever direction the man named Pete pointed them. In the drag was a little red filly, ears up and eyes alert, following the gray enigma with all her concentration.

Pete laughed out joyously to see that gray run, but more so to watch the woman who stayed with him. "That takes guts, to start over like that."

Roy smiled a genuine smile. "Courage. Courage rides a gray horse."

Pete glanced at Roy. "I guess my job here is done. And since my string kindly returned themselves, I suppose nothing keeps me. You can take what is rightfully Addie's to her for me."

Roy furrowed his brow. "Bull shit. Your job isn't done. Not all the horses are started yet. I think you could make a go of it in this country easily."

"Well, it's mighty tempting seeing as the cooks back," Pete chuckled as he reached for his pouch of makings to roll his own. "Say, how'd you know, you know, 'bout that gray?"

Roy turned serious. "That's difficult to explain. I guess you could say I had a winter of dreams. Many nights I was led to this moment, by a gray horse."

Roy laughed and slapped Pete's back. With a string of ten, Pete and Roy started down the slope towards the Brady homestead.

The gray closed the gap from one end, Tom the other. As Tom came up a short rise, he stopped and waited the brief moment until the gray slid to a halt. With green eyes shining, Addie looked down at Tom. Reaching for her, he grasped her around the waist and pulled her to him, crushing his lips to hers. The length of her body settled against his, her breasts against the planes of his chest. Wrapping her arms around his neck, Addie kissed Tom Brady back with everything she had. Molly yipped as they embraced.

When they broke apart, Tom raised Addie high above him, the strength in his chest and arms lifting her. Looking down at him, Addie saw his joy, brightly shining forth from the tears in his eyes. He let out a joyous laugh before he lowered her against him again. In the distance, she could hear the shouting of boys as they made their way to Addie, grateful that some prayers are indeed answered with a yes.

As the boys made it to them, Charlie called out, "Aaaiiee!"

Something inside Addie surged. Thinking back she remembered Fett's words again, *"You'll have strong sons all around you."* While it wasn't what he meant at the time, Fett had predicted life for Addie in an undeniable way. And although he wasn't going to be there to give it to her, Tom would be. Despite a beginning founded on derision, Addie had come around to appreciate Tom for all that he had buried within himself. He was a good man, even when he chose not to be. But now, as time has a way of doing, he was brought back to allowing himself to love, and open up to the risk of losing. For the benefits of love were far worth the risks.

The wind wandered its way through the of the grass, the golden sunlight refracting back in answer from the rolling hills as they cascaded across the desert. The warmth of the sun was deeply comforting as puffy white clouds drifted aimlessly in the vivid blue.

Addie stood on the rise looking out at the land and folded her arms across her chest. She closed her eyes and waited to hear them, steady in their four-beat rhythm, the constant of their movement as they thundered on. She inhaled deeply, the wind tickling the loose wisps of hair at the back of her neck. This place was free of time, free of constraints, free of burdens.

The wind paused in its casual sighing to still the air in anticipation of a single voice.

"I hear You," she whispered. "I hear You."

A meadowlark sounded from where it perched precariously on coarse stalks of bunch grass.

Bowing her head, Addie spoke into the now stillness of the late afternoon sun, which seemed to gather light from everywhere: from the sky, from the four directions of the wind, from the ground beneath her.

"I am at Your mercy, and I beg for You to keep me....just as You have all along. What You have shown me will take a lifetime to understand. But for now, I go on with You at my lead. I can't 'xpect the rest of my livin' will make any more sense than the livin' I've already done."

Gripping her shoulders in her palms, Addie pictured Fett. His broad smile and blond hair, the way he raised his hat to wave at her from a distance atop Buck. He was so very much alive.

"I haven't the strength to let him go, but I understand I really don't have to. All I ask is that with time, I can think on him without crying or

416

feeling such deep loss. To find comfort in knowing, I'll see him again. That he goes with me, just as You do."

The sun caressed Addie with tenderness. "And won't You tell Mama, I'll see her again?"

The meadowlark again trilled, just before a great thunderous sound reverberated through the valley below her. Opening her eyes, the gray stood before her, an empty saddle on his strong back, romal draped around the horn. In his mouth was an intricately carved silver bit. His black etched ears were trained on her, until he saw she'd opened her eyes. Then, with wisdom, he looked to the valley below him.

They came in all colors, fanning out as they carried themselves across the empty valley, heads held high and proud, tails riding on the wind in waves. The shrill sounds of air as it left flared nostrils echoed across the distance. Addie raised a hand to shield her eyes from the blinding light around her. The gray moved to her.

With tears in her eyes, Addie pressed the tips of her fingers to her lips. Fighting the sob that rose from deep inside her chest, her vision blurred. The gray rested his head against her shoulder. She lay her head on his.

Below, in the valley beneath the mountains that cragged and dipped, climbed and peaked, rounded and timbered, those horses ran on.

It's time, Addie girl.

Wiping her eyes, she tried to see them clearly. And there he was, climbing the slope that led down to the valley. The horse he rode holding an easy lope, covering the distance with ears forward and feet sure. The sound of a steady four-beat rhythm growing louder with their approach.

Addie let out a watery laugh as she watched them come, a surge of joyous life coming from her soul. The gray raised his head from her to watch the duo. He looked back at Addie and nickered softly to her.

It's time, Addie.

With shining brown eyes, the little red filly carried Tom Brady to the top of the hill and slowed as she came to Addie and the gray. With a smile radiating out from his neatly trimmed beard, Tom stepped off the filly. She nudged him gently with her nose as he stepped past her. He took his hat off in a single motion as he looked at Addie.

Wiping a tear from her cheek, she tried to look serious. "Ya know, I'd really appreciate it if you didn't ride the life outta my horses."

Tipping his face to the sky, Tom let out a heartfelt laugh. As he looked at the beautiful young woman who stood before him, shining green eyes and auburn hair, the fullness of her life and body, he lost his words. So in reply, he softly said, "Yes ma'am."

Tom took her hand, and they both looked to the valley below. As the bunch moved on, one by one the boys appeared to the right and left of them, up along the hill sides, Frankie and Charlie following a ways behind, Charlie keeping a tight grip in Paddy's black mane. He rode with sureness. Up to the front, tipping and guiding as they directed the bunch, Pete and Roy held them steady in the direction of the trap.

Brushing his finger gently across the back of Addie's hand, Tom looked down at her. "Come on, sweetheart. It's time for you to join them."

Placing a soft and gentle kiss on her lips, he helped her as she swung into the saddle atop the gray. The gray looked back at her with certainty in his eye. Tom squeezed Addie's leg where it resided inside Fett's old pants. Putting his hat back on, he then moved to the red filly in two strides. After he settled into the saddle, Tom looked over to Addie.

Resting his elbow on the horn, he said, "After you, Mrs. Brady."

Smiling at him, she moved as one with the gray down the slope, Tom following closely behind.

A meadowlark called again, and in answer another called from an adjoining butte. The surest sound of spring echoed across the valley and out into the stunning sky. As it followed the contours of the land, the song of a simple bird painted the earth with a color so vibrant and clear, only the heart could see it.

The sky held the golden light, long after the sun began to lower closer to the mountain. Its radiance covered the range in manifested glory, bright and gold, living and seeking. It covered everything, lit everything, and with the purest of gold, made everything visible, long after the sun waned. The radiance spread across the vast and open country, following the bands of running horses and the people that tended to them, guided by an unseen hand.

*L*ook at the sun, bright as it is in the skies,

He comes in golden splendor, God comes in

awesome majesty.

Job 37: 21-22

Photo Credit Jolyn Stewart 2016

Being a native of the American west, Lyn Miller has lived out her life among the people and traditions that make this great country the envy of the world. With her husband and three children, Lyn spends her time immersed in the true grit and determination of the cowboy spirit and among horses. It is this grit and determination that drove her to begin writing novels, and tell a story the world hasn't heard. May you enjoy reading it as much as she enjoyed writing it.

Made in the USA
Columbia, SC
08 November 2018